Dear Betty

you enjoy

NECESSARY
VENGEANCE

NECESSARY VENGEANCE

A Novel

CLIPPER LAMOTTE

Lamborn House Press

Necessary Vengeance is entirely a work of fiction. All incidents and dialogue and all characters are products of the author's imagination and are not to be construed as real. Any resemblance to persons living or dead is entirely coincidental.

2014 Lamborn House Paperback Edition
Copyright © 2014 by Clipper LaMotte

Published in the United States by Lamborn House Press
West Grove, Pennsylvania

LIBRARY OF CONGRESS CATALOGING - IN - PUBLICATION DATA
LaMotte, Clipper.
Necessary Vengeance: a novel/Clipper LaMotte

ISBN: 0990709558
ISBN 13: 9780990709558
Library of Congress Control Number: 2014919199
Lamborn House Press, West Grove, PA

Printed in the Unites States of America

Cover Illustration by
David Stewart Brown Rainstorm Design

Author's Photograph by
Stacey Hetherington
Stacey Hetherington Photography

Creative Design and Marketing by
Nita Greer
Greer Creative Communications

www.clipperlamotte.com

For My Children

"A story should read like music sounds."
Dad

TABLE OF CONTENTS

PART I

MURDER

CHAPTER 1

He pushed the ignition button, and the engine hummed. Virginia Wetherill rested her left hand on his arm. "Look at me, Taylor." The interior lights that went on when the car doors opened were fading out. "Are you all right to drive? You had a fair amount."

"I'm safe. I've driven far worse than this."

"That's not much comfort, but I won't argue. My contact lens is bothering me, and I don't want to drive." She started to rub her right eye but stopped. "I can't wait to get home and get the damn thing out." Taylor Warner backed the car from its space and drove to the exit.

In one minute they were on the street and heading home. Wetherill sank into the bucket seat, took a long breath, and exhaled. She noted the time glowing on the instrument panel. "Can't believe it's only ten. I'm tired." Warner turned on the radio. The second movement of Bruch's violin concerto washed through the speaker system and enveloped them. He wished he could shut his eyes and listen.

They moved through the night without speaking. The windows were tinted as dark as law allowed. No one could intrude on their privacy. Warner concentrated on the road and the music. Wetherill replayed with satisfaction her performance that evening. That's what it was, a performance. Eventually she said, "Too bad we have to hold these fundraisers in B hotels. Can't afford to look too extravagant, but that food is awful."

Warner chuckled, "At least a Dewar's and soda is the same everywhere, even if the chicken isn't."

In fifteen minutes they were through the last traffic light and on a county road with only three miles and four stop signs to their real home west of Philadelphia. They had spent little time there since Wetherill had been elected. She liked the pace of her life in Washington.

There was almost no traffic. Warner could see the lights of only one car in his rearview mirror. The first stop sign was about a mile ahead when Wetherill abruptly sat up. "This lens hurts too much, something's in there. I've got to take it out. Turn the light on for me." Warner reached up and depressed a button on the overhead panel. Soft light illuminated the front of the cabin. Wetherill removed a lens case from her purse and unscrewed one cap and placed it and the case on the dashboard in front of her. She picked up the drops, unscrewed the top, tilted her head back and dropped two drops into her right eye to moisten the lens. "Keep it smooth, Taylor," she said. "I'm taking it out."

With practiced fingers she slid the lens off her pupil, pinching it between her thumb and index finger. She blinked several times, closed her eyelids, and rubbed her right eye with the fingers of her left hand. "Oh, better," she sighed. "It felt like a cinder." She opened her eyes, glanced at Warner, then focused on moving the lens toward the case on the dash. She dropped it. "God damn it! I can't see it," she said, looking into the shadowy dark carpet. Warner said nothing. He knew she was irritated and would pounce on him if he commented. She took a small penlight from her purse and switched it on. She played the light where her eyes were searching.

Seeing the focused beam, Taylor asked, "Now can I turn off the light?"

"You mean before I find it?" she answered acidly. Then her tone softened. "It helps I think." He watched her scan her shoes for the lens with no success. Then she moved the seat all the way back and tucked her left leg underneath her on the seat, exposing most of the carpet to her search. Taylor shifted his foot from the accelerator to the brake to slow for the stop sign that, in the dark, appeared to advance toward the car. Wetherill bent forward and down to get her eyes closer to the carpet. Warner saw nothing coming either way on the crossroad, but on the slim chance that the car behind was a policeman he came to a full stop, glancing in the rearview mirror as he did. To his surprise, he saw that the following car did not stop but drifted right and was snugging into the narrow space between his car and the road bank. This was so curious that instead of moving on, he watched. The car pulled even with his and stopped.

He managed only, "What the hell is he...."

Sharp pain seared Wetherill's ears as she felt more than heard the shattering explosion. At the same instant stinging fragments of glass drove into the skin on the back of her head. The lethal mass of shot that had exploded the window sped over her and slammed into Taylor Warner's head and neck. Wetherill emitted a cry and tried to disappear. The best she could do was turn slightly and drive the right side of her body into the space below the dashboard. She jammed the right side of her face against the center console. Her bent left leg and hip had to stay on the seat. They seemed impossibly high to her, exposed.

A second, deafening explosion sent another wall of shot slamming into Warner, this time splattering Wetherill with a sickening back-spray of blood and flesh. The force of the shot drove Warner's body hard against the driver-side door. As if in protest, his right hand flew off the steering wheel straight back toward the shooter as far as his extending arm would permit before dropping limply onto the seat.

Wetherill's eyes were close to Warner's body, and she saw it jerk violently. She did not see his foot jump off the brake and drop to the floor. The delicate bones in her ears were so traumatized by the first two explosions that the third and fourth sounded almost muffled. Most of the murderous pellets flew through the car and on into the night since less of Warner remained to stop them.

Wetherill felt the car moving slowly, but she was frozen. Then, through the ringing, she heard the squeal of tires as the killing car peeled away. Still she did not move. Finally, she forced herself to focus. *You have to do something!*

She raised her head slightly, causing wet ooze that had landed atop her forehead to dribble down her face. She shifted her right knee and felt sharp fragments of something dig in. She could see Warner's right hand on the seat, only inches from her. Blood was seeping from under the white cuff of his shirt and pooling in the palm of his hand. Bile rose into her throat. She made a guttural noise but the sound was eerily all within her head, blocked from escaping by the continued ringing. Her senses were overloaded by her terrible proximity to the mutilated corpse.

The car crept slightly faster. Willing herself to move at least her left arm, she brought it over her head, grasped the steering wheel and pulled down. In her mind's eye she could see the car gradually arc around the familiar intersection and into the bank on the right side of the crossroad. Once there it dug and slid against the resistance of the bank. Wetherill knew she had to do more. She pushed off with her right elbow and turned her head to see the ignition button on the dash near the wheel. She released the wheel, reached and pressed the button, and snatched her hand back to protect herself from the body. The car's grinding movement stopped.

The silence that followed was worse. She pushed herself back onto the seat. Try as she could to avert her eyes, her peripheral vision flashed the message that there was far less to Warner's upper body than there should have been. Still squinting, she carried out her last task. She reached a finger up to the overhead light and pressed it off. *Merciful darkness*, she thought. But the darkness made the darker shape of the body loom closer and seem more menacing.

She turned toward her door and threw herself at it. It opened a foot and then was stopped by the chewed-up bank. "Oh God, why?" she exclaimed. Desperate to exit, she stayed turned, her back to the body, and inched back toward it until she felt the space separating her bucket seat from his. Still facing her door, she arched herself over that narrow opening. She was terrified her back would touch the body or, worse, that it would fall against her as her effort to squeeze over depressed both seats toward her. It was an awkward maneuver and seemed to her to take forever. But finally her legs and feet were through the opening. She struggled to her knees on the back seat, ignoring the pain in her right one, and pulled the handle on the door behind the body. It opened, and she threw herself out, dropping hands first. She awkwardly scrambled for balance to prevent her bleeding knee from scraping the macadam. She had lost one shoe in the car and kicked off the other. She lunged to her feet and ran down the center of the dark road back in the direction from which she and Warner had come and toward the welcoming beams of an approaching car.

The teenage boys saw a disheveled figure in the middle of the road running toward their car, arms in the air, eyes wide, and mouth moving. The one driving instinctively slammed on the brakes. The woman kept coming, and now they could hear her screaming, "Help me! Help me!" They jumped out and jogged into the headlight beams. Wetherill aimed herself at the silhouette that appeared from the driver's side. She ran straight into him, clutched at his shirt, and buried her head in it. "My husband's been murdered! They shot him! They shot him in the car!" She sank to her knees and wrapped both arms around the boy's left leg. "Don't leave me!" She commanded. He bent at the waist and laid his hand lightly on the back of her head. He had no idea what else to do. His companion pulled out his cell phone and called 911.

CHAPTER 2

T had turned his tired forty-two year-old eyes toward the clock radio. It was 11:48. He'd been staring at the dark for fifty minutes, unable to entice sleep. Even the tequila nightcap hadn't worked. He kneaded his forehead with the strong fingers of his right hand.

"How could she do that?" he asked the darkness yet again. He hadn't seen it coming. No storm clouds on the horizon. "I'm leaving." That was it. Just, "I'm leaving." He couldn't get a handle on it. There had been no explanation and no histrionics. Not even tears. *So cold,* he thought. His efforts to dissuade her were heartfelt but lame because he didn't know what he was fighting, and she wouldn't engage him. He felt dismissed like an errant schoolboy. He was really going to miss her.

He ingested a healthy dose of self-pity. *Couldn't have been a today thing,* he told himself. He was sure. *You don't bleed out all emotion in just a day.* He thought back two nights before to the cocktail party she had thrown for some of their friends. All appeared sweetness and light then. She had been

so attentive. *Maybe a little overboard,* he thought in hindsight.
Her girlfriends probably all knew I'd been sentenced to death.
No doubt they enjoyed watching me walk the plank. And I
didn't even know I was on it! He glimpsed himself, tethered
and blindfolded, disappearing off the edge and into a roiling
sea. He held that image for a moment, but then it dawned
on him that the unexpected loss of her wasn't the only thing
unnerving him. She'd managed to hide her feelings for
how long? Two days? A week? Longer? He had no idea,
but he knew he'd missed signals. *Have to be signals when a*
relationship disintegrates, he told himself. He was supposed
to be good at detecting signals. *Aren't I a big deal FBI agent?*
Big deals aren't supposed to miss signals.

He thought about it. *Maybe my intuition turns on me like*
a double agent in matters of the heart. Makes sense, he mused.
Emotions interfere with intuition. That thought struck him as
moderately insightful, and he wondered if he could claim it as
original, *or did I read it somewhere?*

Thaddeus Ignatius Pennock, Chief of the FBI's District
of Columbia Regional Office, grew up on a Pennsylvania
horse farm. His name reflected his Quaker heritage. Thad,
as everyone called him – he broke the nose of a classmate in
the ninth grade who, picking up on his middle name, called
him Ignats – regarded himself as a pretty genuine guy who
tried for real relationships. His one marriage had been very
good for a long time, but turned sour as his wife increasingly
felt displaced by his career. She had been right. Since his
rancorous divorce he'd had several good relationships. Until
today, that is. This last one no longer looked so good. The
image of walking the plank returned. He grimaced and
slowly shook his head. Street sounds outside his Georgetown
townhouse were barely audible, augmenting more than
breaking the troubled silence within.

Then Thad did what he always did to pull himself together. He reached within for the lesson he started learning by foxhunting at the age of twelve alongside his parents. Legs squeezed tightly against his pony's sides, he would charge across the countryside at a gallop surrounded by the larger, thundering horses of the grown-ups, everyone following the hounds in full cry as they, in turn, chased the hunted fox. He had to avoid holes that would take his pony down and drive him head first into the ground, jump post and rail fences, line fences, coops, logs and other obstacles sometimes four feet high, plunge down banks into streams and creeks, struggle up their slippery far sides, and weave through woods at a gallop avoiding trees that would crush his kneecaps if he rode too close and branches that would swipe him off or slash his face. If he fell, he was expected to get right up, remount, and carry on without so much as a whimper no matter how frightened he was or how much he hurt unless he broke a bone and couldn't.

Over the years of his youth he did fall, but just as many times he made himself get up and thus came to believe that he always could. So, on this disappointing night he picked himself up and remounted. It still hurt, but he would live. As welcome sleep drifted in like mist, he even caught himself thinking of some of the pleasures of being unattached, *even though*, he admitted, *I didn't exactly have a vote on the matter.*

CHAPTER 3

It took four rings for Thad to realize that the sound he had been trying to place in his already forgotten dream was his phone. He travelled the rest of the way to the surface in an instant. He glanced at the clock. *Jesus! Only 12:30?* With less than an hour of sleep, he felt groggy and irritable, and his mouth was pasty. He ran a strong hand through his thick, brown hair and then picked up the phone. "Who is this?" he barked.

"Your wake-up call, Thad my boy," proclaimed the good-natured voice on the other end, "from your friend and colleague, Charlie. Tell me how delighted you are." Charlie Townsend was Thad's counterpart in the FBI's Philadelphia office.

"Christ Charlie, its twelve thirty in the morning! Somebody nuke the Liberty Bell?"

"Ah," Townsend soothed, "Not half bad for someone not yet entirely in command of his faculties." Then his tone turned more serious. "I wouldn't bother you if we didn't have a doozy here. Blood and brains all over the road from drive-by shotgun blasts into the front seat of a car carrying a Congresswoman and her husband. The Congresswoman has been investigating drug traffic here in our fair city, but he's the one sprayed onto the road. She wasn't hit. Pretty good ingredients so far, don't you agree?"

"Whoa," Thad interjected, rubbing his temples. "Rein in a little."

"Okay," Charlie said before summarizing what he knew of how the murder took place. He concluded with, "Representative Wetherill is at the University of Pennsylvania Hospital, sedated up to her eyeballs."

"I've seen her several times on the news. A looker. Her district's not too far from my farm in Unionville."

"I'm told she's a real bull dog. Interesting thing is that lately she's been beating the drums in the press and in a subcommittee she chairs on the Hill to clean drugs off the streets around here. Without real proof she keeps pointing her finger at a guy named Leonard Moretti. She claims Moretti controls all the hard street drugs in the Philadelphia area and has vowed to pull him down. She's just begging him to sue her for slander. Ballsy woman. The D.A. here, you know Everet, is pissed. He's quietly been trying to connect Moretti to the mob for some time. Now there's nothing quiet about it."

"I remember Moretti from my own days in the D.A.'s office," Thad said. "He's into lots of businesses. Low profile. Pretty smooth. Was always on the periphery a couple of steps removed."

"That's him. It's not clear what she has on him, if anything. But politically it hardly matters. By focusing on a live person, she's made her crusade up close and personal. She's got herself a hot button that jump-starts the hearts of her constituents. She's clever, and can she work a crowd!"

He paused and then added, "Look, with the murder happening in my yard, I normally wouldn't call you, but I've no doubt that our good Congresswoman will see to it that the center of gravity of this little drama is DC. So you might as well be in on it from the beginning. Have I got your attention?"

———

It had taken Thad a few side trips to figure out what he wanted to do with his life. He grew up with his mother and father and an older sister in the farm country of southern Chester County, near the Pennsylvania village of Unionville. Little changed over time, its rolling hills, woods, horse farms and fields of corn, soy beans, and hay would have looked familiar to Washington's ragged troops who marched through it two hundred and thirty years earlier. Yet, by car it was only an hour from Philadelphia and forty minutes from Wilmington, Delaware.

Thad's full name announced to the world that he was the product of several generations of Quakers on his father's side. His mother's family derived from the gentry in England who had driven the Quakers to the new world. His Quaker forebearers had been farmers, but as the generations passed, more became professionals – doctors, lawyers, engineers, and teachers – many still living on the land but leasing the actual farming out to others. His father had been a neurosurgeon practicing in Wilmington. His mother had a Ph.D. in biology but early on decided she wanted to be at home while her children were young. Later she worked with the Stroud Water Research Center devising ways to save and reclaim rivers and streams and creeks. Raised in Quaker traditions, Thad valued hard work and understatement. But there was nothing prudish or melancholy about him. His parents had been energetic and light-hearted. He remembered his home as bustling with activity and laughter, and in this he realized he was fortunate.

When he was sixteen, he went off to the same New England boarding school his father had attended and from there to Yale, as his father had. It was just expected. He pursued education more to achieve family benchmarks and fulfill a sense of duty than to feed an intellectual curiosity. In his senior year, having not the slightest idea what he wanted to do other than drink beer and pursue girls, he was counseled to go to law school on the sound ground that it couldn't hurt. Surprising himself, not to mention his parents, he caught fire at the University of Pennsylvania Law School, graduated with high marks, and eagerly went to work at a large Philadelphia law firm where he specialized in white-collar crime.

But after three years, he found his enthusiasm waning, and he thought he would much rather send bad guys up the river than defend them. He landed a job as an Assistant U.S. Attorney in Philadelphia and spent four years prosecuting criminals. He was good at it, achieving a high conviction rate. But gradually this too began to feel like just a job.

He was stuck. He had considered only careers involving the actual practice of law because he had spent three expensive and fairly challenging years of his precious youth training to be a lawyer, and his Quaker conscience kept reminding him, *you can't waste that!* When he finally realized that the years ahead and not those behind were the important ones, the career he coveted became obvious. He didn't care about defending or prosecuting the bad guys. He wanted to catch them.

It had been ten years since he joined the FBI, and he was still on a high. In that time he had had about as many promotions as were possible with talent and luck, and the previous year the Director appointed him Chief of the District of Columbia Regional Office. This brought him close to the FBI's nerve center. His office was in the main FBI building one floor below the offices of the Director and the Deputy Director, to whom he reported. He took the promotion with the understanding that he could delegate non-essential administrative tasks to others so he could spend half his time doing challenging fieldwork.

———

Charlie Townsend's middle-of-the-night invitation was for Thad a high hard fastball right over the middle of the plate, and his smiling blue eyes were now alert and shining. Without a pause he said, "I'll be on the 0700 Acela with Owens. Have somebody meet the train."

"Why am I not surprised?"

"How are you handling the Congresswoman, Charlie?"

"No one gets in her hospital room except medical staff and family. Oh, and her Chief of Staff, a young woman named Veronica Patterson. Wetherill insists on that. No one else, not even Philadelphia's finest. They're probably pissed but they have no choice. I've got two agents on her hospital door from now until we get there in the morning."

There was a pause. Then Thad asked, "Charlie, did I miss something? You telling me this was a shotgun from the passenger side, the husband was driving, and the Congresswoman wasn't hit?"

"That's right, she's got some cuts from flying glass and pieces of the interior that ricocheted around like shrapnel, but nothing big. Happened to be hunkered down close to the floor looking for a contact lens she dropped, would you believe?" Thad shook his head. "That's one lucky lady."

"Understatement of the year, my friend," Townsend replied. "See you tomorrow." They rang off.

Thad propped himself up on his right elbow and punched in another number on the phone. *Bet the ranch on only two rings*, he thought. Before the phone rang a third time, he heard the familiar sonorous voice, "Owens here." Thad smiled to himself. *How does he do it every time? Doesn't even sound sleepy.*

"Did I wake you?"

"Yes Chief," came the straightforward reply.

———

From the time five years before when Thad first partnered on a case with Special Agent Robert Owens, he had maneuvered to work with him regularly. He had come to believe that they were better agents when working together, at least he was better. Owens was his invaluable sounding board.

Owens was the grandson of immigrants from Northern Ireland and the son of an honest Chicago policeman. He was raised to be loyal to his country, respectful of the law, devoted to his family, and a good Catholic. He studied hard through the Chicago public school system and earned a scholarship to the University of Illinois where he qualified for the undergraduate Honors Business Program. In his senior year, the FBI recruited him. Now at fifty-four he was a Special Agent in the DC office under Thad, aspiring like his father before him to nothing more than do his job every day as well as he could. The day before Thad's middle-of-the-night call, Owens and Sally O'Brian Owens celebrated their thirty-first wedding anniversary with their two sons, daughter and son-in-law, and first grandchild.

Most likely Owens could no longer pass the FBI entrance physical. The inevitable first impression of him was that he was round. Not soft or fat, but round. His head was round and capped by still thick but graying hair. His face was pure Irish, green eyes, light complexion, pink-hued cheeks, a prominent nose and an expression that at rest was a slight smile. His thick eyebrows were a shade grayer than his hair. He was five feet nine inches tall when he tried very hard. His legs were short relative to his torso, which also appeared to be round. His bottom and thighs were ample. His suspenders, which he wore daily, had two jobs - holding his trousers up and his barrel chest and stomach in. His neck was short and seemed to disappear altogether beneath the collar of the habitual white shirt and blue and red striped tie. When he was not asleep, reading glasses perched half way down his nose. Owens didn't exactly look like Santa Claus, just like everybody's "Uncle Bob."

But among his friends and colleagues within the FBI, he was neither Robert nor Bob. He was "Owens," as if it were not his last name but an appellation of particular respect. For this friendly and gentlemanly man was recognized within the Bureau as a keen judge of human nature, and that talent was about to be sorely needed once again.

———

"Somebody fired a big bertha execution style into the front seat of a car in which a Congresswoman named Virginia Wetherill and her husband were riding. She wasn't hit, but he was blown away. Happened about three hours ago outside of Philadelphia." Owens was typically silent, so Thad continued, "She may have been the intended target. Will you get us two tickets on the 0700 Acela? Get the club car so we can talk. Bump somebody if necessary."

"Will do."

Thad continued, "Charlie Townsend will email us everything they learn so we'll have the travel time to review it. See you then." He started to ring off, but paused. "And Owens?"

"Yes Chief."

"Were you really asleep?"

"Yes Chief."

"You amaze me Owens." Then he hung up. He lay back and, as earlier, looked toward the dark ceiling that he could sense but not quite see. This time he caught himself smiling, and at that his smile broadened. "All right Pennock," he said out loud, "bad guys to catch." He closed his eyes and within three minutes was sound asleep.

CHAPTER 4

By the time the ambulance carrying Congresswoman Virginia Wetherill arrived at the emergency room entrance, the news had spread among the doctors and nurses on duty that she was on her way with some wounds and that her husband had been killed by gunfire. She got royal and sympathetic treatment. Pieces of window glass had superficially cut her right palm and knee and some were shallowly embedded in the back of her head and neck. It took half an hour to clean and dress these wounds. A plastic surgeon stitched a deep but narrow cut high on her forehead caused by a splinter of plastic from the car's interior. Because she appeared to be in shock she was admitted and sedated. She spent the night in a drug-induced sleep.

The shooting occurred just late enough for the story to miss the early edition of the Philadelphia and national papers, but it was all over the morning news shows and the Internet news. The first pictures taken were cell phone pictures by good, or just curious, Samaritans who happened upon the scene.

The most scintillating visual came from a cell phone camera showing the Congresswoman, illuminated in headlights, collapsed in the middle of the road and gripping the leg of a young man bending over her. Other footage was background, Wetherill and Warner at the fundraising dinner earlier that evening, several other shots of Warner, footage from some of the Congresswoman's subcommittee hearings, and some background on Warner. Speculation as to the reason for the attack was swirling. The most popular theory was a busted gangland-style hit intended for the crusading Congresswoman.

Veronica Patterson expected the story to be sensational, but that interested her little. She never left Wetherill's hospital room that night. She drew her chair close to the bed to look into her boss's face and hold her hand. Occasionally she caught herself nodding off, but most of the night she silently watched over this singular and powerful presence that, even in sleep, held her own world together. The rhythmic rise and fall of the white sheet covering Wetherill comforted her. She thought of the events of the night, imagining herself in Wetherill's place. *So courageous*, she thought, and her devotion welled up like...*like what?* She couldn't articulate it and had never been able to. Ever since she could remember she had to feel passionately about something or someone, as if the intensity of her feelings served a purpose of its own, preventive, a high-voltage shield that kept in check some dark internal force she did not understand.

Well into the night, when there were no hospital noises, she leaned close to Wetherill's nest of red hair and whispered, "You are so brave."

CHAPTER 5

Thad and Owens settled into the back seat. Townsend was in the front with his driver. By resorting to flashing lights and sirens, the driver could get to The University of Pennsylvania Hospital complex within two minutes, but Townsend was content to crawl along with the morning rush hour traffic. He needed the time to brief his colleagues on the latest information.

He began, "No doubt that jurisdiction over this one will be federal, but the state's CSI guys got to the scene quickly, and they're very good, so we've just been monitoring while they do the analysis." He continued, "Preliminary findings from them and the coroner's office show that Warner died from blasts of shot from a 12 gauge at five to six feet. Most of his head and neck were exploded away."

"Warner was six feet tall and as you saw from the pictures I sent you kind of movie star handsome. Apparently he was his own man. Had a successful career owning and breeding mares to stallions with good records on the track. Traveled to Argentina, Dubai, Japan and other racing hotspots. He and the Congresswoman were apart almost half the time, but no indication the marriage suffered. They had their separate interests, hers politics and his horses.

"Prior to the shooting, the victim had been in good shape. All internal organs were normal for a man of fifty. His bad cholesterol was a little high, and his liver enzymes were slightly elevated."

"Probably enjoyed a glass or two of wine," Thad said.

"Not just booze," Charlie smiled. "Blood, urine and hair tests were positive for coke. The levels as well as the condition of his nasal tissue indicate moderate, social use. The guy wasn't an addict, but used. That's basically it on the victim's physical condition so far."

"Anything from the crime scene?"

Charlie flipped to another page of his notes. "Blood, brains, and bone fragments were everywhere, as you would predict. Also glass, metal and plastic fragments, and paint chips – all from the victim's car. It's fancy, a 745 BMW. On the floor of the passenger seat and the back seat there are traces of the Congresswoman's blood. Nothing from the shooter's car except pellets of buckshot."

He continued, "There are scratches on the passenger side door just at the base of the window. Possibly they were made by the edge of the barrel of the murder weapon striking Warner's car. The killer was that close. If so, we might get some idea of what oil was used to clean it. There should also be some residue from the gases escaping the barrel after the shots were fired. On the ground were four shell casings, one of them run over by the shooter when he left. They're Federal two and three quarter double-ought. Also some tire marks. We're checking.

Owens interjected, "That all says to me it was a tactical shotgun. The barrel would have to be short for the shell casings to eject onto the ground rather than into the shooter's car. Both that gun type and the buckshot load are standard fair for mob executions."

Charlie nodded, "Yeah. Besides, the tactical weapon would be a lot easier for someone sitting in a car to maneuver." He checked his notes again. "Okay let's see. In the car was a contact lens case and pen flashlight still on but dying out. A woman's small purse was wedged between the front passenger seat and the console. It contained nothing surprising – comb, lipstick, eye shadow, handkerchief, breath mints, wallet, cell phone. All this was returned to the Congresswoman, or more precisely to a lady named Veronica Patterson who is the Congresswoman's chief of staff. Warner has a daughter who lives in Dallas and a brother in Seattle. Wetherill has no siblings or children, and it appears this Veronica, she goes by Nikki, is a close friend as well as her chief of staff.

Charlie flipped a page of his notes as they rounded the long bend before the entrance to the hospital. He continued, "In the victim's suit pockets were an I-phone, wallet, reading glasses, and a handkerchief and some change. The wallet contained a hundred sixty-four dollars cash, American Express platinum card, Citigroup Visa card, driver's license, medical insurance card, a card for passing through electronic security, probably at his office, we'll check, and several of his business cards."

The car pulled to a stop at the front door of the hospital. Charlie added, "Our geek squad will run the phone and all computers in his home and office. Could take a while. And that's about it. With the background material I emailed to you first thing this morning, you now know what I know."

Inside, at the main desk, Townsend flashed his badge and got the room number for Wetherill. The three men took the elevator to the fourth floor, found the nearest nurse station and went through the drill again. This time Thad spoke. His assumption of the lead role required no communication with Townsend. He addressed all three nurses there, assuming that the one in charge would respond. "I'm Thaddeus Pennock of the FBI." He disliked using titles. He thought they created a barrier and impeded communication. He gestured toward Charlie and Owens, "This is Agent Charles Townsend and Agent Robert Owens. We're here to see Congresswoman Wetherill if her medical condition permits. I believe we're expected."

Thad unconsciously shifted into a more formal speech pattern when he spoke with the authority of his office. But it was a quiet, confident authority, complimented by his physical appearance. He was six two, weighed 195 pounds and kept in shape.

A gray-haired nurse who wore a tag that read, "Barnard, R.N.," stepped forward and shook Thad's hand. "I am Alice Barnard," she announced. "There are agents outside the Congresswoman's room who told us you would be here and would want to question her. Doctor Milstein saw her about half an hour ago and left word that she was awake and alert. He said you could be with her for ten or fifteen minutes, no more. The condition is that I be in the room to monitor her in case your questions upset her too much."

"Fair enough, we don't want to jeopardize her health."

Nurse Barnard continued, "The Congresswoman has a head staff person whose name is Veronica Patterson. Her presence seems to comfort the Congresswoman. She stayed in the room all night and is there now, and Doctor Milstein said it would be best if she remained during the interview." Then she added, "I believe you are likely to get a better result that way anyhow."

"Well," Thad responded, "I would like the three of us to be present. That makes five in the room altogether. Will that work?"

"Yes, I suggest you address your questions from the foot of her bed and that Ms. Patterson be permitted to sit beside her. I will stand close to the head of her bed where I can observe the patient and monitor the instruments. The other gentlemen should stand away a little, perhaps just inside the door."

"Okay with you?" Thad asked.

"It works," said Townsend. Owens nodded.

"All right then," said Nurse Barnard. She purposefully led them down the main corridor and around a corner where four people stood before the closed door of an end room. There were two uniformed police officers and a man and a woman in business attire. Thad smiled to himself. *Why do FBI agents look just like FBI agents? Might as well be wearing neon signs.* There were introductions all around. Nurse Barnard looked at Thad and said, "I'm going in to ask Ms. Patterson to come out and meet you, so that everybody knows the procedure when we go back in." Thad nodded, and she disappeared into the room. Thad took the moment to tell the room guards what would happen inside.

Soon an attractive but obviously fatigued woman came through the door. Thad had trained himself to catalogue his first impressions in as much detail as he could. He trusted first impressions. He observed that Patterson's hair was pulled back and gathered behind her head with some kind of band. It looked to Thad like she was a natural dirty blond, her hair color, skin tone, and eyebrows all in synch. Her features were well proportioned, and her intelligent blue eyes were guarded. She was slightly tanned, like someone who is in the sun to draw in health not color. She wore a well-tailored skirt and jacket under which was a white, collared shirt. A night of tossing and turning in a chair had wrinkled them all. *Tasteful business dress*, he thought. *She's between thirty and thirty-five,* he guessed. Looking at her low-heeled shoes, he guessed again. *Maybe 5' 6."* *Good looking shoes*, he thought, *better looking legs. In good shape. Looks smart, but all business.*

Thad stepped forward extending his hand, "I'm Thaddeus Pennock with the FBI. You are...?"

"I am Nikki Patterson, Congresswoman Wetherill's chief of staff. I'm the one closest to her," and added, looking right into his eyes, "living."

She definitely wanted to make that clear, Thad registered. He introduced the others. Nikki continued, "You should know that Virginia," she caught herself, "Congresswoman Wetherill will force herself to look and act stronger than she is. Please don't be fooled by that. This has rocked her. She is convinced that she was the intended victim, so she's dealing with guilt." *Sure of herself and in charge*, Thad thought.

"Why does she think that?" he asked. Nikki's eyes widened slightly, and she set her head back as if she had gotten a whiff of an unpleasant odor.

"Why it's common knowledge that she's zeroing in on the drug bosses in Philadelphia; besides, there's no reason why anyone would want to kill Taylor. He was nice to everyone."

"Have you talked to the Congresswoman since the shooting?"

"Not really. I've been in the room with her nearly the whole time, and as the sedation has worn off, she's said things like, 'My God, it should have been me.'"

Turning to Townsend and Owens Thad said, "When I'm through, I'll look over and you let me know if we need to cover something I missed, all right?"

Both men nodded. They walked quietly in and took their agreed places. Thad noted that it was an ample, corner room. Large windows on two sides provided plenty of natural light. *Can't be too many rooms like this in the hospital*, Thad thought as he moved to the foot of the only bed in the room. He could see Wetherill's face well. She was propped up on pillows directly facing him, and she would not have to make the effort of turning her head to see or address him. He glanced at Nurse Barnard and nodded. She returned his look and smiled. Then his gaze returned to the Congresswoman, and he began his ritual of tallying first impressions.

When they had entered the room, Wetherill had opened her eyes but had not moved. Now that Thad was facing her she looked directly at him. He was struck by astonishing green eyes flashing under long lashes backlit by a mane of blazing red hair splayed on white pillows. She had the light complexion of a natural redhead and a sprinkle of freckles. She wore no makeup he could detect. The top sheet was pulled up under her arms and tucked in, so that only her arms, shoulders, neck and head were visible. Her impossibly long fingers rested on the tight, white sheet that was molded to the shape of her sleek body under it. She was motionless yet projected beauty and power that dominated the room.

Thad began, "Congresswoman Wetherill, can you hear me all right?" There was a silence of about five seconds. She remained perfectly still.

A quiet but rich, "I can."

"I'm Thaddeus Pennock of the FBI. Charles Townsend and Robert Owens by the door are also with the FBI. We're involved in the investigation that will bring your husband's killers to justice." He saw a slight eye flutter at that, but nothing more.

"I am very sorry for your loss. This is a difficult part of our job – imposing at a very private and painful time. But we must find the persons responsible. The odds of doing that tend to lessen with the passage of time, so I cannot wait as long as respect for your ordeal would normally dictate." He was not aware that his speech pattern had again become formal, almost stilted. He paused, but she clearly had nothing to say. He continued. "Many questions can wait until later, but some cannot if we are to do our job. I hope you understand. Do you believe you are up to answering a few questions?"

During this little introduction her eyes had strayed, and her gaze seemed to go to that middle distance where they look upon thoughts not surroundings. But with his question they returned to his face. There was a pause just long enough to indicate who would control the pace of the conversation. "Continue," she said in the same low-pitched voice, like a monarch to one of her ministers.

He began. "Tell me as best you can recall what happened from the time you left the Marriott."

"I don't want to talk about seeing my husband. I may never be able to. I fear I will remember him like that and never rid my mind of that image." "Rid my mind" struck Thad as curious. *A problem solved by willpower rather than a wound she must rely on time to heal. Controlling?* He wondered.

"Fair enough, let's just see how it goes. What time did you leave the hotel?"

"I don't know exactly, nine-fifty, maybe a little later."

"The car was yours?"

"Yes, well my husband's. It's a BMW, larger than my car so we often take it when we must get gussied up." "Gussied" struck Thad as a curious choice, and it was the first word she had spoken in other than a simple, flat tone. *Cynical?* He asked himself.

She continued without prompting. "Normally, I'm the driver after parties. Taylor drinks more than I, so we have that agreement. But last night, one of my contact lenses was acting up. I didn't have glasses with me. So he drove." Thad caught her use of the present tense, "Taylor drinks more...." How often he had seen that in loved ones immediately after a death, particularly a sudden, unexpected death. She continued, "Anyhow, he was not in bad shape at all. We drove along for some time, and my eye got too uncomfortable. I needed to get the lens out."

"Were you talking at this point or did you have the radio on?"

"Yes for the radio, no for talking. After the mindless chatter you endure at those functions, silence is welcome. Anyway, I wanted him to concentrate on the road."

"What function was it?" Thad asked.

"A typical fundraiser, a necessary evil of politics."

"About how far had you gone when you took the lens out?"

"Shortly before we reached that stop sign. The lens dropped off my finger before I got it into the case. I couldn't tell if it dropped on my shoe or on the floor. I think I said, 'damn it,' or maybe worse. I carry a little pen flashlight in my purse and used it to try to find the lens."

"I didn't see it on my shoes, so I maneuvered around, sat on my leg so I could see more of the floor when I leaned down. If you've ever seen someone look for a lens, you would get the picture. You go through a methodical sequence of search steps." She paused and then went on. "I felt the car slowing down. We were stopped only a few seconds when ...." she stopped. Thad sensed that she was not waiting for a question, but gathering herself to continue. Her eyes shut tightly. With their allure curtained, his gaze shifted to the near perfect shape and proportion of her nose and mouth. Then those long fingers closed on the bed sheet, gathering it in a movement to which the prior absolute stillness of her body imparted exaggerated significance. A silent moment passed, and then her eye muscles relaxed, letting the gathering moisture well under her lower lids. In her left eye a tear formed and grew heavy. It adhered briefly, trembling, and then slid down her high cheekbone and dropped and disappeared into her fiery red hair.

She took a breath and continued. "I heard Taylor start to say, 'what is that . . . .?' Then everything exploded over my head, literally. I dove for the floor and got as much of me there as I could. There were several explosions. Maybe four. Glass and..." she paused, "wet...were everywhere." She paused again. Thad nodded, but waited. "I was frozen and just trying to be safe." During this description, her eyes moved to the white sheet covering her. It seemed to be the screen onto which her mind's eye projected the scene.

After a moment she quietly said, "It was meant for me. Taylor should be alive." Silence again. She was deep in her thoughts.

"You are too hard on yourself," Thad heard himself say. She slowly shook her head sideways, shut her eyes, and then opened them at the same time as she set her jaw.

"No, no!" she said forcefully. "The windows of that car are darkened. You cannot see in. Whoever shot at us would have thought I was sitting in the passenger seat rather than groping around on the floor like an idiot for a contact lens. No! It was meant for me, Agent Pennock!" Then she let the tension out of her shoulders and relaxed into the pillows. Her eyes looked over Thad's head. He was struck again by her beauty and was immediately irritated with himself. *This is work, asshole,* he told himself. She was quiet.

"Congresswoman Wetherill, who would want to kill you?" With that question, she came to life. Still glistening, her eyes widened. Color replaced her pallor, and he could sense animation even in her stillness.

"That's not the place to start Agent Pennock. The question is who would want to kill Taylor? He's very successful, and I'm sure the envy of many in his business." *She's using the present tense again,* he noted. "There have been a few lawsuits over the sale of this or that horse, but that leads at most to mediation or litigation. Nobody gets killed over it. The fact is there is no one on this earth who would gain anything from killing him."

Nikki Patterson *made the same point before we came in the room,* Thad recalled, without attributing importance to it. He pressed, "What about people he came into contact with socially or through sports or hobbies?"

"I know many of them, and I know the type. They would be even less likely murderers than his business competitors. I can't think of one."

"Okay, did he have relatives who stood to benefit by his death, possibly a brother, sister, son, or daughter in financial trouble?"

She shook her head. "No, I've met his brother, and to be frank, even if he needed money badly, he wouldn't have the balls to kill him." Thad was slightly startled by the street slang, so antithetical to the impression she otherwise made. She continued, "His only child is a daughter who loves him, or thinks she does. I'm the one she doesn't like because I came into Taylor's life, and she thinks I crowd her out. It's the classic stepmother syndrome. Maybe she would kill me, but certainly not her father." Then, she added, "Actually, she wouldn't kill me. She derives too much pleasure being irritated by me. It keeps her happily sour. She is so unlike Taylor! It's hard to believe she's his daughter."

"Congresswoman Wetherill, here is one of those . . ."

She broke in and with a dismissive flick of her hand said, "I'm tired of hearing 'Congresswoman Wetherill.' Just use 'Virginia.' We'll finish more quickly that way." He didn't like the informality of "Virginia" despite her invitation, so he ignored it.

"I have one of those questions I have to ask. Did your husband have any extramarital affairs? Is there possibly a jilted lover or lover's husband out there?"

"Impossible!" she said pointedly. "The ladies love him, and he certainly got around before we were married. But," she looked directly into Thad's eyes, "he couldn't do that without my finding out. I know him too well. Besides, he wouldn't." Thad thought, *she said that like 'he wouldn't dare,' not like 'he loves me too much'.* He noted that yet again she spoke of him in the present tense. But this time it did not sit well. *How could she be unconsciously thinking of her husband as alive if the question she's answering is "who killed him?"* He filed the thought away, one of the many unplaced pieces of the puzzle.

Thad continued, "You mentioned that your husband drank alcohol. Did he use drugs – for example, marijuana or cocaine?"

"Certainly not!" she snapped in irritation, her head and shoulders tensing for an instant. "He knows drugs are anathema to me. He told me that there was a time when he smoked marijuana and he said he had experimented with cocaine, but this was well before we were married. He occasionally drinks more than I wish, but that's all." Thad and Owens exchanged a quick glance that said, *so Warner had a secret.*

Thad knew they had been talking for close to his allotted time. Yet, he got no sense that the Congresswoman was physically taxed or uncomfortable. "May we now go back to my earlier question? If you were the intended target, who would want to kill you and why?"

She looked at him quizzically. "Have you been following at all my investigation of the drug underworld in Philadelphia? Do you realize that more drugs come into the east coast through Philadelphia and Newark, New Jersey, than any other port? Not Miami," she continued, "not New York, but Philadelphia?"

He found himself wanting to explain why he didn't know yet irritated for feeling defensive. "My job is to catch the killers not stop the drug trafficking itself. I'm sure our drug units and the Drug Enforcement Agency are following it more closely."

Nurse Barnard interjected, "Agent Pennock, we must obey the doctor's instructions."

"Of course, but I would just like the congresswoman to finish the comment she was in the middle of." Without waiting for a response Thad looked back at Wetherill expectantly, and she continued.

"I received a threat in the mail about two weeks ago. It came in a plain envelope mailed from Philadelphia. The address on the envelope was a taped-on cutout of my official Washington address printed off my website. The letter consisted of words cut out of newspapers and glued to blank paper. It said, 'Understand clearly. If you do not stop sniffing around, you are going to lose your nose and the rest of your pretty face.' That was it exactly."

"Where is the letter now?"

"For heaven's sake!" she said, again irritated, "the FBI has it! You have it! Don't you fellows communicate with each other?"

Thad felt sheepish and wondered if he visibly reddened. *Jesus! How in hell did we miss that?* "This is news to me Congresswoman," he said in his best "I apologize" tone.

"No matter," she said, with another flick of her fingers. "Your high-tech experts couldn't make anything of it. Better up your budget request for next year."

Thad's brow furrowed. "Have you any idea who might have sent it?"

"I have no proof but I know." She took a deep breath. "Leonard Moretti!" she hissed in a tone she hadn't used before. Then her head and shoulders came off the pillows and her eyes flashed. She pointed a long index finger at Thad and angrily exclaimed, "I'm damn sure not backing off! Not after losing my husband to the bastard! Moretti and his gorillas made a big fucking mistake not killing me!"

That was enough for Nurse Barnard. She briskly moved toward Thad saying, "All right, time's up. The patient needs her rest."

He didn't resist. He looked at Wetherill and said, "Thank you Congresswoman Wetherill for seeing us. I'm sure you understand that we will need to continue soon."

Wetherill dropped heavily back on her pillows. She was through. Just as Nurse Barnard reached him Thad said, "Just one more thing." Wetherill did not turn her head or otherwise move and Nurse Barnard stopped.

"It looks from the scene as if the car following yours took advantage of the stop sign to pull alongside between your car and the shoulder. The window had to be down because there is no evidence of car glass at the scene other than from your car." In the corner of his eye Thad could see indecision written on Nurse Barnard's face. She was torn between pushing him toward the door and learning the gory details.

He continued, "The damage to your car suggests a straight-in trajectory for the shots. No angle, so either the driver was the shooter and stopped his car even with yours, or the driver pulled his car forward of yours so a shooter in the back seat could aim straight in. After the shooting, it looks like the driver immediately turned right and got away with no one identifying a license number, make of the car, or even the color. Did you notice a car following yours, or did you see the car pull up next to yours, or possibly see a face, or see the car leave?"

The Congresswoman gave a slow sideways nod, eyes still on the ceiling, and said, "You don't wear contact lenses, do you Agent Pennock?"

"I don't."

"If you did you wouldn't need to ask those questions."

It was his turn to nod. "I see," he said.

Now Nurse Barnard sternly pronounced, "I must insist Agent Pennock."

"I'm very sorry for your loss Congresswoman, and I am convinced that you should not blame yourself for your husband's death. The weapon used was powerful, and there were multiple shots fired. If you had been sitting in a normal position in your seat, in all probability it would not have saved your husband. Both of you would have been killed." He resisted Nurse Barnard's push for an instant, waiting for a reaction to his words.

Almost inaudibly she said to the ceiling, "But you cannot know that for sure."

It was not a question.

CHAPTER 6

A dozen reporters and several camera crews lay in wait as they exited the hospital. This was Townsend's jurisdiction and his responsibility to deal with the barrage of questions. From experience he knew simply to wait silently until the gaggle got the message that nothing was going to happen until they shut up. It didn't take long.

Townsend was an easy communicator. "Good morning to you," he said. "I'm Agent Charles Townsend of the FBI, as some of you know. With me are Thaddeus Pennock and Robert Owens of the DC office of the FBI. Representative Wetherill's doctors allowed us to spend a few minutes with her. She appears to be recovering. I hope that when she is released, you'll give her some space. She's been through a rough time."

"I expect you know the drill. I'm not going to answer substantive questions. This is an ongoing investigation. We're in the process of gathering the facts. We'll set up briefing sessions for you and will tell you what we can when we can. It may not be all we know. That's it for now."

They moved toward the waiting car, and the questions began again.

"Do you have any suspects?"

"Was the husband the target?"

"How did Congresswoman Wetherill avoid being hit?"

At this one, Thad leaned toward Charlie and quietly said, "If we don't address this one, Lord knows what crazy speculation there will be." Townsend nodded and turned and raised a hand, palm out. "Okay," he said, "I'm going to violate my 'no comment' rule and give you one piece of information we know." An eager silence fell immediately.

"The Congresswoman was not in the line of fire. She had taken a contact lens from her eye and dropped it in the process. So she was bent over looking for it on the car floor when the killer opened up." He then thought of Wetherill's comment and borrowed it. "If any of you wear contact lenses, you get the picture." There were several smiles and nods. Someone said out loud what most were thinking, "My god was she lucky!"

Then a voice from the back remarked, "She's lucky she didn't just bolt upright from surprise with the first shot."

"No, she kept down. She has some cuts from flying glass and splinters but fortunately these are not serious." He raised both hands palms out. "Okay, that's it now." They walked the rest of the way to the waiting car. That one comment stuck in Thad's mind. "She's lucky she didn't bolt upright in surprise...." *Would someone really do that?*

CHAPTER 7

When they were in the car, Thad said, "Let's map this out back in your office Charlie, and for heaven's sake let's find out why they didn't tell us about that threat letter!"

Since early morning he had been in problem-solving mode, absorbing each new fact, guessing at its significance. Now he wanted a minute to de-concentrate, as he called it, and see what bubbled to the surface. Alternating images vied for his attention. One was of Congresswoman Wetherill lying still and controlled in the quiet of her hospital room, where everything but her blazing red hair and green eyes was white and neat and ordered and where her strong will dominated. The other was of her huddling near the car floor trying to protect herself while everything above her was violently blown apart by a succession of shotgun blasts.

He was struck by an incongruity. A prominent man had been murdered in a most brutal manner. Yet, so far, the dead man seemed to be just a bit player. Such was the commanding presence of Congresswoman Wetherill. He thought about this but it gave rise to no insight. So, he did what he usually did when he was stuck.

"Owens?" He said. More elaborate communication was unnecessary.

Owens touched his chin, a habit, and offered his observations. "It seems to me that Congresswoman Wetherill is unusually ambitious and disciplined. That leads me to believe she is telling the truth when she says she doesn't use coke or other drugs. Politically she can't afford to. She also can't risk having them around her. That means Warner was hiding his coke use from her. Maybe he snuck into the garage to sniff, but I don't think so. Coke is a social drug so the odds are he used with other people. I think he probably had some social life he was hiding from her. Maybe the killer comes from that secret life. If we get lucky, his phone or computer will give us a lead. If not, we need to discover it somehow." Heads in the car nodded at the logic of this. *What would I do without the round man?* Thad said to himself.

Then aloud he said, "Charlie, I agree it makes sense for me to be involved in this one." Charlie knew that was Thad's way of saying he would run the show, which was no surprise. Charlie had assumed as much when he called Thad the night before.

In Townsend's office in the Federal Building on 9th Street, close to Independence Hall, the three of them spent ninety minutes with coffee and donuts sketching out the investigation matrix and manpower needs. Then they adjourned to a conference room where they met with agents in the Philadelphia office and conferenced in agents in the DC office and assigned investigation responsibilities between the two offices. Once all the parts were in motion, Thad stood up and said, "Now let's take a look at the car."

CHAPTER 8

The Philadelphia Police Department and Pennsylvania State Police jointly operated a warehouse on Patton Avenue in which vehicles involved in a crime were impounded. It contained an onsite laboratory where analysis and tests were performed to discover and preserve evidence. When Charlie, Owens, and Thad arrived, two state crime scene investigators, alerted by a phone call from Charlie's office, were waiting. The taller one extended his hand. "I'm Lieutenant Peter Hurd," he said, "and this is Corporal Sam Rosen," pointing to his colleague.

When introductions were completed, Thad said, "Lieutenant, I read your initial report. Anything new?"

"Yes, Agent Pennock. The car may have been run through a car wash as recently as yesterday. We've confirmed only two sets of prints, the victim and his wife. No prints outside except around the two front doors. But as you know from our initial findings, there are scratches in the paint right below the window that we thought might have been caused by the murder weapon. Since then, we've identified traces of gun oil and the gases that always escape out the barrel of a shotgun when it's fired."

"As I expect you know, the gases that settle around the window well are more protected from the elements. We swabbed that area and picked them up. We're still analyzing them."

Thad asked, "They won't tell us much by themselves, right?"

"Probably not Agent Pennock, but if we get the other car, who knows?"

Charlie offered, "Doesn't surprise me that there are no other prints on the exterior. From what we know the killer left the scene pretty fast."

"Got anything else?" Thad asked.

"No sir."

"Okay," Thad said, "let's have a look."

Corporal Rosen produced latex gloves. The FBI agents stretched them on and slowly walked around the BMW twice in silence. They saw little damage on the passenger side, just a small sliver of glass left in the bottom right hand corner of the window, and the scratches on the paint just below the window. But the interior of the driver's side of the car was another story. It was smashed and mangled and sprayed with dried blood and tiny dried pieces of flesh and gray matter.

Finally, Thad looked at Hurd and asked, "Lieutenant, do you have any doubt that if the Congresswoman had been sitting in the passenger seat, she would have been killed?"

"No doubt."

Thad continued, "If she had been in the line of fire, that is, sitting in her seat in a normal way, what do you think the odds are that Warner would still have been killed?"

"Well, if the Congresswoman had been sitting normally, we're talking four loads of buckshot moving at fourteen hundred feet per second with the barrel within maybe eighteen inches of her. There wouldn't have been much left of her to stop the second, third and fourth rounds. Mr. Warner would have taken them pretty much full force."

"Wouldn't the result have been the same if the shooter had been on the other side of the car? What I mean is, so long as he shot straight across the front seat, they both definitely die regardless of which side the shooter is on. Have I got it right?"

"No doubt in my mind," said Lieutenant Hurd.

Owens then spoke, sounding almost absent-minded. "So most likely the shooter was driving and is right-handed." Hurd and Rosen, who did not know Owens, looked puzzled. Thad and Charlie cracked nearly identical smiles. Thad said to himself, *Here he goes. He's going to solve it right here and now.*

Aloud he said, "Mind letting us mortals in on it?"

Owens' cheeks pinked slightly. "Well..." he began, touching his chin, "There was no need for the killer to maneuver his car between Warner's and the bank if two people were in his car. Much easier for the driver to pull up on the left as if he was intending to pass. The shooter would shoot from the back seat. That makes the approach and the get-away much easier. But if the driver is the shooter, unless he's left handed, he would want to shoot right-to-left across his body with his right arm and hand controlling the weapon. So Warner's car would have to be on his left. Besides, that way the gun barrel would be outside of his own car when he fired and closer to his target. He wouldn't have to shoot across his own front seat and out his own right window." He stopped and there was a respectful silence.

Charlie shook his head in admiration. "We are in the presence of Sherlock Holmes himself." Owens smiled and lowered his eyes. Thad added, "You get used to it. Annoying habit of his. He takes the fun out of solving crimes." Then turning to Corporal Rosen, he said, Corporal, you're built thin like the Congresswoman. Would you get in the passenger seat and tuck your left leg up under you and bend down like you're looking on the floor for a contact lens? Looks to me like the passenger side door still works fine." Thad opened the door for Rosen and paused, "If he gets in there, he's going to be sitting on some blood stains. Any problem with that Lieutenant?"

"No, we've taken all the samples and photos we need."

"Lieutenant, do you know if the seat positions on either of these front seats have been changed since the shooting – up, down, forward, backward."

Sounding offended, Hurd answered, "No way! This is an evidence car."

"No offense meant, just checking."

Corporal Rosen got in, tucked his left leg underneath him on the seat and pushed his buttocks up against the door. This exposed more of the carpet on which to look for an imaginary lens. He bent his shoulders and head down into the open space. His rounded shoulders, the highest part of his body, were several inches below the window ledge. *Safely below the scatter pattern of the shot,* Thad concluded. *And someone the exact size of Wetherill would probably be lower.* Satisfied, he said, "Thank you Corporal." Then he looked around the group. "Anybody know the weather forecast for tonight around 10 PM?"

Corporal Rosen spoke up, "Should be about the same as last night. Weatherman says we're in a high pressure trough for another day or two."

"I don't care about temperature so much. It's the lighting conditions."

Charlie said, "We can get weather info that'll be very specific about that."

"Can your people also find a dealer who has this model BMW with the same tint in the glass? The Federal government would like to borrow it."

"No doubt," Charlie answered.

"And do you have a female agent or someone on the payroll with roughly the same height and frame as Wetherill?"

"So long as you don't need the same face and figure I can fill the bill. Anything else? Want to give me a hard one?"

"Can't think of one. Since Owens won't tell us the name and address of the killer, we'll just have to plod along."

———

At 9:45 that evening, a glittering, new BMW 745i with smoked windows pulled up to the intersection where Warner was shot. The driver and his female passenger were FBI agents. Charlie had come through. The female agent, Nancy Baxter, was Wetherill's size. The agent driving stopped within a chalked area indicating the spot at which Warner had stopped his car the night before. Charlie, Owens, Thad, and Charlie's driver followed in an FBI sedan. The driver pulled to the right of the BMW, which forced the right wheels of the car well onto the shoulder. He tracked the tire marks left by the shooter's car so the distance between the two cars would be identical to the distance between Warner's car and the shooter's. He stopped when his window was even with the front passenger window of the BMW. Because of the grade of the shoulder, he sat slightly lower than the occupants of the BMW.

A state police patrol car followed and stopped behind the BMW. Two troopers, one male and one female, got out and placed low red flares on the road to alert oncoming traffic of the stopped cars. The flares were far enough away from the cars not to alter the shade of the darkness enveloping them. Thad got out of the back seat of the FBI car and walked around to the driver's side. There was just enough room between the cars for the driver to open his door and squeeze out and for Thad to squeeze in and take his place. Owens was in the passenger seat beside him. The driver opened the trunk, removed a Mossberg 12 gauge tactical shotgun and a Remington 12-gauge hunting shotgun and handed the Remington to Thad through the open window.

Sitting in the driver's seat, where the killer would have been, Thad tried to point the gun at the closed, passenger-side window of the BMW, but the barrel was so long that he had to lean back into the car to create enough space to level the barrel. The casing ejection chamber was within the car so that ejecting shells would land inside not outside onto the ground. Thad then repeated the exercise with the Mossberg tactical gun. When he brought it to his shoulder and pointed it at the dark window of the other car, he found he would have to lean out only slightly for the tip of the barrel to contact the other car, rendering feasible the theory that the scratch on Warner's car was made by the murder weapon. He also saw that the casing ejection chamber was positioned just outside his own window. Owens spoke aloud the thought all three shared, "Whoever did it was a pro or wanted us to think he was a pro."

Thad looked hard at the dark window of the BMW for about ten seconds. He had asked Agent Baxter to sit in a normal position in the passenger seat, but he could not see her. "Can you see inside at all Owens? See any outlines of people or movement?" Owens peered over Thad's shoulder.

"Nothing."

"Me either," Thad said, "and I'm right on top of the window. Not until I blow it out would I see inside."

He leaned out and tapped the window of the BMW, which promptly tracked down. "Couldn't see a thing," he said. "How about you?"

"We could make you out," Nancy Baxter said. "Enough to shoot you both," she added with a smile. He smiled back.

She might not look like Wetherill but she has a better sense of humor.

"Okay," he said. "This time, Nancy, you look for the lens on the floor like we practiced. Do you have the penlight?"

"Right," she said as she closed her window.

Thad looked hard at the BMW's window. "Look different to you?"

Owens stared for several seconds. "Looks the same," he said. "I can't see shadows or movements."

"Me either. The penlight's beam is too weak, and her body blocks it." Again he tapped the BMW window, and Nancy lowered it. "Still nothing," Thad said. "Was the penlight on?"

"Yes," Nancy answered, pointing at the floor. Thad sat thinking for a moment.

"Nancy, leave the window open and get down again looking for the lens." She did so.

With the window open, the BMW's interior dimly glowed from the red LED backlights that illuminated the many dials, numbers, and other controls on the dashboard, center console and overhead. The sill of the BMW's passenger door was slightly higher than the sill of the door of Thad's car. It blocked his sight line to the BMW's floor. Thad could see the driver as a dark but definite shape, but Nancy Baxter was almost out of sight. Only the top of her hunched shoulders, the parts of her body farthest away from him, were vaguely visible. The only way he could see more of her was to raise his own body up well off the seat of the car and look down into the other car.

He put the shotgun to his shoulder. He found that the gun barrel blocked his view of Nancy even more. As he held that position a piece of the puzzle took shape in his mind. *If the shots were rapid, as Wetherill says, stuff would be flying all around. The killer might have squinted so as not to take a flying shard in the eye. And if he left quickly after shooting, it's possible and maybe likely he never saw Wetherill, even with the flash that each shot would make.*

He pulled the shotgun down and sat thinking for a moment. Then he turned toward Owens next to him and Charlie behind Owens and said, "Unless he's a moron, the killer knew the chances were high that both Warner and Wetherill would die even if only one of them was his target. So he's not thinking about shooting to get one and miss the other. The only thing he needs to know for sure is that his target is in the front seat of that car. How does he do that?"

Owens didn't pause, "He has to see them getting in or been told by someone who saw them get in."

"Right. He not only has to identify the car he's going to follow but also be certain who is in the front seat. So, he knows before he ever pulls up next to the car that both are there and both are going to be killed. Besides, killing both of them leaves no witness who might see his face or the car or get the license number."

"Sounds right," Charlie commented. Owens was silent.

Thad continued, "The point is, he's not trying to miss anyone, so he doesn't need to see in before he starts firing."

From the back seat Charlie offered, "That's the real world. The guy pulls up and just starts firing."

Owens frowned and held his chin. Thad waited. He knew Owens was circling the problem, as he always did. Before Owens began, Charlie spoke up, "The shooter was expecting two people in the car. He blew out the glass with the first shot and saw only Warner. If the Congresswoman was his target, he needed to locate her and do the job. Get out of his car to do it if necessary. He didn't do that. So he must have been after Warner."

Thad shook his head. "Maybe, but I'm not so sure. Imagine you're the shooter. You've gotten off four loud rounds and maybe that's all you loaded. But something's happened you didn't expect – only one person is visible. You haven't rehearsed this one, haven't considered the options or weighed the odds." He gestured out his side window. "That house over there is within earshot of a very loud noise and maybe someone will look out a window or maybe another car is approaching. You might be seen. Besides, you might have to reload. You'd only have to expend a few seconds trying to decide what to do and whether you could do it quickly before your indecision decided it for you. So you might leave without killing Wetherill even if she was your target."

Owens and Charlie both nodded at the logic of this. Then, as if on cue, Thad and Charlie looked at Owens, who had not yet spoken. The round man pushed his glasses up his nose and quietly began. "Maybe not seeing Wetherill was proof that he'd killed her." Both Thad and Charlie looked puzzled. This had not occurred to them. Their theories assumed just the opposite.

Gesturing toward the BMW, Owens continued, "That first shot at the window would really blow things apart right in the shooter's face too. All he would see is the muzzle flash and the window exploding in and he wouldn't see even that if he were smart enough to close his eyes against flying glass. We know from Wetherill's statements that the shots were in quick succession. He probably saw Warner the second or third time he pulled the trigger and saw his head explode and his body slam into the door. It might flash through his mind that he didn't see Wetherill, but the devastating effect of his shots on Warner's body would provide the explanation."

"Remember, he believed that Wetherill had been sitting right on the other side of the window before his first shot, maybe eighteen inches from the barrel of his gun. It would not occur to him that his first shot missed her. He likely would conclude that it disintegrated the top of her and blew the rest of her down below the door out of his sight. And if he did catch a glimpse of her body hunched over on the floor, it's where the body ought to be. Why else would it be there? Mission accomplished."

He stopped, looked at Thad, then at Charlie, and then back at Thad, who pursed his lips and nodded. "Could have happened like that. Could have," he said.

"Could have," Charlie echoed. "And that means what we know so far doesn't tell us which one of them was the primary target.

"That's right," Owens said. "And one other thing. Lieutenant Hurd said it this morning. Even if Wetherill had been in the line of fire, two shots at that range were plenty to kill them both. And maybe you take one more just to be dead sure." Thad winced at the unintended pun. "But four? That fourth shot isn't necessary. It's like the killer took that shot for some other reason."

There was silence as the other two absorbed Owens' observation. Then Owens put into words what all three were thinking. "We don't know enough to know the significance of what we do know."

There was another silence. Finally Thad said in a near whisper, "This will be a tough one. It may take us a while. Whoever the shooter is, I hope he's done all the killing he needs to."

"Amen," Charlie added.

They got out of the car. The two troopers were still positioned ahead and behind to direct traffic. The other agents were standing at the rear of the BMW and talking. Thad approached them. "That's it. Thanks for your help."

"Well, was it any help?" Nancy Baxter asked.

"Yes, it actually was. It's quite possible the shooter left the scene thinking he had killed both of them. Before we went through this little exercise that seemed farfetched. Not anymore."

They started toward their respective cars, but Nancy Baxter stopped and said, "You know, maybe it's just me, but it sure was some coincidence that the Congresswoman happened to be bent down out of the line of fire precisely when the shooter pulled alongside and opened up." Everyone was silent while that sunk in. Until she spoke, the many voiced reactions to Wetherill's ordeal had all been variations on the same innocuous theme – how lucky Wetherill had been. But Nancy Baxter was coming from a different angle, one with its own set of implications. *Hmmm,* Thad thought. *Hell of a coincidence.*

CHAPTER 9

The doctors did not release the Congresswoman until the following morning. She had instructed Nikki to make sure the press was tipped as to when she would leave, so thirty to forty members of the press and well wishers greeted her at the entrance of the hospital. She had spent a considerable amount of time before the mirror in the bathroom of her hospital room deciding just how she wanted to look. As usual, her talent for making exactly the impression she desired did not fail her.

She emerged and slowly made her way to the microphones, leaning just slightly on a cane. She smiled wanly. Her red mane was slightly unkempt. She wore large dark glasses and no makeup so the abrasions and the bandage covering the plastic surgeon's work were plainly visible. She looked like she wanted to look – a little banged up. She wore black shoes, black slacks, and a black blouse with a black and green scarf at her neck – clearly dressed for mourning, but with a green flair. Her legs were spectacularly long relative to her shapely upper body, which just served to emphasize her legs. As she well knew, she could not wear slacks, whatever the color, without making a stunning visual statement. The television lenses captured the image of a woman who had suffered a brush with violent death in which she tragically lost the husband she loved, and a woman who, by the way, was a knockout.

Reaching the microphones, Wetherill bowed her head and held her forehead with her free hand for a few seconds, which focused all eyes on her beautiful hair. Then she raised herself tall, shook her head and began. Her voice was uncharacteristically soft, which gave her delivery greater impact as everyone strained not to miss a syllable. "I hope you will understand," she started. "My heart feels like an open wound. I ask you to give me the privacy you would want if you were in my place. I'm not up to taking questions." She paused to give them all time to silently make that promise to her.

"I was very lucky to escape." Another pause. She straightened away from the cane and stood as erect as she could. When she continued, her voice was stronger. "My husband died because he was with me. Taylor died in my place. I do not want him to have died for nothing, and I rededicate my life to bringing to justice the heartless drug suppliers and dealers in our community. This vicious and cowardly attack proves that we are getting close." She swept her finger in an arc in front of her and more loudly said, "You members of the press, be sure they get the message that the only way I'll be stopped is if they finally succeed in killing me."

"Thanks to all of you who came out to support me and all those well-wishers who have sent me messages. These gestures are a great comfort to me." She leaned on the cane again.

Reporters' voices rose in a chorus of questions. At the same time, the gathered citizens broke into applause and shouts of encouragement. With one hand on her cane and the other on Nikki's arm, Wetherill passed through the friendly crowd to a waiting car, repeating, "No questions" and "thank you very much."

Charlie later described the scene to Thad over the phone. "You might want to catch it. I'm sure it'll be on the news and Internet. This is one tough lady." When he rang off, Thad immediately began a search for Wetherill's comments and soon found them. As he watched, he thought, *Can't tell. Just can't tell.*

His read at the hospital had been that she loved Warner. But *was it a present love or a past one invoked for the occasion? Maybe I'll find out,* he said to himself. One thing was clear. She had no qualms about turning his death into a golden political opportunity. *But is that anything other than fulfilling a promise to him, "so he will not have died for nothing?"*

The only certainty was that he couldn't read her, not yet anyway. So his attention turned from Wetherill to another player. He called Owens. Before the third ring he heard the dependable voice. "Yes, Chief?"

"Owens, let's see if Mr. Leonard Moretti will have a little chat with us. We need to take the measure of the guy."

CHAPTER 10

The following Monday, about 9:00, Thad set out from his Unionville farm to Bucks County and the country home of Leonard Moretti. Late Saturday afternoon he had driven from his DC townhouse to spend the balance of the weekend on the farm and felt refreshed by even so short a stay. It never failed to recharge his batteries.

Charlie had set the meeting up the previous Friday using Thad's presence "in the area" as a reason to press for Monday. He, Charlie and Owens had discussed what Charlie should say about the purpose of the meeting and had decided to keep it simple. The Congresswoman's husband had been murdered under circumstances indicating that she may have been the target. Moretti was in turn a target of her investigations, rightly or wrongly. Therefore, the FBI would like to talk to him informally about his knowledge of the Congresswoman, her husband, and the Committee's investigation.

They expected him to decline and refer them to his lawyers, so they were surprised when he agreed. They were further surprised when he asked them to meet him at his home rather than his office in downtown Philadelphia or the offices of his lawyers.

Thad wanted Owens also to see Moretti first hand, so early Monday Owens took the Acela to Philadelphia where one of Charlie's agents met him. Thad and Owens linked up at a Starbucks and reached Moretti's home punctually at 10. They had agreed that three were too many, so Charlie was not along.

As they approached Moretti's property, they already had a detailed mental picture of it based on research done for them. The property of fourteen acres was enclosed within a high fence of vertical, black, iron poles ten feet tall, two inches in diameter and set nine inches apart. They were capped with pointed bronze tips. Set far back from the road, visible through a stand of old red oak and sycamore trees, was the large, grey stone house. Just inside the main entrance was a gatehouse, literally a small house, where Thad assumed guards were stationed around the clock. Security elements and the imposing fence aside, the estate was not unlike scores of others in the "Main Line" area west of Philadelphia.

Owens looked at Thad and commented, "Except for the fence, the place fits right into the neighborhood." Thad nodded. As they approached, the gates electronically opened and an informally but neatly dressed man, carrying no weapon they could see, smiled and waved them down. Thad lowered his window.

"Good morning," the man said pleasantly. "Are you Agent Owens and Agent Pennock?"

"We are," Thad said. "Would you like to see some identification?"

"Not necessary," the man said smiling. "Just follow the road to the main door, someone will meet you there. Have a pleasant day." With that, he moved back from the car and turned so it could continue. Through his outside mirror, Thad could see the man put a phone to his ear.

The driveway flowed into an elaborately landscaped circle in front of the main entrance to the house. Thad chuckled, thinking of the contrast between this and the unadorned country circle at his home. Not that it was shabby; it was just simple. They drove three quarters of the way around, parked, and got out. Another man, dressed like the first, came down the front steps. He didn't offer to shake hands, but pointed politely to the front door saying, "Gentlemen, please go in. Mr. Moretti is expecting you."

They climbed the three broad steps to the front door, which opened as Thad reached for the brass knocker. "Gentlemen," the man said, "please come in. Welcome to my home." They shook hands. "Welcome Special Agent Owens," he said and turning to Thad asked "And how do I address a Regional Chief?"

Wants us to know *he does his homework,* Thad registered. He responded to this as he nearly always did, "'Agent' always works Mr. Moretti."

"Then welcome Agent Pennock."

"Thank you," Thad replied. "Agent Owens and I want to thank you for seeing us in this informal way on such short notice."

"Well, I'm glad I was available. A planned business trip was canceled at the last minute, so I took advantage of the opportunity to make it a three-day weekend at home with my wife and enjoy the weather."

His tone was cordial, neither cold nor falsely friendly. As he spoke, he led them through a drawing room and then a library that opened on to a terrace beyond. In the doorway was a slight but attractive woman in slacks, *maybe five feet four inches* Thad guessed. She waited easily for them to approach. "Eleanor, I would like you to meet Agents Pennock and Owens of the FBI. Gentlemen, my wife Eleanor."

Thad noted that she had a firm handshake and looked him directly in the eye while smiling and saying, "Oh, this is quite a treat for me. I've never met real FBI agents before. I think of you as leading rather mysterious and romantic lives, doing lots of dangerous and heroic things." She laughed and asked, "Am I right?"

Thad smiled in return and said, "Mrs. Moretti, there was a time when I thought of us in exactly the same way. Needless to say, it was before I signed up."

She showed disappointment and said, "Agent Pennock, you could have done me the courtesy of fibbing just a little to permit me my fantasy."

Moretti broke in, "Eleanor, let's offer our guests a seat."

"Oh of course," she said. "Please come to the terrace gentlemen, and we can enjoy the day." As he followed her, Thad said to himself, *not what I expected,* which was some version of the buxom, bottled blond or brooding dark Sicilian that were caricatures of the mobster's wife.

She had a trim figure, real blond hair cut short and waved, and an intelligent, pretty face. He knew from the research that she was forty-one. She was dressed in tailored slacks and a light green blouse with a darker green sweater over her shoulders. *This is Mrs. Junior League President,* he thought.

The terrace was old brick, with trellises overhead laced with a green plant bearing white flowers. Thad was hopeless with names of flowers and plants. He loved to look at them, but once past a basic six or seven, he was lost. The sun filtered through the trellis, mottling everything under it. Gray wrought-iron furniture and tables dotted the veranda in nests. It was inviting. Eleanor directed them to a cluster consisting of a coffee table, a love seat, and several chairs tastefully and comfortably cushioned. Eleanor took the loveseat and motioned to Thad and Owens to sit to her left and right. Moretti sat opposite his wife.

Thad was surprised that Eleanor appeared to be settling in as a participant. No doubt Moretti understood the purpose of the visit. This was murder, unpleasant business. His eyes turned to Moretti, the first time he had had a chance to study the man, although he had studied many photographs. He knew he was forty-six. He had thick black hair, trained straight back. He was neatly dressed in casual but expensive slacks and a long-sleeved red shirt. *No gold jewelry,* Thad noticed. He was about five feet ten inches tall, a strong build but not heavy. His features were proportioned, and he would have been ruggedly handsome except his facial muscle tone was slightly slack, slightly puffy, giving the impression of softness. *Just a bad gene,* Thad thought. *Nothing soft about this guy.*

As they engaged in small talk for the first few minutes, Thad observed that Moretti held himself upright but not stiff and spoke softly and evenly, with minimal inflexion. *Not going to be able to read him by how he speaks,* Thad thought. *And he'll be careful what he says.* He noticed that Moretti's gaze was piercing when he held it, but he tended to move his eyes repeatedly left to right, right to left. Each time his eyes swept across his listener's face, they would lock eye-to-eye for a split second, then continue their sweep. This habit, if it was a habit, sent contradictory signals, shy and sincere, shifty and secretive. Otherwise, Moretti's body was still while he spoke, no gesturing. When he did move, the motion was deliberate, paced, and economical. `He's watching himself all the time,* Thad thought.

A door opened at the other end of the veranda, and a maid emerged with a silver tray holding four tall glasses of lemonade. She placed one on the table in front of each seat and left as quietly as she came. Moretti raised his glass, gestured first to Thad and then Owens, and said, "To your health gentlemen."

"And yours," Thad returned. He took two swallows. "That is very good Mrs. Moretti."

"Why thank you."

Thad unconsciously began speaking in the formal manner he lapsed into on official business. "Your home is very beautiful, and you have welcomed us graciously. But as pleasant as this is, I am sure you know this is a business call." He paused and looked at Eleanor. She looked back, not moving.

Moretti, understanding, explained. "Eleanor is a business partner as well as my wife. She can hear anything you have to say; indeed, she may be able to help with whatever it is you seek to know, although I think neither of us knows very much about the topics the agent who called us spoke of. So, please proceed with your questions."

Still perplexed that Moretti did not have a lawyer present, Thad began. "Agent Owens and I are investigating the killing several days ago of Taylor Warner, husband of Congresswoman Wetherill. You, Mr. Moretti, have been mentioned more than once by Congresswoman Wetherill as a prime target of the investigation by her subcommittee into drug trafficking in the Philadelphia area." He thought that blunt start might bring a denial from Moretti, or some comment by Eleanor, but it did not. They both simply waited.

He continued, "Often people who may have no connection with a crime unknowingly have knowledge that can help lead to its solution. That is why Agent Owens and I are here. We have no evidence that you were involved. If we did, we would be advising you to have a lawyer present."

Moretti interjected evenly, "If you did, I would have a lawyer present, but I doubt I would say anything."

Thad nodded. "Although this is an informal visit, you understand that nothing said is off the record?"

"Of course," Moretti said.

Thad continued, "Did either of you know Mr. Warner?"

"You mean the man apparently murdered?" Eleanor asked.

"Not apparently Mrs. Moretti. It would be hard to be more murdered than Mr. Warner was."

Moretti said, "I don't think I ever met the man Agent Pennock."

"I didn't either. I certainly don't remember meeting him," Eleanor added.

Thad thought to himself, *why don't they ask me why I'm asking them?* He continued, "Did either of you ever meet his wife, Congresswoman Wetherill?" They both shook their heads from side to side.

"I have seen her on television and on tape, but not in person," Moretti said.

"Ever talk to her by phone or communicate by email, letter, or in any way?"

"No. I received a subpoena, indeed several, to appear before her subcommittee, but my lawyers were able to get them quashed. That is my only connection."

"Why did you resist appearing?" He would have bet this question would get him a reaction or maybe a declination. It was close to asking for information protected by the attorney-client privilege.

"The subpoenas as I understand were for many, many documents as well as for an appearance by me. A subcommittee like that, with an agenda like the Congresswoman's, is just a hungry political animal that should be starved, not fed. And no one on the subcommittee is playing politics with it more than Congresswoman Wetherill. Do not misunderstand me.

The stated purpose of the subcommittee is laudable, but in practice it is merely a means to a very selfish and personal political end."

"What do you mean by that?"

Moretti responded, "I encourage you to watch a few committee hearing sessions Agent Pennock. It should be obvious to any objective person, which I assume you are."

"So, you have watched the hearings?" Moretti took just a little longer to answer, and his eyes had ceased their back and forth motion and were looking into the distance. *He might be out of his rhythm,* Thad thought.

"I have seen excerpts of tapes of some of the sessions," said Moretti as his eyes began moving again.

Thad asked, "By tapes, you don't mean the nightly news, you mean actual tapes?" There was another slight pause.

"Yes," Moretti said.

"Are they hard to come by, the tapes I mean?" He knew the answer, and he suspected that Moretti knew he knew, but he wanted to hear how Moretti would respond.

"Very easy. Anyone can order them."

"You said you saw excerpts. Can you order excerpts?"

"I don't know." I ordered and got tapes of several sessions. Not every session, but several, and I think you cannot order tapes of parts of a session. I don't know. I never watched a whole session."

"Mr. Moretti, you told me those hearings were just politics, why then did you order tapes and watch portions of them?"

Moretti, unflustered, asked calmly, "Are we discussing these hearings Agent Pennock? I thought you were investigating the death of the Congresswoman's husband. I do not see a connection. Perhaps you will tell me what it is."

Thad thought to himself, *why is he playing dumb? It's so obvious.* But he decided to go along. "The person who killed the Congresswoman's husband used a shotgun at very close range; only due to sheer luck was the Congresswoman also not in the line of fire. If she had been, she would have been killed as well. So she may have been the real target."

"Oh my," Eleanor said, her hand to her breast – a reaction that appeared genuine to Thad. He circled back to the tapes.

"Did someone excerpt the tapes for you?"

"Actually, yes."

"Would you let us see those excerpts?"

"I do not have them. Once I looked at them, they no longer interested me, so I threw them out."

"You mean just threw them out? Literally, like into the garbage?"

"Yes," Moretti said evenly. "Why not?"

Thad leaned forward slightly for the next question. "What subjects did the excerpts that you wanted to see cover?" To Thad's surprise it was Eleanor who answered.

"Now Agent Pennock, let us not beat around the bush." Moretti made no effort to stop her. She continued, "The purpose of the hearings ostensibly is to identify the people who are not only involved, but who are actually in charge of the illegal drug trafficking, if that's what it's called. I suspect you asked to see us because a few disreputable people have testified, without any evidence whatsoever I might add, that businesses we have an interest in have been used to launder money. That was a complete surprise to us and from what we know is absurd. So we obtained the excerpts to hear exactly what was said and by whom."

"It turns out they were convicted drug dealers trying to get their sentences reduced or drug dealers under indictment trying to do the same thing, and they had no facts – just suspicions or alleged facts they claimed someone else told them. In every case, they could not identify or remember the source or the source was conveniently dead. Believe me, if we had any facts indicating these companies are involved with illegal drugs, we would immediately go to the authorities."

Impressive speech, Thad thought, glancing at Owens, *and great teamwork. Hold her back and then trot her out for the big answer.*

Thad shifted the subject. "Mrs. Moretti, may I ask, what is your role as a business partner of your husband? What exactly do you do?"

Now it was Moretti's turn to interject. "Eleanor graduated Magna Cum Laude from the University of Pennsylvania with a combined finance and law degree. She is an officer of many of my companies, helps with many of the technical legal issues, and also advises me on a variety of business matters and decisions. Really, she is my right hand."

"I see," Thad said, "very impressive." He looked at her and smiled. She smiled back. Moretti smiled. *Everyone smiling and everyone playing games now*, Thad thought. *Time to go.* He turned to Owens and asked, "Anything further?"

Owens, characteristically silent until now, added, "Best lemonade I ever had."

"Why thank you Agent Owens," Eleanor smiled, "Real lemons and honey, not sugar, that's the secret."

"Ah," Owens said, "I've learned something useful."

As they rose from their seats, Thad said, "Oh, just one more thing if I may." Both Morettis stopped halfway up and sat down again, shooting each other a quick glance. "Do you know why anyone would want to kill Congresswoman Wetherill?" His eyes moved back and forth from Moretti's to Eleanor's, wondering which of them would field the question.

Looking right at Thad, Moretti said, "Agent Pennock, how would we know?" Thad thought, *first rule of diversion, answer a question with a question. He doesn't get off that easy.*

"I'll give you a very simple hypothetical, Mr. Moretti. Let's say a drug boss thought a congresswoman was moving in the right direction towards pay dirt, and if she continued, she would likely get a breakthrough. Wouldn't that be a motive to kill her and wouldn't it be the right time to kill her?"

Thad waited. Rotating his palms outward like a supplicant, Moretti again asked, "Really, how would we know? It would be rank speculation."

"Understood," Thad said, "please guess." He glanced at Eleanor, her eyes were wary now. Thad thought, *Is hubby about to go off script?*

"Just as a matter of logic I would suppose that killing the Congresswoman would lend credibility where there had been none. The hearings would acquire some legitimacy. If the criminals involved felt exposed, killing the Congresswoman would increase that exposure rather than eliminate it. It should be the last thing they do." He paused and smiled, "That's my guess." Thad glanced at Eleanor. She was again relaxed.

Now Thad was certain that he had gotten everything he was going to get from this interview, little as it was, except for distinct impressions. They left Eleanor on the veranda, and Moretti escorted them to the door. "Thank you again for your time, Mr. Moretti."

"Yes, thank you," Owens echoed.

"Good luck with your investigation gentlemen," Moretti offered, smiling.

"Well?" Thad asked Owens as he drove out the main gate and on to the road. His partner inched his glasses up his nose. "People, even sophisticated people who've been around the block and around the world, are a little apprehensive when the FBI comes calling. They're not quite sure what's going on. They're nervous or anxious or curious or all three. It shows in their voices and gestures and expressions in little ways. They want to help; they go out of their way to appear cooperative; they over answer questions. They're thinking, 'what do these FBI guys think of me? I hope they believe I'm trying to help.'"

He gestured behind him with his thumb. "Now those two? Very different. Everything was perfect. They were perfect. They were guarding secrets. And they were guarding them by pretending they had no secrets, by pretending they were just normal folks. There's a world of difference between acting normal and pretending to act normal. I don't know what they're hiding, but that's what they're doing."

Silence for a moment. Then Thad added, "They're careful. I don't think they take chances. Moretti sounded believable when he gave us his 'guess.' What do you think?"

Owens took a minute and then said. "I can't read him. He has mastered the mask. So has she."

"If Moretti thought the subcommittee was getting warm, getting close to his operation, he'd have to weigh the chances that some politician on the subcommittee, or some other politician for that matter, might see great benefit in swooping up the flag from the fallen Congresswoman and lead the charge against him as the obvious killer. In fact before Moretti decided to kill her, he'd almost have to conclude that that wouldn't happen. And how could he ever be that sure?"

Owens turned the argument around. "You're saying he'd be crazy to do it because he'd be the natural suspect. Sure enough. But maybe he's doubly smart. He knows he'd be the obvious suspect and so everybody would agree he'd be crazy to put himself in that position. But that's exactly why he can do it." They were silent again.

Finally, Thad asked again, "Well?" Owens gazed ahead at the road and the traffic on it.

"I don't have anything helpful to say."

They were back in Washington by 3:30 that afternoon. The murder was now several days old, and the trail was getting cold. While Owens returned to overseeing various aspects of the investigation plan that he, Charlie, and Thad had devised, Thad met with his superior, Deputy Director Lewis Porter, reviewing in detail what they had learned and how they planned to proceed.

Thad had full authority to run the investigation and did not need Porter's approval. Formally he was keeping his boss apprised of the status of the case, but both men understood that Porter felt the heat from the Director, and Porter was not a man to displease.

He was one of a kind. Everyone marveled at how this unorthodox and irreverent man managed to land such a lofty job in an institution in which adherence to protocol was normally indispensable to advancement.

He was six three, totally bald, had massive shoulders, and was about as conventional as a camel on a putting green. But no one questioned his capabilities or his performance. His ability to anticipate and thereby avoid problems was uncanny. He kept his job simply because he got better results than could reasonably be expected from a mortal. He set the standards, was merciless when exposed to incompetence, and was fiercely loyal to his group. And he had an uncanny ability to be two different people, publicly sophisticated and urbane and privately rough and profane.

Chomping down on his perpetual, unlit cigar, he looked up from the summary report Thad had prepared and barked his infamous blue vocabulary through clenched teeth. "You got it set up right Thaddeus, so go to it. But remember, this little mother of a case is high profile, God damned political hand grenade! That douche-bag Moretti is green slime somebody needs to wipe off the wall. And that redheaded congresswoman with the tits and the legs and the big mouth? Please don't piss her off. I've got enough troubles for Christ's sake."

Thad had long ago mastered Porter-speak. "We're together on that, Lew."

CHAPTER 11

It was nearly 8:00 by the time Thad got back to his Georgetown townhouse. In his own environment, he let down enough to notice the tension he had ignored all day. He knew its source was frustration with the lack of progress in the investigation. He went to the refrigerator, took out a Stella and popped the cap. From the freezer he took a Lean Cuisine fettuccine Alfredo and chicken. He did not immediately zap it in the microwave. Instead, he sat down heavily in a kitchen chair and took a swallow of the refreshing beer.

Gina was on his mind too. The edge had worn off his hurt. His initial reaction to her curt "I'm leaving" had been to write her off, forget her. But with the passage of time during which he had been absorbed in the new case, that now seemed more a protective response than a resolve. He wanted to talk to her, at least to understand what had moved her to so suddenly and adamantly reject him. *Bullshit*, he confessed to himself. That was a nice excuse and maybe even a good opener, but what he really wanted was to change her mind. Bottom line, he missed her enough to risk rejection again.

He took his cell phone from his shirt pocket, punched in the code for her number and listened to the rings. *Bad time of day*, he thought to himself, *probably on a date with some asshole.* But she answered.

"Thad," she said evenly, alerted by caller ID, "why are you calling me?" He wished for some hint of emotion in her voice. *Even a little anger would do*, he thought.

"Hi, Gina, great to hear your voice. Two things, really. First, I miss you and I hope you miss me. I'm sorry I did whatever it was that angered you. Second, if you don't miss me, please at least tell me why you closed the door on us without any explanation." He thought that was a pretty fair try. But for about five seconds Gina didn't reply.

Then she said, "'First, second,' do you always have to sound like a goddam lawyer in a court room?" Flashing through his mind was the totally extraneous thought, *how could anybody say "goddam lawyer" with no emotion?*

Gina continued, "Never a conversation with you, Thad, always an oral argument. So, 'first,'" she mimicked, "I am doing my very best not to miss you and succeeding admirably thank you. 'Second,' you know perfectly well why." There was silence. Thad furrowed his brow, perplexed. "I do?" he asked. Icily she replied, "Oh yes, Thaddeus, you do." *Finally some emotion*, he thought, but his intuition told him not to be glad about it. When she called him Thaddeus, it was not a good sign. He protested, "Actually, I don't," feeling a little silly that he couldn't move the conversation a little way along. "Well," she said, "if you can't figure out why, I'm doubly glad that we're through, because if that doesn't occur to you as a reason, you certainly don't think much of me or our relationship, or should I say didn't think much of me or our ex-relationship."

He scrambled to follow the thread, if there was one. "That?" he asked. "Yes," she said impatiently. "That."

Genuinely without a clue, he asked, "Gina, what is 'that'?"

"Don't play games with me, Thad. You know damn well what 'that' is, or, more precisely, 'who' 'that' is!" *Real venom in the "who"*, he thought. Totally at sea, he could only manage, "What?" "Oh, screw you Thad," she exclaimed impatiently, "and your little hussy Gretchen!"

Silence. He envisioned Gina's brown eyes flashing and her lips drawn tight over her beautiful white teeth in a grimace of anger. *Uh oh...* he said to himself. Then, impulsively to her, "Gina, how . . ." and trailed off. *Too late.* He knew she knew there was only one pertinent sentence that could begin with "How," and it wasn't "How are you?"

The reason for Gina's fury was now crystal clear to him. So Thad's puzzlement shifted from why she was furious to *how in bloody hell did she find out? How could she?* That little tryst with lusty Gretchen had lasted only three days while he was on assignment in San Francisco for a week almost a month before. He had returned to DC, she had gone back to LA. That was that. They had not seen each other or talked or emailed, and he had no plans to. *Hell, she came on to me!* he said to himself, feeling exonerated for a nanosecond. *Okay, I could have said, "No." But it's not like Gina and I are married.* That was also lame, and he knew it.

Still not pulled together, but certain his "How...?" followed by his silence were condemning him, he began again before figuring out the finish. "Gina, I didn't know, I mean how did . . ." *Bad start!* Gina picked it up. "How did your darling Gina know?" Her tone was downright menacing. "Your hussy Gretchen happens to have a very good friend in LA, and she told this very good friend all about the wonderful lover she had in San Francisco and all the interesting things this wonderful lover did to make her feel sooo good. Sooo orgasmic." Spewing fire now, Gina almost spit her next words into the phone, "I'm sure by now you've guessed who Gretchen's friend in LA is, lover boy?"

Thad wasn't curious anymore. He just wanted to be somewhere else. He could see the train about to hit him, closing in at warp speed. He didn't know that many people in LA, but he knew one lady very well. Sure enough, Gina yelled into the phone, "Your so charming ex-wife, that's who! And did she ever enjoy giving me every disgusting little detail! God it was humiliating!"

She was at the top of her lungs and out of breath, with nowhere to go. So she stopped. To salvage the hearing in his right ear during that salvo Thad held the phone at full extension of his arm, and it was still amazingly loud. His mind diverted for an instant. *Can you blow the speakers on these phones?* Then he was back. It wasn't that his first wife was unfriendly. She just wanted to prevent every other woman in the world from making the same mistake she had made. *How unbelievably unlucky can you get?* He said to himself. *Is this a test from God? I don't even believe in God. Well, not in church God, a God who tests man with unbearable trials and tribulations. But this sure feels like a test from God!*

Awash in guilt, Thad petitioned, "Gina, that... believe me, it meant nothing to me, absolutely nothing."

"Nothing!" she was screaming now. "Nothing? That is supposed to make me feel better? Our relationship meant so little to you that you threw it away on 'nothing'?" Again he had to hold the phone away from his ear. He closed his eyes. He marveled. *Would she feel better if I said Gretchen had been the best lay of my life?*

He tried again. "Gina, what I mean is I have no feelings for Gretchen. I don't think of her. I think of you. I only have feelings for you." Silence on the other end for a short moment, just long enough for a spark of hope to kindle within him. Then, quietly, in a voice as taught as a violin string at the snapping point, she snuffed the spark out.

"And I have feelings for you too Thad... I hate you!" And the line went dead.

Thad stared at the silent phone for several seconds, the outburst still reverberating in his right ear. He felt battered. That was a side of Gretchen he'd never seen. Slowly he lowered the phone into his pocket, marveling at how the female mind, that one at least, worked. His eyes fell on the bottle of beer, coated with comforting condensation and patiently waiting. He felt a twinge of affection as he reached out and closed his hand around its coolness. He and his beer were going to enjoy a few minutes together, and it wasn't going to yell at him.

Halfway through his third beer he felt lucky to have escaped a life with that temper snuggled up next to him.

CHAPTER 12

It was six o'clock on the evening of the sixth day, and Thad was about to leave the office, go to the gym and work out. For two days there had been no developments. Charlie Townsend's unit and the Philadelphia Police Department had followed up all possible leads to the identity of the shooter. The police and the FBI shook down every contact they had on the street. These efforts yielded nothing.

Shell casings and shotgun pellets at the crime scene were their only connection to the shooter, and they told them nothing. The lab report on the threat letter sent to Congresswoman Wetherill revealed that the paper was a common bond sold for desktop printers. The text had been cut from a newspaper, the Washington Post. The glue used was Elmer's. There were no fingerprints. The person who prepared the letter undoubtedly had worn gloves, probably latex. It was Owens of course who asked the only question any of them could think of about the letter. "It was mailed from Philadelphia. Then why were the words and letters cut from the Washington Post?" No one had an answer or any idea whether the answer would be helpful.

Charlie confided to Thad that unless they got a break, the killer was going to walk.

Thad's phone rang. It was Charlie. "Thad," he said, "my geek boys, working with RCFL, pulled some interesting stuff off the victim's iPhone and computer." At the mention of RCFL Thad's mind's eye uploaded an image of the FBI's Regional Computer Forensics Laboratory in Radnor, Pennsylvania. Charlie continued. "It gave them a clue where to look. Unless you've got something really important to do, you ought to hear this now."

"Nothing is more important than this," Thad answered, taking his feet off his desk and leaning forward with anticipation. "I want to grab Owens. Where can I call you back?"

Four minutes later they were on conference room speakerphones at both ends of the call. Charlie began, "I've got Elliot Foster and Joan Strauss with me. I've told them who you are, and Elliott will run through this for you."

"All right," Thad said. "Elliott, we're all ears."

Foster began, "Hello Agent Pennock. Nice to meet you. We've been running through all of Mr. Warner's electronics, his office computer, home computer, house phone, fax and iPhone. This guy Warner really got around. He had more business and social contacts than anybody I ever researched. He went all over the place, Buenos Aires, Santiago, Madrid, Paris, London, Dubai, New York, Saratoga, Wellington."

Thad broke in, "Wellington? Are we talking about Australia or the horse park near Palm Beach?"

"The latter. Also Lexington and San Diego. He was into buying and selling brood mares and yearlings, both in partnerships where he had shares and for other owners." Some really big time owners like Arab sheiks used him as a bloodstock agent."

"Some of our guys talked to a number of his friends and they all said pretty much the same thing. He was a stand-up guy. He was apparently very likeable, and honest too, which got emphasized like it was a rare trait. Apparently he had a great eye for the potential in a horse. His friends also liked the Congresswoman. They seemed to understand why he had been attracted to her even though the two of them spent more time apart than most couples. He loved the fact that she was beautiful and a congresswoman to boot. Liked the idea of it and so put up with the reality of it, which was that she was busy with her own thing much of the time."

"Am I reading through the lines that he might have been a little unhappy that she didn't give him more time?"

"You're heading in the right direction, sir. From what we learned, he loved having a good time, and he was disappointed that she wasn't there for many of the good times. Like watching his horses race, going to horse sales, watching polo matches, being entertained by big timers around the world. He had lots of those kinds of occasions when the Congresswoman couldn't be with him. This shows up in some of his emails to his friends as well as from the interviews we've conducted so far."

"So was there another woman?"

"Well, here's the thing. The victim had a nucleus of maybe ten really good friends. All married except for two women, both living in Lexington. One of them was actually an ex-girlfriend of his, and the other has a steady squeeze. But Buenos Aires figured big in his life. Many of his brood mares were located near Buenos Aires, and his business kept him there a lot. It added up to over three months of the year. The Congresswoman was hardly down there. Maybe just couldn't fit it into her schedule."

"Plenty of opportunity to step out and not be caught."

"Not really," Elliott said. "He knew a lot of people in Buenos Aires and he would have had to be really careful. He couldn't risk going to polo matches, the race tracks, any of the good restaurants, or even walk the streets alone with a woman without some real risk of being seen by someone he knew."

"Where are you going Elliott? You have a punch line for me?"

"Agent Pennock, we've been pretty much through everything, checking out everyone that makes sense. We didn't find anything direct. But Joan here, who is one of our best diggers, found a snark."

The FBI had a penchant for what it thought were imaginative terms, often borrowing from other disciplines. "Snark", an unexplained computer event, entered the FBI lexicon about five years earlier and stuck. In FBI lingo it meant an unpredicted, unexpected, but significant event.

"Let's hear it."

"His iPhone was synced with his office computer. Contacts on one were also on the other. He had many business contacts that included name, address, phone numbers, email addresses. One of those contacts was a Guillermo Artiges, whose business was Artiges & Co. It's a big outfit that sells leather goods like saddles, bridles, halters, polo gear. A natural for Mr. Warner. Here's the thing, there were two phone numbers under Artiges and the second wasn't associated with Artiges or his business. It's the cell number of an Argentinian woman whose name is Maria Isabella Loperena."

"She's thirty-six and an Argentinian blue blood back five generations on her mother's side and nine on her father's."

"Nine?"

"Nine. She went to college in the United States at the University of Virginia. Graduated with honors. She was married at twenty-seven and divorced at thirty-one. She has a seven-year-old son who is autistic. She's raises a lot of money in Argentina and the U.S. for autism research and clinics. So she's in the states regularly and spends most of her time while here on that project."

"But she's also a great sportswoman. Rides horses, shoots, has some racehorses, even plays polo. I'd describe her looks to you, but other than saying she's beautiful I couldn't do her justice, so I emailed you a color picture, and you can decide for yourself."

As if on cue, there was a knock on the conference room door, Thad's long-time assistant, Gloria Sharp, entered, handed Thad a color picture and said in her efficient way, "Just received." Then she turned to leave, and Thad, who thought of her as the lady with the smile that lights everything up, said, "Thanks Gloria, but what are you still doing here? It's 6:15?"

"Just catching things up. Leaving now. Goodnight."

"Hold up, Elliott, I just got the picture." Thad saw a dark beauty looking straight at the camera, confident and slightly bemused. It was a knees-up shot. She wore a sleeveless knit turtleneck, revealing round shoulders and arms proportioned to her lovely neck and head, then tapering to a small waist and contoured hips. Her breasts were striking, but not too large. Her face looked like 1,000 years of perfect breeding, thick black hair pulled back, a high smooth forehead, unblemished smooth skin, a chiseled nose, high cheekbones, full shaped lips and large brown eyes. The whites of her eyes seemed to enlarge them. Her lashes were long, and her eyebrows were dark and reached toward the bridge of her nose, another feature that set off her eyes. Her skin color had a hint of bronze.

My, my, he said to himself. *Not sure I've ever seen anything like this.* He was surprised that he could feel his heart beating. He pulled himself away from the picture and the impression it made on him. He resisted commenting on it aloud and wasn't sure why. "Go ahead, Elliott," he said.

"From appearances she didn't seem to have a particular man in her life. She has a group of friends she goes out with, but no one guy. She and Warner ran in the same crowd, but didn't appear to be a duo. Same goes when they were both in the U.S. Most of that overlap was in New York and Wellington."

"So far, Elliott, I'm a little underwhelmed."

Elliott answered, "What we've got is some statistically significant information. Joan worked it up. Warner was in Santiago for three days in June, supposedly to look at some horses. Guess who happened to be staying at the same hotel? And there wasn't any society or sporting event going on then, and she wasn't raising money. They were also at the same hotel in Lima in late July for four days. Nothing special was going on there. In neither place did the local society papers or blogs mention she was there. We think there's no way that's a coincidence. They probably met quietly in Buenos Aires too. But since you don't need an airline ticket to go from one part of the city to another, it's tough to put them alone together."

Thad's intuition kicked in. "Do you know if Señorita Loperena happens to partake of illicit drugs?"

"One of the Buenos Aires trash rags claimed that its reporter caught her snorting up at some society party," Charlie piped in.

"Bingo," Thad said quietly, looking at Owens. He paused, thinking.

Owens picked up the slack. "Charlie, has anyone talked to her? Does she know we know?"

"Couldn't," Charlie said. "The pictures of her are secondary sources, society magazines, society sections of newspapers, stuff like that. We hit up the airlines for her travels and the hotels where she stayed. Same for Warner. And, of course, Google, blogs. Lots of hits on a woman like this. But nothing we did could tip her that we're looking at her."

"Anything else?" Thad asked.

"That's it," Elliott answered.

"Okay," Thad said. "Terrific work, both of you. Right now she's our best bet. Charlie, where is she?"

"Buenos Aires as of today," Charlie answered. "She has no commercial airline bookings for three weeks when she heads for New York."

"Can't wait that long," Thad said. "Where was she the day of the murder?"

"BA, as far as we know. Had been there about six days. Before that, she was in Wellington about a week and as it so happens Warner was there most of that time."

Thad asked, "For the South American stuff, who did you work through, CIA?"

"The CIA and our embassy in Buenos Aires, but mostly the Argentinian National Police Interpol Division, ANP. They were real good, very efficient and no bullshit."

"Doesn't surprise me. They've got a great reputation. Joan and Elliott, again, great work. Glad I don't have to try to hide from you two. Now, send me everything you've got on Señorita Loperena and just keep supplementing as you find more. I also need her contact information in Buenos Aires."

He looked at Owens. "Go there, right?" He was only half asking.

"Have to, Chief."

Thad looked at the speakerphone. "Okay, Charlie, I'm taking a little trip to BA. Send me the contact at ANP and let them and the embassy know I'm coming in. I'll get down and back as soon as I can. In the meantime Owens will be in charge here."

"No problem," Charlie said, "and thanks, Thad, you just won me twenty bucks."

Thad knew this was a set-up of some kind but he couldn't resist. "How's that?"

Charlie said, "I gave Elliott and Joan two to one that you wouldn't pass Señorita Loperena off to anyone else."

Elliot had the last word. "Joan and I just lost twenty bucks Agent Pennock."

CHAPTER 13

T had believed Argentina would be one of the great powers of the world were it not victimized by a long history of corruption at every level of its formidable bureaucracy. Despite this, it was a beautiful and bountiful country, and he considered Buenos Aires one of the world's great cities.

His flight from Dulles touched down at Buenos Aires International Airport at 5:50 p.m. local time. As the plane taxied to the gate, he recalled, bemused, Lew Porter's reaction to the picture of Señorita Loperena and to Thad's recommendation that he interview her.

"Holy Mother!" Lew had said, unconsciously removing the ever-present, unlit cigar from his mouth. "This is one luscious piece of overhanging ripe Argentinian fruit!" Eyes glued to the photograph, he thrust the cigar back into his mouth and through clenched teeth continued his stream-of-conscious monologue. "Tell you what Thaddeus. I'm nixing your trip. I'm getting the Director to appoint you to my job, and I'm taking yours. I'm doing you a favor, my boy. This is way too much woman for you. You could get hurt. You walk up to her? You're gonna trip over your pecker and bite your tongue off when you hit the ground." He looked up at Thad and shifted the cigar. "If this is the way they breed'em down there, Christ, we gotta go talk to Immigration and get a boat load of Loperenas into this country. It's our goddam solemn Constitutional duty!"

Thad was met by a Colonel and a Corporal in the ANP. They bypassed customs, took Thad to a waiting squad car, and got from the airport to ANP headquarters in Buenos Aires, with lights flashing but no sirens, in forty minutes. *The only way to travel*, Thad said to himself. As was planned, he had a brief meeting with Major Varella, Superintendent of ANP Interpol Division, Colonel Hernandez, Deputy Superintendent of the ANP major crimes unit, and a public relations officer. They spent ten minutes going over ground rules about Thad's visit, such things as no statements to the press without ANP approval, all obvious and acceptable. They reviewed the plan for the next day. Señorita Loperena had agreed to be interviewed at her home at 10:00 a.m. She had readily admitted to knowing Taylor Warner. Thad would conduct the interview with Colonel Hernandez present.

When the meeting broke up, Thad and Hernandez went to dinner at Lola, across a small park from the famous Cementerio de La Recoleta, crowded with the crypts and mausoleums of Argentina's upper class and famous dead. Over drinks they exhausted the topic of Señorita Loperena and then consumed a fine Argentinian malbec and beef.

He said goodbye to the Colonel at the restaurant door. After thirteen hours in the air, the cars, the meeting, and the restaurant and wine, he needed to walk. He was familiar with this part of the city. Twice he had taken horseback trips with friends in Patagonia over the Andes into Chile, and on each occasion he had spent time in Buenos Aires. A third time he was there to visit an Argentinian woman whom he had met in New York and dated on and off for about a year. *It's a great lovers' city,* he remembered. *Wonder what she's doing now?*

It was March, and the end of the Argentinian summer. He strolled the Pres. Robert M. Ortiz, a two-block walkway of restaurants with outdoor tables under shade trees. Street musicians played, instrument cases open, inviting tips. Young Argentinian men and women confident in their good looks meandered this route to be seen. He recalled pleasant hours sitting at a table here with friends and drinking wine and gazing appreciatively at the young bodies who in turn were taking pleasure at being watched.

He turned right on Av. Alvear, a street of fine shops and flower stalls. *They love their flowers here,* he thought. Five pleasant blocks later he turned right on Panera and entered the tiny lobby of a very small hotel on the left side of the street with the grand name Embassy Plaza. It was comfortable and old, tucked in like a row house in a fashionable part of town. It accommodated at most one hundred guests on its five floors. It would not have earned a five-star rating under any standard except Thad's, who had only three criteria, a comfortable bed, no noise, and great water pressure in the shower.

He also liked it because of its intimacy and two ancient elevators. These were located at either end of the small lobby behind what looked like two closet doors. The elevator inside was just a metal cage, barely large enough for one person and a suitcase. The clangy cage door collapsed to one side so the guest could squeeze in. If the guest didn't shut the closet door as well as the cage door, it wouldn't go. During the time it took one of these relics to rise from the first to the fifth floor or to descend the same distance, countless important events took place throughout the world and all living things aged significantly. To Thad these rickety cages were stubborn little redoubts against the three-headed juggernaut of modernity, efficiency and sterility, and they never failed to buoy his spirits.

So, as tired as he was, he was smiling when he worked his way out of the cage on the fifth floor. Shortly thereafter, contentedly steeped in the sights and sounds and food and wine of the city, he slipped into sleep.

Sometime during the night his dream world darkened. He was a pair of disembodied eyes lying open and unblinking on the floor of Taylor Warner's car close to Warner's right leg. He saw the man's body above soundlessly jump, as in an early silent movie, and saw in slow motion his head burst from unheard explosions that shattered the man and the car door and splayed glass and metal and bone and blood. Then all was still, except for gravity-ruled rivulets of blood that silently dripped into the stinging eyes he could not close.

CHAPTER 14

The Park Plaza happened to be only one and a half blocks from the home of Maria Isabella Loperena on Libertad just before that small street flowed into the beautiful Plazoleta Carlos Pelligrini. Her home was a perfectly restored granite house built in 1842 by a wealthy banker. It was one of the smaller homes on this row, and while others were grander in scale and more ornate, to Thad's Quaker taste none was more architecturally and aesthetically pleasing.

As planned, Colonel Hernandez and Thad were at the front door at 10:00 a.m. Señorita Loperena opened it herself.

———

Thad, like most men, had thought some about why he was attracted to certain kinds of beauty more than others. His theory was that every man was prewired to respond to a particular beauty that he can neither visualize nor describe until he sees it, if he ever does. When he does, he realizes with a jolt that the image before him has all along resided in his subconscious, latent and unseen, and, until that moment, present in his conscious mind only as an ill-defined expectation. That the stranger is immediately familiar makes the encounter seem preordained. He knew his theory was too romantic, but he rather liked it.

———

When Thad beheld Maria Isabella, he felt the jolt. He also knew with certainty that she had seen his reaction. But because it was spontaneous and therefore neither an affront nor disrespectful, she was not offended. Their eye contact lasted a second longer than normal, and in its wake Thad had the sensation that they shared a private oscillation, like the sound wave of the lowest E on a double bass bowed only for them, barely audible, and felt more than heard. Then the instant passed, and Thad was again the observing FBI agent.

He saw in her face an intensity of suffering far greater than Wetherill's. It seemed to emanate from a heart not yet able to reconcile the finality of her lover's death with vivid, living memories of him.

While her mouth smiled politely, the rest of her did not. Thad could see the darkness under her eyes, the redness in the whites of them, and the slight puffiness around them. Despite this she was more beautiful than the pictures he had seen. In the flesh, her vitality was palpable even as she grieved, bringing her beauty to life and rendering her sensuous and desirable. He had the irrational thought that it was his responsibility to hold her in his arms and assuage her grief.

After introductions she silently led them through a high-ceilinged main hall, past modestly sized drawing rooms on either side, past a formal dining room (Thad registered ten chairs at the table), and then to the right into a library of rich paneling, leather books, and a large fireplace. She did not stop there, but went through a door at the end of the library to the right of the fireplace, down two steps and into a light, high-ceilinged garden room with slowly turning ceiling fans designed to bring the delights of the outdoors in. Two sides were nearly all glass overlooking a private, walled-in yard and flower gardens. The natural light made the room cheery.

But instead of wicker furniture with soft, gaily-colored cushions, the room contained an array of business and office machines, papers, ledgers, two computers, a printer-fax-copier, a telephone with three lines, and a disk player and speakers. There were two sets of shelves with stud books going back twenty years, and on one of two desks were catalogs of this year's major horse sales in North America and Europe. This was a working room.

There were two comfortable chairs in front of the larger of two desks. Maria Isabella motioned Thad and the Colonel to those. Thad, who had minored in the history of architecture, would have bet that hers was an 18th century French secretariat. As they settled in he said admiringly, "Your desk is beautiful." She responded simply, "Yes, it is beautiful." Her voice was naturally low-pitched and rich. She looked squarely at him and waited.

Her gaze was disorienting. He began stiffly and haltingly, surprised at her effect on him and his lack of concentration. "Señorita Loperena, you are gracious to..." he paused, "mmm... receive us on short notice." Another pause, then he caught his stride. "I have come to Buenos Aires to see you because I am in charge of the investigation into Taylor Warner's death and intend to see that the persons responsible are apprehended." At the mention of her lover's name the muscles along her high cheekbones contracted, rendering her vulnerable just for an instant. *Still plenty raw,* he thought, *be careful. You're not here to compound her grief.*

He continued. "We're talking to many people who knew Mr. Warner, but our investigation indicates that you and he may have had a special relationship." He had thought about how he would get to the heart of it, but now, in her presence, he wanted only to be straightforward. She smiled, this time including her eyes.

She looked squarely into his. "I believe we did, Agent Pennock," she said in a quiet, strong voice. Her first language was obviously Spanish. But her English was excellent, tinged with a melodious accent.

Thad continued, "I am going to ask some questions that pry. It is not something I enjoy, but I have no choice." When she next spoke, she shocked both men.

"Please understand," she said, still smiling, "If it would insure the capture of Taylor's killers, I would appear naked on the evening news broadcast." Both men smiled. Thad felt himself relax. *That's why she said that,* he thought and admired her even more.

"Thank you," he heard himself say.

"Of course," she replied quietly.

Now he knew they would speak candidly. "Do you have any idea who may have wanted Mr. Warner dead?"

Her eyes locked on his. "Agent Pennock, I do not know a person who even disliked Taylor. He radiated happiness everywhere he went. That is why I loved him. It is why I found him irresistible even though he was married. It is why I pursued him until he gave in to me. And it is why I did all I could to make him love me." *Whoa,* Thad thought, *so artlessly forthcoming.*

Thad asked, "Did he love you?" She looked at him intensely, compelling him to understand that whether or not his question was serious, her answer would be.

"Yes, he did. Very much."

"Did he love his wife?"

She did not hesitate. "Yes, but I believe he suspected there was more to love than he was receiving from her. I hoped that in time he would be convinced." Her eyes glistened with moisture, but courage nevertheless radiated from her.

"Was he going to leave her?"

"He had not faced that. It was not a thing to be rushed given the constraints upon our relationship." Thad continued to be amazed by the candor of her answers and the self-awareness they revealed. He thought of Owens. It was a trait of his. She continued, "We had been intimate for only four months. And during that time, we were separated for many weeks at a time. That intensified the yearning, but was not the model for an enduring relationship. We had to hide our feelings anytime we were not alone. It was all still a great challenge and adventure, and both of us love adventures." Grief swept her face. "Loved," she corrected. Then, as swiftly, she willed that grief back down deep within her and composed her face.

Thad asked, "Who knew about it?"

"I know of no one."

"Surely, someone must have known how to reach you when you were away – the person caring for your son for example."

"Cell phones," she answered. "It is very easy as I am sure you know. You arrange for a cell phone that works wherever you are. Also understand that the people who work for me simply do not ask questions. They understand that if they perform their jobs well, I will be appreciative, and their jobs do not include what I do with my life. There have been many times that my employees have been approached by others wanting information about me. My employees are loyal, and they know that their jobs depend upon my ability to travel, whether around the city or to another country, in as much privacy as I can create. They are my friends and take pride in protecting me."

"Señorita Loperena, will you provide us with the names, addresses, dates of employment, and any other information you have about your employees?"

"If you think that is necessary, of course," she answered, "but you must alert me beforehand so I may give them permission. Otherwise, they will not talk to you."

"Agreed. How many do you employ?"

"There are six, not counting those who care for my horses. I have two professionals, a man and a woman, who attend my autistic child, Rodolfo. He lives here with me. I love him. But I lack the skills to allow him to progress to the extent possible or even the ability to make him as comfortable in his environment as these professionals can. They are second parents to him."

"I have a part-time secretary-bookkeeper. I have a gardener and two maids, one of whom is also my cook."

Thad asked, "Which of your employees would be the most likely to have access to your, well, your life. For example, your life as reflected on your computer, your secretary?"

"No doubt," she said.

"Does she prepare your bills for payment?"

"Of course," she said. "Agent Pennock, if I understand the thrust of your question, any arrangements necessary for me to be with Taylor were made by me, not my secretary."

He pursued, "How long has she been with you?"

"Not a she; Matias was with me four months, and I must say he is very good, was very good."

"Who did he replace?"

Señorita Loperena's face darkened. "Ah," she said, "my dear Camila. She had been with me more than thirteen years.

We cannot control our fate, can we Agent Pennock? She was a plain girl, I would say, but very beautiful inside. She was on holiday. I am told she went for a swim alone in the hotel pool late at night and drowned. Her good friend was asleep in their room and had no inkling until the morning."

"Do you know her friend?"

"Not really, but I know she was a long time good friend."

"Señorita Loperena, this may sound strange, but do you know if an autopsy was performed?"

Surprised, Señorita Loperena asked, "Should one have been? I have no idea."

"It depends on the jurisdiction and a variety of other factors, and I am afraid I am incurably a policeman seeing evil deeds everywhere. Just checking. Are you now without a secretary?"

"Yes, but I did replace dear Camila with Matias Correa." Señorita Loperena sounded impatient for the first time. "I want to help in any way, Agent Pennock, but this seems like..." she paused, "like a somewhat tangential line of inquiry." Thad could not remember when the "secretary" road had ever led anywhere but to a typewriter. In hindsight he could not have explained why, but notwithstanding his total-waste-of-time experience, he asked another "secretary" question.

"How did you find this Mr. Correa?

"He found me. He called and said he was a long-time friend of Camila, and he was devastated to hear of her death. But he said something like, 'I feel somewhat guilty asking this so soon after her death, but I am an excellent secretary and believe I could fill her position.' I use my lawyers to investigate the background of anyone whom I employ, and Matias had excellent qualifications, and, I add, he is, was, very good at his job. Discrete and professional. I was sorry to lose him."

"Lose him?"

"Yes, he decided to move back to Cordoba, where he has family."

"When did he leave?"

"Three weeks ago. I am about to hire a replacement that has been vetted – is that the word you use? – by my lawyers." Thad looked at the Colonel and then back at Señorita Loperena.

"We need to have all the information about Matias Correa that you and your lawyers have."

"Yes, of course, but why?"

"No specific reason yet. Do you know how extensive the background check was that your lawyers' pursued?"

"As I mentioned, with any person I am considering hiring for any job, I have my lawyers get referrals and as much information as they can. They cleared him, so I hired him and was not disappointed, except he was almost too conscientious. He hardly took a day off."

Out of the blue a thought popped into Thad's mind. "Do you still use the cell phone you had when you met with Mr. Warner?"

"Yes, I have the same phone."

"Does it have a GPS device?"

"Do you mean can I put in an address to which the phone will guide me?"

"Well, let's start there. Does it?"

"Yes it does."

"Does your phone have a device which would permit someone else to identify the phone's location?"

Señorita Loperena looked puzzled. "If it does I do not know about it. Is that possible?"

"There are such devices," Thad answered.

He continued, "Did Mr. Correa ever have access to your cell phone?" Señorita Loperena looked as if she would protest, but then closed her eyes and for a moment sat perfectly still. That freed Thad's own eyes from all restraint, and they soaked up her image. *By God she is a beautiful woman*, he exclaimed silently.

When she opened her eyes, she said, "I've been thinking about our daily routine. Yes, I think there were times when my cell phone was here in this room when he was here and briefly I was not. There could have been occasions where I was out of the room for as much as one hour." The Colonel and Thad exchanged glances.

"Will you permit us to have a technician examine your phone?"

"Of course, if it will help. As I mentioned before, I would do anything."

"Thank you," he smiled.

Thad returned to his earlier line of questions. "Did Mr. Correa have access to records indicating where you traveled? Specifically, the times you were away with Mr. Warner."

"He of course knew when I was away, but he could not know where I was when I was with Taylor. I have several charge accounts. He services all but one. That one I personally control and all my expenses when I was with Taylor ran through that account."

"Do you have a credit card for that account?"

"Yes."

"More than one?"

"No."

"Where do you keep it?"

"In my wallet."

He thought for a moment. "When you are at home, where do you keep your wallet?"

"Nearly always in a dresser drawer in my dressing room."

"Do you lock that drawer?"

"No, but I hardly leave the house without my wallet, so I am here when my wallet is in the dresser."

"When he was here, where did Mr. Correa work?"

"In this room. He used that desk."

"What were his hours?"

"Monday, Wednesday and Friday, ten until two."

"Were you here then?"

"Most of the time, yes. Much of what he did required my presence. I instructed him on payments and dictated letters. Perhaps half of the time he was here, we would be together. Normally the first hour or more and then the last half hour, when I reviewed what he had done and signed letters. I have a great deal of correspondence. I prefer letters to email, which I view as cold and impersonal."

"Did you ever send a letter to Mr. Warner?"

"Never."

"Not even to his office?"

"No. We agreed on that. No letters from either of us. We used email sparingly, always deleting the message after reading it. We used the phone."

"Señorita Loperena, would you show me the way to your dressing room from here?" She smiled, and this time her eyes smiled too. She had already concluded that Thad was smart and thorough and that he would capture Taylor's killer. That was a great comfort and lifted her spirits, awakening her innate playfulness and sense of humor. Besides, there had been that first look.

"If Colonel Hernandez will chaperone us," she said with mock gravity.

Colonel Hernandez swallowed a chuckle. But Thad dropped his eyes and felt shy for the first time since he could remember. He rose to cover his discomfort, but not before it reached his cheeks.

"Is that a blush, Agent Pennock?" She asked, with a little laugh. "Come, I'll show you the way." She spoke as they walked, "There is a main staircase and a back stairs off the kitchen. The quickest way is the back stairs, and it couldn't be more private. I'll show you."

It took only a minute to pass through the kitchen to a back hall, walk up the stairs, traverse another hall past two bedrooms, and enter the master bedroom, and, from there, the dressing room. She showed him the dresser and opened the drawer and removed her wallet. "Here," she said, taking a platinum AMEX card from the wallet and handing it to him.

Thad and the Colonel exchanged glances. Someone handy with a computer, who had the number, expiration date, and four-digit safety code, could probably access that account.

"Tell me Señorita Loperena, are you aware that it is possible for someone to access their account on line and view the detail of charges on the card?"

"I understand that to be so," she said, "but I prefer dealing in hard copies."

"So, you receive a bill in the mail every month and send in a check?"

"Yes, I do that for all my accounts."

"Who opens your mail?"

"I do, invariably, except for specific mail I let my secretary open, such as certain bills. Other than that, my employees have strict instructions not to open anything, no exceptions. My privacy is important to me."

Thad asked, "How long have your other employees been with you?"

"Anywhere from five to almost twenty years." Thad's intuition flared like a sunspot. *Has to be Correa.*

"Señorita Loperena, do you keep copies of the monthly American Express statements for your private account?"

"No, not after they are paid. I do not want them lying around."

"How do you get rid of them?"

"I have a shredder." Then he had an idea.

"I would like to go back to your PC and open an online American Express account for your private card. I want to print out all the charges on it since you began . . ." – he was about to say "seeing Mr. Warner," but for some reason that struck him as too shallow, too ordinary – "began," he repeated, "your relationship with Mr. Warner."

"You will have to instruct me how to do that," she said.

"Bring your credit card with you," Thad said and started back to her office.

Once there, he sat at the computer, and she pulled a chair up beside him. The Colonel stood behind them both where he could see the screen. She was very close, her arm brushing Thad's. She was oblivious of it. He was not. It sent a hot rush through him. He got busy.

He brought up the American Express website, clicked on "my account," then clicked to the question "do you have an online account?" "Now we will open an account for your card," he said. In response to the sequence of instructions, he entered the card number, the expiration date, the four-digit code, and the account name as it appeared on the card. The next instruction was to create a password requiring at least seven digits, including at least one letter, one capital letter, and one number. "What do you want me to enter," he asked.

"I do not care," she said, "I will not be using it."

"All right," he said and typed in BA65432 twice, as directed. Then he clicked, "open," But as the three of them watched the screen, it did not open. Instead, in red letters the message appeared, "incorrect password, try again." He looked puzzled, re-entered the password again twice, and clicked "open." Same message. He shook his head.

"What is wrong?" she asked.

"It will not let us in, it's acting as if you already have a password."

It hit him. He looked back at Colonel Hernandez, who was nodding that he also had immediately understood. Then he looked directly into her inquiring large brown eyes so close to his. "Señorita Loperena, someone else has been in your account."

She stiffened, "No!" she resisted, offended at the invasion of her privacy so jealously guarded. Then, as doubt seeped in, her eyes seemed to grow ever larger, "Are you certain?"

"Let me put it this way," he answered. "American Express may have an innocent explanation for this, but I cannot imagine what it would be."

They were silent. He knew what she was thinking but could not short circuit it. The implication washed over her like a hot acid. "Oh, my God!" she whispered. Her right hand went to her mouth, and her left hand gripped Thad's arm. Maybe it was the phone, maybe the card, or maybe both. She had let their affair be exposed, and perhaps that was linked to his death. She stifled a sound from deep within before the two men could identify whether it was a nascent scream or a moan. She sagged toward Thad until her shoulder rested against his arm. She sobbed, her body's way of forcing her to breathe.

Her touch and distress expelled all else from Thad's thoughts. He neither moved nor spoke. Colonel Hernandez, not so affected, quietly asked her a question to draw her away from her grief. "Who are your attorneys? I wish to obtain from them the information they have about Matias Correa." Señorita Loperena controlled her breathing and gave him the firm name. Hernandez left the room to make the call.

They did not speak. She did not move away. She was acquiring strength from their contact or hearing in her heart some unspoken message of comfort from him. Thad didn't want to move, but soon she pulled herself together and straightened without speaking or looking at him. It all felt natural to Thad, none of it awkward. He looked at her and in a strong but kind voice said, "Señorita Loperena, the information was stolen from you. Stolen. Do not forget that." She looked into his eyes. *How is it I know this man?* She asked herself.

"Thank you," she replied. "I will not."

Colonel Hernandez returned and said, "I have made the call to your lawyers. Understandably they ask that you call and give your consent. Kindly do that and I will follow up from my office. Also, I will have someone contact you for an early time to examine your phone. With that, I think there is nothing further we can do here. We will keep you informed of what we learn, Señorita Loperena. You are entitled to know." He added, "I do not believe you are in any danger. You were a source of information not a target." She looked at Thad. He nodded agreement.

Then he heard himself add, "And I will call you."

He instantly reprimanded himself. *What did I say? What reason would I have to call?* But she looked at him and answered his thought. "That will help," she said.

As the Colonel and he walked down the front steps to the curb and their waiting car, Thad felt as if he had left something of himself behind and was carrying away a part of her, and that silly and ridiculous notion seemed neither silly nor ridiculous. It was simply something that had happened.

On the other side of the door she had just closed Isabella stood with one hand still on the doorknob and the other pressed against the rich wood of the door. Her eyes were closed. By nature she was fearless and brutally honest and so examined her thoughts without judging them. Some unsought event had just occurred. So soon after the death of the man she loved she had caught herself hoping she would see Agent Pennock again. She did not feel guilt at this little hope. Indeed, to deny it or mask it with an absolving guilt would to her have been dishonest. More than anything, she was surprised. Given the depth and genuineness of her love and grief, she would not have thought such a feeling, however innocent, possible. *So curious,* she said to herself. *The human spirit, however badly crushed, will respond to the sun whenever it breaks from behind the clouds.*

CHAPTER 15

T had phoned Lew Porter from his room and filled him
in. "Son of a bitch!" Porter exclaimed through his ever-
present cigar. "Murder Loperena's secretary to get a plant
in her house? Create references for Correa that hold up to
investigation by Loperena's lawyers? That's no little romp
in the friggin park! Sophisticated and expensive operation
I'd say just to freeze-frame Warner snorting and screwing
with someone other than his wife. The bastard running this
show is highly motivated, Thaddeus. Hi–lee! Now who do
you suppose that might be?" They both knew. Lew asked
questions for a full ten minutes more exploring every detail
of the interview. Finally he said, "Okay Thaddeus, let's get to
the really important stuff. Is she as luscious in the flesh as
she looks in print?"

Thad let a second or two pass as if the answer wasn't
clear and he needed to think about it. "Well, Lew, I'd say on
the whole it was a little disappointing. She's beginning to
go to seed just a hair. Make-up can hide a lot in a photo, but
in person? Mmm...bloom's off the rose somewhat. Maybe

I was expecting too much." He stopped, surprised he had not cracked up while talking. He waited several seconds for Porter's reaction. He could not see Porter's pursed lips gradually expanding into a great smile.

Finally he heard, "Damn, Thaddeus! That good?"

As his plane flew north high over the Atlantic, Thad worked through the implications of the facts that had surfaced so far. A sophisticated surveillance plan had been executed a hemisphere away. As capable as the Congresswoman was, he could not see her engineering this. Besides, she wouldn't need to. If she had suspected something, she could have hired Kroll or any other good detective agency to tail Warner. *No, he told himself, Lew's right. Wetherill was not the mastermind here. She was the ultimate target.*

When his plane touched down that evening at Dulles, Thad checked his phone messages and saw that Colonel Hernandez had called. He immediately called back and learned that Correa had indeed returned to Cordoba and to the same apartment he lived in before going to Buenos Aires. He never gave up the lease. As yet there was no hard evidence that Señorita Loperena's previous secretary, Camila, had been murdered, let alone any link between Correa and her death, so there was not much for the ANP to charge him with. Thad and the Colonel reconfirmed their decision to keep him under surveillance for a time to see if he would lead them to the mastermind pulling the strings.

CHAPTER 16

The morning after his return Thad called the Congresswoman and was not surprised when he was put through to Nikki Patterson. "Hello, Agent Pennock," she said pleasantly. "I hope you are calling to say there is progress on the case?" He didn't want a long conversation, and he wanted it to sound like a routine request.

"Still working with scattered pieces we can't fit together yet," he said. "I'd like to meet with Congresswoman Wetherill sometime today, preferably sooner than later. Every once in a while I think of additional things to ask."

"I don't think that's possible," Nikki answered. "She has a full schedule through dinner and an after dinner meeting. Staying busy is a help to her now. If you could talk to her by phone instead, it would be better because often a few minutes open up here or there. I just can't predict when. If that happens, she could call you."

Thad was puzzled. *You'd think finding Warner's killer might have some priority.* But his response hid this thought. "I'm a man of habit, Ms. Patterson. I prefer face-to-face.

Kindly ask the Congresswoman if she could find half an hour for me. You never know what little fact might move the case along. I'll make myself available any time today."

"I will tell her you think it might be important." *Still fishing,* he thought, *very good at protecting her boss.*

"Don't get her hopes up. At this stage I'm not prepared to say what's important and what's not. Call me on my cell after you've talked to her. You still have that number?"

"Yes," she said, "I'll get back to you, but it will be at least another hour before the meeting she is in is scheduled to break up."

"Thanks," he said and hung up.

Something about her, Thad thought. *She's efficient, loyal and protective of her boss, exactly what the Congresswoman would want. Hell, what I would want if I were in the Congresswoman's shoes. So, what is it?* He shook his head.

At 3:15 Congresswoman Wetherill, still the image of a grieving widow in a black skirt and jacket, black stockings and shoes, and black scarf around a white shirt, rose from behind her desk and greeted Owens and Thad. The black clothes set off her red hair. She gestured towards leather chairs facing the desk. Then she returned and sat behind her desk while Nikki took a chair against the wall to Thad's right, about fifteen feet from the desk, so that she faced the three others in profile. She had a note pad and pen in her lap. *Her spot when the Congresswoman wants a witness,* Thad thought. The large, imposing mahogany desk was a barrier shielding the Congresswoman, who looked at him with sharp green eyes and a sad smile. "Agent Pennock, I hope you are here to tell me there is progress in identifying my husband's murderer."

Thad began, "Congresswoman Wetherill, Ms. Patterson tells me this is a very busy day for you so I'm grateful you could squeeze this meeting in." Wetherill turned slightly, looked at Nikki and then back at Thad.

"Nikki's job is to protect my schedule, and thank goodness she's good at it. Otherwise I would be overrun and get nothing accomplished. But nothing is more important to me than finding my husband's killer. I will make time for you day or night." *The perfect response,* he thought, *explaining Nikki's reticence on the phone.* "What can you tell me?" she asked.

Thad looked at Nikki, then at the Congresswoman. "We treat communications with the spouse of a murder victim as confidentially as the spouse wishes. I'm going to tell you some things and ask you some things that involve your relationship with your husband. Things that most people would consider to be intimate. Having said that, I leave it to you whether you wish our conversation to be in private." He looked at Nikki, then back.

Nikki made no move to leave or speak. The Congresswoman nodded. "Yes, I appreciate the advice and your sensitivity to your protocol. But when you work as closely as Nikki and I have for as long, little remains private. It's like chartering a sailboat with friends. You may fully intend to respect each other's privacy, but the environment is such that by the end of the trip, you have all probably seen each other naked or going to the bathroom or both. Besides, Nikki was by my bed in the hospital when you asked me questions that I certainly thought were personal. I'm comfortable having her here. Who knows, maybe she knows something I don't that will prove helpful."

Sounds just like Moretti's little speech about his wife's presence, he said to himself. But he had hoped for this outcome. The Congresswoman would surely discuss with Nikki anything she wanted Nikki to know anyhow, and this way he and Owens had the opportunity to see any spontaneous reaction to their questions and comments.

The only problem was the seating arrangement. Owens and he could not look at both of them at the same time, could not read both of their immediate reactions to the news they were about to hear. So, Thad tried to change it. "Makes sense," he said, "so if it's all right with you Congresswoman Wetherill, I would like to ask Ms. Patterson to come join us, so I can feel I'm talking to both of you. It's a little awkward with you here," he gestured, "and her there." He started to rise to adjust the one empty leather chair.

The Congresswoman raised her hand. "Never mind Agent Pennock. This is what we are accustomed to, and after all, Taylor was *my* husband, and I think you asked to see me?" Turning to Nikki, she said, "Nikki, if you think there is anything to add as we talk, please speak up."

"I shall, Congresswoman, thank you," Nikki said.

Lost that one, Thad said to himself. Without any prompt from Thad, Owens shifted his chair so he could observe Nikki in a non-obvious way while Thad addressed Wetherill. Thad began, "Congresswoman Wetherill...." but got no further before she put a hand up in a "stop" gesture.

"I think I recall telling you in the hospital that 'Congresswoman Wetherill' is a mouthful. We will save a good deal of time if you simply call me Virginia and Nikki, Nikki."

"That is gracious of you, but I am far more comfortable, since this is a professional visit, following our protocol, which calls for last names."

"Whatever," she said, flicking her hand with mild annoyance.

Thad wanted to jolt her immediately. "Did your husband use cocaine?" For an instant, Wetherill's green eyes were green ice. But she quickly relaxed and gave a little laugh. "I admit I was fuzzy in the hospital, but haven't we covered that?" Before he could respond, she leaned forward. "Oh, sorry Agent Pennock, I forgot to offer you and Agent Owens something to drink. Coffee, tea, a soft drink? Since you are on the job I bet you abstain from anything harder. Probably have a protocol for that too?" She smiled, "But I have it if you want it."

"No thank you," the two agents said in chorus.

"Well," she said, "don't hesitate to pipe up if you suddenly have a craving for a boiler-maker. Now, sorry, didn't we cover that before?"

He thought to himself, *buying time.* He had caught her a little off guard, but she was back in stride. "I think I told you that is preposterous. Taylor loved to take a drink and could drink too much on occasion, but I never saw him use cocaine. He didn't even talk about it. Why do you pursue this?"

Sounding as official as he could, Thad said, "The autopsy showed without question that there were chemicals in your husband's blood and hair follicles consistent only with his ingestion of cocaine between two and four days before his death, probably by inhaling through his nose rather than by injection, but there is no 'probably' about whether he took it. The science is solid."

As he was speaking, Thad saw the Congresswoman's face tighten and her look sharpen. It was now the look of the other boxer in the ring. She was now a challenger, an adversary. He waited for her to speak. She said nothing for a full ten seconds. During that time, her look softened again. *Was this a mask or real,* he asked himself. He was unable to tell.

Flicking the air with a hand, which Thad now recognized was a habit, Wetherill said, "Why, I can't believe it. I mean, it's so hard to believe. Using drugs is...," she paused, "anathema to me. Taylor knew that. I don't know what to say." Thad sensed real feeling in these words, *but were they first time feelings or prior feelings revisited for the occasion?*

Thad turned his body to Nikki and asked, "Ms. Patterson did you ever see Mr. Warner use cocaine or any other drug?"

The Congresswoman interjected, "Of course she hasn't. Nikki and Taylor haven't been alone together for more than ten minutes ever. If I never saw him using, she didn't either." *That sure as hell tells Nikki what to say,* Thad thought.

"That's right," Nikki confirmed, looking at Thad. "I was hardly alone with Mr. Warner, and I never got any indication he was using any drugs." Thad thought, *whether they are telling the truth or lying, their stake is now down. They didn't know. OK, drop the next shoe.*

"Congresswoman, have you ever heard of Maria Isabella Loperena?" *No reaction,* Thad observed. "Who is she?" Virginia asked evenly and with measured curiosity. "Please search your memory," he said. She looked over Thad's head, as if she were mentally scanning through her contact list.

"It's a lyrical name. I meet so many people, but it doesn't mean anything to me. Have I met her?" Thad thought, *if she's lying, she's good.* "Who is she?" Wetherill repeated. *Here goes,* Thad thought. *Going to be interesting.*

"We have hard evidence that this lady, *yes, 'lady,' damn it,* he said to himself, and your husband were having an affair during the four months leading up to his death." There was silence as Wetherill's jaw opened and her eyes widened.

"What!?" she exclaimed, slapping her right palm on her desk and leaning out over it towards Thad. Her flaming hair seemed to come alive. "Hard evidence?" Wetherill harshly demanded, "What the fuck is 'hard evidence?'"

Slowly and professionally Thad answered. "Principally records from hotels in various cities, her cell number disguised in Mr. Warner's contacts list, many calls to that number, and...," he paused, "confirmation of the affair by Señorita Loperena."

"God!" she exclaimed angrily, closing her eyes, rocking, and pressing her temples. "How could he humiliate me that way! How could he!" These were not questions. She was venting. She sank back in her chair, eyes still shut. "How could he...?" she repeated, this time more in bewilderment. Tears seeped from under the corners of her eyelids. Several seconds passed. Nikki started to get up, but changed her mind. Then the Congresswoman's glistening eyes opened, and she leaned forward again, long fingers pressing on the edge of her desk. "Did she do it? Did she kill him? I tell you I will kill her!" Thad thought, *we should just let the Congresswoman mete out justice in this country, and we could shut down our costly penal system.* He knew his sense of humor could be a little on the morbid side, but it had the virtue of clearing his head of emotion just when it could get in the way.

He thought about her question. If she was innocent, it was a logical question, indeed, *the* logical question. So far, Wetherill was saying all the things she would say if she wasn't complicit in the murder. If it was a performance, it was good.

Thad answered evenly. "No, we are quite sure Señorita Loperena . . ."

Wetherill broke in, angry again, "Just call her by her real name Pennock – 'Whore!'" Then she flicked her hand again in that dismissive gesture, leaned back, closed her eyes, and shook her head side to side in a prolonged, "I can't believe it."

Thad continued, "We are quite sure she is not involved in the murder." The Congresswoman was silent for a long moment. Then, eyes still closed, she very quietly said, "Ah... for just a moment," another pause, "I let myself believe that perhaps . . .. Perhaps the shots were meant for him. That's awful to say, but . . ."

Then Wetherill opened her eyes and sat up. "Well, it's been a very edifying little chat so far," her words dripping with sarcasm. "Any other pleasant news for me about my murdered husband? I feel so much better about the whole thing!"

He responded respectfully, "I can show you what we have if you wish."

She shook her head quickly side to side emphatically, her hair flouncing, her hand warding off any proof. "No, no," she said. "I certainly do not wish."

"If at some point you change your mind . . . ." He let that offer trail off, and, altering his tone, began afresh. "Let's move from facts to motive," he continued. "Our theory has been that anyone wanting to see you lose the next election would be very glad to get their hands on . . ." he was about to say *dirt like this*, "information of this kind," he continued, "and spin it against you. Better yet, the extortionists would come to you first with the evidence to get you to agree to retire in exchange for deep-sixing the information. I expect you would have refused, told them that you were not afraid of it, maybe even told them you were going public with it yourself to put your own spin on it. That would leave them only one alternative. Kill you."

"But," he continued, "Since you didn't know any of this, it means you weren't approached and our nice, logical theory is out the window. I confess it's puzzling. Surely, Moretti or whoever acquired the information would have tried one way or another to use it to stop you before resorting to murder. So, maybe we're back at square one. Maybe someone else hired the shooter or maybe your husband actually was the target."

Wetherill's face was a mask while Thad spoke. When he finished, she ignored his obvious effort to bait her and instead threw it back at him. "Well," she said impatiently, "if his whore didn't do it and Moretti didn't do it, who the hell did?"

Looking first at the Congresswoman and then at Nikki, he said, "We don't know."

Wetherill's eyes moved past Thad and focused pensively on thoughts. He was surprised by her next softly spoken words. "I'd take the humiliation from his affair over the pain from his death in a New York minute. How could I not see it?" Then her gaze came back and met his. "It's got to be Moretti. It was so brutal. Who else but a heartless mobster could do something like that?"

After the session, Owens and Thad compared notes on the body signals and facial reactions of the two women. They were dwelling in the realm of gut feeling and intuition, but both men believed the gut could be a smart detective. Bottom line, they agreed that Wetherill had seemed genuinely surprised at the news of Warner's affair and cocaine use, and neither man could read Nikki. Owens ventured a glimpse into Nikki's thoughts. "I got the impression Nikki was more concerned about the impact of the information on her boss than about the information itself. But I don't know what to make of that."

CHAPTER 17

At 2:00 p.m. the next day, Thad ushered Nikki into a small conference room near his office. Owens was already there. Nikki wore a blouse, vest, and skirt, with mid-heels. Her hair was pulled back and held by a simple comb. If she had make-up on other than lipstick, Thad couldn't tell. *All business, as usual*, he thought. He tried to picture what she would look like if she made the effort. *Pretty nice I bet.*

Nikki had called that morning and asked to see him. "My boss doesn't know I'm coming," she said. Thad and Owens had huddled about that. In case this signaled a rift, they would be informal, call her Nikki, be friends.

Pointing to a chair, Thad said, "Have a seat Nikki. Like some coffee?"

"No thanks," she said, with a worried look.

Owens chuckled, "Nikki, that expression tells me you've had our coffee." She made an effort at a smile, but lost it quickly. She seemed nervous.

"Okay," Thad began, "what can we do for you?" She looked at Owens, then back at him. "Do you tape your conversations in here?"

"Not without your permission. Do you want what we say taped?"

"No, no," she quickly said.

"All right, no tape."

"And just think of me as another piece of furniture," Owens added, "and from the looks of things in this room, I'm badly needed." *Works every time*, Thad thought to himself as Nikki smiled and relaxed a little.

Then Nikki countered, "Agent Owens, I bet that works every time." Owens' grin widened. Both he and Thad got the message Nikki had pleasantly delivered. *Don't bullshit me.*

Nikki sat straight-backed, legs together and canted slightly to the right from the knees down. She looked straight at Thad and began. "Four days before the murder, I got a phone call from a lawyer I've never heard of. His name is Alfred Kirk. He said he had been instructed to ask me to come to his office and pick up a package. I asked what package and from whom? He said he didn't know. It was sealed. He said there was a separate letter addressed to him, which he opened. The letter said he was not to open the package and was to contact me and say to me, 'This information will ruin Congresswoman Wetherill's political career.' He then told me the letter also says that if I refuse to take the package, copies of its contents would be made public in a way calculated to get the widest distribution. He added, 'This is not in the letter, but I am requesting that if you take and open this package and the content suggests that some crime has been or is likely to be committed, you will let me know promptly, and we'll take it to the authorities.'

"I was comforted by that. It made him seem on the up-and-up. He also told me that there was a payment of $3,000 in the envelope to him to do what the letter instructed."

"Because he seemed honest I agreed to take the package. He said his office was in the Watergate building and asked me to pick up the package at his office. He said, 'Just Google me, Ms. Patterson. I assure you I'm real.' I did, and he is real. I figured I'd have a better idea what was going on once I got a look at what was inside. I was about to sign in at the security desk at the entrance to Watergate when a man came up to me and said, 'Mr. Kirk had to go out and asked me to wait for you here in the lobby and give you this package. You can call him tomorrow if you want to talk to him about it.' So I took the package and he left. I never did talk to Kirk."

At this point Nikki stopped and looked at them as if asking, "Any questions so far?" Thad looked at Owens and then said to Nikki, "You just go along. If we want to ask something, we'll let you know."

Nikki nodded and continued, "Then I went straight home, where I had privacy. In block letters the package was addressed to Mr. Kirk and his firm. There was a notation 'by hand delivery,' and it said 'personal and confidential, to be opened only pursuant to the attached instruction letter.' When the package was given to me, a letter was taped to it. On the envelope it said, 'To be opened only by Mr. Alfred Kirk, Esquire, personal and confidential.' I opened that envelope first. It had been opened before and then taped shut. The letter said exactly what Mr. Kirk told me it said, so I concluded that Mr. Kirk just gave me everything he had received."

"Still have the letter and envelope?" Thad asked.

"Yes, and the big envelope the contents came in – everything, I still have everything."

"Where?"

"In my apartment. The only things in the package were photographs, very vivid. They show Taylor and another woman, the same one in every picture." She paused, looked down, took a deep breath and looked up again. "They're eating alone or kissing in a corner, or snorting coke...." Another pause where she dropped her eyes. "Or having sex." She shook her head wonderingly, "How do they get those?"

Owens chimed in. "You would be amazed at what passes for a camera these days. Very easy to get shots without anyone having a clue. And if you know someone's room number, or some other place you know they'll return to, you can plant cameras."

"All I can say," she continued, "is they look like the real thing. They're the kind of pictures tabloids would dribble out for weeks. From what you told us yesterday, I guess the woman is Loperena?"

Thad was glad Nikki had not brought the package with her. He was not disturbed that Señorita Loperena had had a husband and lovers. He knew that's the way the world works. Nor was he bothered by any mental picture he could conjure up of her having sex with Warner. But an actual photograph? That was different! Looking at it was too risky. He might not be able to forget the image. *Damned unprofessional*, he berated himself. But he knew he would never look at the pictures if he could help it.

"Have you shared them with anyone?" Thad asked.

"No way! I hope they never see the light of day. I haven't... I didn't know what to do with them. There were no instructions for me, nothing saying show them to the Congresswoman. No blackmail note. Nothing saying, 'If you don't give us X dollars, we'll go public.' No nothing." She lowered her eyes, "I think I made an awful mistake. Maybe they thought I would show them to her. But the photographs would have so devastated her." She looked up at them again.

"I didn't know what to do. I thought that Moretti or whoever was responsible would get back to me. But I guess they thought the Congresswoman was stiffing them. She didn't even know . . . ." Her voice trailed off, "I didn't show them to her." She looked down and was silent. Thad asked, "Why do you say Moretti is behind this?" She brought her eyes up again. "I . . . because Virginia...," she corrected herself, "the Congresswoman is so confident he ordered the killing."

Thad was surprised at how composed Nikki seemed, but in case this was ripping her up inside, he decided to offer some comfort. "Well, you heard my theory yesterday at the Congresswoman's office. I'm certain she would not have knuckled under. She'd take the bull by the horns, go public and disclose the extortion attempt and spin it to help her investigation and minimize the damage from the scandal. If I think that's likely, you can bet that whoever is behind this thought so too, particularly after not hearing anything back. So, I think it would have played out about the same way regardless. Can you really see your boss giving in?" Nikki, who had continued looking down, raised her eyes to Thad's.

"No," she said, "I can't. But that's a lot different than knowing for sure."

Thad thought back to Wetherill's final words to him in the hospital, almost identical. Then Nikki said, less a question than a statement, "I've got to tell her all of this, don't I?"

"You have no choice. She needs to know you were approached. But I want Owens to be with you and that should help."

She sat for a moment and then said, "At least I won't be the first one to tell her about the affair."

"Thanks," Thad said sarcastically.

Then his tone changed. "Look, Nikki. There's another aspect to this. Why didn't you come to us right after the murder? Why have you waited, what is it, six days now?"

Nikki seemed to have anticipated this question, because without skipping a beat she said, "I was hoping the affair would never come to light, she would never know Taylor cheated on her. But after yesterday . . . ."

"Head in the sand never works, Nikki. Never. Anything else?" Thad asked.

"No."

"All right, Owens will go with you to your apartment, and you are to give him all the materials – package, envelope, everything. Has anybody touched it besides you after you got it?"

"No."

"The odds of getting meaningful prints off the package or its contents are nil, and I'll bet the source of the package will be untraceable.

"Then I want you to come back with Owens and give him a full statement of what you have told us today. Go through the photographs in the package that you actually looked at."

"I looked at them all," she offered, looking surprised that he might have thought otherwise.

"After that, you and Owens sit down with the Congresswoman and you tell her what happened. But the pictures don't go. They will remain here in an evidence locker."

Then his tone became stern. "But, understand something. You didn't think this through. Yes you were trying to spare your boss's feelings, but the fact is you withheld potential evidence for six days and would have continued to do so if we hadn't had our little session with the Congresswoman yesterday. You get a pass this time, but if I find out you're holding back anything else, I'll come back on this and, believe me, you will be in serious trouble. Understood?"

"Yes," she said, flushing at the severity of both tone and message.

Turning to Owens, Thad said, "Have someone see Kirk and check him out. See if there's a record of Kirk or anyone in his firm representing any known mobster. See if anyone in that firm knows who delivered the package. I'll bet the real Attorney Kirk knows nothing about any of this and the bad guys just pulled his name out of a hat. And check in with me after you and Nikki speak to the Congresswoman. Tell her she is not to go public with any of this, at least until she clears it with us."

"Okay Chief."

Thad turned back to Nikki and said in a kinder voice. "Look, Nikki, there's a way you can help. The Congresswoman counts on you. Help her stay cool and calm for a while and let us know the slightest thing out of the ordinary. Who knows? Maybe Warner's death was a warning. Maybe they'll approach her again. Will you help us? I also think it's the best way to help her."

"Yes, I'll try."

Ten minutes later as Thad was returning to his office, his cell phone rang. It was Colonel Hernandez. "Well, my friend," he said, "our man is moving. This very morning, Correa got on a plane to Philadelphia through Miami, under the name Enrico Lopez. He did not alter his appearance, so video monitors caught him at the departure gate in Cordoba and then again in Santiago, where he changed planes." He gave Thad the particulars of the flights.

Hoping this might be the break they needed, Thad said, "Colonel, we will try to do as fine a job on our end as you have on yours. Maybe Correa is the hound that will open on our fox. We'll follow every move and keep you informed."

Later, Owens reported back that the Congresswoman had not wanted to see the materials given to Nikki or even hear a description of them. And she displayed no anger towards Nikki. "She was actually excited," Owens said, "because she considered this proof that Moretti was the murderer. 'I knew it,' she kept saying, 'I knew it!'"

When Owens finished, Thad told him the news from Hernandez. Then, leaning back in his desk chair, he asked, "Tell me, wise one, what will go down?"

Owens, sitting across the desk, went through his habitual routine. He paused, looked down, pushed his glasses up his nose a millimeter, raised his head and began, "Only a guess, Chief. Correa insisted on getting paid in the U.S. in person in U.S. dollars as a condition of doing the deal. He probably has a plan to invest it here after putting it into accounts here that whoever is paying him cannot trace. Or there's a problem, and he's come to resolve it. His risk is that they decide it's better to send him to the shredder than pay him, but he's got that risk whether he's here or in Cordoba."

"How do you think they'll make the pass?" Thad asked.

"In a crowd so nobody notices. Big bills, maybe an envelope. Small bills, maybe a gym bag." There was silence for a moment, and then Thad spoke.

"So even if we see the handoff, we're not going to be able to link it to Moretti or whoever ordered it?" It was both a question and a statement.

"Not if they do it right. Some guy down the line. We could peel back his fingernails and even if he wanted to he couldn't tell us who gave him the money or where it came from." He paused, then continued, "Maybe somebody will make a mistake. If he's come to negotiate, maybe it will be someone we can link to Moretti."

Thad exhaled, "Lots of 'maybes.' Okay, we need a faultless tail, no screw-ups. And maybe we need to bend the rules a little to discover that link. I'll talk to Lew and contact Charlie."

CHAPTER 18

Correa stepped out of the plane onto the exit ramp to the terminal and saw two ramp attendants. He didn't know there usually was one. When he passed, one of them said something into his radio and fell in line three passengers behind. From that moment until Correa got into a yellow cab at the Terminal B cab stand, the FBI had at least one pair of eyes on him.

As Correa's cab moved away from the curb, a car parked thirty yards in front also pulled out. The passenger was brushing her hair with her right hand and holding a mirror up in her left. Another cab with two male passengers pulled from the queue and settled in behind Correa's cab. The three cars exited the airport on to I-95 north toward Philadelphia. The car in front was moving too slowly for the driver of Correa's cab so he passed it. It never occurred to Correa that the man and woman could be tailing him.

The three cars drove over the Penrose Avenue Bridge, turned left at the first light and soon merged onto I-76 west, cutting through West Philadelphia near the University of

Pennsylvania complex and Penn Station. A series of exits led downtown – University Avenue, South Street, JFK Boulevard, and finally the Ben Franklin Parkway. If Correa was headed downtown, he would take one of these.

One of the radio channels available only to the FBI had been cleared for the tail. The Philadelphia Police and the Pennsylvania State Police each had a high-ranking officer monitoring the channel so they would have real time knowledge of the situation in case Charlie, who led the operation, needed local help. The protocol was strict silence on the channel except for Charlie and the agents who at any given time were the tails.

Correa's cab exited I-76 on to the Ben Franklin Parkway and proceeded straight to the Ritz-Carlton Hotel. The car with the coiffed passenger passed the entrance and the tailing cab pulled in right behind Correa's. One of the two agents jumped out, walked into the hotel lobby, and moved to a house phone from which he could see the reservation desk. Correa moved at a more normal pace. He waited for the porter to retrieve his suitcase from the trunk and paid his fare. He barely noticed that a man in the cab behind went into the hotel before he did. The second tail pretended to pay the fare to the agent portraying the cabbie then picked up his overnight bag, declining help from a porter. He did not want to beat Correa to the reservation desk but did want to be right behind him so that he could hear the name Correa gave for the reservation. The name was Enrico Lopez.

When Correa moved away from the reservation counter and towards the elevator lobby, the first tail placed the house phone in its receiver and walked to the elevators. He followed Correa and stepped deep into the elevator so Correa punched his floor first – "9." The tail, not looking at Correa, stepped forward and pushed "10." Then he stepped back. No point in inviting Correa to study his face. Correa got out on the 9th floor, and the tail watched until the elevator doors closed, but he had no chance to see Correa commit to any particular room. "Ninth floor, but no room number," he radioed.

When the door opened at the 10th floor, the agent stayed put and pushed the button for the lobby. It had gone smoothly, but he was disappointed. His day as a close tail was over. Cardinal rule – once the mark sees an agent and other agents are close by, the first agent is backed off. When he got his assignment originally, he knew that if Correa went to a hotel, the elevator ride was it for him. He would now be back-up.

As soon as Correa moved away from the reservation desk and toward the elevators, the second tail flashed his badge at the attendants and asked to see the manager on duty. He showed his badge and asked for and got the room number for Enrico Lopez. He told the manager that the FBI needed to watch Lopez. He asked for a room on the ninth floor between 909 and the elevators, registered it in his name and took two keys. He told the manager exactly where the agents on the job would be located and the type of hotel personnel they would pretend to be. The agent told the manager this was a need to know operation and he should tell no one without first getting FBI approval. He gave the manager Charlie Townsend's cell number and his own cell number.

Room 909 had to be watched; otherwise, a well-disguised Correa could slip out of the hotel undetected or a critical meeting or exchange could take place in another room in the hotel. So a particular electrician and a particular housemaid, who had been in an FBI van awaiting instructions, were ordered to the ninth floor of the Ritz-Carlton to observe room 909.

An hour after checking in, Correa left his room and went to a bar in the hotel for a drink and to check out the women. He considered himself a lady's man. The electrician on the ninth floor deftly picked the lock of room 909 and quickly searched the few belongings Correa had brought with him. Correa had taken his cell phone and wallet with him, so there was nothing of interest in the room except a piece of note paper on which was written "32 Degrees, eleven, red cap, Mickey, Mantle." The agent memorized the note. Then he bugged the room and the room phones, a detail that the hotel manager didn't "need to know." It was not likely Correa would use a room phone, but they might get lucky. One of the bugs sent a signal when the door to 909 was opened. The electrician was in and out in less than ten minutes, but while he was busy, two agents moved into room 906, across the hall, with monitoring and communication gear and set up shop. They would know when Correa came and went and what he, or anyone else for that matter, said in room 909.

Correa spent eighty minutes in the bar. The tails watching him reported on his obvious interest in women. He returned to his room alone and did not leave again until 9:30 the next morning. During the night he made no calls from the room phones and the only voices heard by the listening agents came from a television.

The information on the paper scrap was a small break. "32 Degrees" was a nightclub on Second Street. The tails would have followed Correa there in any event but now Charlie's team could place agents there beforehand.

32 Degrees exactly met the description of the type of place Owens thought the meet would occur. It was either the spot for the transfer of Correa's payment or the contact point from which Correa would be taken elsewhere. If they took him elsewhere, according to Owens, it would be to make sure that Correa had not been tailed, or, as Owens put it, "To eliminate him. Cheaper that way."

"So 'eleven' probably means the time of the meet?" Thad asked. Owens nodded. "What's 'red cap,' 'Mickey', and 'Mantle?'"

"Pure guess. Either Correa or his contact or both will wear a red cap. 'Mickey' and 'Mantle' are the code words that link them up. Pretty basic stuff."

"Suppose the pass doesn't happen there but the connection takes him through some door to the back?" Thad asked. "So where are we? Can we get to someone who works there?"

"No good," Charlie piped in. "We try to buy somebody, we probably tip our hand. Only thing we can do is cover all the exits."

Owens added, "My guess is it's going down on the dance floor. Correa goes through back doors only if somebody working there or an owner is in on it. That's unnecessary risk."

"I agree," Charlie added, "If you're in the middle of the dance floor in this joint, guaranteed nobody is paying any attention to you. Ever been there? Strobe lights and wall-to-wall, shoulder-to-shoulder capital P pussy. You could pass off a fire truck in there with the siren going and nobody would notice."

Thad frowned. "So if we just watch, we won't learn a damn thing." He was silent for a moment, thinking. Finally he said, "Well, this may be one of those times we do what the FBI doesn't do. We bend the rules a little. He fancies himself a ladies man? How about something like..." and he told them.

When he finished, Charlie said, "I've got the agent who could pull that off. She's the first person you'd notice in a room full of beautiful women and the last person you'd suspect was FBI."

CHAPTER 19

The next day Correa wandered around the city and into several shops. At one store he bought a red baseball cap. He returned to his room about 4:00 p.m., and at 7:00 he left again wearing the red cap. He killed time in a series of bars hitting on women. He wasn't bad looking, and with his Argentinian accent he attracted some interest. But he kept moving. At 8:30, he went into a sports bar and had dinner. He switched from Tequila to beer and stayed with it. He watched a soccer match, frequently checking the time. At 9:45 he paid his bill and walked the four blocks to 32 Degrees.

He hadn't counted on a line. For a few minutes he stood in it, gauging how fast it moved. *Not fast enough,* he said to himself. He saw that the bouncers called a few of the better-looking girls to the front from time to time. There were three of them, and they were big and serious. At 9:55, he took some bills from his wallet, walked up to the bouncer furthest from the door, and slipped the money into his hand. It was enough. The bouncer signaled to his companion guarding the door and nodded to Correa. Seconds later he was in.

The place was wall-to-wall hands, upper bodies, biceps and breasts, gyrating to the sensual, heavy-rhythm music. Large spheres hung from the ceiling, spinning slowly and reflecting in all directions flashing colors from pulsing strobe lights that provided most of the light and atmosphere of the room. He worked his way through the undulating bodies, eyeing the women he brushed by with a self-satisfied grin pasted on his face. He uttered an occasional, "Hey, Señorita, looking good." When he reached one of the long, crowded bars, he found a spot and ordered tequila on the rocks with a lime and turned around leaning his elbows on the bar. He looked right and left and then into the gyrating flesh on the dance floor.

A tail wearing a collared shirt, dungarees, and sunglasses squeezed into a space next to him, faced the bar, and ordered a beer. The loud, throbbing music continued to seduce the dancers into elemental movements. A second agent squeezed in on the other side of Correa and ordered a drink. One of the two agents was a placeholder, but it was too early to know which one.

Neither tail was going to strike up a conversation with Correa or even utter a greeting unless Correa spoke first. But Correa wasn't interested. He was waiting. Five minutes later, a hard looking, full bodied girl with dark hair and racially mixed color elbowed her way to the bar next to him, forcing the agent on Correa's left to push down the bar a step. She was in tight slacks and a halter-top. She wore a baseball cap backwards. It was red. The agent on Correa's immediate right, away from this girl, now knew he was the placeholder.

Both tails saw Red Cap order a drink, turn her head, and say something to Correa, who still faced the dance floor. They couldn't hear it. Correa turned and looked first at the hat and then at the woman's face. He said something that neither tail could hear over the din. But there was no doubt, contact made. Correa turned so he and Red Cap faced the bar shoulder to shoulder.

The agent whom Red Cap had pushed aside was looking at the back of her head. He spoke quietly into his shirt collar and within ten seconds a 5'6" blond knock-out with big blue eyes worked her way to the bar on the other side of Correa. The placeholder agent there moved away from the bar making room for her. She ordered a drink, and said, "Hello," to her right and left with a smile. Correa, hearing the pleasant voice, turned away from Red Cap and took in Blue Eyes. His face lit up. "Hola bonita," he answered. Blue Eyes widened her eyes and flashed a smile of beautiful white teeth. Correa, egotistical enough to believe he could interest her, said smoothly, "Please excuse me, I'll be just a minute. I hope you will not leave." She said nothing, but continued to smile at him. He looked at that smile for a full three seconds and then turned back to Red Cap.

Blue Eyes could only see Correa's hands on the bar since he was leaning forward and away from her, but the agent on the other side of Red Cap, much taller than she, had a good view. Red Cap did the talking, or rather whispering close to Correa's ear. Then Correa opened his right hand, which was on the bar. Red Cap put her smaller left hand in it for just a moment and then removed it. Correa closed his hand and slowly put it in his right pants pocket. Both agents saw the pass. Red Cap abruptly left and disappeared into the dancing bodies.

Correa immediately turned back to Blue Eyes, his back to the tail at the bar. He didn't notice the tail move slowly away from the bar, speaking into his shirt collar. "Couldn't make what it was, but Red Cap slipped something into the mark's hand. I think we've just had a hand-off."

Charlie ordered, "Stick to Red Cap."

"On it," the agent answered, but he would have given a day's pay to watch Blue Eyes go to work on Correa.

Blue Eyes put her arm on Correa's. She flashed her smile, moved her curvy body in a little closer under his eyes and murmured, "I love your accent; it drives me crazy." Putting her lips to his ear, she breathed into it. "Dance with me." She did not wait for an answer, but hitched her fingers in his belt and urged him into the dancing throng. Once there, she faced him and moved her body into his in rhythm with the music. She smiled up at him, locking her eyes on his like the radar of a guided missile. Her hands were in motion on his back, his shoulders, his chest, his neck. She gave him no time to think. With her hands behind his neck and their bodies moving up and down, she threw back her beautiful head and laughed. Then she drew his head to her and sucked his lower lip into her mouth. She took his arms and put them around her back, left them there, and then returned hers to his hips, her body working his.

Then Blue Eyes stepped it up. Again she threw her arms about his neck and began kissing him, this time with passion, and as she did so she pressed her groin tight into him. She moved her hands teasingly around his body, to the middle of his back, around his hips to the side of his legs, grazing his loins. Correa was beginning to feel very lucky. Just as he settled into the rhythm and pleasure of this, she ducked underneath his arms and rotated until she was behind him. She pressed against his back, compelling him to move with her while her arms and hands brushed his hips, his loins, and, although he had no clue, his right pants pocket. Then she whirled to face him again, pulling his head down and into another full-mouthed kiss as she continued her rhythmic movement. Correa, eyes half closed, was swept along by the delicious seduction.

Suddenly, in mid-embrace, she broke off and pushed back. Her blue eyes were wide, and her left hand went to her mouth. Looking right and left and then directly at Correa, she blurted, "Oh, I have made a fool of myself! What an awful embarrassment. I am so ashamed." Then she ran off into the crowd.

Correa didn't move for a few seconds watching in amazement as she disappeared into the sea of bodies. Only when she was out of sight did he realize his arms were still outstretched where they had opened to release her. He dropped them to his side. His penis, engorged and pressing against his pants, slowly softened. It had been a bewildering performance from beginning to end, and he had no idea what to make of it. As he continued to stare in the direction she fled, he absentmindedly put his hands into his pockets.

An instant later, the tail still watching saw him jump like he had touched a high-tension wire. Suddenly his hands were all motion, in and out of his pants pockets and then his shirt pocket two and three times. His eyes grew wide, and his expression progressed from surprise to concern to fury. He stormed into the crowd where Blue Eyes had disappeared.

Blue Eyes had hurried to the club entrance. Just inside the door another agent held out to her a long coat, which she quickly put on. The agent handed her a cap and sunglasses. Blue Eyes donned the sunglasses and quickly tucked her blond hair under the cap as the two of them briskly exited the club and hurried down the sidewalk about forty yards to a double-parked van. The agent opened the rear door, and they both jumped in. The van pulled away. Blue Eyes opened her right hand and, with a proud smile, displayed a key. "This has to be the key to the drop," she said.

The other agent, grinning broadly, said, "Jesus Sarah, I've never seen anything like that. I'm amazed the guy didn't come in his pants. I see you in a whole new light!"

Agent Sarah Morton smiled at him and said, "Only when I'm on the clock, Pat." She then gestured for a radio another agent held. "Chief Townsend," she said into it, "this is Agent

Morton. I am in the van with Agent Steininger. The mark was given a key. I have it. It says 'Penn Station' and has the number 203. It looks like a locker key of some sort. It went straight from Correa's closed fist into his pocket and then into my hand. I don't think he ever got a look at it.'"

"Okay, I'll be back on in a minute," Charlie said and clicked off. He turned to Thad and Owens. "The city is experimenting at the train station with a secure area with lockers where travelers can leave suitcases and other bags for up to 48 hours. The idea is they can tour the city and see the Liberty Bell without dragging stuff around. Screening machines provide security so no one leaves a bomb. That facility has only been open about three months. Did you notice it when you trained in?"

Thad nodded, "Can't miss the signs touting it. They're all over the station." Thad looked right at Charlie, "We have to assume that Red Cap told Correa the location and locker number. Maybe she didn't, but we can't take that chance."

"Not just that," Owens added, "Moretti's people may be watching Correa or watching the lockers or both. If Correa gives Moretti's people the word that the key is gone, who knows what agent Morton will be walking into?"

Charlie barked orders into his radio. "Team one get Agent Morton to Penn Station ASAP. She's making a locker pickup. Teams four and five get to Penn Station ASAP. Deploy as you see fit to watch her back and get her out safely. Team three stay with Correa."

"Agent Morton, you personally have to make the pickup. In case Moretti's men were watching the club and are at the lockers it has to look like a solo con job and not the FBI. Whoever is watching has to see the girl that stole the key use it. Whatever is in that locker, get it fast. We'll have your back."

"Yes, sir," Agent Morton said, and then asked, "How do you want me dressed?" Charlie looked at Owens.

"As she is now," Owens said. "A good con would keep the coat and hat to draw less attention."

"Hear that Sarah?" Charlie asked, slipping into use of her first name.

"Yes sir."

As the van approached Penn Station, Charlie spoke again. "Listen up teams four and five. Agent Morton gets an Academy Award, but we have no idea what to expect. Nobody get sloppy. Protect her."

Just then a member of team two radioed in that Red Cap had gone straight from the nightclub to a tall, pockmarked black dude who was a known pimp and whose street name was Soapy. "Ah," Charlie said, "I know that creep. He's got a sheet longer than the Baja Peninsula, all drugs and prostitution. He's one of those cowardly low-lifes who are afraid of everything so they prey on desperate, female drug addicts.

"Smart," Owens commented. "Use a strung out prostitute and a pimp who know nothing from nothing."

"We'll leave them out there," Thad said, "Bringing them in only tips the people we're after, and there's only a slim chance they know anything anyway."

CHAPTER 20

Correa, full of rage and confusion, elbowed his way through the dancers, knocking two down in the effort. He forced his way to the nightclub's entrance and then to the street. He looked both ways, registering everyone in sight, including a girl in dark glasses and a cap and long coat moving to the back of a double-parked van. He turned to the bouncers, and, in an animated state, tried to get them to tell him in which direction the sexy blond with the blue eyes had gone. None had even noticed such a girl.

Correa waived his arms up and down in frustration. His feet moved in place, and once he turned a complete circle, uncertain where to go next. To anyone watching, it would have been comical. Then he picked a direction and started running. At the corner he looked all four ways. No sight of her. When he realized he would not catch her on the street, his mind immediately went back to Red Cap and her words – "the lockers at Penn Station. The number's on the key, but don't look at it now. Just put it in your pocket until I'm out of here."

Then he was all motion again, frantically gesturing to stop a taxi. Forty long seconds later he was in a yellow cab, leaning forward, pounding on the back of the front seat and exhorting the cabbie to, "move, move faster, faster." Soon the cab was heading west on Walnut Street, speeding when it could, running yellow-red lights when it could, and taking dead aim at Penn Station. The cabby didn't mind the bellowing passenger pounding away. He lived for tips the size this maniac had promised.

As soon as Correa hailed the cab, the team following him got on the radio and reported. Charlie listened and turned to Owens and Thad. "He's in a cab. He must be headed for the station." Then he got on the radio. "Teams 4 and 5," he said, "the mark is on his way. We'll keep you posted, but you aren't going to have more than four or five minutes to get in place and probably not that if he's lucky hitting the lights."

"Confirmed," said the leader of Team 4.

Charlie continued, "Where is Agent Morton now?"

"She's just now heading to the lockers."

Charlie continued, "See anybody suspicious or anyone watching her?"

"Not many people here at this time of night. Maybe fifteen to twenty people, including workers. She actually got here just in time. Locker area closes at eleven. There's no one in the immediate vicinity except one guard manning the screening device and a shoe-shine guy by his stand near the entrance to the lockers." It did not feel right to Thad. He glanced at Owens, who shrugged.

Agent Morton, without the sunglasses, walked casually to the entrance to the lockers. She smiled and exchanged greetings with the security guard. She showed the key and widened her smile. "Picking up my things." He let her through. The shoeshine man sitting by his stand looked over the top of the newspaper in his hands. His eyes followed the good-looking girl moving into the locker area.

The tail following Correa radioed in to Charlie. "He's flying. Not paying much attention to the lights. We're falling behind. He'll be there in ninety seconds unless a city cop stops him."

Charlie, his voice now tense, passed the word along. "Teams 4 and 5, you have no more than ninety seconds."

Sarah stopped in front of locker 203. A pro, she did not glance around, but simply went about her business. She inserted the key and opened the door. She reached in without hesitating. It would appear to anyone watching that she knew exactly what she would find. She removed a brief case.

Charlie's sharp voice crackled over the radio, "The mark is almost at the east entrance. Get the hell out west." Sarah did not hurry. She exited the secured area and turned right. A man and woman, arms locked and gazing lovingly at each other, moved from her left and walked in the same direction five yards behind her. Another man hailed the couple and waived and jogged to catch up with them. Soon the three were talking and laughing together and providing a moving screen three bodies wide.

As the heavy granite mass of Penn Station loomed larger before him, Correa pounded harder on the seat. Finally, the cab squealed to a stop at the east entrance of the great hall of the station. Correa jumped out and half handed, half threw the cabbie some bills, rushed to the entrance, and burst through the double doors so forcefully that they swung hard and slammed into the granite wall with a loud report that echoed around the cavernous lobby. Most of the people there turned their heads at the noise, but not all did.

Wide-eyed like a hawk, Correa searched the turned faces quickly, scanning left to right. As his eyes moved, he registered three people, two men and a woman, walking away from him toward the opposite entrance. *Too tall to be her,* he concluded. He thought there might be another person beyond them, but he could only see snatches of color, maybe a coat. He continued scanning.

His inventory of the hall took perhaps five seconds. He was a man in a hurry. He bounded over to the entrance to the lockers. He couldn't see all of the room beyond, but the portion he could see was empty. He carried no luggage so the security guard let him pass. At that instant agent Morton and the team protecting her walked out through the west exit. She jumped into the van idling there and the others walked another thirty yards and got into their van.

The lockers not in use were unlocked, and some were partially open. For the next twenty seconds Correa frantically moved from locker to locker, trying each one in the ridiculous hope that maybe his package would be behind an open door. His behavior caught the attention of the guard. "Hey buddy!" he yelled. "What are you doing there?"

Correa hurried back to the guard. The shoeshine man watched. Correa held out a $10 bill, and in his Argentinian accent he politely but urgently asked, "Señor, have you been at this post for the last five or ten minutes?" The man looked at the bill, then at Correa.

"Yeah," he said slowly, cautiously. "Why?" The guard wasn't sure he could take money for information and didn't want to lose his job. *But, who's to know?* He thought.

Correa asked, "Did a pretty blond with blue eyes and short skirt come through and get something from the lockers? She's about five feet five inches tall."

The man looked at the $10 bill then at Correa. "Nope," he said, shaking his head. "The only good looking five-five girl in here was wearing a long coat and cap covering her hair. Couldn't tell if she was a blond."

It took only a second to hit him. *The woman getting into the van! That's why I couldn't find her!* Then a more ominous thought flashed into his mind and burned there. *She had help! What the hell's going on?*

Eyeing the $10 bill, the guard added, "It looked strange. Good looking broad dressed to party and carrying that briefcase."

Correa grabbed the guard by the shoulder and leaned in. "How long ago?" Seeing the guard recoil, he added, "Please, here." He offered the bill, "It's very important."

The guard relaxed and smirked, "She steal your briefcase?"

"Please..." Correa tried hard to contain himself and keep calm. "Please. How long ago did she leave?" "Oh, about thirty seconds before you come flying in here."

"What!" Correa blurted, "You really mean thirty seconds?"

"Well, no, more like twenty."

"Through here?" Correa asked, incredulous.

"Yeah, same way you did, mister."

Correa replayed his scan of the great hall. His mind's eye stopped on the two men and the woman walking away from him and then on the visual fragments he had glimpsed through them. *Another person...a long coat. Damnation!* He forgot the guard and raced toward the west exit. He needed to run, to exert effort to keep from exploding with rage. But even as he did so, he knew it was futile. A second time within the span of twenty minutes he would be too late! He charged through the doors and stopped. He stood in the night air with his back to the building and took a quick look left and right and then slowly scanned everything he could see left to right. She wasn't there. He shut his eyes and clenched both fists in front of his face. "Chanta!" he roared. *What the hell is going on?*

The shoe shine man had watched Correa from the time he banged open the doors of the east entrance until he ran out the doors on the west side. He waited a moment to see if the frantic man would return. When the man didn't, he removed a cell phone from his shirt pocket and punched in a number. He had started to make the call as the girl with the briefcase walked by him on her way out but stopped when Correa literally burst onto the scene.

In a moment someone answered, and the shoeshine man succinctly reported everything he had seen. When he finished, the man on the other end said simply, "Shut down," and rang off. The shoeshine man reached behind his stand and retrieved a sign that read, "Closed." He propped it on the front of the stand and walked away. Apparently, no one had stopped to think how unusual it was for a shoeshine stand to be manned at that time of night.

———

The cell phone of a man in Moretti's home rang. The man first looked at the caller ID and then answered. "Yes?" He listened to the person on the other end for about thirty seconds, rang off, and walked to the closed door of the library. In addition to several guards around the property, Moretti had two of his men inside his home when he or any of his family were there. These were trusted, capable lieutenants. The man about to knock on the library door was one of them. He knocked twice, paused, and knocked once. The other lieutenant on duty was in the library with Moretti and a male secretary. He opened the door and motioned the man in. It was eleven o'clock, but Moretti was at his desk.

"Mr. Moretti, I have a message from Antonio."

Moretti nodded, looked at the secretary and politely said, "Raymond, please give me a moment."

"Certainly sir," the secretary answered as he rose and left the room. This was a pattern that had played out many times

before. Moretti, again politely, motioned the lieutenant with
the message to stand next to him behind his large desk. The
man did so immediately, and when he rounded the desk, he
leaned down close to Moretti's ear and quietly spoke to his
seated boss until he had recited to him the events at the train
station. When he finished, he stood straight and backed a
pace away.

Moretti's mild expression never changed as he listened to
the report. It almost never did. He had disciplined himself
to keep a polite and pleasant countenance always and to
speak with polished diction, perfect grammar, and measured
tones. He did not believe he could do this when it was most
important unless he did it all the time, even in the privacy of
his library. It was not enough to practice these affectations.
He had to live them. The image he cultivated was so counter
to the public image of someone suspected of being associated
with organized crime that it was the best refutation of that
suspicion. In manner and appearance, he could have been the
head curator of the Philadelphia Museum of Art.

He sat thinking for a moment and then turned slightly in
his chair and looked at his lieutenant. "Is there anything else
Thomas?"

"No sir."

"Then, I thank you, and you may leave." As Thomas
turned to go, Moretti raised his hand, "Please wait." He
motioned him to return, and when Thomas had again bent
down to him, Moretti asked, "Is Mr. Correa staying at the
hotel we recommended?"

"Yes sir," Thomas answered.

"Given this development, he must return to Argentina
promptly. Ballotti is still the only one here who has had
contact with him?"

"Yes sir," Thomas answered.

"Then it is Ballotti. He should promptly meet with Correa and find out how it came to be that this woman obtained the key from him. Ballotti must persuade him that his mistake and his loss place no additional obligation upon us in his favor. He must return to Argentina immediately. And, Thomas, Ballotti must learn from him everything he can about this woman. Was she working alone or with others? Who is she? Are my instructions to Ballotti clear to you?"

"Yes Sir."

"Very good. I should like to hear a report of Ballotti's meeting. Thank you." This was a dismissal. Thomas bowed slightly and left.

As a businessman, Moretti kept impeccable records, although for many of his ventures there was more than one set of books. But when he dealt with what he thought of as "family" matters, he wrote nothing down. His instructions were oral, and there were always two or three of his men, nearly but not always men, layered between him and any independent contractor like Correa. Unless one of his lieutenants turned on him, he would always be insulated, and his lieutenants were well aware of the inevitable, unenviable fate of a turncoat. So Moretti knew that a soured Correa would not be a threat that could expose him personally. But that assurance was insufficient. He had a business to run. *I will not risk a mad dog in the street*, he said to himself. Then he raised his head and looked pleasantly at his other lieutenant standing near the library door. "Stephen, kindly ask Raymond to return."

CHAPTER 21

The next morning, showing signs of little sleep, Correa left his hotel and walked three blocks, periodically looking behind him. Then he turned around and walked back, searching each face he passed. He walked three blocks beyond his hotel and reversed course again. Except for hawkers or people who were simply standing on the street or in a doorway, he did not see the same person twice. Passing the hotel again, he walked two blocks, turned left, walked another block, and then took a cab.

The tails had little trouble with Correa's unsophisticated maneuvers. They were on him. The cab dropped Correa in front of a parking garage on Sansom Street, barely more than an alleyway between Chestnut and Walnut Streets. He took the stairs to the third floor and there began looking for parking spot number 316. The car in that space was backed in against the wall so any occupant could see who passed by on foot or in a car. The car was unlocked and empty. Correa got into the front passenger seat and waited. Five minutes later,

Joseph Ballotti appeared and got into the driver's seat. He stared at Correa. "You don't look so good."

"You wouldn't either," Correa shot back in his accented English.

Ballotti forced back a grin and asked, "Any sign that you are being followed?"

"I wouldn't be here if there was," Correa said with irritation caused by embarrassment he felt but refused to acknowledge.

When Correa got to his hotel room the night before, he saw a note that had been slipped under his door. It told him to leave his room and call a certain number. When he did, he received the instructions that led him to this place at this time.

Correa, still testy, said, "I was about to call you when I got your message."

"You're lucky you didn't. Your instructions are never to call."

"Your instructions?" Correa retorted, "We are way beyond 'your instructions'. I have none of the money I earned. Isn't that curious? Out of the God damn blue thirty seconds after I'm handed the key, a good-looking con comes on to me and steals it! And she's got help! A coincidence? Some fucking coincidence! The whole thing was planned. Planned!" He looked hard at Ballotti. "You know what I think Ballotti? I think she works for you. Nobody else knew I was here, let alone why I'm here. Yet she shows up right away and knows just what to take. Imagine that!" Then with heat he said, "It was a set-up, and you owe me my money!"

Ballotti took a breath and slowly and deliberately spoke, "Correa, listen very carefully. I'm going to pretend you never said that. Be grateful for that, because it is very important to your health. Do you understand me?" Correa just glared at him. Ballotti continued, "I knew last night that you had screwed up. Not because we stole from you, but because it's our business to know what you do when you work for us." He paused, "Now, tell me all you know about this woman who took the key. Everything."

Correa, exasperated, yelled, "I don't know shit about her. She was just there, right there next to me when the hard little bitch in the red cap palmed me the key. But no way anyone saw the key. Even I didn't see it.

"I don't know who she is, where she came from, or where the hell she went. She was blond and wearing not much. She did a number on me that would make a telephone pole of your dick and melt the rest of your Goddamn body around it. She was too good for it to be a coincidence, too good. I ran out of the club after her and didn't see her. The bouncers didn't notice her leave. But I did see a woman in a long coat and cap climb in the back of a van with some guy. The security guard at the lockers described the same woman taking a briefcase from a locker. She didn't pull this off alone. You planned the whole thing. You owe me my money!"

Ballotti, looking at him in wonderment, shook his head side-to-side. "I know you heard what I told you. I know you should have understood what I told you, because you are not an idiot." He took a breath and exhaled heavily. "I'm going to try just one more time. Listen carefully. We are businessmen. To be successful – and we are very successful – we need to call on contract players like you from time to time. So, when someone does the job he was hired to do, like you did, he gets paid. If we didn't pay, word would soon get around, and it would be difficult for us to get people to help us do business. So, we pay. Understand? We paid you Correa. We delivered the payment into your hands, and it was you who lost it. So, we kept our bargain. You screwed up because you let all your blood drain from your brain into your dick. Tough! Now we don't want you bouncing off walls around here calling attention to yourself, so you are going home right away. Got that? It's not complicated. Business done."

Correa's anger grew as Ballotti made this speech, and by the end his face had visibly reddened. "Done? You say we're done? I didn't get a dime for delivery! I took care of the secretary, took her place, and got you what you wanted, and who knew I was here but you? Nobody. So who could have set the sucker's punch up but you? Nobody. I don't like to be double-crossed. I will leave after I get my money, and if I don't have it by the end of the day, who knows who will hear about this. You cannot scare me off. Understand something. I have letters in certain hands. They need to get a call from me when my plane lands in Argentina. If they do not, my letters go to the press."

Ballotti's face was now hard and his stare icy. "You will go to the press and say a man named Ballotti hired you to kill a secretary and take her place to get information proving that the Argentinian woman screwing the husband of Congresswoman Wetherill was a junky or maybe a dealer? Do I have that right?"

"So far, but you didn't include the important part. My letters say you work for Moretti. He wants the heat off the investigation, so he threatened the Congresswoman with exposure of her husband's druggy whoring.... Beautiful!" He leaned in and thrust his finger into Ballotti's unreadable face. "You stole my money from me. Stole it! And I want what I bargained for. Have it at my hotel room by ten tonight and all will be well. I will need two days to place it, and I assure you I will then be gone. You can trust me, which is more than I can say for you." He was convinced he was back in control.

Ballotti looked at him in silence for a brief moment. Then he quietly said, "You know, Correa, I was wrong. You are an idiot. I don't know Mr. Moretti, but if you release crazy statements like that, you're likely to wake up dead no later than the next morning. Just get on that plane."

"Oh, I plan to get on a plane all right. One way I have my money invested, the other Mr. Moretti makes headlines. Your choice, Ballotti." He got out, walked toward the stairs and disappeared behind the line of cars without looking back. Ballotti started the engine, but remained parked. He made a call and briefed the man on the other end.

CHAPTER 22

When Correa got into Ballotti's car and it became clear that the two would talk there rather than drive away, two of the agents who followed Correa to the parking lot slowly drove past the parked car, appearing to look for an open space. The agent in the passenger seat was operating a concealed camera. She got good pictures of the two men together. When Ballotti finally pulled out of his parking space, the tail split into two squads – one followed Correa and the other the new player. They got the license number and ran it. It was an Avis car rented to a Joseph Ballotti at 412 Locust Street.

The name and address were entered into every database to which the FBI had access. Ballotti's only criminal record was a conviction years back for illegally running cigarettes. He had fingered his source, which got him a suspended sentence. Otherwise, he was clean. But the search hit pay dirt. Ballotti had been employed for the past five years as a sales representative at Bristol Manufacturing, a company owned by Bristol Holding Corp. A limited liability company called Bristol LLC owned a majority of the shares of the holding company, and the holder of record of the rest of the shares was Leonard Moretti.

Thad made a beeline for Lew Porter's office with the report. There it was, the first provable link between Moretti and the attempted shakedown of Congresswoman Wetherill. Porter sat quietly absorbing the facts and their implications. Only his jaws moved as he chewed the end of his cigar. Finally he looked up and said, "Good stuff my boy, good stuff. Not evidentiary proof yet, but good stuff." He paused and then said, "Let me ask you Thaddeus. If Moretti went to all that trouble and expense in Argentina, including probably the murder of Señorita Loperena's secretary, is there any doubt that he's behind your basic drive-by of Taylor Warner?" He put up his hand. "Don't bother. Rhetorical question. Keep digging. Get taps on Ballotti's phones, hack into his computers, tail him. Sooner or later my boy, sooner or later we'll have Moretti by the gonads. Just make it sooner."

CHAPTER 23

Correa spent the remainder of the day in an aggressive, spirited mood, moving from bar to bar. He finally picked up a perky off-duty nurse about 6:00 p.m. and spent two hours rolling around with her in his room. But by 8:30 he was bored and asked her to leave. She did so pleasantly, wanting nothing more from him than she had already taken. Now, he was hungry. He had just over two hours to wait for his money and wanted to be available in his room. He ordered the sirloin steak on the room service menu, although he did not have great expectations for it. He was accustomed to Argentinian beef. He ordered the better of the two malbecs on the wine list, turned on the television, and when his order arrived, he contentedly watched, ate, and drank. By midnight he had not had a delivery from Ballotti, and he began to be concerned. *"Tomalo con soda,"* he told himself. *There is still time.*

At 3:15 a.m., the ringing hotel phone startled him awake. The FBI agent monitoring the phone also awoke. Correa had fallen asleep in his chair with the television droning on. He shook off his grogginess enough to hit the off button on the remote. Then, picking up the phone, he said, "Hola," still too groggy to click into English. He didn't have to. The female voice at the other end spoke in Spanish. "Is that you Matias?"

Instantly he was fully awake. It was his sister, Pilar, and there was no way she would know how to get in touch with him. Yet, it was her voice, and she sounded upset. "Matias?" she repeated, the tension in her voice palpable.

"Pilar, how did you find me? Is something wrong?"

The pleading voice answered, "Matias, you must help. You must!"

"What," he demanded, "What is it?"

"Two men are here in my house at five in the morning! They say that Florencia and Lucas are very beautiful children and should be allowed to grow up and have long and happy lives."

Correa went cold. The image of his sister was replaced in his mind's eye by his seven and five-year old niece and nephew. His hand went to his lowered forehead, and he squeezed his temples. *I have to think,* he said to himself. *Think.* "Are they all right?" he asked in a demanding tone, frustrated at likely losing control of the situation. Pilar did not answer that; instead, she focused on what she had been told to say to him.

"These men say they hope you will just get on a plane tomorrow and come to see Florencia and Lucas. They say that they will be very interested in the news stories in Philadelphia for a long, long time, and that I have beautiful children. Matias, I do not understand why this is happening, but . . . but Florencia and Lucas!" *He had to think!* Unable to bear the silence and what it might portend, Pilar pleaded in his ear, "Matias, tell me you will do it. My children!" Correa searched for a way out for another few seconds, even as he came to know with certainty that there was none. "Matias!" his distraught sister demanded. *No time!* He had lost. He choked back his anger.

"Pilar, I will be on the plane tomorrow and will come to see you and the children right away. Be sure the two men know that. Kiss the children for me."

He hung up, not waiting for Pilar to respond. He didn't want to hear her frightened, pleading voice again. He leaned back in the chair and closed his eyes. He was sick at heart. When he so confidently told Ballotti that he knew Moretti was the mastermind, he had been guessing. *Who else would want dirt on the Congresswoman's husband?* Now he knew he had guessed right but had overplayed his hand. He thought of $400,000 in untraceable bills that he would never hold. A feeling seeped into his chest that he had not had in a long time, a very long time. Fear. And it stayed with him until the wheels of his plane lifted off the runway the next day. It should have stayed with him longer.

The FBI heard the whole conversation. Thad was awakened and it was played for him over the phone. He instructed the agent who called him to contact Colonel Hernandez and play him the tape so the ANP could identify the children and protect them. He woke Owens. "I'm worried for the kids," he confessed. "Only a powerful and connected person could have so quickly found Correa's sister and had her 'visited' this way."

"But Chief," Owens said, "Those kids are far more useful to Moretti healthy. The threat of harm is better leverage against Correa than actually harming them. Correa is going to put this whole thing behind him like a bad dream. He'll start thinking about how he's going to make his next buck. Probably already is. Guys like him leave wreckage behind and don't think twice about it. I don't think those kids are in any danger."

"I want to believe that, Owens," Thad said. "Will you follow up with our friends at ANP? They'll get it right."

The next day agents of the FBI and lieutenants of Moretti, unknown to each other, watched Correa board his flight.

Thad was content enough with the results of the tail. Short of catching Correa talking to Moretti himself – which never would have happened – the tail had served its purpose. Correa led them to Ballotti, and Ballotti was only one step away from Moretti. In time, Thad thought, the ANP might learn enough to nail Correa for the murder of Maria Isabella's secretary and maybe then he would sing. Then maybe Ballotti would sing. *Lots of maybes,* he told himself. *So, Correa,* Thad said to himself, *for now your* chapter *is closed.* He couldn't know that it would never reopen. Five days later, Correa burned to death in his bed in Cordoba. Traces of a cigarette were found. He didn't smoke. The ANP, frustrated, could find no evidence of the foul play they knew had killed him.

CHAPTER 24

T had spent the next weekend on his farm, and he agreed to meet Maria Isabella Sunday night in Philadelphia. She took the train down from New York where she had been raising funds for autism research.

He had not seen her since that morning interview in her home in Buenos Aires, but he had called her regularly. Keeping her informed was well justified on a professional level, given her relationship with Taylor Warner and the fact that a criminal had worked his way into her home as a secretary. But the normal information channel would have been from the FBI to the ANP and then to her. When Thad made his first call to her, he had told himself it was to fulfill his promise to her to do so, after which he would leave communications to the ANP. But that call had ended with an unstated but mutual expectation that he would call again. Four more times he had called, and the most recent one had lasted half an hour, notwithstanding that there was very little new to tell her about the case. They were both bemused by this budding telephone relationship since distance and their very different lives gave rise to no expectation that anything could come of it. They had simply enjoyed getting to know each other.

But now that they were about to see each other again, each experienced, unknown to the other, an unexpected sense of anticipation.

Thad arrived at the Four Seasons Hotel shortly after 7:00PM. He called her from a house phone. "I suggest you come to my suite," she said matter-of-factly. "We will not have to be concerned about being overheard."

"All right," he replied, mimicking her matter-of-fact tone, and then, deadpan, "that means I'm still batting 1,000 getting into your bedroom."

Her laugh was warm. "And that is to be considered an achievement? You'll be disappointed to learn that my suite has a lovely sitting room. The number is 701."

"Ah, the Four Seasons suite, the best in the hotel."

"You know it?" She was playing now.

"I've stayed in it several times, it's lovely."

"So," she said coyly, "you've even been in my bed."

He laughed, "Yes, well, timing is everything. I'll see you in a moment."

The Four Seasons suite was on the northwest corner of the top floor of the hotel. Nearly the entire north wall was glass, looking out over the Benjamin Franklin Parkway to the perfectly sited Philadelphia Museum of Art and the Schuylkill River beyond. In the darkening evening the lights along the broad parkway and the yellow lighting of the grand Greek revival museum at its end created a stunning tableau. But to Thad, it paled in comparison to the beauty within the suite. In Buenos Aires she had been dressed for business. This night she was dressed for dinner, and the sight of her sent a charge through his heart like a huge dose of adrenalin.

Thad thought it curious that someone as well trained in observation as he was supposed to be could have so much difficulty describing a dress – its fabric, its cut, its folds, its whatever. Hers was black, with something expensive-looking sparkling in the fabric. It was sleeveless, with a deep but tastefully narrow cleavage. *"Cleavage" doesn't sound like the right word,* he thought. There were folds across the shoulders and down the front that he couldn't describe more accurately. It was shaped to her waist but not tight on her hips, merely touching them and falling to just below her knees. As it fell, it seemed to be composed of layers of exquisite black material, each layer diaphanous, so that when she moved, the effect was one of ever-changing hues of black. *That's not bad,* he thought.

As lovely as she had seemed in Buenos Aires, he now had much more of her to admire. Her legs were astonishing to him. Long, with just enough shape – like the legs of a thoroughbred. He thought of the sculptures of Bernini in the Borghese Palace in Rome. Daphne in the flesh. Well, not quite. Viewed separately each of the features of her face carried some imperfection, except for the size and shape of her eyes and the extraordinary whites of them. Almost blue-white. But blended together, those features created the most alluring woman he had ever seen.

Her voice jarred him loose. "Well, Agent Pennock, I must charge a fee for that look."

"I apologize, Señorita Loperena," he said, "but in all candor, I think I have never seen such a beautiful sight. It deserves some study," he smiled.

"Well, in small doses it is flattering to be admired, but quite discomforting to be ogled. Come, have a drink and sit down and tell me what you have learned." She had champagne opened, which was fine by him.

Because of their regular phone conversations they were both at ease. For twenty minutes Thad talked about the case in great detail, motivated in part by a desire to hold her attention longer and, perhaps, impress her. As he spoke, her eyes were on his, but she was really looking at his words and their meaning. She wanted to understand.

When he finished, they were silent a moment. "So," she finally said, "you have a prime suspect in this man Moretti, whom you likely will never be able to prove was responsible, and you have no other real suspects?" She had distilled it down to its unpalatable essence.

"I won't say 'not likely', but it will be tough. We're going to have to get lucky." She sipped her champagne. He was drinking in details of her lips on the glass and the movement of the muscles of her beautiful throat guiding the liquid inward.

"You know," she offered, "if Virginia had not been in the car, I would be suspicious of her. Taylor's death makes her a more sympathetic figure and news of my affair with Taylor less of an impediment to her career."

He raised his hand slightly and his index finger slightly more. "But" he said, "don't forget that she didn't know about the affair until after the shooting."

She looked directly into his eyes and with a slight smile quietly asked him, "And you are quite certain of that Agent Pennock?" He said nothing for a moment, and she continued. "That depends, does it not, on whether you credit Nikki's story about concealing the package from Virginia?" Thad noticed her use of the familiar "Nikki" and "Virginia." *Undoubtedly because Warner would have referred to them that way,* he thought.

She was implying a great deal – that Nikki and the Congresswoman had been complicit in the murder and the Congresswoman played a very risky part to assure she would not be a suspect. Thad turned his eyes from Maria Isabella to the window and the great columns of the distant art museum. But he did not see them; his mind's eye was replaying the shooting. He did not notice getting up and walking to the window.

Of course he had considered that possibility many times, but had concluded that the Congresswoman's presence in the car during the shooting presented an unacceptable risk to her life. But had it really been that dangerous? If she were the mastermind, she would have known exactly when the shooter's car would draw alongside and when to be below the line of fire. Once there, was she really at risk? Then he noticed where he was. He turned.

Maria Isabella sat erect, with her hands in her lap, looking at him and patiently waiting. "Sorry," he said, "I was on a walk-about for a moment."

"Several moments," she smiled. "But I could sense the wheels of a brilliant mind turning in earnest."

"It was your brilliant mind that got the ball rolling, diverting me from your delightful company."

"Enough," she laughed. "We have both gone over the edge. Are we now through with business? Shall we have dinner?"

He did not answer immediately, but then asked, "Señorita Loperena if I may, I would like to pick your brain a little more." Then looking at his glass, "But I seem to be out of necessary fuel." After she removed that impediment, he took a sip and asked, "Did Warner ever talk about the Congresswoman? What she was like, their relationship, any insights about her?"

"Some," she said. "But you must understand that his loyalty to her was exaggerated by his guilt at betraying her with me. He would not have articulated it that way; indeed, he would not have thought of it that bluntly. But I am certain that was his mental state. He could not criticize her because that would have been disloyal to her, and he could not praise her because that would have been disloyal to me. So he spoke of her very little. When he did, it was as if he were describing a stylized person, a manikin. I did not press. Taylor would tell me a lot about Virginia when he thought he was talking about himself. However, it was an entirely different story with Nikki."

"Oh?" Thad asked, "How so?"

"They were, as you say, oil and water. Taylor disliked her and from what he said, she felt the same about him. It was all the more surprising to me because that was not Taylor's way. He found the good in everyone and excused the bad. It was one reason I loved him so much. But he constantly expressed his frustration with Nikki."

"What was the problem?"

"Nikki was proprietary about Virginia, as if Virginia were her property, not his wife. Taylor thought that Nikki went far beyond the scope of her job, scheduling and influencing all aspects of Virginia's life, including her private life with him. It infuriated him."

"Give me some example of that interference if you can?"

"Well," she began, "Nikki would send him memos or emails about Virginia not getting the right nutrition or enough sleep or that she was getting run down because she was trying to please Taylor by going to his polo or racing parties on top of her own active schedule. Once or twice she even canceled dinner reservations he had made for the two of them without consulting Virginia or him, saying that Virginia was too exhausted and needed her rest. She simply told Taylor she had done it. It was Nikki, not Virginia, who was condescending to Taylor, even though Taylor's relationship with Virginia should have been none of Nikki's business."

"Well, did he just take it or did he confront Nikki or mention it to Virginia?"

"He would confront Nikki, but she would simply say, 'I'm doing my job as best I can. If that is not good enough for the Congresswoman, I expect she will let me know.' Then, when he complained to Virginia, she was sympathetic and comforting and calmed him down, but Taylor never got any indication that Virginia ever spoke to Nikki about it. At least, there never was a change in her behavior. On the other hand, Taylor recognized that Nikki was very skilled and a great help to Virginia. So he avoided a final showdown."

"But you know Thad" – his name flowed so easily and naturally from her lips for the first time that his heart skipped a beat – "perhaps if I had not come into his life, he would have been more confrontational and brought the problem to a head. Instead, I think he used the problems with Nikki to feel a little discontented, which made it easier for him to feel less guilty about our relationship. Does that make any sense?"

Thad was again impressed by Maria Isabella's openness and honesty about her role as the other woman. She continued her train of thought. "I really think, at bottom, Nikki took her cue about Taylor from Virginia's attitude toward him. I am persuaded that Virginia has the ability to compartmentalize her life to an unusual degree. When she was in her Taylor compartment, she really wanted him there and treated him with great affection and respect. When she was busy with other things, which was often, she did not think of him or what his needs might be. He simply did not exist for her. Her life is all about Virginia. Nikki understands that. Taylor did not. Given his personality, such a thing was inconceivable. So when she was in a compartment that did not include him, he felt alone and like a part-time husband, but did not really blame Virginia for his feelings."

"Can you think of anything else about Nikki or the Congresswoman or Taylor that might shed light on the dynamics of their relationships?" This was the lawyer training in him, wrapping up a detailed deposition with a "can you think of anything else" question.

She replied smiling, "Well, if I do, I will surely ring you up. It would be a nice excuse." And that was the signal that the remainder of the evening should not be lost to business.

"Okay," Thad said. He sat back and slapped his knees with his hands. "I vote for putting work behind us for the evening. One of my rules is never to work after two glasses of champagne. Of course that's a new rule, but I think a good one for tonight at least."

"Do you care for more champagne then?" she asked, knowing full well the answer.

"It's a necessity." When their glasses were again adequately filled, they found themselves standing close to one another, neither feeling inclined to sit. He looked into her eyes, dazzled by the whites of them. Given what he sensed was happening, he suddenly needed to confront the one bogey man that had been invisibly standing between them since he first looked into those eyes.

"Maria Isabella, I want to ask you a personal question."

Cocking her head slightly, she said, "You want to?"

"Yes, for me."

"And if I say to you, you have no business doing so?"

"You would be correct, but" he paused, "I still would want to know." She permitted her face to assume a particularly stern expression, although her eyes continued to smile.

"It is highly inappropriate for you to expect me to answer a personal question . . .," she paused for emphasis, "while still referring to me as Señorita Loperena or Maria Isabella. You must call me simply 'Isabella.'"

It could have been nothing more than the gracious gesture of a thoughtful woman. But he intuitively knew it was more. Thad recalled the moment he first saw her on the threshold of her Buenos Aires home and the instantaneous chemical bond between them. He felt it again now. His gyroscope wobbled for an instant. The important world was slightly altered, the point of equilibrium shifted. Committing nothing, Isabella had created potential between them. Now he assuredly needed to address the bogey man. Bowing slightly, he said "Isabella."

With a smile she nodded slightly. And then she said softly, "Very well, Thad, let us get on with your personal question."

Visibly taking a breath he went right at it. "I know you use cocaine." He paused, expecting that she might comment. She cocked her head slightly again and shifted her right hand to her right hip. Her eyes never left his. He waited a moment, but she said nothing. He continued, "It doesn't fit. I've seen enough of you to know it doesn't fit. So I don't understand it." She cocked her head even further so her hair fell away exposing a sculptured ear. In her eyes there was no fear, no anger or annoyance, just searching into the depth of his.

"Thad?" she asked. Her voice was soft, yet demanding.

"Yes," he answered, drinking in the tone, but half dreading her next words.

"Where shall we dine? Here or the very excellent dining room?" He downshifted to negotiate this unexpected turn and managed it well.

"Isabella," – he pronounced the "s" as an Argentinian would, "s," not "z," so the sound of the name was strong as well as lyrical – "please choose."

"Here, I think." She moved away from him and toward the phone. Changing shades of sparkling black danced in her dress with the sway of her hips and motion of her legs. He marveled at the sheer beauty of her movements. She asked for menus and a waiter. There was a pause as she listened. Then, "That will not do. I have with me Agent Thaddeus Pennock, Regional Chief of the FBI in Washington DC. We therefore require dining room menus and a waiter, not room service. Agent Pennock has a schedule to keep. How soon may we expect the waiter?" A pause, then cheerily she said, "That will do nicely," and she hung up.

Turning her magnificent figure half towards him, she said, "My goodness, you are an influential man! Barriers disintegrate at the mention of your name." Thad just shook his head side to side, grinning.

They moved to a clutch of furniture around a small table. She chose the end of a sofa and he the chair nearest her. She held her champagne glass in her right hand and leaned her left arm on the sofa arm. She turned her upper body to her left towards him and crossed one beautiful leg over the other. *This vision is like a drug,* he laughed to himself. Hers was a deep, irrepressible beauty. She radiated vitality, an essential ingredient of joy.

It was not the repartee that inched them closer to each other, but the underlying respect and the paradox of honoring limits. The waiter arrived. They ordered, and the waiter left. "How is your drink?" she asked, leaning toward him. He nodded contentment. He could not recall a more erotic moment. She leveled her eyes with his, not eighteen inches away, and calmly spoke. "Yes," she said, "I have used cocaine very modestly from time to time ever since I was eighteen. But I go long periods, years sometimes, without it. In fact before meeting Taylor, it had been three years. He enjoyed it on occasion, so I joined him. I also drink wine, champagne, and like beer. But I always stop before it compromises my judgment. I like control over my faculties, so moderation is easy for me." Here she threw her head back and gaily swept her left arm in an arc before her, a double gesture that lifted toward Thad her alluring breasts tantalizingly concealed within the bodice of her dress. As she did so, she laughingly continued, "Having said that Agent Pennock, over the course of this evening you may observe that I might enjoy more wine than I would in a less predictable situation?" She was now irresistibly flirting. "Because I am with a gentleman who would never take advantage."

Thad smiled. "Isabella, if there is one thing I've learned, it's never to say 'never,'"

She laughed again at his predictable response. "Really? I've not learned that yet. Something to look forward to!" She took a sip of champagne and became serious. "I do not make light of cocaine. I have read and studied a great deal about it and have no illusions. There is no healthy level of indulging. You have not asked me this, quite appropriately I add, but it lies behind the question you did ask. So, I will say it. I cannot tell you I will not use it again some time." She paused, wondering if he would comment. He said nothing, so she continued, "But I have no craving, no habit, and...." She paused again, only this time it was to search for the words that would permit her message to be at once a neutral statement and much more. Finding them she looked into his eyes, "And I can confidently tell you that if the person I care about does not enjoy it, it no longer exists for me."

He noticed they were physically closer. He could not say that she had moved her body toward him or he his body toward her. Rather, it was as if a vacuum had appeared and her body filled it. Her gaze stayed steady. The thoughts she had expressed to him resonated with the power of clarity and unvarnished truth. That was rare in and of itself but more so on such a topic. He took a deep breath. She had banished the bogeyman, almost. She could never banish it entirely. He lived the culture of the FBI, and he had seen too many addicts and too much carnage. Nevertheless, he felt relieved enough.

"Thank you," he found himself saying, fully expecting her not to understand why.

"You are welcome." A knock at the door broke a spell of which neither had been aware. The waiter entered with the first course and an excellent burgundy.

They would go on to two more courses, more good wine, and then coffee. During the evening they talked of their pasts and their mutual love of horses. She spoke animatedly about the clinics for autistic children she had established and her desire to see them adequately endowed. He spoke of his early attempts to find a career and his passion for his job, matched only by his passion for foxhunting. She promised to visit his farm and to foxhunt with him. Eventually, she saw him to the door and laid her hand on his arm. They did not kiss, despite the increasing intimacy of the evening. They both knew this was in deference to a more meaningful kiss in the future, the not too distant future.

Later, Thad fell asleep excited about the potential of life, all things possible suspended in anticipation of tomorrows.

CHAPTER 25

This time Moretti met Thad and Owens in Moretti's office downtown. Thad had called and advised him that he should now consider himself a person of interest in the investigation based on information gathered since they last met. Moretti then asked what that new information was, and, of course, Thad declined to disclose it. "I would like to speak to you again Mr. Moretti, and I advise you to have your attorney present."

Moretti paused and then said, "You know, under these circumstances I can refuse to talk to you. Persuade me why I should."

"Because if you are innocent, you may be able to help us solve the crime sooner." The line was silent for a few seconds.

Then Moretti said, "You are persuasive, Agent Pennock. I will be available Monday morning at ten if you wish to meet me at my office."

Thad and Owens arrived right at 10:00 AM. Moretti was businesslike in his greeting and introduced them to his attorney, Desmond Quill. For Thad and Quill it was something of a reunion. When Thad was a young Assistant District Attorney in Philadelphia, he had met Quill several times. Quill had a flourishing white-collar crime practice and a reputation for being tough but honest, civil, and independent. If there was sleaze on his clients, he did not permit it to rub off on him. Tall, thin, gray-haired, and wearing round steel-rimmed glasses, Quill looked typecast for his occupation. True to form, he let Moretti run the meeting.

Moretti, unsmiling but polite, opened the conversation. "You gentlemen asked for this meeting, so please proceed." Thad and Owens had discussed exactly what Thad would say and how far he would go.

"Mr. Moretti, this case seems to be breeding dead bodies – murdered people in two hemispheres. In no particular order, a very nice secretary whose name was Camila Lorenzo found floating in the pool at a Bariloche hotel, a not very nice man who went up in smoke in his bed in Cordoba, and, of course, Taylor Warner, blown away in his car near Philadelphia. Add to this the possible attempted murder of Taylor's wife, Congresswoman Wetherill, and I'm well over my quarterly allotment of carnage, a problem I do not like to have. So, I need to remedy the situation." He stopped. Owens closely watched Moretti as Thad spoke. That the FBI should even know about the murders of Lorenzo and Correa, let alone link them to Warner's death and possibly to him, should have shocked Moretti into some involuntary visible reaction, however subtle. But Owens, experienced in what to look for, saw nothing.

Moretti raised his eyebrows, smiled slightly, and spoke in his even voice. "Really? Argentina? If I am a person of interest, as you say," he looked at Quill and then back at Thad, "It means that you suspect that I had something to do with these incidents. Should I be flattered to be thought capable of orchestrating such far-flung events? I do have some influence Agent Pennock, but far less than Congresswoman Wetherill's pathetic little investigation would lead one to believe. But more importantly, having influence is one thing, how one exercises it is quite another. How may I convince you that focusing on me is a waste of your time and the taxpayers' money?"

Thad smiled and said, "Convince me. Do you know something I do not?" Moretti again looked at his lawyer for permission to answer and then back at Thad.

"Yes I do," he answered. "I know with absolute certainty that I did not order anyone to shoot at Congresswoman Wetherill and her husband. It follows that I know with the same absolute certainty that someone else did. Therefore, you waste your time, not to mention mine, by pursuing me as a suspect. Look elsewhere. As for the deaths you mentioned in Argentina, I know nothing and have not the slightest idea what they have to do with, in your words, 'this case.'" He stopped speaking and calmly looked Thad directly in the eye. Thad sensed something important in Moretti's speech. *Why did he deny the murders in Argentina in different words than his denial of the Warner murder?* Giving Owens a quick "think-about-that" glance, Thad said, "I was hoping for something more concrete, some lead. You have sources I don't have." Moretti was silent, offering nothing more. Thad quietly added, "You may be sure, Mr. Moretti, we will get the persons responsible."

Moretti responded in a level tone. "To do so Agent Pennock you must look elsewhere. And were I you, I would not so easily assume that the Congresswoman was the target." At this, Thad's eyes narrowed slightly, "Do you know something I do not, Mr. Moretti?"

"I will repeat," Moretti said, "I am the one person who with absolute certainty knows that I did not order the shooting of Wetherill or Warner. If you accept that, where does it lead you?"

Realizing that his client had just made a bad mistake, Quill interjected to control the dialogue. "Thad, do you have any specific questions you wish to ask my client?"

"Not at the moment, Desmond," Thad answered, rising. "But I hope you will contact me if Mr. Moretti can think of or runs across something helpful. Thank you both for your willingness to see us."

"Not at all," Moretti said politely, motioning for Thad and Owens to precede him out of the room.

Thad took a few steps then turned to Moretti. "Ah, I nearly forgot to ask. Do you know an Argentinian named Matias Correa?"

"No," Moretti said evenly, "I do not." In planning this meeting Thad and Owens did not think the name would draw any reaction from Moretti because Thad's earlier comment about someone going up in flames would surely alert Moretti that they knew about Correa. But the purpose of the question had been only to set up the big surprise.

"How long has Joseph Ballotti been working for you?" Thad asked. Despite all of Moretti's training to discipline himself he could not entirely suppress a visible sign of the shock that the mention of this name gave him, particularly coming right after the mention of Correa. It was only an instant, but both Thad and Owens caught the darting motion of Moretti's eyes to the left and the involuntary constriction of the muscles at the corner of his mouth.

"What is the name?" Moretti asked, buying time to regain total composure. "Joseph Ballotti?"

"Yes," Thad answered, "Joseph Ballotti."

"You mean working personally for me? I do not have anyone by that name working for me."

"No, as an employee in one of your companies, Bristol Manufacturing to be precise."

"Well, it could be. At the moment the name rings no bells. I certainly do not know all of the employees of each of the companies in which I hold an interest. Why do you ask?"

Before the meeting Thad and Owens had discussed whether they had anything to lose by letting Moretti know that they had linked Moretti with the Argentinian events through Ballotti and decided it was worth it. If Moretti was not behind the murder of Warner, he would have more incentive to convince the FBI of that. But if he was, he might think twice before making a second attempt on the Congresswoman's life. They were certain that just mentioning Correa and Ballotti was enough. They wanted to leave Moretti wondering how much they really knew. So in answer to Moretti's question Thad said simply, "To see if you would lie."

"Did I?" Moretti parried.

"Ah," Thad said, with a smile, "perhaps, perhaps not. We shall see." He nodded to Quill, "Nice to see you Desmond." The two agents left Quill and Moretti staring at their backs as they left, escorted out by Moretti's secretary.

As soon as they were alone in the car Owens said, "Did you catch it, Chief?"

"Catch what?"

"His mistake. We know Moretti is behind the attempt to extort the Congresswoman, and now he just told us he is the only one who would be trying to kill her."

"Jesus, I missed that completely! What did he say?"

"He told us not to assume that the Congresswoman was the target. He could only conclude she wasn't the target if he knew he was the only one who would be considering killing her. If he didn't order the hit, it leads him to the conclusion that Warner probably was the target. Quill caught it immediately. That's why he jumped in."

"Owens," Thad said, "Do you know how depressing it is to be in the presence of someone constantly demonstrating superior intelligence?" They fell into silence until they were pulling into Penn Station to catch a train back to DC.

"You know, Chief, just the way he put it. He said, 'I know for a certainty I didn't order the shooting, and therefore I know for a certainty that someone else did.' You just don't hear a denial put quite that way."

"Yeah," Thad said, and repeated the words silently to himself, *for a certainty someone else did.*

They did not talk much on the Acela from Philadelphia to Washington. They each spent time on their own paperwork, their smart phones, and their respective thoughts. They had worked together for so long that they were easy with long stretches of silence. But just as the train was leaving Baltimore, its last stop before DC, Owens quietly said, "What do we really know about Nikki Patterson?"

"Nikki?" Thad said with some surprise.

"Yes Nikki."

Thad inventoried what he knew. His mind's eye saw her at the fundraiser, leaving at the same time as Warner and Wetherill, saw her in the hospital next to the Congresswoman's bed, heard her on the phone protecting the Congresswoman's schedule, saw her sitting attentively to the side in the Congresswoman's office, saw her take the package of photographs from someone claiming to be acting for Kirk, and saw her sitting in his office admitting that she had kept the photos to herself. Until Owens' comment, Thad had not appreciated the number of scenes of this little opera Nikki had been in, and not just as a member of the chorus. *And she has no alibi,* he thought, *just her word that she had gone straight home.*

He recalled Isabella's comment the previous night at the Four Seasons when he mentioned that the Congresswoman did not know about Warner's affair until after the murder. *"That depends, does it not, on whether you credit Nikki's story about concealing the package from Virginia."* He turned and looked at his partner's kind face. All he said was, "Why didn't I think of that, Owens?"

He saw the cheek crinkle and the crow's feet appear as Owens' facial muscles shaped a smile. Owens kept his eyes forward, pushed his glasses slightly up his nose, and answered, "You soon would have, Chief."

"Get the geeks going on it right away, an A to Z on Patterson. Shouldn't take long since she is a congressional staffer."

"Will do."

Owens rose and walked to the lavatory at the rear of the car, entered and shut the door.

He pulled his telephone from his shirt pocket, punched in a number, and to the person answering gave the order for a complete background check on Nikki Patterson.

CHAPTER 26

The next morning at 10:00, while Owens was supervising the A to Z on Nikki, Congresswoman Wetherill's office announced that she would hold a press conference at 3:00 PM "to reveal to the public further information concerning her late husband and his murder." It would be held on the lawn of her home in Bucks County. Her office staff got the word out to television, cable news, news agencies, and numerous newspapers and magazines.

Thad was alerted to it by Gloria, his secretary, who learned of it by way of coffee break conversation, still the fastest communication channel of the modern era. Thad was furious. It was never an advantage to have the bad guys know more than the FBI wanted them to know, so he wanted to control the flow of facts to the public. He'd asked Wetherill to say as little as possible about anything related to the murder, but he couldn't order her not to disclose information she learned independent of the investigation, including the pictures sent to Nikki and the story they told.

He figured she probably could do no actual damage because he had already dropped Ballotti's name to Moretti, thereby letting Moretti know that he knew about Moretti's link to Ballotti and Balotti's link to Correa and, therefore, Moretti's link to the blackmail pictures of Warner and Isabella together. *Still*, he simmered, *I did ask her.* She was blowing him off and her arrogance irked him.

He called her cell number and was surprised when she answered. He was blunt. "This is a bad idea Congresswoman. The less..." She cut him off.

"They sent Nikki the pictures. They know I know. What's to hide? This sleaze will leak out one way or another and I'll be damned if I'll let the press shape it. I'm doing this Pennock. Now I've got to go." She rang off. He looked at the phone. *What did I do to deserve her?* he asked himself.

The media descended. Security guards checked credentials. Some curiosity seekers tried to get in, but were turned away. Thad debated letting Charlie handle it, but his intuition told him he ought to go. There was something about Wetherill in person that he still needed to understand. He took the 11:00 AM Acela back to Philadelphia, and he and Charlie Townsend had no trouble getting admitted. The two of them stood at one side of the group to watch everything in profile, Thad's favorite vantage point.

Iced tea, lemonade, tea sandwiches, and pastries were being consumed in great quantities when, at 3:15 p.m., a door to the veranda opened, and Congresswoman Wetherill emerged, flanked by Nikki and several staff members. They walked slowly to the stand of microphones at the edge of the veranda looking out to the lawn filled with eager news professionals. Thad counted five television cameras close to the microphones. He observed that Nikki was dressed in her usual skirt and jacket with minimal makeup and jewelry.

Congresswoman Wetherill wore black pants, a white blouse, and heels that accentuated her long legs. Her waist was pulled in with a stylish, wide belt, hitched with a large, intricate gold buckle. As she had since Warner's death, she wore large sunglasses. Her shoulder-length mane of curly red hair looked slightly windblown on this windless afternoon. She was all legs and red hair. She had just the effect on the crowd she wanted – an unapproachably beautiful woman, powerful politician, and grieving widow, a mix of strong and contrasting impressions. When she began, her expression was somber but her voice strong. "Thank you for coming," she opened. *Short and simple. Just right,* Thad thought. She smiled the tragic smile she had practiced before her mirror.

"The facts you will hear today are, for me personally, deeply saddening, embarrassing, and humiliating. Were I a normal citizen with no public duties, I would do all I could to bury them and keep them private. But I have responsibilities to my constituents and a commitment to my cause, which, as you know, is the destruction of the debilitating trafficking in drugs that plagues this nation and, particularly, my beloved Philadelphia. I have said publicly before that I believe the shotgun blasts that took my husband's life were meant for me, and today I will show you that this is not the speculation of a hysterical woman who was just made a widow."

At this she paused, biting her lower lip, communicating a brave effort to maintain control. "The facts you will hear are known to the FBI and other law enforcement agencies involved in investigating and solving this horrible crime. I want you to know them so that, in case something should happen to me, or in case I should lose the next election due to the personally embarrassing nature of these facts, there will remain the greatest chance that the crusade to destroy the local drug cartel will not disappear with me. That is the sole purpose of this press conference, the sole objective I wish to achieve."

Thad thought to himself, *by the shear impact of her looks and delivery, she makes what otherwise would be pure schmaltz sound genuine. Hats off!*

Turning to look at Nikki, Wetherill continued, "I want to introduce you to my Chief of Staff, Nikki Patterson, whom many of you already know. I admire and respect her intelligence and character, and I'm grateful to her for so excellently and loyally coping with the demands I make upon her and the responsibilities that I shift to her shoulders. You will hear of the difficult judgment call she had to make and of the misplaced guilt she carries for my husband's death."

Here Wetherill paused. Thad watched the crowd absorb that little bombshell. Jaws that an instant earlier were munching tea sandwiches froze in mid-bite. "I have assured her," Wetherill continued, "that the outcome would have been no different had she acted differently, and I only hope I would have had the courage to make the same decision she did, had our roles been reversed." At this, Wetherill turned to Nikki and said simply, "Nikki?" She stepped back a pace giving Nikki center stage.

As Wetherill surely intended, questions were swirling in every head. Thad said to himself, *the "curiosity meter" on this lawn just jumped into the red zone.* Nikki moved closer to the microphones and began. Heads leaned forward in unison to catch every syllable. Her serious demeanor matched Wetherill's. Her voice was steady, and, to Thad, the tone and deliberate pace seemed rehearsed.

Nikki told the mesmerized gathering essentially what she had told Thad in his office. When she described the contents of the package of photographs she was handed outside Kirk's office, Thad saw eyes widen again and pens freeze. Gazes shifted to Wetherill for an instant, then heads lowered and pens scratched faster than before. These were professionals who sensed a story with spectacular public appeal but took no pleasure in the personal humiliation they thought the Congresswoman must be feeling.

Wetherill showed no reaction as Nikki spoke. She appeared to be looking right at Nikki, but behind those glasses her eyes were scanning the crowd, and all of her political sensors were feeding information into the political mainframe in her brain. She liked the read-out. She saw enough heads nod up and down to convince her that the group had gotten the point in spades. Whoever sent the photographs had one objective, force her to drop her investigation or her husband's drug-hazed philandering would hit the front pages and her career would be toast.

Nikki then described her three-part dilemma, whether to keep the threat and the package to herself, tell the Congresswoman, or go to the police. "I agonized for three days without reaching a decision because I knew Mr. Warner's conduct would cause Congresswoman Wetherill untold anguish. The night of the third day, Mr. Warner was killed. By not deciding, I unintentionally elected the first option – keep it to myself. Then, it was too late."

She paused. She didn't have to add the big conclusion. It was obvious to every listener. Rebuffed, the bad guys tried to murder the Congresswoman and failed. She was the target; Warner was collateral damage.

Nikki continued, "After the murder, I took my information to the FBI. They told me I had no choice; I had to tell Congresswoman Wetherill everything. A detective and I met with her and showed her the materials, and I told her everything about how I got them. I felt so responsible, I just cried. But Congresswoman Wetherill told me that it would have made no difference whether I had told her sooner. She would never have stopped her investigation. She said nothing good ever comes from acting against your beliefs and that while she and Mr. Warner might or might not have worked things out, they surely would not have done so if the price to either of them would have been sacrificing what they thought was right. It was a great comfort to hear that." She paused, "And that's all there is." She backed away from the microphones, looking over her shoulder at the Congresswoman as she did so.

There was an approving buzz and a swarm of waving hands and shouted questions. Wetherill, smiling at Nikki, squeezed her hand for an instant. Then she moved to the microphones and held her right arm in front of her, palm out, hand open. Thad noticed again how long *and lovely* her fingers were. She stood like that, silent behind the sunglasses, until the noise wound down.

"I have little to add except that I am fortunate to have Nikki working for me. I loved my husband. I was shocked and devastated by his infidelity and drug use. But if that strong and wonderful man could be induced into taking drugs, with the horrible errors in judgment that follow, how much easier is it for cunning dealers and desperate users to lure our children into tragedy. Whoever wants me to stop my crusade," – *the perfect word*, Thad thought to himself – "and they know who they are, and I believe I know who they are, and . . . ," pointing a long finger toward the crowd and lowering her voice for dramatic effect, "I believe you know who they are. They will have to kill me or buy an election to stop me!" Thad heard scattered applause. He and Charlie exchanged glances. "Unbelievable," Charlie murmured.

It got quiet fast. They wanted more, but Wetherill's calculation was that more would be less. "Thank you for coming," she said. "I think you understand why I will take no questions. I will never talk publicly about my relationship with my husband, and I will not talk about an ongoing criminal investigation." *You just did!* Thad silently shouted. Wetherill continued, "However, subcommittee hearings reconvene next week. If you want to do some real good, follow those hearings and get the word out. Now please stay and enjoy the refreshments. Thank you again." She waived and with her cadre of aides following, she turned and walked into the house. A number of reporters tried to follow and were politely but firmly stopped by security guards.

Thad and Charlie had witnessed the performance from one end of the veranda, observing Wetherill and Nikki in profile and the reporters and other newscasters on the diagonal, like observing a theatre performance from off-stage left. "Well?" Thad looked at Charlie as they walked out together. Charlie shook his head slowly sideways.

"I bet you those two sunk a hook deep into the brains of ninety five percent of those reporters so they won't be able to think straight about all this. Damn near convinced me," he smiled.

There was no one close enough to overhear them so Thad followed up. "Try this wild one on, Charlie. Nikki pulled the trigger and Wetherill planned it. They seemed such a team out there."

"Problem is," Charlie began, "that show we just saw is exactly what Wetherill would have put on either way – if she had had nothing to do with the killing or engineered it. It's good politics. Exploit the situation. Appear willing to risk death. She hints that dirty drug money will try to buy the next election out from under her. She establishes the themes of her campaign." He held his hat in his right hand and slapped his left hand with it in grudging admiration of the performance. They continued their walk to their car in silence.

———

Inside her large and expensively appointed home, Wetherill and a group of staff and advisors gathered in the library. She wanted their feedback on the impression she and Nikki had made. Then they strategized and planned the next steps to capitalize on the swelling support they saw building for the Congresswoman and her investigation. The session lasted almost an hour. When it broke up, Wetherill thanked them all and within their hearing asked Nikki to stay for a few minutes to iron out some scheduling details. When the last staffer had left the room, Nikki closed the door.

As she did so, Wetherill moved from behind her desk to the large sofa near the fireplace, sat and looked at Nikki as she approached. Nikki eased down close to Wetherill and took both of her hands in hers. Neither spoke. Nikki leaned in. The Congresswoman turned her head to Nikki and closed her eyes. The kiss was long and tender.

When their lips finally parted, they stayed close enough to feel each other's breath. Nikki looked deeply and longingly into Wetherill's eyes and whispered, "I would do anything for you."

"You already have."

"I would do it again tomorrow if you asked me," Nikki said a little louder, her voice choked with emotion and desire.

Wetherill shook her head slightly side to side as she said, "No. I will never ask anything like that of you again." She released her left hand from Nikki's and moved just far enough away to gently touch Nikki's forehead and begin to stroke her hair to the side. She added, "You did so well out there...." They were silent as she continued stroking.

When she spoke again, the usual competitive edge in her voice had softened. "Dear Nikki, you've exposed yourself to great danger for my sake. I will do everything in my power to protect you."

"I know you will, but I did it for both of us. Don't worry, they'll never link me to Taylor, and even if they do somehow, they won't catch me, ever. I've planned."

Wetherill stroked the side of Nikki's face again. "I will protect you," she repeated.

As the two women drew even closer to embrace again, the vivid photographs Nikki had seen of Isabella and Taylor in a lovers' embrace suddenly filled her vision. She clutched Virginia's arms, shut her eyes and visibly shuttered. Then she opened them and took Wetherill's face in both of her hands. Turbulence riffled her body. "This is not our doing, Virginia! Our lives were perfect with Taylor at your side. That selfish whore had no business making a fool of him and ruining things. She is wicked. If I lose you, I swear I will find a way. Believe me I will find a way to cut out her heart!"

Before this outburst, their bodies had been tense with anticipation, like runners poised on the starting blocks waiting for the report of the starter's gun. Now their kiss exploded with passion, and their bodies hungrily melted together. For them, this room, this expansive sofa by the fireplace, was a favorite place to make love.

CHAPTER 27

The news media feasted on the sensational story Nikki Patterson told. They pounded on it from every angle. It was a moneymaker, and they were not about to let it go before the last reader was saturated with it. Reporters tried to get to Moretti for comment, but could not. Finally, Quill made a brief statement. "Mr. Moretti knows nothing about any pictures or other information that might be compromising to the late Mr. Warner, or an Attorney named Kirk. He does not know anything about the use of any information to influence Congresswoman Wetherill's subcommittee's investigation. He knows nothing about Mr. Warner's murder. He has spoken to the FBI, cooperated with them, and will continue to do so."

The reporters also hounded Thad for any comment on Nikki's story. His response to all of them was the same. No comment on a continuing investigation. When the time came to release information to the public, he would let the press know. Yes, Ms. Patterson had given them a package of information indicating a relationship between Mr. Warner

and another woman. No, they would not release the pictures.
No, they would not release information on "the other woman,"
including her name, except to say that she was not a suspect
or even a person of interest.

CHAPTER 28

A to Z was shop shorthand for a thorough background check, "from conception through tomorrow," as Thad often said to emphasize his demanding standards. Records of all kinds, birth, schools, social security, passports, driver's licenses, employment records, criminal records, military records, bank accounts, tax returns, credit cards, credit ratings, Google, Facebook, and every place that any of those searches led.

A lot of Owens' work had already been done for him, at least through the date on which Nikki became a member of Wetherill's staff. She was required to have a "Secret" grade security clearance because staff members were likely to have access to certain levels of classified information. "Secret" clearance required a rigorous background check by the Defense Industrial Security Clearance Office.

So only two days after the Congresswoman's sensational press conference, Owens estimated the A to Z was 98% complete. The few lines of inquiry remaining related to tangential information, so he was ready to report.

Thad looked up when Owens entered his office. "Well?" he said. Owens knew that eloquent monosyllable encompassed a warm greeting, the wish that Owens was well, and an invitation to sit down and tell Thad what he had learned. If Thad could have made it shorter, he would have. Owens handed Thad a copy of the report, keeping his own copy in his lap. Thad leafed through the report to get a sense of its contents. He would study it thoroughly later. Right now he wanted to hear Owens' take on it. Owens had been living with the investigation, and if there was something to see between the lines, he likely would have seen it. When he finished his quick review, Thad looked up.

Typically a man of few words, Owens underwent a transformation when he was giving a report as part of his job. His personal high standards of performance simply overrode his natural reticence. He likely did not notice the difference himself. It would not have occurred to him to compare his manner of speaking when required to give a full and thorough report to his everyday style of speech.

He began, "Not your typical shrinking violet. Nikki Patterson is a tough, smart cookie who has accomplished some impressive things in her thirty-three years."

"Was born in '80. Parents were both Ph.D.'s who taught at Berkley. Both radical activists in the 60's. Parents divorced when Nikki was nine. Father moved to UCLA and Nikki stayed with her mother, but apparently neither parent was much interested in her. Nikki was bright and athletic. IQ is 130." Thad gave a low whistle. Owens continued, "Mother remarried when Nikki was twelve. Nikki and her stepfather didn't get along. Suddenly at fourteen she began to get into trouble, changed her attitude about school, was rebellious. So at fifteen she was packed off to boarding school in the East – Phillips Exeter, academically demanding."

Owens continued, "According to school records and reports, getting away from home was good for her. Mostly A's in school work, and she was a starter on the varsity women's field hockey and lacrosse teams her junior and senior years. From the school pictures, she was pretty good looking, but socially pretty much a loner."

"Now it gets interesting. Her stepfather, who is now dead, had some pull with the Senators from California, and she got into West Point." Thad's face showed interest for the first time since Owens began. "She lit the place up, finished eighth in her class. Won a couple of awards. One was an academic award, and the other was for marksmanship. Third best cadet, man or woman, on the range with an M16A2." Owens paused there, letting the full impact sink in. The two men just looked at each other in silence for a full five seconds. They knew the M16A2 was a sophisticated weapon. They knew that if Nikki was a marksman with it, she could fire a 12-gauge shotgun with effect in her sleep. Thad nodded for Owens to continue. "On graduation they picked her for Spook School in Army Intelligence. You know, training how to spot and ferret out spies, infiltrators, terrorists. How to detect false I.D's and passports, interrogation methods, tailing and surveillance – that sort of stuff. But after four months they let her transfer out. She wanted combat instead. She shipped to Iraq in 2004 as a Humvee driver, which is as close to combat as a female can get."

Thad jumped in, "Christ! That is combat. Sitting ducks. There couldn't have been many women doing that. I thought that was a first line combat position."

"Apparently not quite, but she still tried to pull every trick she could to get an assignment that would let her shoot. Couldn't get it done of course. There weren't any of those positions for women. So, after her first tour, she didn't re-up. She looked for something demanding to do. Apparently, while still in the Army in Iraq, she was pulled out of the Humvee for a few days to chauffer around some members of Congress visiting on a fact-finding mission. One of these was the freshman Congresswoman Wetherill. The group got caught in a crossfire when an unexpected fire-fight broke out. Nikki kept her cool and got them out safely. This little embarrassment was hushed up on the theory it could give aid and comfort to the enemy. But the Congresswoman was so impressed by Nikki she told her to look her up in Washington if she ever wanted a different kind of job.”

"Nikki took her up on her invitation. The Congresswoman hired her on as one of her legislative researchers. Within three months she had become Assistant Chief of Staff and two months later, in April 2009, Chief of Staff. Has had the job ever since. She's a fanatic for work. On the job seven days a week. Apparently loves it. Is a stickler for routine. Works out most mornings. She's also the registered owner of a Browning Cynergy 12 gauge over and under, and when she can manage it, she shoots at the Prince George's County Trap and Skeet Center.”

"Obviously not the murder weapon," Thad commented, "shoots only two rounds and doesn't eject casings." Owens nodded and continued, "Not much social life. Apparently tells interested guys that right now she has the best job in the world and she'll have time for other things later.”

"Gay?" Thad asked.

"Nothing to affirm that," Owens responded, then continued from his notes. "One final thing Chief. Both her stepfather and father are dead. They left her well off. She doesn't need to work. She had securities worth over one million and a hundred fifty thousand dollars in mutual funds, money market funds, and a savings..." Thad interrupted, "What do you mean 'had'?”

Owens looked up from his notes. "Four days before Warner was killed, all that was liquidated, and we can't find where it went.”

Thad's intuition was now firing. Slowly he said, "son... of...a...bitch." He held out both hands toward Owens. "Well?”

Owens thumbed his suspenders, gave his glasses a little push, and began. "It played out like this. Correa was Moretti's contract man. We know that, even if we don't have evidence to indict. He got the goods on Warner for Moretti, and Moretti used them to try to back the Congresswoman off the investigation. But given Wetherill's personality, Moretti figured the Congresswoman should hear the bad news from a friendly source so she wouldn't react compulsively. You know, kill the messenger. Moretti wanted Wetherill to think about it and not just blow a gasket and find herself backed into a corner. That's why Nikki, not Wetherill, got the call from a Moretti guy pretending to be a legitimate lawyer, Kirk."

Owens shifted his weight and continued. "Nikki tied her future to the Congresswoman's political future, and if the Congresswoman picked her marriage over her career, where would that leave Nikki? A Valkyrie with no god to protect. So she'd do anything to protect Wetherill's career. She knows what a firefight is. She's not afraid to eliminate Warner. She knows her guns and munitions and can easily do it. But the hard part is to do it in a way that looks like Wetherill is the target. Otherwise you can't point at Moretti and say, 'He did it.'"

"So Nikki had to show the pictures to the Congresswoman and get her involved. Wetherill is royally pissed off at Warner, sees her marriage as over, and sees the political damage she'll suffer when his affair and coke use come out. A faked mob hit is the perfect way out. Wetherill had to be in on it. No way Nikki could be sure she'd miss Wetherill unless she knew exactly when Wetherill would be hunched down below the line of fire. It worked. Nikki is our triggerman, Chief. We just have to figure out how to prove it."

Both men were silent for a moment, taking it in, thinking about the next step.

Finally, Owens spoke again with more animation than usual. "She pulled the trigger four times! Four times when once and surely twice would have been plenty to do the job! God knows what those extra shots were for, Chief. She's one dangerous lady!"

CHAPTER 29

It was 6:30 in the morning. As usual, Nikki had awakened at 5:30, gone through a rigorous workout, showered, had a light breakfast, and was getting ready to leave for Wetherill's office. Her doorbell rang. She was puzzled. That never happened at this hour. She walked the short distance from her kitchen to the door and opened it.

"Morning, Nikki," said Thad in a pleasant voice. "I wonder if I may ask you a few questions before you start your day. May I come in?" Nikki did not move and was quick to respond.

"Agent Pennock, I must be in the Congresswoman's office by seven fifteen ready to go. Just follow me down there, and at some point I'll have a chance to talk to you. Or call me there and we can set up a time."

Thad, still smiling pleasantly, brushed past her into her apartment, saying, "Not necessary." When he was a good ten feet further in, he turned and continued, "Won't be more than ten or fifteen minutes, if that." He looked over her shoulder to the door and said, "As you can see, Agent Owens is with me." Owens moved into the room, tipped his hat to Nikki and offered, "Good day." Her hand still on the doorknob, Nikki considered protesting their interference with her schedule but Thad had already planted himself well inside.

Thad continued, "Only a few minutes, I assure you, and we can finish a lot faster here where you will not be distracted by your many obligations. Now, I understand you have a very impressive military record and are considered a fine marksman, or is it marksperson?" He was intentionally being overly pleasant. She could tell, and he knew she could tell. That is what he wanted. Nikki was immediately wary, not liking how this was starting off.

"What does that have to do with anything?" she asked, sounding defensive.

Thad did not offer to explain, but continued. "You have a shotgun registered in your name. Is it here in your apartment?"

Nikki's emotional response to danger was unlike that of most people, but she did not know that. Fear or apprehension became anger. Testily she protested again, "What's this about, Agent Pennock."

"Is it here?"

But Nikki was feisty now. "What has that to do with anything? I've been shooting all my life as is well documented in the background check I had when I went to work for Congresswoman Wetherill. In my opinion, it happens to be the best gun available to marks*men* who are serious about trap shooting." She emphasized the "men" sarcastically. "I practice every few days so, yes, it's here."

"Would you be willing to turn it over to us for twenty-four hours so we can perform some ballistics tests?" Both he and Owens were studying her carefully, looking for any reaction to this accusatory request. What they saw was controlled anger.

"Why? It's a perfectly legal gun. I have a permit."

Thad kept coming, "Will you give us that permission? That will save time. We could get a warrant, but that means delay and is a hassle that we would like to avoid." Actually, he doubted he had enough evidence to show cause why the search warrant should issue. Getting her to consent to their request was likely the only way they were going to get access to the weapon.

Nikki weighed the request for a moment and replied, "I'll agree if you tell me why you want to test it. I have nothing to hide. I only use it for sport. That's what it's made for. It's a sport gun."

"Deal," Thad said quickly. "Get us the gun, we will give you a receipt, and I will tell you why." Nikki climbed the stairs and disappeared. In a moment she came down carrying a leather rifle case by its handle. She leaned the case against the hall wall. Owens handed her a receipt in duplicate, which he had already signed and which Nikki read through word by word. Owens then handed her a pen. She signed both copies, kept one, and returned one to Owens.

"Okay, the reason we ask this is simple. We don't know who may have been involved in the murder of Mr. Warner. In such situations it is protocol to cast a wide net. Given your close relationship with Congresswoman Wetherill you are well within that net. We have to run all the traps all the way. We know your rifle is not the murder weapon. However, the oil on your gun might match the trace of oil on the driver side door of Mr. Warner's car. We're looking at things like that. We would be soundly and justifiably criticized if we didn't actively eliminate people as possible suspects."

Nikki shook her head sideways. She sarcastically said, "So that's it? So if the oil is the same, that narrows it down to the million or so gun owners who use the same oil? Good thinking, gentlemen. Now what's really going on here? There must be more to this visit than you're telling me."

Owens asked, "Do you let anyone else shoot it?" Nikki answered, "Occasionally at the range we will shoot each other's guns. So, yes, others have shot it. But I have never let anyone borrow it if that's what you are asking."

"So," Thad said, "to be clear, you have always been present when anyone else was shooting it. Is that right?"

"Yes, that's right."

Consulting his notes, Thad said, "Let's see. Registration says you bought it at Miller's Gun Shop in Wilmington, Delaware. Is that right?"

"Yes. Miller's has been around a long time. They're knowledgeable, and Wilmington is on the way from DC to my real home outside of Philadelphia. Also, there is no sales tax in Delaware.

"Where do you buy ammunition?"

"Usually Atlantic Gun Shop in Silver Springs."

"Any place else in the last six months?" Nikki thought a moment. "In the last six months I don't think anywhere else," she said.

"How do you pay for your ammunition?"

"A credit card, American Express," Nikki answered easily. It struck Owens that Nikki suddenly had decided to be cooperative, her earlier antagonism checked.

Thad moved to the gun case, unzipped it, and looked at the weapon.

"Do you have any other guns, registered or not?"

"No. I would not have an unregistered gun." She looked at her watch. "Are we through? You promised."

"You're right," Thad said. "Just one more question. What did you do when you left the fundraiser the night Warner was killed?"

"You know that," she snapped, suddenly irritated again. "We've been through it. It's in my statement. I was at the fundraiser. I left when the two of them left."

"Where did you go?"

"Home, I was finished for the evening."

"Did you see or talk to anyone from the time you left the fund raiser to the time you went to sleep."

"No, I was through for the day."

"Did you drive?"

"Yes, my own car."

"Same car you drive today?"

"Yes."

"What is it?"

"A Toyota Camry. You know all this. Why are we going over it again?"

"Is that how you plan to go to work today?"

"Yes," Nikki said, visibly exasperated now. "That is exactly how I plan to go to work. I will get in the car that you already know about and drive to work. Now, please take the gun and go."

Thad said, as gently as possible. "Please Nikki. Understand we're just doing our job. We ask you to please cooperate. We also need to examine your car to eliminate the possibility that it was the shooter's car."

Nikki looked like she was going to explode. Thad reflexively extended a calming hand. "I have two men who will take the car for examination and return it late this afternoon. Another is right outside your door in a car with the motor running authorized to turn on the flashing lights and siren and get you to work in no time. At the end of the day we'll pick you up or pay for a cab, whichever you wish. I know this is an inconvenience but I hope you see that one way or another we have to do this. Touch all bases. If you consent, it's less hassle for you and everyone and it'll be over and done."

"It's insulting!" Nikki burst out! Thad shook his head.

"Nikki you're smart. There's a big difference between suspicion and elimination. We're going down a checklist. Period."

Nikki gritted her teeth and shut her eyes for a few seconds. "When she opened them, she said, "What a pain in the neck. Have my car back by six!"

Thad didn't hesitate. "We'll do that."

Owens reached out his hand. "Here is the consent form for the car. Please read and sign it."

She shot back, "I don't have time to read it! I'm late!"

"Your call," Owens said. "The form states that your signature means you read it or waived reading."

"Give me the pen again," Nikki said. She took it from Owens and quickly signed. "Now if you please, get me to work."

A moment later Thad and Owens watched the car taking her to the Hill disappear down the street. "You played that perfectly, Chief," Owens said. "We never could have gotten warrants if she refused." Thad looked to the sky and opened his arms.

"Praise the lord! A compliment from the Master!" Owens chuckled. "Let's hope the gun or the car give us something to work with."

Both were silent for a moment. Then Owens asked, "want to talk to the Congresswoman now?"

"I don't think so. We really don't have anything solid on Nikki. Moretti is still the likely suspect." Recalling Lew Porter's plea to him, he added, "Besides, Wetherill would likely make an awful stink." Then he added, "Can you think of anything that makes a case against the Congresswoman?"

"I don't see it yet."

"Well why not, wise one?" Thad asked with a smile.

CHAPTER 30

J ust after 6 PM two days later, Thad was closing his office door for the day when he heard the phone on his desk ring. He walked back, sank into his desk chair, and picked up the phone. "Pennock", he said. The pleasant voice on the other end announced, "Agent Pennock, this is Amy Ferguson from the lab. I have the results of the tests you requested on the car belonging to Ms. Patterson." Thad's mind's eye saw the smart young woman who had already gained a reputation for being a crack technician. He straightened in his chair, fully alert.

"Hello Amy, nice to hear your voice. What have you got?"

Amy began, "A couple of things. First, there is only one set of prints in the car, but we got some clear ones. They match the set for Ms. Patterson that the FBI has on file as part of her security clearance. No surprise there. Next, there were gas residues inside the window well in the driver's side door. These are gases identical to ones that would emit from a shotgun when fired." Thad felt adrenalin shoot through his system. "If the barrel is outside the window when the gun is fired," he asked, "how does that residue travel backwards and into the car?" He thought he knew the answer but was always hoping to learn something new about the science.

"Doesn't travel backwards, Chief. Some residue is still being emitted for a few seconds after the round leaves the barrel, and although it's barely visible, it just starts falling until it adheres to something. Where four shots are fired quickly, the barrel is really smoking. On many models of cars, including this one, after four quick shots we would expect trace amounts to sink into the window well when the gun barrel was drawn back into the car.

"The car's been washed at least once and maybe more since the shooting. On the outside there were traces of soap and fluids typically used in automatic car washes. The inside of the driver's door was also wiped with some cleaner, but whoever cleaned it did not think to clean the inside of the window glass or the window well. Probably because the person cleaning knew the window was down when the shots were fired and didn't think the window could show evidence of gunshots. That window well would have been hard to clean anyhow unless you flushed it, and that's messy. How am I doing so far Agent Pennock?

"You have my full attention, Amy!"

"We also found the same gas residue on the passenger seatbelt strap."

"Where did you say? Passenger side?"

"Yes, you know, the strap is affixed to the right support beam or whatever you call it between the front and back side windows. In fact the stuff we found was on the back side of the strap. This may seem like a curious spot, but I've thought about it. I was given the dimensions of the shotgun you guys think was used. If someone in the driver's seat was holding that shotgun and wanted to put it down to drive away, it would be logical to prop the gun against the passenger seat with the stock on the floor and the barrel kind of leaned away toward the far door. The end of the barrel would be right about where the seatbelt hung."

"Sometimes those straps are twisted with the back side front. Maybe that happened here. Someone clearly made a real effort to get the carpets, seats and everything squeaky clean, but whoever did the cleaning missed the back side of the strap because, get this, we found there not only the gas residue but also trace amounts of gun oil and a really tiny paint chip. The paint is the type used for car exteriors."

Thad's adrenalin was pumping now. "Please tell me you've done the comparisons with Taylor's car."

"Yes Sir. I actually phoned the Philadelphia lab and had them retest the samples from Warner's car so samples from both cars would be tested on the same day. Not only did the particular composition of the gas residues match but the degree of degradation was almost identical. Ninety percent certainty that the gas residues in both cars came from the same barrel at the same time."

"Amy, where have you been all my life!" Thad said.

"There's more, Chief. The paint chip matches the paint on Warner's car, so the paint and gas residue tests support each other. No doubt in my mind. The gun that killed Mr. Warner was fired from the car we tested."

Thad curbed his excitement in order to think straight. The news was almost too good, and he wanted to be sure of it. "Any problems with these tests? Are the procedures established ones, nothing experimental or quirky?"

"No problem. The tests have been around for some time, and the chain of custody is good."

"How soon can you get me the report on this?"

"By noon tomorrow."

"Do better than that if you can. Set a record."

"That would be a record."

Thad laughed. "All right, Amy. Can't ask for more than that. Great work. If you were here I'd give you a big hug and kiss and take my chances with HR's sexual harassment team."

"Who's going to tell them?" Amy answered.

Thad hung up for two seconds and then dialed Owens' extension. After one ring Owens answered. Unwilling to contain his excitement Thad jumped to his feet and bellowed into the phone, "Got her, Owens!"

A minute later Owens was sitting in Thad's office across the desk with a note pad in his hand. "Listen to this," Thad said and gave him the news from Ferguson. Then he added, "Let's see. We don't have the weapon and probably won't find it, but we have Patterson as a crack marksman totally comfortable handling guns. We have her telling us she drove her car away that night at the same time the Congresswoman and Warner left and that she was alone the rest of the night, and now we have the murder weapon fired from her car."

When he finished, he waited for Owens' reaction. It didn't come right away. His methodical mind was carefully processing and cataloging the information, then assessing its significance. Eventually his eyes returned to Thad's, and he said simply, "That does it." Thad grinned. If Owens was sure, he was sure.

"Let's take it to Lew first thing tomorrow. He should know before we pull the trigger. But should we pull it? If the Congresswoman is complicit, will leaving Nikki out there give us a better chance of getting something solid against her, or do we bring Nikki in?" Owens didn't hesitate, "In."

CHAPTER 31

That night Thad felt like celebrating, but celebrating alone was a little like making love alone. Better than no celebration at all, but just not the same. He thought of Isabella. Although it was nearly 10:00 PM in Buenos Aires, she answered his call. He told her they were close to solving the murder and that he could tell her more soon. Then he told her he missed her. She laughed, and he felt her laughter envelope him. They talked about the next time they might see each other and anything else that came to mind. It didn't matter what; they were drinking in each other's voices. Twenty minutes later they said good night.

As he was sinking into sleep, his thoughts drifted out of focus like shapeless clouds. But just on the edge of sleep those clouds took form and pulled him back. He saw Congresswoman Wetherill bent to the car floor looking for her contact lens as the first explosion went off above her. *What was it?* Then he recalled the comment of one of the reporters outside the hospital, and a little experiment came to mind.

CHAPTER 32

The next morning, Lew Porter could not see them until 8:30. At 8:15, Thad looked in on Owens, who was occupied with paperwork. As Thad approached, Owens looked up. They exchanged their usual expansive greetings.

"Owens."

"Chief."

"Join me."

"Sure."

Owens rose. Thad led to one of the records rooms where he randomly picked up several heavy notebooks of papers. He walked out with them followed by a puzzled Owens, who patiently waited for an explanation. Thad walked to conference room 2 and pushed the door open with his shoulder. Thad asked Owens if he would sit at the table. Owens did. Thad stood beside him, put the notebooks on the table, took a pencil from his pocket, handed it to Owens and then picked up the notebooks again. Owens sat with the pencil, his body turned sideways so he could see Thad's face.

"Now, Owens," Thad said, "please drop the pencil between your legs just underneath the table and then pick it up." Even for the patient Owens, this was a bit much. He remained turned and looking at Thad.

"You serious, Chief?"

"Very." Owens nodded, turned in his chair to square with the table, and dropped the pencil between his feet, which were under the table six or eight inches. Owens again glanced skeptically at Thad, who nodded to proceed. Owens began pushing his chair back so he could more easily reach over his stomach for the pencil.

"No, no, put the chair back where it was. Just get down and reach for the pencil as best you can." Owens looked at him again, but said nothing. Then he nudged his chair back to the table. So positioned, he had to duck his head sideways and down to the left until his head and right shoulder were below table height. Then, staying low, he moved his head and shoulders back to the right until he was squared, his chest and belly pressed down on his thighs, and his face beginning to redden. In this position, he reached down for the pencil. As his fingers closed around it, Thad slammed the heavy notebooks down on the table. They made a percussive *bang*.

Owens' shoulders and head instinctively jerked upward toward the danger not down away from it, and they collided with the underside of the table. "Ahh!" He blurted. He dropped down again enough to permit his right hand to rub the back of his head. At the same time he pushed the chair away from the table with his feet to get his head and upper body vertical again. Then he rose to his feet still rubbing the back of his head.

With as much indignation as he could muster, which was never much when addressing Thad, he asked, "What was that about?"

"Owens, my apologies, but a very helpful experiment. Let me ask you," he continued, "When you reacted to the impact and noise above you, why didn't you simply drop to the floor away from it?"

"I didn't think about it. I was surprised. It was instinctive."

Thad nodded. "You were bent over in an unnatural and vulnerable position. My guess is that the unexpected threat triggered an instinct to get back into a posture from which to defend yourself even if that meant moving toward the threat. But if you had been expecting me to slam the notebooks down? If it wasn't a surprise?" He shook his head sideways and turned and walked toward the door. "See you at 8:30," he said, "and keep the pencil." Still rubbing his head, Owens watched him leave. Then he made the connection, as Thad knew he would.

CHAPTER 33

At 8:30, the two of them fast-walked to Porter's office. When they arrived, Porter's secretary led them to the Deputy Director's conference room where Porter sat talking with Lacey Leroy, an alert, attractive, middle-aged woman who had years of experience as a public relations manager with the FBI. "Glad you fellows could finally make it," Porter said through the ever-present cigar. "Lacey here was getting goddam bored just listening to me. Sit down, sit down. You can't believe the fucking flak...sorry Lacey, coming down from the White House to solve this thing like today. My guess is the president can't stand to see a politician in the other party get so much high visibility sympathy for so long. The Congresswoman has all the headlines. I need a goddam foxhole. Sorry, Lacey."

He chomped on the cigar. "It's getting bizarre, that performance by her and her sidekick." He shook his head in disbelief. "Damndest thing I ever saw. It's like Warner's murder was political manna from heaven, like the guy himself was born to die that way to serve the higher cause of the red-haired howitzer." Then he shook his head and, more slowly for emphasis, he added, "She's one tough bitch. Sorry, Lacey."

Thad nodded, recalling that "performance" was the way both he and Charlie had characterized the press conference. "So what have you guys got?" Porter asked. "Better be good. Can't waste Lacey's valuable time, can we?"

Thad began, "Owens and I are together on this, Lew, but he can speak for himself." Then Thad went through the background check on Nikki, the lab findings, and Amy Ferguson's opinion as to the certainty of the results. As he spoke, Porter's body became increasingly still until nothing moved, not even the cigar, while his eyes shone brighter and brighter. When Thad finished, there were several seconds of silence finally broken by Lacey. "My goodness!" she exclaimed, "unbelievable!"

Porter took a mighty chomp on the long-suffering cigar. "Son of a bitch! Bloody one hundred eighty degree turnaround! You couldn't script this." Then he looked from one to the other of his agents. "You fellas know what this means? The Congresswoman's in the sewer pipe, too. Has to be! What do you have on her?"

It was Owens who answered, "She has the perfect alibi; she's in the car. Even if Patterson rats her out, it's her word against the Congresswoman's. I don't know if it comes across on TV, Lew, but the Congresswoman could shoot the judge dead in front of twelve jurors, then look them in the eye and say, 'I didn't do it,' and seven of them would believe her. She's that good. We're going to have to get lucky."

Porter was silent while Owens spoke, his gaze on middle space, his mind churning. Then he refocused and looked from one to the other of his agents. "You suppose they're lesbies? Be a goddam waste! Sorry, Lacey."

"We have no evidence of that. Patterson seems to go overboard to smother her appeal for whatever that's worth." Porter turned to Leroy.

"Lacey, you're a woman..."

"Thanks for noticing, Lew," Lacey snuck in.

"Oh, believe me I notice! But I'm gonna leave it right there! No kidding, can women spot lesbies better? Are these two lesbies?"

"I have no way of knowing, Lew. Patterson shows some of the signs, but Wetherill's been married twice, and she really is tuned in to how to project her sexuality. Maybe she goes both ways? I just don't know."

Porter leaned forward with elbows on the table. His gaze once again went inward. The cigar migrated, his jaws slowly working on it. The motion reminded Thad of a ruminating cow. Then Porter sat up, his decision made. "Take the case to Jake. If he gives us less than seventy percent chance of conviction, we leave her out there and hope she does something to implicate Wetherill or maybe we'll bring her in and squeeze her to give up Wetherill. If we get seventy, we arrest her and have the wonderful press conference that Lacey will script for us."

"Lacey, we have to rewrite the PR playbook on this mess. Be thinking about it." He rose to leave but stopped with another thought.

"And Lacey?" he paused, looking right at her.

"Yes, Lew" she answered, anticipating another instruction.

He removed the cigar from his mouth, squinted at her, and broke into his best Jack Nicholson grin.

"Watch your mouth around me please."

Lacey, always polite, saw her rare chance to have the last word.

"I'll do my fucking best, Lew."

CHAPTER 34

Jake Corcoran was an experienced Assistant District Attorney in the District of Columbia. Patterson would almost certainly be tried in Philadelphia, so Corcoran would not be the prosecuting attorney. But Porter often used him as the litmus test for the likelihood of a conviction. His success rate was unusually high and not because he protected it by trying only the "sure thing" cases. The opposite was true. He was smart, he prepared thoroughly and, most important, juries liked and respected him. Corcoran spent nearly two hours with Thad and Owens. He listened to their summary of facts and reviewed documents in the file, including the lab report that Amy's group had just delivered. He confirmed that the chain of custody of critical pieces of evidence was solid. He asked many questions, most of which Thad or Owens could answer.

Finally, he leaned back in his chair with his arms resting on its arms. "Okay," he said. "The case you present is good. I give it a seventy percent chance of conviction, maybe a little higher. And then he added, "It's a little strange though. You didn't ask me this, but if the Congresswoman hadn't come so close to getting shot herself, I'd find it hard to believe she wasn't in on it."

CHAPTER 35

Porter alerted the Director that Patterson's arrest was imminent, but as usual he left to Thad the decision of where, when, and how it would be done. Thad, in turn, gave that responsibility to Owens, who decided to avoid the hoopla of an arrest on Capitol Hill. So, at 9:30 that night Magistrate Judge Helen Winslow issued an arrest warrant for Nikki and a search warrant for her apartment. At 10:30 the arrest team was in position and knocked on her door. No answer. They called to confirm their orders and were told to go in. They breached the door and quickly canvassed the apartment. No Nikki. They phoned Owens, who immediately saw his mistake.

It was a rare Owens' oversight. Always professional, his demeanor remained unchanged, but inwardly he chastised himself. *How could I miss that!* "All right," he said, "We need an arrest and search warrant that are good for her home in Delaware County and get the Pennsylvania state police to stake it out until the agents with the warrant get there."

At 10:40, Nikki was just about to undress for bed. Late that morning Wetherill had asked her to stand in for Wetherill at a Republican Party barbeque in Wetherill's home district outside of Philadelphia. She drove rather than take the train. The trip gave her the opportunity to spend the night in the condominium she had bought close to Virginia's home.

The barbeque had been a raucous affair lasting longer than she hoped. Now she was unwinding. Her cell phone rang. "Darling girl!" a familiar voice said. She smiled as she recognized Gerry Humphries, the handsome, gay piano-bar player who occupied an apartment next to hers in DC. Nikki liked the merry man. She could relax in his company and not worry whether she would have to fight him off.

She clicked on the loudspeaker and rested the phone on the table by her bed and began to undress. "Hi Gerry! What a nice surprise. How are you?"

"Oh my dear, you just don't want to know! It would take hours, maybe days to tell." He laughed, and Nikki laughed. Gerry's self-proclaimed purpose in life was to lift the spirits of those he cared about and do so by exaggerating his own misfortunes. Everyone was in on the gambit, but it nevertheless worked because Gerry wore it all on his sleeve.

"What's up?" Nikki asked cheerily.

"Well, dear girl, I called so *you* could tell *me*. I just got home, early for me, as you know all too well. My date was the absolute pits! Whatever did I see in that boy? Gave me the creepy crawlies! Anyway, here are the police; no, actually, the Feds like in FBI! They're in *your* apartment and are taking *your* computer and lots of other stuff out. I couldn't believe my eyes. I asked them what they were doing but they wouldn't say, so I had to call, absolutely had to. What's happening? Where are you? Is my Nikki all right?"

She was not all right. She was not prepared. Despite her contingency planning Nikki never believed it would really come to this. And it came out of nowhere like a spear arcing silently and unseen through a black sky and striking and penetrating deeper than a mortal wound, piercing her soul with the certainty that her life with Virginia was over. *They know!* She told herself. *It's finished...!* She sank on to her bed. *My God!*

She had killed to preserve that life. *Why wasn't that enough?* Her obsession with Virginia had been the shield against feelings and memories long buried deep in her subconscious and too painful to bear, and now as if tripped by a switch they rushed into her consciousness and overwhelmed her as quickly and unexpectedly as the remembered events once had. "Oh, my God!" she wailed.

"Nikki? What is it? Nikki! Are you all right?" Nikki's cry bore so much pain that Gerry was afraid of what he might hear next. But Nikki couldn't listen or think.

A debilitating shame shackled deep in her subconscious broke free and spread swiftly through her like a sepsis. Awaking with it was the awful memory of its cause. *Oh God, no! Oh no!* Her mind screamed as she helplessly began reliving the never-ending minutes in another bedroom many years before when she had been so young and the demon had fallen upon her.

She felt again his heavy, sweating, grunting, liquor-saturated body pressing down and pinning her as he forced her coltish legs apart and his throbbing shaft into her. With every fierce thrust he physically and mentally shredded her. The pain nearly split her in two, but it was nothing compared to the shame and humiliation that crushed her spirit. She could hear him panting and felt his lips smear his saliva on her neck. Those course lips wet her ear as he slurred, "I know you want it. I see it in your eyes and how you walk and sway your hips around me. I can tell you're asking me for it! Oh, I can tell!"

Her mind protested again as it had years before when she had been trapped in his grasp, *I'm not asking! I didn't ask! I don't want to ask you! I don't know how to* ask *you! Do I ask for it? Oh God! Do I ask?* She had to escape the shame. She threw her head back, clamped her eyes shut and knees together and balled her hands into tight fists and wailed into the room, "Get out of me! I deny you!"

On the other end of the phone, Gerry the piano player was dumbstruck. "Nikki! What's happening? Such terrible words! Nikki?" She did not answer, but his voice had broken through, and she struggled to break free of the memories.

Her mind flailed about for any purchase that might check her free-fall. It cast out random thoughts like grappling hooks in every direction. One after another they simply sank into the void until suddenly one caught and held. *Vengeance!* She did not immediately know why or how that offered her a lifeline, only that it did, and so she clutched at it.

For years the prospect of revenge against her stepfather had been the anesthetic that had kept the pain of her despoliation from driving her to suicide. She wanted him to die and told herself she readily could have dispatched him in some conventional way...gun...knife...poison. But that would not suffice, not for what he had done to her. She wanted to physically dominate him as he had her, throw him to the ground, wrench his limbs from their sockets, smash in his jaws with her heels, crush his testicles in her hands, and slice through his penis with a dull knife. She wanted to inflict the kind of pain and humiliation he had so cruelly visited upon her. She bided her time until she would be strong enough and skilled enough. Vengeance was her obsession, and obsession was good; it parried suicide.

When her stepfather offered to use his influence to help her get into West Point, she relished the irony. There, she could acquire the combat skills she needed. And she did. But she deployed to Iraq without creating the opportunity to wreck the havoc upon him she dreamed about. In truth, had she been able to fully know her mind, she would have recognized a lurking reticence to complete the task. What would there be to live for afterwards? What would hold her together then? She never quite formed these thoughts but they influenced her actions.

She left the army and was hired by Virginia. She delayed and delayed. Plotting and planning in anticipation of the deed seemed to suffice. She worked tirelessly to become indispensable because it was good cover for what she still told herself she wanted to do, but she soon became fascinated by the power, manipulation, and cynicism of Virginia's world and by Virginia herself. It was a good fit; her shame deprived her of self-worth so she felt at home in an environment where there was little of real value. More and more she found herself wanting to fill her life with Virginia's.

The morning after Virginia elevated her to chief of staff she got the call from her mother that her stepfather had died unexpectedly but peacefully in his sleep. Suddenly revenge was no longer possible. It had for so long been the pin preventing the hand grenade within her from going off. Now the pin had been pulled.

But the mind does not easily surrender to suicide. It seeks an alternative without being fussy about how much reality it will cost. Her subconscious solved the survival problem. The instant Nikki comprehended that her stepfather was dead her mind clicked as if changing channels on a monitor. She was infused with a feeling of devotion towards Virginia that was such an overwhelming obsession that it suppressed all memory of the rape and buried her shame so deep in her subconscious that it manifested itself only as a source-less tension. Her conscious reaction to her stepfather's death was sympathy for her mother and an absence of feelings for him.

From that moment her devotion to Virginia was unconditional, but she had no comprehension of the greater purpose this devotion served. When the day came that Virginia and she viewed with shock the disgusting pictures of Taylor and that whore snorting coke and fornicating with such obvious pleasure, she readily accepted Virginia's verdict; Taylor's selfish, drug-induced philandering had placed in Moretti's hands a guided missile with which to shoot down Virginia's career. Whatever needed to be done to neutralize that threat should be done.

Perhaps when she sited down the barrel of the shotgun and then fired four blasts into Taylor's car, the man she saw was her stepfather. In any case that conscious act of murder was her ultimate demonstration of devotion to Virginia and seemingly forever sealed the memory of her rape in an inescapable tomb in her subconscious. Until Gerry's phone call it was never a serious thought that she could not be at Virginia's side. Now that thought was reality. Her guardian obsession was suddenly powerless to protect her, and she was about to be devoured by her own undeserved shame.

Vengeance! It was an abstract thought at first but even so it promised hope. It began pulsing at her temples and gradually it pounded louder and louder until it was a mantra gone berserk, shouting down her demon. *Vengeance!* Nikki's mind strained to make it crystallize into a specific course of action.

Suddenly, she seized upon the memory of her pledge to Virginia made in that moment of passion in Virginia's library. She had taken Virginia's face in her hands and had looked into her eyes. At the time, the pledge was a grand emotional gesture, a declaration of undying love. But now, fulfilling the pledge was a necessary act, another proxy killing of her stepfather. She would be the instrument of retribution, punishing that

Loperena Whore for destroying the triangular equilibrium in which Virginia and Taylor and she had thrived.

She felt her connection to Virginia reviving. It did not matter that she could not be with Virginia; indeed, avenging the dishonor done to Virginia required that they not be together. But she must remain alive and free to carry it out. No need to look beyond that.

"Nikki! Please! What's happening?"

She didn't know how long she had not been listening to Gerry, but she didn't care. In a thin-edged voice she quickly dismissed him, "Have to go, Gerry. Don't be upset."

"But dearie," he implored, "upset is my natural state!" But Nikki had moved beyond any further conversation with him. She had a message to deliver to someone else. She shouted her pledge to the black night, "Whore! I will cut out your heart!" Gerry's eyes widened and his mouth was agape as the line went dead.

Like a violent thunderstorm clears the air, Nikki's exclamation dissipated the turmoil triggered by Gerry's call. Her thoughts were ordered. Her memory was sharp and clear, but altered. She had no recall of her stepfather's use of her. It was buried again, carrying with it the unbearable shame. She felt invigorated by the challenge before her. She checked her watch, 10:55 PM. She assumed the police would soon arrive and was grateful for the screen of night. She calmly walked out of her home and to the car with nothing but her pocketbook. She fairly burned with anticipation. She knew exactly where she was going. *How well I plan ahead!*

PART II

VENGEANCE

CHAPTER 36

Marvin Adelman was rightfully proud of his business. He had begun eight years before at an industrial site outside of Ardmore, Pennsylvania, with only twenty-five rental storage units. He had worked hard, and now he had four hundred units – row after row of garage-like structures. Four hundred! Each had a lift-up garage door that could be securely locked. Each could hold a car and a good deal more. He had a comfortable on-site office, and a ten-foot chain link fence secured the entire property. *Man, he thought, was that fence ever expensive! Nothing schlocky about my fence!* It was his best advertisement: "Adelman's Security is double security."

And his key system was sophisticated too, like hotel room key cards that could be changed by computer at any time. A renter got a key card that opened the main gate and the rented unit. *Man! Was that key system expensive too!* But now he was 80% rented. The loans for these investments were almost paid off, and when that day came, nearly every dollar from rent after his mortgage payment would drop to the bottom line as profit! He didn't even have to be in the office all the time.

Marvin was an affable man. He liked nearly all of the people who rented from him and really liked that Hot and Easy blond shicksa Mary Ellen Duross, P. O. Box 469, Ardmore, PA. Nice hot little car too. Three weeks earlier she had rented Unit 217. It was on the far side of the property, out of sight of the office. Too bad cars going back there don't pass near the office. He'd like to feast his eyes on her when she came in.

Nikki got out of her rental car at Unit 217, slid the key card into its slot, heard the click, pulled up the garage door, and turned on the light. It illuminated the dark green two-year old Audi with tinted windows. *Like the BMW windows,* she recalled matter-of-factly. She entered and lowered the door. She retrieved the keys to the Audi from a small box under a blanket in a corner and remotely unlocked it. She lifted the trunk and removed a suitcase and two gym bags. She unzipped the suitcase. On top were an expensive blond wig, large brightly colored sunglasses, low-cut jeans, a sleeveless, fitted knit turtleneck, open-toe high heels, dangly costume jewelry, and a cosmetic bag. She used the contents of the cosmetic bag and the lighted mirror in its lid to apply lots of eye shadow, eyelashes, lipstick and other heavy makeup. She then donned the wig and got into the clothes, which, in the case of the jeans, took some doing. But when she finished, Nikki had disappeared. The person in the mirror was "Hot and Easy" Mary Ellen.

She reached into a side pocket of the bag and retrieved a passport and wallet. The picture in the passport and on the Pennsylvania license in the wallet was "Hot and Easy" herself. The wallet also contained five bankcards and a social security card all in the name of Mary Ellen Duross. Getting the documents was not hard, just expensive. But she could afford it.

She had opened accounts in five different banks in the name of Mary Ellen Duross and deposited $50,000 in each and ordered cards to draw against those funds. In a side pocket of the bag was a cell phone and charger. She would charge it during the long drive. She checked the glove compartment of the Audi for the registration and insurance card.

She closed the suitcase, which contained more "Hot and Easy" clothes, and put it back in the Audi trunk. She checked the two gym bags to assure herself the nearly one million dollars was still there. She took $13,000 out and carried the bags to a corner and draped her discarded clothes over them. Then she drove the Audi out of the unit and the rental car in. She took one satisfied look around the unit before closing the door. *I plan better than anyone!* She exulted.

She had picked Marvin's storage company because there was a security gate and not a security guard. The only time she had seen Marvin was the day she rented the unit. And she had paid cash for six months rent. She was certain no one could link Mary Ellen and Nikki. In the unlikely event that the police would be showing Marvin a picture of Nikki, he would not recognize her. They might even ask who had rented a unit recently. If so, he might describe Mary Ellen and the green Audi. She had made a point of being "Hot and Easy" with Marvin, so she was sure he would remember her as different from any description of Nikki the Feds would give him. Getting the Audi into Unit 217 had not been difficult. The night after she rented the unit, she drove it in, walked a quarter of a mile to Lillian's Diner, and called a cab. She had it take her to downtown Philadelphia, and from there she took another cab to her condominium.

So, she was set. She closed the garage door with Nikki's possessions inside, including the money. Before pulling away, she set her GPS for Chicago's O'Hare Airport and looked at her estimated arrival time many hours ahead. She already had a plan. She adjusted the seat slightly, settled her body into it, and mentally programmed herself for the long ride. *The sequence is critical*, she reminded herself, *the sequence of steps in a plan*. She felt invisible and unhurried.

When she was well away from Marvin's, she looked at the hot girl looking back at her in the rear view mirror and laughed aloud. She was Mary Ellen, and she was going to enjoy it! She turned on the radio and sang along with three songs in a row. An hour later she used Mary Ellen's cell phone and a credit card to call Chile's airline, LAN, and book a flight to Santiago with an open return.

CHAPTER 37

As Hot and Easy was closing the door of Unit 217 at Ableman's Storage, Congresswoman Wetherill was showing Thad and Owens into the library of her Georgetown home. It was midnight. Although she had been awakened by Thad's phone call telling her, not asking her, that he and Owens were on their way, she was dressed, coiffed, and alert. She moved to the chair behind her desk and gestured to them to take the two seats facing her. It occurred to Thad that although the desk projected power, it also offered protection. *Did the Congresswoman ever really doubt herself?*

"Agent Pennock," she began, "you assured me this late night meeting was essential; indeed, that I had no option. Were I not used to such curious, nocturnal ultimatums from the Majority Leader, I might have been annoyed. Is there a breakthrough?" Thad did not hesitate. He wanted her to get both barrels at short range so Owens and he could see her reaction.

"More than that, we know who the killer is. We just don't know if she was working alone. Nikki Patterson murdered your husband."

Thad and Owens looked for a hint of fear, and neither could detect it. Her mouth opened for an instant and shut again. Her green eyes were wide. Her expression was one of surprise, but to the two of them it looked like surprise at their utter incompetence. Her own alibi was so rock solid. "Absurd," she finally said. "That's absurd. I'm at a loss to know how you're spending your time. A real chance to finally get Moretti, and you come up with this? What could you possibly be thinking?"

Thad, embarrassed that they had blown Nikki's arrest, was in no mood to hear he was a fool as well as careless. Whether this was an excellent act by a murderer or the genuine surprise of an innocent, he did not appreciate being insulted. "No doubt, absolutely none. You will have to live with it," he said. "There is irrefutable evidence that the murder weapon was shot from Nikki's car into your husband's car. She's liquidated her investments and we cannot trace the proceeds."

The Congresswoman responded as if an impossible scenario was nevertheless more likely than Nikki being a murderer. "Well," she protested, "someone else must have used her car. She wouldn't do this."

"Wrong," Thad declared quickly, not letting up. "We have her sworn statement that she left the fundraiser in her own car right after you did. The only question is whether she acted alone." He stopped, letting the unstated accusation hang in the air.

"But why would she do such a thing?" the Congresswoman exhorted, sidestepping the implication. Thad kept pressing, deference to her high office gone.

"You tell us," he said, staring right at her.

"Me, how would I know?"

"How would you not know? Would Nikki really kill your husband without your consent? Would she kill him the way she did without your knowing when the shots were going to come through the window? Would she have risked killing you? Wasn't it for you that she killed him?"

There it was, the direct accusation, and it got the response he had predicted. The Congresswoman shot up from her chair, her red hair and green eyes on fire. "How dare you! How *dare* you! That is preposterous! You are out of your mind! You disturb me in the middle of the night with this claptrap? The Director will hear about this first thing in the morning. In fact I'm of half a mind to roust him up. Now, get out." Pointing a long finger at the door, she hissed, "Get out, both of you."

Neither agent moved. They sat calmly, coldly looking at her. "Where is she?" Thad asked authoritatively.

"I told you to get out!"

"Congresswoman Wetherill," Thad said formally, "Nikki Patterson is now a fugitive from justice wanted for murder. I have asked you where she is. If you refuse to cooperate and you know anything that may lead us to her, Congresswoman or no Congresswoman, you are guilty at the least of aiding and abetting a murderer after the fact, which is a very serious felony. Now sit down and tell us where she is."

Confusion flickered in her eyes for an instant. His exercise of authority had trumped hers. Then she recovered and her anger returned, "You have no right to accuse me!" But she lowered herself into her chair. In a wounded voice she said, "She stood in for me tonight at a political affair in Bucks County. She drove because she wanted to stay at her condominium for the night. If you want to talk to her, that's where you'll find her."

Thad kept pressing, "No. She was not there at eleven twenty when our team arrived, and she hasn't been there since." At this news the Congresswoman lost most of her anger. She looked puzzled, seemed to be thinking and, uncharacteristically, was silent.

Thad decided to shift gears, unapologetic but no longer threatening, "Why would Nikki want to kill your husband?" She put her long fingers on the table in front of her and looked right at Thad.

"The conclusion that Nikki murdered Taylor is so irrational to me that I cannot conceive of a rational motive." Her gaze seemed to move to some indeterminate point in the room beyond Thad and Owens. Then she threw Nikki under the bus. "The only thing that comes to my mind is . . .. I have felt for some time that Nikki loves me like. . . . like a lover would, although out of respect and certainty that I would find that repulsive, she has never made an overture of that kind. Maybe . . . ." she paused then continued, "maybe when she learned of Taylor's mistake with that whore, she thought it would ruin my career if it ever came out, so killing him that way might make me a sympathetic figure if it did. I don't know. I'm guessing. The guess makes me sick. I cannot possibly believe she would do such a thing. I'm taking your word that she is the killer, but in my heart I still don't believe it."

Man! Is she ballsy! Thad said to himself. He glanced at Owens and could read his same thought. She had articulated the real motive for Warner's death and attributed it entirely to Nikki. The truth and the half-truth were a powerful defense that guaranteed that in the mind of any juror there would be reasonable doubt of her guilt. Thad had a sinking feeling that the Congresswoman ultimately would get a pass. "When did you last speak to her?" he asked.

"She was driving. It was right after the fundraiser. I had asked her to report in to me, and she did. She confirmed she would drive back early in the morning."

"Call her," Thad said, not asking. "Find out where she is and what she is doing. Use your speaker so I can listen."

"Now?"

Wetherill instinctively resisted precisely because Thad had given her an order. But she needed only a few seconds to see that as folly. She dialed Nikki's cell phone from the phone on her desk and depressed the button for the speakerphone. All of them heard the unanswered rings until the call shifted to voicemail.

Thad said, "Ask her to call you ASAP." She did and then broke the connection. Thad told her, "We'll trace the location of the phone. My guess is she's dumped it."

Thad pressed, "If she were on the run, where would she go?"

"On the run?" Wetherill asked, as if this had not occurred to her.

"Yes," Thad said, "on the run." Wetherill was silent for a moment.

"I have no idea."

"Does she have favorite places she likes to go? A cabin in the woods, a hotel at the beach?"

"I don't know of any," Wetherill answered. "She never really took enough time off to go anywhere like that. A day here or there at the most. She has no siblings, her father and stepfather are both dead, and I never felt she was close to her mother. I can think of only one time she took two days off to visit her."

"What languages does she speak?" Thad asked.

"A little French and Italian and quite good Spanish." A slight pause, "I still can't believe this."

"Believe it," Thad said unsympathetically. "And believe this too. You are now a person of interest, and we better not find out that you are holding something back." Wetherill stiffened and began to protest again, but Thad held up his hand. "Because you are a member of Congress, we will not publicize that you are a person of interest, but do not think you can make a phone call or two up the line and make this go away. God could not get that done for you. And one more thing, you hear from her and don't tell us, that's jail time. Are we together, Congresswoman?"

Wetherill looked at him, the fury behind her eyes returning. "It is time for you to leave, Agent Pennock. Nikki is a good and loyal worker and my friend. I do not take kindly to any of this, and I have no doubt you will come to understand that you have made a grave mistake about her. I only hope it's soon."

Thad had delivered his message, and there was no doubt that she had gotten it. He was not the type who needed the last word just because it was last. He rose, repeating, "If you hear from her or think of anything that might help us locate her, call me immediately." She did not respond, but simply stood behind her desk. They let themselves out.

CHAPTER 38

Despite the hour, Owens and Thad headed back to the office. Owens spent a few minutes on the phone. When he rang off, he reported to Thad. "I have the Pennsylvania, Maryland, New Jersey, and DC police looking for her car. We're checking Amtrak, Philadelphia, BWI, Dulles, Newark, and National airports and checking with all the airlines to see if she has booked. Nothing back yet on any of those."

Thad took a deep breath. He had faith in the scientific evidence pointing to Nikki. Still, certainty about whether someone was a killer had for him an emotional component. Her disappearance served to supply that. He now knew in his bones she was the killer. "Okay, make it an APB, everything. Planes, trains, TV, internet, the whole nine yards."

"Got it."

Thad then made a call he wished he could skip. He woke up Lew Porter and brought him up to date, but with no mention of who had been responsible for failing to put the collar on Nikki. "Christ, Thaddeus, this is a world class screw-up! Tell me I'm still dreaming! Tell me you're just yanking on my wonker. We look like the goddam Keystone Cops!"

"I know. And, Lew, we'll have to make some announcement first thing in the morning. You want me to do it?"

"Damn straight I want you to do it, but I don't have that luxury. Our compassionate Director would accuse me of hiding beneath your skirt, and that's not a location on my bucket list!"

"But why should I be worried?" he continued sarcastically. "I've got the best and brightest agents right on top of this goddam dung heap. Don't I? And before we have to totally humiliate ourselves before the media in the morning, they'll have dived in and not come up for air until they've pulled out this little bag of shit and clasped her to their bosom. And that will happen before I wake up bright-eyed in the morning. Am I right, Thaddeus?"

"We'll do everything we can, Lew."

"Now there's a comforting thought! Does this mean I can now return to a lascivious sleep and dream of bonking a delicious movie star instead of being corn-holed by someone looking suspiciously like the Director?"

It wasn't really a question so he continued, "Wake up Lacey, Thaddeus, and tell her what we need by eight AM, which is when I'll see your sleep-deprived body in my office."

Thad followed up.

"I suggest we cut off questions or speculation about the Congresswoman if it comes up. We can accurately say that we cannot rule out the possibility that Patterson had one or more accomplices, but at this point we have no evidence of that."

"Unfortunately, that has the ring of truth. Now, any more good news or is that everything you have to tell me?"

"That's it," Thad answered.

"Bullshit Thaddeus. You know it's not." Thad was silent. After a pause Porter added, "But that's why you're a class act." Then he hung up.

He put his face in his hands, squeezed his eyes shut, and took a deep breath. *Where the hell is she?* He asked himself. Nothing came, so he called Owens back to his office. When the round man was seated, Thad said, "Well?"

"Disguise, new ID, hid the car. Only two choices; bury herself deep or leave the country." He paused and then added, "Just doesn't seem to me the type to hole up somewhere."

"Agreed," Thad said.

"Even if she's disguised, New York, Newark, Philly, BWI, Washington airports are too close, too risky. Maybe Boston, Atlanta, Chicago, or maybe she slips into Canada or Mexico and launches from there."

Thad's desk phone rang to cut Owens' speculation short. Thad was surprised. *Who would call this phone at this time of night?* He asked himself.

"Agent Pennock, this is Corporal McKinstry, DCPD. My chief told me to call you directly. He gave me your direct line"

"Wait," Thad said and pressed the speaker button. "You're on the speaker. Agent Robert Owens is with me. Go ahead."

"O.K. gentlemen. I'm on the team assigned to help the FBI in DC in its search for the fugitive Veronica Patterson. We just interviewed a man in one of the apartments next to Patterson's, a Gerald Humphries. He said he called her last night on her cell around 10:30 to find out what was going on. He was just coming home and saw your guys force an entry into her apartment. He says he really likes Patterson, and this sight, in his words, 'distressed him.' So he called her cell number and told her what he was witnessing."

"This Humphries fellow said that she was very pleasant at first, but when he described the scene at her apartment, she seemed to go a little crazy, first wailing 'Oh my god!' and then yelling, 'Get out of me! I deny you!' He says those were her exact words, 'Get out of me! I deny you!' – and they scared the daylights out of him. He asked her what was wrong, and after a minute she says, 'Got to go now. Don't be upset.'"

Thad and Owens looked at each other grimly. That was it. Gerald's phone call had tipped Nikki, and she surely was on the run.

"Did she tell him where she was going?" Thad asked.

"I asked that," McKinstry responded. "She didn't."

"Did she say anything else?"

"Nothing about where she was going, but he did say she yelled something at the end that freaked him out. Not only what she said but how she sounded."

"What do you mean?" Thad asked.

"Well," McKinstry continued, "you know how, excuse me, those guys like him, I mean he's got gay written all over. They're real sensitive, like the canary in the coal mine?"

"Go on," Thad said.

"Well, he says that for stretches of time she wouldn't answer him. Says he was frantically trying to get her to say something, but she wouldn't. Like her mind wasn't on the phone. That's how he described it."

"But what did she say?"

"Well, he remembers exactly because, he says, she shouted it like she wanted to wake the dead."

"What was it, Corporal?"

"He says she shouted, 'Whore, I will cut out your heart!'"

"Say that again, Corporal?"

"She shouted, 'Whore, I will cut out your heart!' and then her phone went dead. That's exact. I wrote it down."

Thad and Owens looked at each other.

"That's it?"

"That's it, Sir."

"Anything else, Corporal?"

"No Sir."

"Did you get his statement Corporal?"

"Yes, Sir, I did."

"Submit it through channels. Good work, Corporal."

"Thank you, Sir." They rang off.

Thad looked at Owens, and his eyes asked the question. Owens lowered his head and moved the back of his fingers over the whiskers on his chin and cheek. They sat in silence, both knowing that Owens' mistake was looming larger. He should have ordered a simultaneous arrest attempt at Nikki's Bucks County condominium just in case she was there. They would have her. But Thad's deep respect for his partner and friend meant that he would never point the finger at Owens. In Porter's words, "a class act."

Thad just waited. Owens finally looked up, and when he spoke, Thad was surprised but pleased that Owens had moved past his mistake and had gotten into Nikki's mind. "Chief, the Congresswoman repeatedly referred to Señorita Loperena as, 'that Whore.' That's the only reference to 'whore' we have. So, we look for tickets booked any time after ten thirty last night in any name, man or woman, to Buenos Aires, probably with an open return."

Thad went cold. *Kill Isabella!* But what he said was, "Jesus, Owens! Took you long enough."

CHAPTER 39

Early the next morning Thad called Isabella.

"Why, Agent Pennock," Isabella teased, "such a surprise! It has been so long since I heard from you." In fact, it had been the previous day. Thad was now in the habit of talking to her regularly. They were interested in each other, intrigued. They both believed, without it being mentioned, that they would soon become lovers. Neither the distance that regularly separated them nor their different lives seemed to be impediments, at least not now.

Thad had called Isabella just before Nikki's anticipated arrest to alert her that Nikki was the primary suspect in Warner's murder. He had not wanted her to hear that first as a news flash. Now he had a more disturbing message for her.

"Isabella, listen to me, where are you?" he asked, no preliminaries, all business.

"Why, thank you, and I hope you are well too."

"No, please listen. Please tell me where you are." She caught the seriousness in his tone of voice.

"What is it? I am still in Buenos Aires, my home, right now in my office."

"We have not captured Nikki yet. We believe she is in disguise and – look, I don't want to alarm you – but there is some indication she may try to . . . " he paused, "harm or even kill you."

"Kill *me*?" she repeated, incredulity in her voice.

"Yes. Revenge for Wetherill, revenge for herself, who knows? We have some indication that she may have gone off the deep end, lost it. Maybe in her sick mind her life with Wetherill started to unravel because of your affair with Warner and maybe she blames you for what has happened. Who knows?"

"Well, that is ridiculous!" she said, offended.

"Of course it is," Thad responded, "but you're reacting rationally. She's not. She's sick, probably really sick, and possibly on a suicide mission. Is there some place where you could simply disappear for a few days until we capture her or at least get a better indication of where she is? She's not going to walk up to you and say, 'Hi, I'm going to shoot you.' She's a trained soldier. You won't get a warning or time to react."

"Thad, you are not serious are you?" She was trying to make light of it. "I am not going to hide someplace. If you knew she was on a plane to Buenos Aires, I might feel differently. But from what you tell me, you have a theory only. Am I right?"

"Owens agrees. He has a lot of experience."

"Still, it is a guess, isn't it?"

"Look," he said, more aggressively, "I can understand your reaction, but I think you have no choice unless you want to be reckless. My gut tells me this threat is real. I feel so strongly that you are in danger that if you won't agree to disappear some place where you really are safe, I'll be compelled to shift my supervision of the case to Buenos Aires and make sure the ANP takes this more seriously than you appear to be!" *No need to tell her I'm coming anyway,* he told himself.

"You will?" she exclaimed with pleasure. "Wonderful, perhaps she will not be caught for a week or two!"

"Isabella, I'm serious!" his irritation now evident in his tone. But she was irrepressible, which was one of her great attractions.

"You expected me to say, 'Oh, that's so much trouble for you. All right, then I will go into hiding.' Well, I am not going to say that. If it takes this crazy woman being on the loose for you to come to me, so be it!"

He was exasperated, "You are incorrigible! I've never met anyone like you."

"Really?" she said delightedly. "I shall assume that is a compliment. When can I expect you? I will happily meet your plane."

"You will not!" he asserted with all the authority he could muster. "If Nikki is coming for you, she has an eight-hour head start. You will stay inside until I arrive. There will be a policewoman with you in your home and police outside watching the house around the clock. I am making those arrangements as soon as we ring off. The men outside will stop anyone approaching your home, front or back. They will ask for identification and call you. You are to let no one in the house whom you do not know and trust. You will have food and anything else you need delivered. The police outside will inspect every delivery."

He did not utter his next thought, *if you refuse me, I'll have you locked up as a material witness. Holy Mother! Would that ever set you off!* Luckily, he did not have to play that card. She did not refuse, but instead answered cheerily, "An adventure! I shall call all of my friends and invite them over, so I can watch them being frisked!"

Thad just shook his head. She was not making it easy for him, but he had gotten her consent. Warmly, he said, "I do not want anything to happen to you. Keep safe. I will call you back to give you the specifics of the arrangements I make and the name of the ANP officer who will be in charge. He will call you directly. I will call just as I leave the States and again when I hit the ground in Buenos Aires."

"I cannot wait," she said, and then added, "and I'll show you my bedroom again. Just you and me and, I suppose, the nice policewoman to protect me." With a laugh, she rang off.

He stood looking down at the phone, plagued by a thought born of his experience. *If Nikki is really after you and willing to die, how the hell can I protect you?*

CHAPTER 40

The media had a field day with the sensational and unexpected twist in the search for the murderer of Taylor Warner. The well-orchestrated speech by Nikki to the press was still fresh in the minds of the public. She had made a convincing case by implication that the drug mob the Congresswoman was pursuing killed Warner while trying to kill her. Now, with a single startling announcement by the FBI, everything about the crime was turned on its head. Warner, not the Congresswoman, was the intended victim, and the alleged killer was not the mob but Wetherill's young chief of staff, who had seemed to be such a sympathetic figure. What the FBI did not offer was a motive.

But Wetherill did her best to supply it before speculation ramped up that she was complicit. Two hours after Porter's public announcement that the FBI was searching for Nikki, she met the press to make her own statement. Behind dark glasses she spoke of her devastation at being awakened at midnight by the FBI and told that the person who had been her right hand in performing her duties in Congress, and whom she had believed was a dear and loyal friend, was the suspected murderer of her beloved husband. "I can only guess that she had some irrational belief that she was helping to protect my reputation." It was a "nearly unbearable irony," she said. "Nikki is obviously seriously ill."

The Washington Post quoted her as saying, "I have lost the two people closest to me in a twisted tragedy." Into the microphones from behind those dark glasses she pleaded, "Nikki, if you can hear me, wherever you are, please give yourself up, and I will do everything I can to see that you get the help you need." One newspaper pronounced this, "under the circumstances, a remarkably selfless and generous gesture."

Some of the scandal sheets did ask the right questions. "Was Patterson acting alone?" was one lead story. Another headlined, "Was Patterson psychic?   Did she know Congresswoman Wetherill was not in the line of fire?" But every legitimate news source gave Wetherill a pass. Thad was incredulous. He called Owens from the airport as he waited for his flight to Buenos Aires to depart. "For Christ's sake, Owens, she's floating above it all! How can that be?"

"Because, Chief, she was in the car and got bloodied up, and, most importantly, there isn't a scintilla of proof against her.   And, Nikki is," he made quotation marks in the air, 'crazy,' right? So maybe she did try to kill them both, right? Wetherill would have all guns blazing at the first journalist that peeped over the barricades. And they all know it. Unless something more points to her, she's still the victim."

"Well God damn it," Thad said, "we've got to find that 'something.'"

CHAPTER 41

Hot and Easy Mary Ellen reached Buenos Aires on Tuesday at 2:00 PM. She had not booked a flight to Buenos Aires; rather, she had flown to Santiago, Chile, and from there had taken the long bus ride from Santiago to Buenos Aires. Owens had not thought of this.

The bus was smooth riding and well appointed, and she arrived feeling rested. She thought that even if somehow the FBI divined that Nikki was stalking the Whore, *and how could they,* the odds of them focusing on a different person flying from Chicago to Santiago and then taking a bus to Buenos Aires were odds she would take any day. True, she had booked an open return flight, which Owens had predicted, but she never intended to use it. *I plan so well,* she gloated as she alighted from the bus onto Argentinian soil.

She had challenges once in Buenos Aires. She needed the right weapon, the right disguise, and new papers for the escape back. She also needed a new name for Mary Ellen and a Canadian passport that she could use to register in a different hotel or boarding house. Although she would still look Hot and Easy, she did not want to be registered as the American Mary Ellen Duross anywhere after the first night.

Her problems were all solvable. They just required money, more money than the $10,000 she could carry with her outside the U.S. without declaration. So she had contrived to get additional funds into Buenos Aires another way. A bank in which she had deposited $50,000 was large, with branches in many cities. When she had reached the Chicago area, she had stopped at a branch, spent some time in the car adjusting her clothes, wig and makeup, and walked in. Forty minutes later, she put her hand on the smitten assistant branch manager's knee and thanked him profusely for his "wonderful help." She was visiting her best friend in Chicago, and the two of them were going on a trip to Buenos Aires. She was, "so afraid of carrying a lot of cash," but wanted to have it there in case she needed it. And, turning up her Hot and Easy burners, she wondered if he could possibly help her transfer $9,500 to some nice bank in Buenos Aires, as she was "just helpless" about such things.

Hot and Easy had gotten terrific service from him. So now she had nearly $20,000 cash in hand to finance her business in Buenos Aires, the $9,500 that the bank wired to a bank in Buenos Aires and $9,900 that she carried in.

Early Tuesday night, her first in Buenos Aires, Mary Ellen got to work in the streets buying information first and then services. By 2:00 AM she took delivery of the Canadian identification papers she would use while there. It was fast work, even the passport, because the forgers could use her Mary Ellen passport photo. By 3:00 AM she had her Bersa "Thunder Pro 9," an Argentinian semi-automatic 9mm handgun, a 2-½ inch suppressor, and three 17-round clips of sub-sonic ammunition, just in case she got into a firefight escaping. Only the middleman who delivered the weapon knew she had it, and he wasn't going to talk. She hadn't planned it this way, *but the bastard gave me no choice.*

The delivery took place at his sleazy apartment. Before she gave him the $1500 back-end payment for delivery, she told him she needed to test the weapon. Then she shot it into his pillow and mattress. The silencer impressed her, but the test infuriated him. He started toward her. "Hey you bitch!" he exclaimed in Spanish, that's my bed!" He was a big man and looked like he was going to swing at her. *You can't risk a commotion,* she told herself. "Stop!" She commanded, but not too loud. He kept coming.

She shot him twice in the face and moved out of the way as he collapsed without a sound. She bent over him and observed with satisfaction that the entrance wounds were exactly where she had aimed, the hollow point slugs, designed to flatten out upon meeting resistance, had not exited his head, and there was little blood. That meant the hardware package she had ordered was working as advertised. Her objective was a silent and very clean hit so that when the Whore fell, it would take those around her a few extra seconds to realize that she hadn't just fainted. Precious escape seconds. Looking down at the body at her feet, she smiled and thought, *Turned out to be a full dress rehearsal.*

Wednesday morning, after four hours of sleep, Hot and Easy Mary Ellen checked out of her hotel and found a modest, smaller hotel where she booked a room as Elizabeth Turner, a Canadian tourist. Then she took a taxi, giving the driver a route that took her past the Whore's home. She had planned a two-stage reconnoiter, the first by taxi and the second on foot, but she never got to the second. As her cab passed Isabella's home, Nikki was startled to see a policeman sitting in a police cruiser parked in front and two men in suits, one on the sidewalk in front of the house and one on the sidewalk directly across the street. They were scrutinizing and photographing every pedestrian.

How do they know? She asked herself. *How could that be?* But her surprise faded quickly. Her sense of mission was so strong, so clearly written in the stars, that she thought it inevitable, even appropriate, that knowledge of it should somehow leak into the world. She instinctively knew that Pennock was behind this and that he would be her adversary. *As it should be,* she told herself. She felt no fear, only a simmering anger that kept her on high alert. *Plan B,* she told herself, and ordered the cabby to take her to a street of shops. Hot and Easy Mary Ellen was going disguise shopping.

She announced to sales clerks, conversing easily in Spanish, that she was going to an elaborate costume party and needed two costumes that made her completely unidentifiable. She told them she wanted to look like a non-descript peasant from the countryside–straight gray hair, stout, round shouldered, calf-length ample skirt, smock with big pockets, wide-brimmed floppy hat, orthopedic shoes, and a big shoulder bag. For her second disguise, she wanted to be a man, maybe thirty-five, with a trimmed full beard, longish hair, slightly elevated shoes, baseball cap and loose-fitting jeans, shirt, and zipper jacket. The sales clerks threw themselves into these challenges, a refreshing change from the boredom of their routines. The make-up specialists in the cosmetic departments were inspired.

Viewing the results, Nikki concluded that no one would pay any attention to either the old woman or the man. Both looked unremarkable and uninteresting, and nothing like Nikki or Mary Ellen. Nikki's eyes danced with pleasure, and she laughed along with the sales clerks as together they admired their handiwork in the mirror.

She left the store in her man disguise, telling the clerks she wanted to practice walking, talking, and moving like a man and see whether people on the street were fooled by it. She had charmed them, and they waived "good luck" as she left. Carrying bags containing all the clothes not on her back, she walked straight to a store advertising passport photos. She knew she was taking a slight risk using the same picture for both passport and driver's license because those pictures are almost never taken at the same time. *But* she thought, *when are you ever asked to show them both at the same time?* She then returned to the hotel and practiced putting on and taking off the disguises.

Early that night she was back in the streets buying more information and making a new contact to whom she gave the passport photo. This time the fakes were more complicated. It was not until 1:00 AM the following night that she took delivery of an envelope containing a passport and Argentinian driver's license and credit card, all in the name Eduardo Parks, a citizen of Buenos Aires. This identity cost her $4,000. But now she was ready to accomplish her mission and safely escape.

CHAPTER 42

On Wednesday, while Nikki was in clothing stores assembling her disguises, Thad was a half-mile away meeting with Colonel Rodriquez Hernandez of the ANP. They were being briefed by Buenos Aires police concerning the murder of a street runner who acted as a middleman for all types of illegal transactions, including gun sales. The senior officer was saying, "It appears that nothing was taken from him, including one thousand U.S. we found in his coat pocket. There were four nine-millimeter casings on the floor and two slugs in the victim's mattress. Hollow point. The two other slugs will be in the victim's skull but the autopsy is not yet complete. The entrance wounds are almost on top of each other, which means that the gun is almost certainly a semi-automatic and the killer knows how to shoot. There are apartments above, below, and on either side of the victim's, but no one heard a shot, so in all likelihood the weapon is suppressed. Put it all together and you've got a quiet killing machine in the hands of a marksman."

"You said U.S. dollars?" Thad asked.

"Yes," the policeman said. "Unusual for him to be carrying around U.S. dollars, at least in that large amount, unless he had just engaged in a transaction in U.S. dollars. I'm guessing, but it is not unreasonable to conclude that the thousand dollars in his pocket was partial payment for the gun that killed him."

The Colonel asked, "Anything more?"

"Nothing, sir," replied the policeman.

"All right then, I will need to be kept up to the minute on anything further you learn from the crime scene or your investigation."

When they were again alone, Thad asked, "Any promising leads from your search for women with a United States passport who checked in to hotels in the city?"

"We continue to work on it, Agent Pennock. You would be surprised at how many there are."

"To the contrary," Thad said, "from personal experience I know that this is a wonderful singles city, so I will not be surprised no matter how high the number gets."

Hernandez smiled and looked at his watch. "Time to see the General." Thad nodded and followed him to the impressive office of General Varella, the powerful Superintendent of the ANP, whose reputation as a brilliant and effective crime fighter was worldwide within the law enforcement community.

As Thad entered, the General rose to his full six feet three inches, extended a long arm and large hand, and greeted Thad warmly. The thought ran through Thad's mind that great men with innate modesty are the greater for it. The General, youthful for his sixty-four years, with thick black hair, a broad face and large features, smiled and said, "Agent Pennock, I am happy to meet you. I have been apprised of your impressive career for such a relatively young man. So from one professional to another, welcome to Buenos Aires again." Thad guessed the "again" was the General's way of saying, "I do my homework."

"General, without exaggeration, your city is one of my very favorites in the world. To be here again and also have the chance to work with you is a privilege for me." The General laughed, eyes razor sharp but twinkling.

"You make too much of it. But now let us address your vexing problem. If you are correct that this highly trained Ms. Patterson is here and perhaps willing to sacrifice her life to kill Señorita Loperena, it is most serious. That she is in Buenos Aires is no longer in my mind pure speculation but a genuine possibility in light of the circumstances surrounding the murder of this small-time hoodlum last night. Therefore, I am willing to invest the time and resources of my department in a ruse of the type I have had some success with in the past. Perhaps this Ms. Patterson will be lured in."

"Please," Thad said. "I am very interested."

"It is simple," the General pronounced. "All effective traps are simple. The society columns Thursday and Friday will, as they normally do, chatter about the weekend social events including the races on Saturday and the celebrities and socialites expected to attend. Since it so happens that one of Señorita Loperena's favorite horses will be running in the Grade One stakes at Palermo, the word will go out that she will attend, which she would be expected to do." The General saw concern in Thad's expression.

"Are you proposing that we use her as bait in a trap?" Thad asked. "Yes and no Agent Pennock, and by way of explanation, I want you to meet someone."

CHAPTER 43

Both Wednesday and Thursday, Nikki spent time in the business centers of her hotels surfing the web for two stories, the FBI's search for her and the movements of the Whore. Wednesday night she found nothing current about Senorita Loperena, but when she hit CNN, the Washington Post and the Philadelphia papers, she found two stories about the missing Chief of Staff of Congresswoman Wetherill. In the first, the FBI confirmed they were still searching and otherwise had no further comment. But the second, a story quoting Congresswoman Wetherill, angered her. *I'm not sick! Is this how you defend me? You make me look pathetic!* For an instant she felt on the edge of a deep and dark sinkhole, but her guardian obsession was vigilant. The sinkhole vanished in a rush of feeling for Virginia. *So smart my love! Deflecting suspicion from yourself. Don't worry. My shoulders are broad. I can easily carry the burden for both of us!*

Thursday evening, as she searched for "Loperena" in the local newspapers, her heart suddenly raced. "Yes!" she said aloud, pumping her fist like a golfer who just sank a 25-footer.

The brilliant four-year-old stallion Torpedo Run, in which Maria Isabella Loperena owned a third share, was running in a Grade One stakes race on Saturday at the Hipodromo Argentino de Palermo, and the buzz was that she planned to cheer him on. *She is surfacing!* Nikki exulted.

Nikki spent Friday reconnoitering the Hippodrome. She searched for a spot where she could get close enough to Isabella and then quickly round a corner or drop into a stairwell, any structure that got her swiftly out of sight. After several hours studying the locations she thought Isabella might frequent, she narrowed her choices to three. The first was the private, glass-walled boxes overlooking the finish line from which the Whore likely would watch the races. She saw that these were protected by security and would be difficult to penetrate and hard to retreat from. She might not get a shot, let alone escape. The second was the paddock, where the Whore surely would go before the race for a last minute look at Torpedo Run and to confer with his trainer and jockey. Nikki was certain the paddock would provide the opportunity for a kill shot but just as certainly would result in her own capture or death. If she did not get away, so be it. She would sacrifice her life for Virginia if it came to that. But this was no suicide mission. Critical to the obsession that sustained her was the unquestioned assumption that she would have a future with Virginia, unquestioned because to question it would be to face the realization that it was impossible.

The third location was on the entrance steps from the street to the main hall of the Hippodrome. She initially rejected this spot as much too open with too many uncontrollable variables. But she kept returning there. She estimated the distance from curbside to the first entrance steps at about forty yards. There were three sets of eight low steps, and each step was wide and deep. As she climbed she took two paces on each step before mounting the next, and she thought that fifteen people shoulder to shoulder could fit on a single step. At the top was the entrance to the main hall. Once there, race goers walked straight ahead to access the grandstand. But the intriguing aspect of this entrance was its proximity to the cavernous gambling area.

Slots players turned right as soon as they entered the hall and walked to the steps leading down to the expansive, low-ceilinged, underground area housing over three thousand slot machines. It was a dimly lit, crowded maze brightened only by the colorful, blinking lights of the slot machines noisily devouring the wealth of the many gray-faced, dull-eyed players chained to the machines by greed, hope, or hopelessness. But the clincher for Nikki was that there were no security cameras that she could discern monitoring the entrance steps themselves. Camera coverage began in the great hall.

This location had another advantage, Nikki thought. The landing between the second and third set of steps was a perfect spot to wait for her prey. She was elevated enough to survey race goers approaching the steps from the ground and yet out of range of the surveillance cameras at the top. She could stand at one end of the landing appearing to be waiting for someone to join her. In fact, one or two other people were doing exactly that as she watched.

She worked through different scenarios, and suddenly her eyes sparkled as she hit upon a plan she thought would work for the kill. Then she ascended the remaining stairs, turned right, and walked down into the gambling area to work out the transition portion of her plot. Finally, she explored exit routes away from the front entrance and decided upon the exit closest to the paddock.

By mid-afternoon Nikki had planned out each minute detail. But she needed one piece of luck. The Whore had to use the main entrance, not a VIP side entrance. *I can't control that,* she told herself and dismissed the thought. Her adrenaline was leaking away, and she felt tired. *If they're protecting her at home, they surely will do so here. I won't know where they are or how many there are.* But she was confident she held the trump card. *They won't know me either.*

CHAPTER 44

S aturday was nearly perfect for racing. The humidity was low, the sun brilliant, and there was little wind. A gentle rain had fallen for three hours the night before, making the condition of the Hippodrome track fast.

At 3:00 PM a limousine with tinted windows pulled up to the curb in front of Isabella's home. Within a few seconds, her front door opened, and a uniformed policewoman stepped out, looked up and down the street, and signaled to Isabella to emerge and follow close behind her to the car. Two plainclothes agents at the curb looked in opposite directions down the street. There were few cars and fewer pedestrians. An unseen person in Isabella's home shut the door after her. Moving quickly to the car, the policewoman opened the door and helped Isabella into the back seat, closing the door behind her. The limousine moved away. Fifteen minutes later, it pulled up near the wide curb in front of the main entrance of the Hippodrome. It had to wait a few moments before a place opened at the curb. When it did, the driver pulled in and stopped. A sizable crowd was funneling into the steps from the parking lot, bus stop, and taxi and car drop-off points.

As it pulled to a stop, the limousine caught the eye of a peasant woman with an oversize shoulder bag who stood looking down from the second landing. Around her were several others also using the landing as a place to meet companions who had not yet arrived.

The peasant woman saw a man in civilian clothes wearing a jacket bearing the name "Torpedo Run" exit the front passenger seat of the limousine. The man surveyed the crowd through dark glasses and then opened the rear door. A striking dark-haired woman smartly dressed and also wearing dark glasses reached out a hand to him and began to climb out. The total body armor concealed under her clothes and wig made that maneuver awkward. To lower her head enough to clear the top of the door, she had to bend sideways at the waist, her back and neck stiff and straight. But Nikki missed this. She had known it was the Whore's car the instant she saw "Torpedo Run" on the man's jacket, so she immediately shifted her focus to scour the crowd around and behind her to detect agents or policemen who might be reacting to the Whore's arrival. She spotted two behind her at the very top of the stairs at the opening to the entrance hall. *Obvious place,* she thought. *They can watch everything on the steps.*

But the lovely woman had not taken three strides on the wide walk to the first set of steps before Nikki's focus was back upon her. The limousine pulled away. In the back seat, unseen by Nikki, Isabella turned to look out the rear window. Grave concern was etched on her beautiful face as she watched the lovely Lieutenant Dominquez gradually disappear into the crowd moving toward the entrance stairs. She whispered a prayer.

Nikki's eyes locked like lasers upon the Whore. She was curious to know this seductress who had so completely shattered the equilibrium of her life. As the pictures had forecast, she was tall and shapely with beautiful legs showing below a deep blue pleated skirt. She wore stylish open-toed shoes of the same color. The lace of her long-sleeved, high-necked white blouse fluttered at her neck and wrists in the slight breeze. A necklace of gold coins fell on shapely breasts, and gold coins hung from each earlobe. On her left wrist was a series of gold bracelets. She wore no rings on lovely fingers beautifully manicured. Her wide-brimmed hat was blue and white, the shades of her blouse and skirt. Her pocket book was the same blue. Large sunglasses hid eyes that, if Nikki could have seen them, looked nothing like Isabella's.

Picked apart and scrutinized, the features of Lieutenant Dominquez were unlike Isabella's, but together they resembled hers closely enough that a mind expecting to see Isabella would reconcile the differences, particularly when the eyes could not be compared. And Lieutenant Dominquez had carefully practiced Isabella's posture, walk, and gestures, all of which reinforced the deception. Nikki grudgingly admitted that the Whore was a stunner. *Well, a dead stunner before she ever reaches the top,* she vowed to herself.

Nikki watched her ascend the first tier of steps. It was not so crowded that there was jostling, but the pace was slow. Behind her sunglasses Dominquez scanned the crowd above her. She saw a plain, round-shouldered woman in a large hat, above and to her right, descending against the current of ascending patrons and appearing to be concentrating hard on the steps she was negotiating. Dominquez passed over the woman and continued scanning for any sign of a suspicious looking person, a person who was going to try to kill her.

Nikki's mind was racing! She had expected a bodyguard that would stick close to the target, but the man in the jacket was trailing five or six steps behind the Whore. He would have both the Whore and Nikki directly in his vision when the Whore went down! Not acceptable! She made a snap decision. *I must get him first!*

When Dominquez reached the first landing, she glanced again at the old woman under the floppy hat, who had by then descended to the same landing. The two women passed within eight feet of each other with three people between them. A few seconds later the man in the Torpedo Run jacket passed the old lady. His eyes were forward, constantly scanning the people around Dominquez ahead of him. He did not see the old woman, now below him, turn, move two paces towards the center, and begin climbing. She was three steps below him and still to his right.

All of Nikki's faculties were locked onto this man, the sole obstacle to the kill that was her mission. She assumed he was wearing a bulletproof vest, *but he is swinging his arms just enough,* she calculated. *Foolish!* Her right hand slipped into one of two slits she had made in the large bag hanging from her left shoulder and gripped the gun concealed there. Head down as if concentrating on the effort to re-climb the steps, the old woman had to visualize aiming the pistol. Anyone watching would have seen her bend even further forward with the effort of climbing, which caused her shoulder bag to tilt slightly and move a little further across the front of her chest. She took one more step, then there was a muffled "phit-phit," as two hollow-point rounds exited almost silently through the slit in the other side of the bag and smashed into the man's body on a slightly upward trajectory just behind and below his right armpit and just above the top of his concealed armor. The sounds of race goers talking and many shoes scraping concrete steps masked the suppressed reports.

The slugs took shards of bone with them as they drove into the man's chest from the side, expanding against the resistance his body gave. The internal damage was instantly mortal. Race goers right behind him saw the man's upper body suddenly lurch left, and then he fell to his left in front of a shorter, stockier man who abruptly stopped, halting those climbing behind him. They waited for the man to pick himself up. Some of those on the steps immediately above and to the sides of him also sensed or heard the unexpected movement and turned. Others, like the stoop-shouldered woman, continued climbing, either ignorant of the fall or disinterested. Dominquez, further up the steps, did not know that her companion, who was supposed to have her back, no longer did. She kept walking up.

The peasant woman measured the distance to the Whore, who had crossed the second landing and was now eight steps from the top and still perhaps twelve feet away from the old woman. *Too far!* Nikki quickened her pace to cut that to eight. Just then two women close to the man who fell uttered cries of concern, not yet screams of fear. The little scene was busy, but not yet panicky. *After all,* Nikki thought, *people do take nasty spills on steps.* Then Nikki saw that her target was aware of the commotion behind her. Dominquez stopped five steps from the top and turned to look back down at the spot where the man should have been. Because the concealed armor she wore prevented her from easily twisting at the waist, she turned her whole body almost completely around. The clutch of people surrounding the fallen man blocked her view.

Nikki knew that not seeing the man would tell the Whore that he was down, but the second longer it would take her to be certain of that was the extra second Nikki needed. She had to close, but still look like all she was doing was climbing to the entrance. As Dominquez completed her turn to face down the steps and begin searching for the man, the first real scream came from a woman at the spot where the man lay.

In the corner of her eye Nikki saw the Whore's facial muscles contract as she comprehended danger. Her eyes darted to her left toward the old woman, now only three steps down and six feet to the left and continuing to climb straight up at a normal pace among a few others still doing the same.

Dominquez's dark glasses masked her eyes, but her body signaled that she was looking right at Nikki, who could almost see her thought. *That same woman!* Nikki saw her body stiffen as she sensed what was about to happen. Dominquez started to open her pocket book and extract her weapon. At the same time she began to turn her head away to the right so the skullcap under her wig and not her vulnerable face would take the bullet. But the constraining neck armor she wore under her blouse required her to pivot her whole body and that took a fatal fraction of a second too long. Nikki visualized aiming her shots at the middle of the Whore's face and pulled the trigger twice, "phit-phit." The first bullet caught Dominquez' turning head in the left temple and the second struck something metallic but unseen with an audible "ping."

Nikki knew that the first bullet struck home, which meant that the Whore's brain was destroyed and that she was instantaneously dead. The impact caused Dominquez's head to jerk slightly, and her knees buckled. She dropped straight down to a kneeling position on the step below the one on which she had been standing but did not immediately collapse further. Her limp torso and head were held unnaturally rigid by her concealed armor. For an instant she looked like she was kneeling in prayer, except that her arms hung limp at her sides and her jaw and eyes were open. Then her upper body slowly toppled like a tree until her unfeeling face struck the shin of an amazed man a step below.

When her brain registered that the Whore was dead, Nikki involuntarily stopped in her tracks. Everything doable was done. She had nowhere to go. She had played out her future. She teetered on the brink of that vast, black sinkhole and was on the verge of disappearing into it. But her subconscious had had years of practice denying stark truths. It quickly devised a little more future for her. *Unless I escape back to Virginia, I've failed,* she told herself. The *back to Virginia* part, the impossible part, didn't have to be faced now. *Escape* was her future. All this took only a second. She began to climb again.

By the time screams from people around the fallen woman pierced the air Nikki had climbed the last few steps and gained the entrance hall. In her peripheral vision she saw the two policemen she had marked earlier, one now not six feet from her, move quickly down towards the commotion. Striding out without appearing to hurry, she turned right with some others and soon disappeared into the underground of slot machines.

CHAPTER 45

Thad, Colonel Sosa, the ranking ANP officer on site, and the others in the security operations room of the Hippodrome had been alerted by cell phone when the limousine arrived with Isabella's stand-in, Lieutenant Dominquez, and her back-up, Lieutenant Ruiz, both ANP officers. Since then, they had been waiting to see the disguised officers appear on the screens of their monitors, signaling that they had arrived at the top of the stairs.

The lovely Lieutenant Dominquez was the person General Varguez had wanted Thad to meet just before the General explained the trap he would set for Nikki. While he waited to see her on the monitor, Thad played back the scene in the General's office.

———

The General's door opened and a striking woman in military uniform entered and saluted. The men instinctively rose. Lieutenant Dominquez turned to Thad. She smiled and coquettishly said to him "Agent Pennock, what a great pleasure to meet you."

Fascinating, Thad thought to himself, *she has captured the essence of Isabella in her demeanor, movements, tone of voice, and with a hint of Isabella's features. With the right makeup, hairstyle and clothes she will trick the eye....* He looked at the General and said genuinely, "Lieutenant Dominquez is impressive."

The General smiled. "Our lieutenant is a great asset. She has had exactly six hours to look at pictures and videos of Señorita Loperena. Six hours! By the time she goes to the races Saturday imagine how closely she will resemble your friend."

The General had said, "Your friend" in the most solicitous way, signaling to Thad that he understood that preserving the life of Señorita Loperena was more than just a professional objective for Thad. *This is one good cop!* Thad thought admiringly. Turning back to Lieutenant Dominquez, Thad searched her eyes to understand her, a beautiful and talented woman in the prime of life about to knowingly risk her life in the most dangerous way.

Reading his thoughts, Lieutenant Dominquez said to him in a quiet voice, "I have played such a role twice before. I will have on a full skullcap that extends down the back of my neck, all under a wig designed to hide it. That will overlap a bulletproof vest with a full neck collar." She smiled, "What you and others will see will be a high-necked blouse. I will be protected down to my thighs, so that I will only be vulnerable to shots in the arms and hands, the mid-thighs down, and a direct shot in the face – temple to temple and forehead to just under my chin." She smiled easily as her fingers outlined the vulnerable frontal area. "If she uses the weapon we think she has, she will have to be very close to me to assure accuracy, so my life will depend upon my own vigilance."

Thad was struck by her professionalism, describing the parts of her body that will be exposed to a lethal assault when she intentionally walks into an ambush as coolly as if she were describing an armored vehicle. The General then spoke, "Lieutenant Dominquez will also be wearing sunglasses that can stop any revolver round, including the hollow point ammunition that killed the gunrunner we found last night. Movement of her neck and upper body will be restricted, but she has practiced moving as naturally as possible with that handicap.

Unless this Patterson woman simply does not care about preserving her own life, and her use of a very efficient suppressor suggests that she does, the likelihood is that she will shoot from behind or the side because that minimizes the number of eyes that would actually see her shoot. From those angles Lieutenant Dominquez will be protected from a lethal shot. Of course we will have a plain-clothes companion just behind her and police throughout the Hippodrome. Having said that, the purpose of this exercise is to draw out Ms. Patterson, so this back-up cannot be obvious and therefore may not prevent shots from being fired."

Impressed, Thad nevertheless found himself saying to her, "You are a very brave lady." He was surprised by her response.

"As the General knows Agent Pennock, what I am is ambitious. This is a fast track to promotions. I have had much training in spotting assassins. If she is in my line of sight, she will not get off a shot. If she is not, someone else will get her or the body armor will protect me from a kill. If I am shot at, I am confident it will not be where the bullet can kill me." *Such confidence!* Thad thought, *Necessary, I guess, or she couldn't do it.* But he worried.

Sudden chatter on the speakers in the operations room snapped Thad back into the present. The disturbance resulting from the first murder had only just rippled its way to the two ANP policemen at the top of the stairs when they saw the second, closer one. They voiced a terse alert into their radios and quickly descended against the flow of the crowd. They had heard no shots and had no idea what had happened or was happening except they no longer could see Lieutenant Dominquez.

As they moved down, a small wave of people that included the old woman moved up and past them. When they reached Lieutenant Dominquez, it took five seconds for them to elbow through the people trying to attend to her and another five to notice the bullet hole in her temple that gave no hint of the massive internal damage. It took another twelve seconds for one of them to reach Lieutenant Ruiz further down the steps and determine that he had also been shot. The two officers reported in a series of short, excited bursts over their radios, and their shocking messages, delivered through the speakers in the operations room, ripped like shrapnel into everyone there.

As he listened, Thad fought the bile rising from his stomach to his throat and reeled from the impact of the tragedy – the sudden, irreversible, irretrievable end of Lieutenant Dominquez's vibrant life. His mind's eye was scorched by vivid images of her body splayed on concrete steps and already decaying in a million imperceptible ways. Thad glanced at Colonel Sosa and saw his struggle for control. Sosa had known the suddenly dead officers well. Helpless to undo what had been done, both men knew from experience that action was the best antidote. Sosa forced himself into action, barking orders to bar all exits until the previously arranged screening procedures were set in place and to cordon off a three block perimeter.

Approximately 25,000 people were inside the complex. The previous evening the decision had been made that there would be no lock down or rush to evacuate if the murderer was on site. Thad had agreed. If patrons knew they could leave, panic would not likely set in. Besides, if shooting started, the fewer people around the better.

Colonel Sosa broke the men and women monitoring the security cameras into two teams. The larger team continued to monitor live activity looking for anyone acting out of the ordinary. The smaller group, including Thad, began to review tapes from the cameras closest to the Hippodrome entrance, the stairs leading up to the grandstands, and the stairs on the opposite side of the entrance hall leading down to the gambling hall.

A single wide-angle camera was mounted high on the wall opposite the entrance to the hall and covered the entire width of the last step up into the hall, giving a face-on view of everyone entering from the main entrance. At its widest angle, the camera's frame took in about ten feet on either side of the main entrance and so recorded those who immediately turned right towards the gambling hall and those who turned slightly left to walk across the hall to the grandstand staircase. The camera could also be zoomed in to a view comparable to standing five feet in front of someone entering the hall. At the wider angle the tape operator could isolate a portion of a tape and zoom in, but the picture got increasingly grainy and facial features were difficult to see.

The camera had been positioned at wide angle during the critical minutes. Thad and the Colonel were looking over the shoulder of the operator of the tape at the monitor in front of them. The man began speaking, "Colonel, if the killer came inside rather than going back down the entrance steps, she must be in the group that was caught by the camera during the few seconds it would have taken someone to walk from the step where Lieutenant Dominquez was shot to the top step. We can see our police starting to move down the stairs toward her, so Dominquez had to have been shot only a few seconds before that time. So if we back the tape up, say, ten seconds before we see them move, we can be sure that the killer is not yet within the range of the camera." He continued, adrenalin flowing, "Our killer will come into view of the camera within no more than, say, fifteen seconds after that starting point. You figure at most fifteen people across every two seconds, that's maybe seventy-five people max, most likely a lot less."

The Colonel ordered the video operators to get that fifteen-second slice of time onto two of the monitors in the room. The Colonel, Thad and one other policeman gathered around one, and the other three on this team around the second one. "All right," the Colonel said, "we look for people wearing clothing or carrying bags that could conceal a weapon or for someone acting suspiciously. Keep in mind, the murder weapon is no derringer. It will be long-barreled because of the suppresser and most likely was concealed when fired. You three focus on the right half of the screen, we will take the left. Freeze the frame every two seconds. If you see a possible on your side of the screen, let us know, and we'll keep the freeze. We'll do the same." In English he quickly summarized for Thad the gist of the conversation.

Three frames in, two members of the second team simultaneously said, "Freeze it!" With the identical screens on pause and the Colonel and all team members looking at the same frame, the Colonel asked, "Where, where Lieutenant Rico?"

"See the man on the right about six in from the end," Rico answered. "That long raincoat. Why a raincoat on a day like today?"

"Okay, slow motion. Let's follow him until he's out of that camera's range." In slow motion, the man in the raincoat, both hands in pockets, walked to his left towards the grandstand area. He was about to walk out of camera range when two young women, late teens or early twenties, ran up to him. As they did so, he turned towards them, obviously having been called by them. He pulled empty hands from his coat pockets and hugged each of them in turn. All three were animated and smiling. They walked out of camera range together. To the tape operator, the Colonel said, "Note the time, we may want to pick him up on the grandstand camera if we can, but for now go back to where we froze it and continue."

Three times more they went through the same procedure, as someone in the group wanted a closer look at a patron. *Four so far,* Thad thought to himself, *but only one a woman, and she was tall and thin, not at all like Nikki.* "Continue," the Colonel said, and the tape operator ran the tape for two seconds then two seconds more and froze it. In that time, another row of people had peeled away and a new one appeared at the top of the stairs.

Thad focused on a dowdy woman. "Colonel, look." She was on the right side of the steps turning to her right, indicating that her destination was the slots. She was round shouldered and looking down. She had caught Thad's eye because her dress and posture hid her.

"Run the tape another second or two," the Colonel ordered, "so we can get a better look."

"Could be," Thad said with anticipation. The hat, tousled gray hair and sunglasses hid most of the woman's face. Her dress was ankle length, plain and full and over it she wore a generous smock. Her feet were in half-calf socks and thick-soled orthopedic shoes. Her actual figure was completely masked. A large shoulder bag hung from her left shoulder and she was clutching it with both arms. *Could shoot right through the bag moving it hardly at all.* Then Thad noticed the clincher. "She's wearing gloves!" he exclaimed to the others. His mind raced. *No powder burns with the gloves. Perfect get-up to disguise the person and camouflage the shooting.* Icily calm now he said, "That's the shooter Colonel. That has to be her.

CHAPTER 46

In the toilet stall furthest from the entrance to the ladies room, Nikki quickly and quietly removed her sunglasses, gloves, hat, wig, dress, smock, sox and shoes, revealing a V-neck cotton blouse and a slightly too tight short skirt. From one large pocket of the smock she took a pair of square-framed, white sunglasses and wedge-heeled canvas sandals. From the other she retrieved a purse containing a make-up kit, wallet and passport. She reached into the bag and removed a blond wig that had served as a nest for the silent, deadly gun still lying there. She put the wig on and adjusted it over her short hair as best she could without a mirror.

Finally from the smock she took an envelope with the words "out of order" printed in rough hand. She stuffed everything but her purse and its contents into the shoulder bag. She flushed the toilet and opened the stall door and looked out. *Here is where I need to get lucky,* she thought. From her careful reconnaissance, she knew the trash bins in the slots area had covers limiting the size of items that could be dropped in. Besides, there was too much risk that someone would see her disposing of a perfectly good shoulder bag. She did not want to be noticed doing something out of the ordinary.

She put the bag down on the toilet seat lid and licked the envelope saying "out of order." She opened the stall door inward toward her and stuck the envelope to the outside of it. She stepped out and pulled the door shut. It opened slightly when she removed her hand. *Will have to do,* she told herself. She left that ladies room and made her way across the expanse of the gambling hall to another on the opposite side. There, she spent a precious but practiced three minutes adjusting the wig and applying her Hot and Easy makeup. She was Mary Ellen again in looks, but the passport slipped to her in the middle of the night identified her as Elizabeth Turner, a Canadian.

She left this second bathroom and wound her way back through the banks of ringing slot machines and up the stairs into the natural light of the main hall of the Hippodrome. Knowing that security cameras were everywhere, she tried to move as naturally as possible. *Now to get out of here,* she said to herself.

CHAPTER 47

"Okay," the Colonel said, "roll it so we can follow that woman until she's out of camera range." As he watched her purposefully move, Thad's confidence increased.

"She's moving towards the gambling hall," he said. "Probably going to ditch the gun and her clothes." He looked at the Colonel. "Are there other cameras we can pick her up on?" The Colonel turned to the operator in front of them, "Can we pick her up?"

"Sure," he said. "The first one will be a camera just inside the entrance of the gambling hall. She should be walking right toward it." He flipped a few switches and up came the tape from another camera. "This is camera 14," he said. "See her, walking right toward it." The Colonel and Thad watched in silence until the woman walked under this camera and out of view. *She moves like she knows where she's going,* Thad thought.

"What's next?" the Colonel asked the operator.

"Let's try camera 16." Again, he flipped switches. Up came a tape of what was clearly a bank of slot machines to the left and a wall to the right. Within five seconds the woman in the big hat came into view at the bottom of the frame walking away from the camera. Before she disappeared beyond the top of the frame she turned right and disappeared into the wall.

"Where does that go?" the Colonel asked sharply.

"That's a ladies room, Colonel."

"Is there a camera inside?"

"No, Sir."

"Why the hell not!" the Colonel barked to no one in particular. "Keep that camera going," he ordered. He turned to address another officer. "Lieutenant, get some people down to that ladies room fast. Get some women officers in there. Comb the place, every trash can, every stall. We are going to find ourselves a murder weapon and lord knows what else."

He looked at his watch, "What time did she go in?" he asked the operator of the tape. The man squinted slightly at the screen then looked at his watch.

"About eight minutes ago."

"Damn," muttered the Colonel, "she won't be there." Then he looked back at the screen. "Fast forward until you see somebody come out and then freeze it." The operator went through the exercise for what he determined was fifteen minutes, fast-forwarding and then stopping each time someone left. In that time twelve women came out, but the old lady in the hat was not one of them. "No surprise," the Colonel said under his breath. "She sure as hell is not in there, but I bet most of her clothes are."

At that instant, the Colonel's radio crackled. "Colonel, this is Lieutenant Alvarez. There are three women in the bathroom right now. We are certain that none of them is the woman we're looking for. None of them remotely looks like the picture of Veronica Patterson. But we have a shoulder bag stuffed with clothes, and we have the murder weapon. It's a nasty looking piece."

"Seal the bathroom," the Colonel barked. "Leave things where they are, and we'll get a crime unit in there pronto. Thank you, Lieutenant." Those close to him were able to hear the exchange, but he summarized it for Thad. Then he and Thad turned back to the monitor to review the women who came out within seven minutes after the old lady went in.

Thad quickly narrowed down the possibilities to two. "Can we pick up these two women on any other cameras?" Thad asked.

"Should be able to," said the operator, "but this one," pointing to the screen, "we saw her go in, and she looked the same as she does here. Must be the other one." Thad resisted because the other one, while about Nikki's size, was so hot and easy looking, so unlike Nikki. Then, recalling the times he had thought Nikki tried to look as plain as she could, it hit him. *Of course she's going to be the opposite!*

He pointed to the screen and said, "That's Nikki, Colonel."

CHAPTER 48

As she crossed the entrance hall to the stairs to the grandstands, Nikki looked at the commotion to her left around the entrance stairs. Police and medics were rushing about, and a crowd with their backs to her stood at the top of the steps, looking down. She slowed her walk as she watched, mimicking the actions of a person who knew nothing of what had occurred. *Appear curious a minute,* she told herself. *Don't hurry.* After several seconds of this, she turned her eyes back to the grandstands entrance and resumed her normal pace. Reaching the main level she did not hesitate. She walked the length of it to the stairs that led down to the paddock area and, beyond that, an exit.

As she approached the paddock, the horses for the next race were arriving, watched by their owners, trainers, jockeys, and a number of spectators and bettors who wanted to get a last minute look before placing their bets. Things were normal here far away from the main entrance.

She walked around the outside of the paddock, attracting lustful stares from nearly every man she passed. She could see the exit about forty yards ahead of her. As she approached it, two armed Buenos Aires policemen ran by her to the attendant at the gate and engaged the man in hurried conversation. The man nodded and gave up his position to them. *So*, she thought, *they will screen anyone leaving*. She was icily calm. Rather than approach immediately, Nikki stopped, turned, and looked at her watch as if she were waiting for someone. She did not want to be the first person to the exit. She wanted to see what the procedure was going to be. A middle-aged man carrying a newspaper and daily racing form approached the exit and was stopped by the policeman. Nikki watched as they spoke to him briefly. He handed them the newspaper, removed his wallet and showed identification. Then the man raised his arms away from his sides, and one of the policemen patted him down. She smiled to herself. *Due process must be a little different here.* Then she thought, *I'm going to be sure that cop enjoys patting me down.*

The other policeman put a small camera, which Nikki had not noticed before, to his eye and snapped a full-face picture of the man. The first officer gave another command that Nikki could not hear. Then, she saw the man nod and unbutton his shirt cuffs and push his shirtsleeves back to his elbows. He held both arms out, hands open, and one of the policemen shone a greenish light over both of his arms and hands. *Powder residue search*, she thought. She smiled. Her mind's eye went back to the long gloves now stuffed into her shoulder bag behind the toilet. *Planning!* She thought about her wig. It had been inside the bag with the gun to mask the shape of the gun and may well have some traces of gun powder in it. That had been a calculated risk. *But they'll never think to shine it on my wig.*

As she watched the policemen's routine, alarms were sounding in her head. *This stop and search is too organized.*

What am I missing? Now she was angry. Someone else was planning well too.

The first officer told the man with the newspaper he could move along, and he turned to the next person approaching the exit. *Pretty nice,* he thought. She was smiling at him through her sunglasses, hand on one hip. "Hi guys, what's going on?" she said easily in quite good but clearly second-language Spanish. Then without prompting, she put out her arms and said, "You really going to search me?"

The first officer gave an appreciative grunt. "No, Señorita," he said, "she is," gesturing toward a blocky policewoman who was just approaching the group.

"Oh," Nikki pouted in disappointment.

"Identification please," the officer said, holding out his hand. Smiling at him, Nikki moved closer than his request required and held up her passport. He looked at the picture and then at her. "Remove your glasses please."

"Sure," she said, doing so and looking right at him with her Hot and Easy look.

"Please look at the camera Señorita Turner," he said, gesturing to the policeman to his left, who efficiently snapped the picture.

"Call me Liza, the other sounds so old. What's your name handsome?" The officer did not reply. He handed the man with the camera the passport, and that man took a picture of it. Miguel then nodded to the policewoman, who gave Nikki a quick but efficient tap down. All the while, Nikki smiled and looked right at the first officer as if to say, *this is the part you should be doing.*

Miguel then said to her, "My name is Miguel, but it is best that you simply call me Officer. Tell me why you are here Ms. Turner?"

"I'm sightseeing, *Officer,*" she exaggerated in good humor. "Don't know much about racing, but I wanted to see this huge slots hall. I like gambling." She smiled.

"When did you arrive?"

"Oh, about an hour ago," she lied.

"Why are you leaving so soon?"

"I said I wanted to see it, not live in it," she laughed and threw her arms open, "And now I've seen it, and I'm off to see something else."

"Hold your arms out in front of you with palms down, Señorita Turner." She held them out but only half way to horizontal so the green light played down on her hands and arms and well away from her wig. When finished, the other policeman looked back at Miguel, shaking his head sideways. Miguel nodded and the other officer handed her passport back to her.

Miguel then asked, "Why are you alone, Ms. Turner? Surely a pretty girl like you should have companions." She was ready with the answer most consistent with her Hot and Easy persona.

"Best way to get to know the natives."

"How long will you be staying in Buenos Aires?" Miguel asked.

"Just playing it by ear. Every time I guess how long I'm going to stay someplace, I'm wrong. Maybe tomorrow, maybe the next day. But," – Hot and Easy again and looking squarely at him – "I'm open to staying longer, Miguel. Oh, sorry, I mean 'Officer.'" Her eyes wide, she made the statement an invitation and the mistake on purpose.

Miguel laughed good-naturedly, and Nikki knew she had hooked him. She was going to make it out. Miguel nodded to the other policeman who then took Nikki's left hand and stamped the back of it with a black ink symbol. Miguel said to her, "Show that stamp if you are stopped again by a policeman. Enjoy your stay. I suggest you not go around near the front entrance to the racetrack. There has been an incident there, and you will be in the way."

Nikki feigned a curiosity she thought an innocent would exhibit. "Something exciting I should see?" she asked.

"You wouldn't get close enough to see anything," he replied. "You would be directed away."

"O.K.," she said and sauntered saucily through the exit. Once through she looked back over her shoulder. "Bye-bye, *Miguel*," she said teasingly and waived to him.

Four minutes later the radios of the three police officers crackled and came to life. It was Colonel Sosa. "The gun, clothing, wig and shoes of a disguise have been found in the gambling hall ladies room closest to the main entrance. The killer is most likely an attractive younger female, shoulder length hair probably blond, and wearing a V-neck blouse and tight, short skirt. She may not show powder residue. A black and white picture from a surveillance camera will be circulated immediately." Miguel and the other two looked at each other and then around to the exit and beyond. The brooding, plain policewoman offered, "I will go after her?" Miguel looked hard beyond the exit. Then his face relaxed into a slight smile. *No way*, he thought to himself.

"No," he answered and turned back looking for another woman fitting the description.

It took another five minutes for a copy of the photo from the surveillance camera to reach Miguel. He quickly compared it to the picture his partner had taken of Elizabeth Turner. "Shit!" he said softly. He immediately radioed to Colonel Sosa and gave him the time the suspect had gone through his checkpoint and her passport information. The policeman with him ran to the security room with his camera and showed the photograph of the woman and her passport to Colonel Sosa and Thad. *Elizabeth Turner,* Thad said to himself. Colonel Sosa turned to a nearby lieutenant. "Notify every hotel and point of departure from the country."

CHAPTER 49

Nikki did not return to the hotel where she was registered as Elizabeth Turner. Instead, she had the taxi drop her at Hotel Dolmen in the financial district. She walked across the lobby to the elevator bank and, once in, pressed the button for the 5th floor. As the elevator rose, she took from her small purse a hotel key card. When the elevator door opened, she walked to room 525, looking both ways to confirm that no one could observe her. Before going to the Hippodrome that morning, she had checked in as Buenos Aires resident Eduardo Parks, gone to the room and changed into her peasant disguise. She was certain the fact that Eduardo Parks resided in Buenos Aires would not arouse undue suspicion. Obviously Mr. Parks would be entertaining a lady.

Nikki slipped the key card into its slot, heard the click, and opened the door. It was not yet 5:00 PM. She made two phone calls. The first was to LAN to book a flight from Santiago, Chile through to Chicago in the name of Mary Ellen Duross, leaving Santiago at 4:00 PM the next day, Sunday. She had no doubt that the police would soon trace Elizabeth Turner back to her twin, Mary Ellen Duross, and she wanted it to appear that Mary Ellen was escaping via the same route she took to enter Argentina.

Her next call was to United Airlines to confirm the round-trip reservation for Eduardo Parks made the night before, leaving tonight, Saturday, from Buenos Aires at 10:00 PM and arriving at 11:00 AM eastern time tomorrow at Dulles International. She did not intend to use the return ticket, but a one-way ticket might have invited attention.

Nikki spent the next hour transforming herself from Hot and Easy to Eduardo. She removed all her clothes and the wig, revealing her own inch long hair. She showered, scrubbing off all makeup. *Goodbye, Mary Ellen and Elizabeth,* she said to herself. She dried herself and applied a man's deodorant. Then, methodically, she glued on the close-cropped beard covering her upper lip, cheeks and chin. She then donned a man's wig, the color of which matched the beard.

Satisfied that the facial hair appeared natural if not studied too carefully, she put in tinted contact lenses to change the color of her eyes to brown. Then, to complete the facial transformation, she glued on thicker and more expansive eyebrows. For an instant, she regretted having a nose scaled to her face, and, therefore, slightly small and refined for the disguise. But she would not dwell on anything she could not change. Next she bound her breasts and dressed comfortably for the flight in a loose fitting shirt, baggy dungarees and modified elevator shoes. Finally, she put on a jacket and baseball cap and slipped the straps of the already-packed knapsack through her arms, settling it on her shoulders. Then as Eduardo Parks, she left for the airport.

It was just dark, and as Nikki watched the lights of Buenos Aires flow by from the back seat of the cab, the face of the pretend Eduardo Parks smiled a pleased smile. She sank into the seat and, for the first time since her triumph, permitted herself to relax. She looked down at the back of her right hand. Most of the black ink stamp had washed off when she showered. Only a light impression remained. *The police put their stamp of approval on me when I was the very one they were looking for!* She envisioned the ANP scrambling to cover all flights and all border crossings between Argentina and Chile when they got word that Mary Ellen Duross had booked a flight the next afternoon from Santiago.

She wanted to cheer aloud and resisted the impulse. But there was nothing to prevent her from gloating in silence. *I cut the Whore down right under their noses!* She imagined how proud Virginia would be of her when she heard the news. *Twice! Twice I've killed for you! And this time, right under their noses!*

The Parks identification papers had been expensive but worth it. They were expertly done, and the concept was clever. There was a real Eduardo Parks who lived in Buenos Aires at the address on the driver's license, and the passport number was the passport number of the real Eduardo Parks. The other precaution her $5,000 had bought was reasonable certainty that the real Parks was currently in Argentina. He would be surprised to know that, as far as the United States and Argentina immigration services were concerned, he was about to take a plane to the U.S.

Chapter 50

Most of the night and all the next morning Thad was with the working group of the ANP. The search that was mobilized impressed him, but so far there was no hint of Nikki's whereabouts other than the booked flight from Santiago. He had pressed General Varella for a total blackout of information on the incident at the Hippodrome so that Nikki would not know that the woman she shot was not Isabella. But it was now noon and with no clear idea where Nikki was, even what country she was in, the counter-pressure for disclosure was too great.

The General called a meeting in his office. He was cordial but firm. "Agent Pennock, to this point I believe we have appeared credible in taking the position that we are continuing to track down leads but have not yet identified a particular suspect, and for that reason, wish to keep everything confidential, including the identity of the victims. However, just before you arrived, I received a phone call from our President. Quite frankly, she is concerned about the ANP appearing inept. This matter has turned out very badly. And if I continue to suppress the facts, we will be accused of trying to cover up a botched job. Which," he added looking squarely at Thad, "it was. As to the identity of the woman shot, we are out of time. Lieutenant Dominquez's family wishes to hold services for her and see her properly buried. The ANP wants to honor both of these fine officers as the heroes they are. So, in half an hour, we go public with their identities and status as ANP officers. That will lead to immediate questions as to what they were doing and why.

"So I am going to lay it out. And that will mean identifying Señorita Loperena and revealing that our main suspect is Veronica Patterson, the fugitive Chief of Staff of Congresswoman Wetherill." The General concluded, "I want our citizens to know that Lieutenants Dominquez and Ruiz courageously gave their lives in the line of duty to protect the life of an Argentinian citizen."

Thad responded, "General, were I in your shoes, I would do exactly what you propose. I ask only one thing."

"Rest assured I will do it if I can," the General responded.

Thad continued, "I believe that Patterson only pulled the trigger because she had been fooled. She believed she was killing Señorita Loperena. To that extent your plan did work. She is unbalanced to say the least, and after your disclosures to the public, it will not be long before she hears that she failed in her mission. That will surely set her off in some significant way, and she might well try again, particularly if she is still here in Buenos Aires. Given what has happened, I have no doubt that Señorita Loperena will be as cooperative as possible, but she will be in as much or more danger than she was before."

The General looked at him somberly. "Please understand, Agent Pennock, Lieutenants Dominquez and Ruiz gave their lives in her place. So, for us, her life now has the value of three. At this moment, there is no life in Argentina except perhaps that of our President that is more precious." Thad felt a mixture of relief and chagrin. The General's response forced him to admit to himself that his own concern for Isabella's safety was personal, not professional. The General had gotten it exactly right. He silently asked Lieutenants Dominquez and Ruiz to forgive him.

As soon as he left the General's office, Thad called Isabella. He had not yet seen her, despite being in the city for several days. He instinctively knew that was the right thing to do, and she had accepted it without complaint. He was there to coordinate with the ANP in protecting her and capturing Nikki. His most recent call to her had been a brief one right after the failed effort to trap Nikki in the Hippodrome. Since then he had been focusing totally on tracking Nikki down. He felt jinxed. The botched attempt to arrest Nikki and now this disastrous failure! *She's smart and she's lucky,* he told himself. *Bad combination!*

As he anticipated, Isabella had been horrified to learn that two people had lost their lives in her place. At least that is how she expressed it. He tried to comfort her but knew that she would have to work through it largely by herself. On the phone now she sounded a little better. Thad alerted her to the upcoming news conference. Her love affair with Warner would surface, and she was likely to be judged harshly by many. She could have cared less. Her mind was on the beautiful lady and vigorous man she had known for the brief time it took a limousine to cover the distance between her home and the Hippodrome. She could still feel the touch of Lieutenant Dominquez's hand.

"I want to see you," he told her. "I will have a little time after the news conference and before my flight back this evening. Will that be okay?" "Thank you for asking," she replied, "but you did not have to. I need you to hold me and tell me that I am not the cause of so many deaths."

Nikki's plane landed at Dulles on time. Eduardo Parks breezed through customs and headed directly for a taxi stand, delaying only long enough to go to the bathroom. Tired from the trip, Nikki had automatically looked for the ladies room, catching her mistake just as she was about to enter. She took a cab from the airport to Union Station. There, she bought a ticket on the 1:00 PM Acela to Philadelphia, arriving just after 3:30 PM. Emerging from Penn Station, she hailed a cab and directed the driver to Ableman's Storage. *This is the tricky part*, Nikki thought, always uncomfortable when not totally controlling events. She needed Marvin not to be on site, or, if he was, not to be in the vicinity of Unit 217.

There was no sign of Marvin. Nikki swiftly exited the cab and unlocked and opened the unit door. The interior was as she had left it. She moved to the back left corner and threw off the blanket covering the two duffle bags. Safely out of the cabbie's sight she unzipped them enough to confirm that the cash was still there. When she originally packed the bags, she had been surprised that they could hold $900,000 in $100 and $500 bills.

She lifted the heavy bags and carried them out to the taxi. She asked the driver to pop the trunk. Had his passenger been a woman, the cabby would have jumped out and handled the bags himself. Instead, he stayed in his seat and pulled the handle that unlatched the trunk. Nikki lifted the bags in, closed the lid, shut the garage door, and got into the cab. She asked the cabby to drop her at Penn Station in Philadelphia.

As Eduardo Parks, Nikki booked the next train to New York City. She thought she knew whom to contact there to buy herself a new identity. This time, very new. She had worked it out. She would alter her appearance so drastically that she could walk the streets and not be recognized. She could be with Virginia.

While waiting to board the train, she bought the Washington Post, the New York Times, and the Wall Street Journal. She figured that if there was news out of Buenos Aires, one of these might have it. Seated on the train, she went through the papers cover to cover, but found no reference to the shootings. While she found that to be curious, she was too exhausted to dwell on it. She settled back in the seat, closed her eyes, and let the muffled rumble of the heavy wheels rolling on the tracks gently rock her to sleep.

The conductor's announcement of the Newark stop woke her, and she dozed the fifteen minutes from there to New York. She still felt tired, very tired. She got into the cab line outside the entrance to Madison Square Garden and, with drooping eyes closely watching the two duffle bags and one small suitcase at her feet, waited her turn. Eduardo Parks, citizen of Argentina, booked a room in the Marriott Courtyard at 866 Third Avenue. Nikki wanted nothing fancy, basic services and little attention from staff. That hotel filled the bill. She went straight to the room and took off Eduardo's clothes, wig and beard. Then she showered and dropped onto the bed. She plunged into a deep sleep. But, several times during the night she was half awakened by the unsettling intimation that something vast and horrible loomed just over the horizon.

CHAPTER 51

T had looked at his watch. Ten minutes until he boarded his flight from Buenos Aires to Dulles. He was confident that General Varella would protect Isabella from harm and that she would take seriously the precautions the General would insist upon. He felt very close to her.

———

They had spent two hours sitting on her sofa and quietly talking. She had needed to talk about her relationship with Taylor, her feelings of guilt in connection with his death and Camila's death, and now the deaths of the two brave officers whose presence in the limousine she could still feel. Thad, in turn, spoke of his failure in bungling Nikki's arrest, letting her slip through his fingers in Philadelphia and slip away again from the Hippodrome. They knew that neither of them had caused these deaths, but they had been participants in the chain of events, and they knew that had they each acted differently at a particular point in time, the course of those events would have been altered and some or all of the victims would be alive.

Then without conscious effort their conversation shifted to the joyful things in their lives. Isabella spoke of her love for her son, her excitement at starting a new clinic for autistic children in Cordoba, the success of the three already in place, and her passion for horses. Thad spoke of his attachment to the rolling hills of Chester County, of the exciting challenges of his job, of his belief that he was making a contribution to a better world, or at least not making it worse, and of his gratitude for knowing and working with fine people like Owens and Lew Porter.

This interlude drew them closer than if they had made love. They did not notice time speeding by and suddenly Thad had to leave or miss his flight. "When do you come to New York?" he asked. "In three weeks," she answered.

Thad bent to her and kissed her on the lips. This first kiss was not passionate but tender. After a moment Isabella drew her head away from him enough to look into his eyes. Then she closed her eyes and slowly bent forward again until their lips just touched, and they remained that way.

Finally, Thad drew back and rose. "I have to go." She stood up close to him. They laughed into each other's eyes. He drew her hand to his lips and kissed it firmly, closing his eyes to augment the sense of touch. She smiled and said, "Thank you, Agent Pennock. Keep safe."

"You will be well protected," he said. "I'm confident of that. See you in three weeks."

———

Thad moved to the departure gate and got in line. His cell phone rang. The call was from colonel Rodriguez updating him and confirming what they suspected. The LAN flight on which Mary Ellen Duross had booked a seat to return to the U.S. had left Santiago without her. Thad had become concerned when there was no sign of her trying to pass through any of the border crossings between Argentina and Chile in time to make her booked 4:00 PM flight. But there was nothing else to go on, so agents in Santiago were planted at the airport at the departure gate on the assumption that she had slipped across the border in disguise. Now Rodriquez was confirming that she had not tried to board the flight.

With grudging admiration, Thad acknowledged that they had been duped. ANP agents were now gathering and reviewing the passenger lists for every plane that had departed from Buenos Aires for the United States within the prior twenty-four hours. It would take time to track down all of the several hundred people, so they prioritized the list, focusing first on American women returning to the United States. The last category was male Argentinian residents leaving for the U.S. with a return flight.

CHAPTER 52

Nikki's alarm startled her awake at 7:00 AM. Hungry, she ordered room service. When the knock on her door came, she entered the bathroom and, with the door cracked open, called to the person bringing her food cart that she was showering and to please leave the food and the bill in the hall. "Yes, of course," the male voice said. She waited a moment and then retrieved the cart from the empty hall.

When she had eaten, she showered and put on Eduardo Park's jeans and shirt. As she had planned, with her inch long hair and bulky clothes, she looked like a female bohemian – at first glance not Nikki or Mary Ellen, and surely not Eduardo. She decided to risk going to the "business center" on the first floor. She was anxious to get news from Buenos Aires, and she couldn't understand why there had been none the day before. She had an uneasy feeling that something wasn't quite right. Since the shooting she had puzzled over the unexpected metallic "clink" her second shot to the Whore's head had made. *That was a ricochet off metal. No doubt a metal headpiece under a wig,* she concluded. She thought about the

Whore's clothes and realized that they covered her entire body except for her face, hands, lower legs and feet. Not even her neck showed. And she remembered the stiff way the Whore had collapsed. All that added up to full body armor. *Could that be?* She asked herself. *What does it mean?* She needed to hear some news.

The business center was small and empty. She rented some computer time by giving her room number. She intended to search for the name Maria Isabella Loperena on websites for Argentinian newspapers, beginning with La Nacion. She never got to the second paper. La Nacion had a prominent headline that unleashed searing pain behind her eyes! "Assassination Attempt Foiled But Two Agents Slain." She read with frenzied haste, the palm of her left hand pressed to her temple to counteract the pressure building there. Soon she became aware that she was screaming aloud and forced herself into silence.

She jumped to her feet, quickly opened the door and stepped outside as hotel personnel alarmed by the shriek ran toward her. Nikki extended one arm in a "stop" gesture and pressed her other hand to her breast. "I am so sorry," she said, in a choking voice that was not hard for her to produce. "I just got an email that my sister has been seriously injured in a car crash, and I lost it." She swallowed a sob. "It's O.K. Please, I need a few minutes alone." The employees who had responded to her screams murmured sympathies and gave her space. She ducked back into the business center hoping that none of them would try to be a Good Samaritan. No one entered.

Despite the pounding in her head she made herself focus on the screen again and read the full story.

In a brief statement at 1:00 PM, General Varella, Superintendent of the ANP, disclosed that the man and woman shot down yesterday on the steps of the Hippodrome were veteran officers of the ANP. He said the official silence until this point had been necessary to insure that nothing would compromise the chances of apprehending the killer. The General said that four days before the shooting, the FBI, (Federal Bureau of Investigation, an agency of the United States government), had alerted the ANP to a possible assassination attempt on the life of Señorita Maria Isabella Loperena, a prominent resident of Buenos Aires. The suspect was Veronica Patterson, an American being sought for the murder in the United States of Taylor Warner, the husband of United States Congresswoman Virginia Wetherill. The General introduced Agent Thaddeus Pennock, Chief of the FBI's Washington, DC office, who is leading the FBI task force seeking to apprehend Ms. Patterson.

General Varella said the attempt on Señorita Loperena's life was thought to be related to her romantic involvement with Mr. Warner. Ms. Patterson is the primary suspect in the killing of Mr. Warner, and the FBI had some indication that she would make an attempt on the life of Señorita Loperena. That led to an elaborate ruse involving Lieutenant Dominquez who looked much like Señorita Loperena.

General Varella reported that Lieutenant Dominquez had volunteered to impersonate Señorita Loperena at the Hippodrome races last Saturday. The ANP planted stories in the society sections of several newspapers reporting that she would be at the Hippodrome on Saturday. The intent was to draw the suspect into the open. The ruse worked but ended tragically.

The killer, a graduate of West Point Military Academy, an Iraq war veteran and a skilled marksman, had sophisticated close-range stalking and shooting skills. The shooting took place on the steps leading to the Hippodrome. Lieutenant Dominquez wore body armor under her clothing and a wig, and the only part of her body that was exposed to a mortal wound was the front of her head. The suspect's bullet struck her in the left temple and killed her instantly. Lieutenant Ruiz was wearing a bulletproof vest, but the two bullets that killed him entered his body under his right armpit above the vest and penetrated into his chest cavity. The General added that these two officers were highly trained and fully appreciated the risks of this dangerous assignment.

The authorities on site immediately began examining security camera tapes, and within ten minutes of the shooting, they identified a suspicious grey-haired woman wearing a large hat, sunglasses, a loose-fitting print dress and smock. She carried a large handbag. These clothes, a grey wig, the murder weapon, and the handbag were found in one of the ladies restrooms in the gambling hall under the Hippodrome. The handgun with a suppressor had apparently been concealed in the handbag, which had openings on each side. According to the General, the killer probably slipped her hand into the bag through one opening, gripped the gun and fired from inside the bag.

She first shot Lieutenant Ruiz, who was several steps behind Lieutenant Dominguez. In the confusion caused by his falling she managed to shoot Lieutenant Dominguez and slip into the gambling hall undetected.

The General said that within twenty minutes of the murders, the ANP had identified and had a photograph of the suspect, who entered the country as Mary Ellen Duross from Chicago, Illinois, USA. The security personnel at the exits were alerted with a description and within minutes had a photograph in hand. Upon receiving the photograph, security personnel at the paddock exit, who were already checking everyone leaving for identification and for gun powder residue, immediately alerted the ANP that the suspect had cleared that checkpoint approximately five minutes before. The suspect escaped, presumably by taxi.

The General added, "We believe the suspect is no longer in Argentina, but has slipped out using another disguise and other identification. However, until that is confirmed, we will continue looking for her here. We have reason to believe that Duross is really Veronica Patterson and that there is no actual Mary Ellen Duross."

He concluded, "Señorita Loperena, the intended victim, is unharmed but devastated, as are all of us, at the loss of our brother and sister officers. They fell in the line of duty as courageous heroes, and we intend to honor them as the heroes they are." The General took no questions.

Nikki stopped reading, but was in a fury. *I can't believe it! I can't believe it! I was tricked!* Her mind traced the moments at the Hippodrome from her first sighting of the woman in blue until her last glance as the woman fell. *I should have seen it!* For several minutes she could do nothing but shift back and forth between the two thoughts. *She's alive! I was tricked! She's alive! I was tricked!* Gradually the reality that the Whore was alive began to take on its original significance. *She's alive! I have a mission!* And she began to feel good, very good.

In that instant Buenos Aires became nothing more than a false start. She would do it right this time. *Patience,* she told herself. The plastic surgery she had planned to undergo to keep her hidden in the open would now serve the additional purpose of getting her close to the Whore to insure a kill. And she would simply wait for the Whore to come to her. It would be far easier to create an opportunity to kill her during one of her trips to the States than try again to slip in and out of Buenos Aires undetected. *Why didn't I see that the first time?* She asked herself. *Too eager, too hurried. Not this time,* she vowed.

Nikki shut down the computer and walked from the business office playing the role of someone coming to grips with news that a beloved sister was badly hurt. She returned to her room, gathered the critical items she would need for the subterranean chapter of her life about to begin and left. She knew how to disappear. It only took money and she had plenty of that.

———

Eight hours after Mary Ellen Duross failed to show up for her flight from Santiago back to the U.S., the ANP finally discovered that Buenos Aires resident Eduardo Parks was in two places at the same time. The Eduardo Parks that had flown to the U.S. was traced through Delta and Amtrak records to Dulles, then Philadelphia, then New York, and through Marriott records to the Marriott Courtyard where Nikki spent the night. When agents arrived, Parks had not checked out. They ignored the "Do Not Disturb" sign and stormed the room. It was empty. In the bathroom they found a fake beard, a wig, and lift shoes. Their dusting showed Nikki's fingerprints were everywhere.

CHAPTER 53

Nikki could not resist taking one big risk. She yearned to call Virginia, to hear her voice. Many times she had relived the moments when she was last in Virginia's library looking into Virginia's eyes, feeling the touch of her skin, and hearing her say, "Dear Nikki, you exposed yourself to great danger for my sake. I will do everything in my power to protect you." She had to hear that voice again, had to receive Virginia's praise and gratitude again. *And*, she told herself, *she'll want to know I'm safe.*

It was 10:30. Wetherill lay in bed reading. Her private line rang. She looked at the number calling. It displayed "Unknown." She was puzzled. This was the confidential line for her own calls, and she gave the number out sparingly. Not more than twenty people had it. She considered not answering but curiosity won out. "Who is this?" she asked not in a friendly tone. "Me, Virginia! It's me!" Nikki exclaimed, her voice charged with longing and anticipation. "It's so great to hear your voice again!"

Ever since Agent Pennock advised her that she had become a person of interest, Wetherill had been concerned that her phones and mail might be monitored or that she was in other ways the object of high-tech surveillance. Her greatest fear was that Nikki would contact her and say or do something that would reveal her complicity in Taylor's death. *It wouldn't take much,* she imagined. *A few wrong words out of her mouth.* So, she had devised and rehearsed a script she hoped would prevent that catastrophe. And now it was show time.

"Nikki, my god! Have you gone crazy? First Taylor and now these people in Buenos Aires! Why are you doing this? What possessed you? Did you want to hurt me? Did you think you were helping me? Stop this madness! Turn yourself in, and I will make sure you get the right kind of help. Nikki, do you hear me, do you understand me?" Virginia abruptly ended the call so Nikki had no chance to respond, but she kept talking into the dead line just in case her voice could still be monitored by a bug in the house or by god knows what. She would take no chances. "Nikki? Nikki are you there? Hello? Nikki answer me." She feigned waiting for a response. Then she dialed Thad and recited the conversation word for word, adding at the end, just to be sure, "She just hung up. I'm sure I screwed it up, but when I heard her voice, I just couldn't help it. I let her have it. Damn it Pennock! To hell with getting her help! I wanted to reach through the phone and grab her neck and throttle her!"

Thad heard himself half-heartedly murmur something like, "Yes, I can imagine," and added, "I'm going to start the process of tracing that call, but I don't have any hope it will bear fruit. Should she call again, try to say things that will keep her on the line and get her to tell you where she is or how you can contact her, if you can. Better yet, say you'll meet her someplace."

"Yes, I'll do that," the Congresswoman replied. But Thad had no illusions. He realized that Wetherill's little tirade was probably calculated. *The last thing she wants is for us to capture Nikki.*

When she realized the line had gone dead, Nikki stood holding the prepaid, throwaway phone only a few inches from her ear. She tried to assimilate Virginia's words and assign to them a meaning consistent with her intense feelings, tried to understand why Virginia had so abruptly ended the call. She fought against the hurt for a long time. Then she heard herself say aloud, "This can't last forever," and she had no idea why she said it or what it meant. She had a foreboding, and for just an instant she felt a surging helplessness during which her mind's eye caught sight of the edge of a black vortex. But the last thing her subconscious would permit was an emotional break with Virginia. That was a death sentence. She concluded finally that Virginia didn't mean those words. *For some reason she had to say them to protect herself.* That explanation was enough. Just enough.

CHAPTER 54

Nikki started with the contact in New York who had provided her with Mary Ellen's passport and other identification. Luckily for her he hadn't changed his phone number. "I'm a customer of yours," she said. "You prepared papers for me. I need advice." They agreed on an isolated place to meet that night.

Despite the darkness he recognized her instantly. "Jesus lady! If I'd known it's you, I wouldn't be here. You're too hot to touch!"

"There's no risk to you," she countered. "I just need some information." He hesitated, looked around and then back at her.

"What information?" She told him. "Good idea," he said, "Your face is everywhere." Again he looked around and then at her. He seemed to be making up his mind. Finally, he nodded. "Okay, I may know a guy who may know a guy. Cost you $500 for me to do the research." She paid him.

"Call me tomorrow at three and use a minutes phone" He walked away.

On the call the next day he gave her a telephone number. "The guy expects the call pronto. Ask for 'Jeb's great uncle.' Just say that. Don't say who you are because I didn't tell the guy and he won't want to know. Nobody wants to know more than they have to. If he says, 'No, this is Sam's great uncle,' stay on the line and he'll run the conversation. If he answers any other way, hang up. Throw the phone away after. There may be other calls. Use minute phones for all of them."

"I've got it," she said.

"And don't mention me to anybody," he added, "I didn't help you."

"I understand." The man was silent. "Anything else I should know?" Another silence. Finally he said, "I can't believe you iced two cops in the middle of a crowd at a racetrack no less and got away. Fucking unbelievable."

"Wasn't me," she lied. "Are we through?"

When she called the number and gave the code, the male voice on the other end said, "This is Sam's great uncle. You're on a throw away phone?"

"Yes."

"You're looking for plastic surgery?"

"Yes."

"What do you want done?"

"I want my face to disappear." There was silence for five seconds.

"That will be a big number. What can you afford?" She wasn't about to bid blind.

"I can afford it if it's a fair price." Another pause.

"Call me back at six tomorrow night," the voice said. "And don't make plans for later tomorrow night. In the meantime get three thousand dollars in cash. Can you make that work?"

When she called the next evening at 6:00, the same voice gave her directions to a school bus stop and told her to be there at 11:00 with the money. She got to the deserted stop five minutes early. The nearest streetlight was half a block away, so from the road she could not easily be seen sitting inside the shelter. At 11:00 a car approaching in the far lane slowed as it passed her. She watched it turn around at the next cross street, slowly return, and stop beside her. The passenger window lowered and she heard the driver's voice. "I'm Sam's great uncle. Did you bring three thousand?" It was not the voice on the phone.

"Yes," she replied.

"Okay. Get in."

"Where are you taking me?"

"We'll drive around. Talk in the car. I'll drop you back here."

When she was in, the man held out his hand without looking directly at her. She gave him the money. He pulled away from the curb keeping his eyes on the road. "All right," he said. "Look straight ahead and not at me. Don't volunteer any information. Just answer my questions. Got it?"

"Yes," she said, liking what she heard. *He wants to avoid recognizing me. Good! All business and anonymous.*

"Tell me exactly what you want."

"I want to change my looks as much as possible." He said nothing. *That didn't surprise him,* she thought.

"You're talking about spending half a million and it has to be cash. Can you do that?" It was more than she expected but not by much and would leave her enough to live on for some time.

"Yes," she said, feeling competitive about this intentionally minimalist conversation, "if it buys me what I want."

"When can you have the money?"

"Tomorrow." Out of the corner of her eye she saw his involuntary nod. *Impressed, aren't you buddy,* she said to herself. She congratulated herself for having the foresight to liquidate her investments before killing Taylor. *Great planning girl!* Now she felt entitled to be more than a passive listener. "For that kind of money your doctors better be good. I'm not looking for a face lift."

"Hah!" he snorted. "Open the glove compartment. There are two photographs right on top. The light in there is good enough for you to see them." As she examined the photos he added, "The lady with the dirty blond hair is 'before.' The other is 'after.'"

Nikki's astonishment trumped her intent to act the cool customer and before she could stop herself she exclaimed, "Wow!"

"How's that for a face lift?" he said smugly, then continued without waiting for her to comment. "Can you get yourself to Key West?" She dropped the photos and shut the glove compartment. *Plane is out of the question,* she thought. *Train or bus that long is too risky. Can't do it in a day. I'd have to rent a car and stop someplace. All too risky. There must be another way.*

"Can someone get me there?"

He didn't hesitate. "Five thousand plus expenses for a guy to drive you with a stopover at a motel. He'll book a single for himself. Get you in. Then stay at another motel. That way you don't have to come up with a name or be seen." He paused and then added, "Except when you stop to pee. But understand, he won't want to know you or want you to know him, so you say as little as possible and don't look at him. That means two days in a car with a guy and you don't look at each other or talk. Can you do that?"

"Yes."

"You have to have all the money with you. In suitcases.

"How do I know he won't just dump me and take the money?"

"You don't really, but you're not the only one who wants a new face. In the long run we do better sticking to business. That's all I can say. Take it or leave it."

"Will it be done in Key West?" she asked.

"Not unless you want your face to look weed-whacked. You'll have to take a trip. It's included. I can't tell you where. If you don't know, you can't slip up. It's that simple. And the transportation is unconventional and not very comfortable, so I hope you're not a complainer."

Nikki was relieved. She had wondered how a well-equipped facility in which skilled doctors performed complicated surgery could be kept secret in the U.S. Now she knew. *Has to be a small plane or fast boat,* she thought, *so I'm going somewhere in the Caribbean.* "I'm in," she said. "No complaining."

As it turned out, it was a fast boat and Sam's great uncle was right. The trip was uncomfortable.

CHAPTER 55

When she arrived and the blindfold was removed, a soft-spoken middle-aged woman with a reassuring smile in a nurse's uniform with a name tag that said "Marianna" told her that she was in an apartment that would be her home for four months. She added that the apartment was part of a hospital complex in which sophisticated plastic surgery was routinely performed and that to protect the privacy of all of the "clients on the grounds," including herself, her movement would be restricted and she would be accompanied by a staff member when not in the apartment. "No other client will see you or know you are here," she said. "Indeed, no one on the staff, including the doctors, knows anything about you, including your name, so we will call you 'Hilary' until you select a permanent name. That's best for everyone concerned." She held up a wristband bearing a number and the name 'Hilary' and fastened it around Nikki's left wrist. "Please do not remove this," she said, "it is so helpful to the staff."

Is it possible *they don't know who I am?* She wondered. *Does it matter?*

Then Marianna gave her a general description of the hospital layout and grounds, "so you will not be bedeviled by curiosity for the next four months." As Marianna described it, her apartment was in a large five-sided, single story white stucco building with red tile roofs set within a ring of trees and gardens all enclosed behind a high pink stucco wall. Ten apartments like hers lined each of four sides of the pentagon. They all had a sitting room, bedroom, bathroom and covered patio looking out to the gardens and the wall seventy yards away. The fifth side and the interior space housed operating rooms, post-op recovery rooms, an intensive care unit, radiology rooms, examining rooms, laboratories, pharmacy, kitchen, laundry, staff dining room, doctors' offices, an IT room, storage rooms and all other operational functions. Her room, like every other part of the building that she would be in, would be kept immaculately clean and sanitized.

Marianna then walked Nikki through the apartment and showed her where everything was and how everything worked. The furniture was comfortable but not elegant. There was an elliptical exercise bike, a rowing machine, a television, a satellite radio, a list of books she could order from a central library, and an intercom through which she could communicate with a service desk. She had no phone or computer or other device by which to interact with the outside world. Meals and laundry would be delivered to her room.

The covered patio was walled on the sides to prevent contact with the occupants of the apartments on either side of hers and was closed off at the end by a high but airy wrought iron gate that was locked but admitted the sights and smells and sounds of the gardens beyond. "The gardens will look very inviting to you," Marianna said, "but the doctors do not want you there. While your face is healing, you must avoid the sun. The patio will permit you to enjoy shaded light and fresh air." The door to her apartment from the interior of the building was also locked, and she would have no key.

Nikki got the picture. She would live in strictly enforced isolation. She wouldn't see other patients and they wouldn't see her. *Fine with me,* she told herself. After Marianna left, she lay in bed hoping to get a little sleep before dawn *wherever I am.* She guessed Cuba although she had seen nothing to indicate Cuba, or any other country for that matter. Cuba made sense. It was secretive and officially closed to Americans. She did the math. Forty apartments at half a million dollars each every four months meant a nice flow of U.S. dollars. *I'll bet the Cuban government takes a big chunk,* she decided. *A little mud in Uncle Sam's eye.*

She had been the only passenger on the nighttime trip from Key West. The powerful speed boat with a crew of two and Nikki had pounded along in the darkness at a high speed with no running lights, bouncing over one wave and slamming its hull down on the next for several hours. She had been required to stay in the small cabin of the boat as they approached a black mass of land, and her trip to the hospital from the shore, although comfortable, had been in the windowless back of a van. At the time it had seemed a little too James Bond, but she understood that it was the only practical way, short of drugging her, to guarantee that nothing she actually saw or heard would identify which of the several island countries the speed boat could have reached in the time she was in it. *For all I really know,* she told herself, *they could have driven the boat around in a big circle and I'm somewhere on the coast of Florida!* She was impressed with the planning and execution so far. *I think they know what they're doing.* She thought of the surgeries she was facing. *They better!*

Her first two days were filled with tests. She had a complete physical examination including a blood work-up. Additional blood and tissue analyses were done to predict her susceptibility to infection and scarring and blood clotting. These were followed by a full body scan and additional scans of her face that provided high-resolution, three-dimensional images of her bone and cartilage.

On the fourth day Nikki sat in front of a computer screen as a technician scrolled through the many different "looks" that could be created from the various combinations of changes the tests showed could be made. Nikki was mesmerized. For fifteen minutes the computer sequenced through image after image, subtle changes cumulating into large ones, until suddenly the person she wanted to be was looking at her. "This one!" she exclaimed. "I want to look like her!"

It was a beautiful face to be sure, but she thought many of the faces she'd already seen were beautiful. There was something else, something more. Her conscious thought was, *she's so fresh!* Her subconscious saw a woman with no shame.

The technician called in the surgeon in charge of her case, and Nikki watched the two of them double-check the technical data to insure that this particular face was within the parameters of feasible change. It was. The doctor turned to Nikki, whom he addressed as Hilary. "You're certain?" he asked. "This will require multiple surgeries and mean a lot of healing pain." She didn't hesitate.

"This is the one. I don't need to look further. I want to look like this!"

"You have twenty-four hours," the doctor said evenly. "That's the protocol."

The next day she and the surgeon and the technician met again. Her enthusiasm had if anything increased. She was adamant. She pointed at the screen. "I am absolutely certain.

Can you really do it?" The surgeon ignored the question. Instead he gestured toward the screen and asked, "What is her name?" as if the image was a person. Without hesitation Nikki shot back, "Oh, its Christa. Her name is Christa."

From the day Nikki had been raped, the name "Christa" would periodically float unbidden into her mind, linger awhile, and then vanish. She didn't consciously summon it this time either. It just presented itself. "It sounds fresh," she told him.

Then the name "Cairns" popped into her head and with no prompting she added, "And her last name is 'Cairns.' She's 'Christa Cairns' because she looks fresh and strong."

The surgeon studied her. After a moment he nodded. "All right. Now your work starts. Look at me please, not the screen. You'll have the rest of your life to look at that face." When she pulled her eyes away from the image and toward him, he held up an index finger and said, "This is important so listen carefully. From this moment until the day you leave here, you must answer only to the name 'Christa Cairns.'" He looked at her wristband and gestured, "We'll change that as soon as we're finished here. 'Christa' is what I will call you and what everyone here will call you. You must train yourself not to react to the name you had before you came here, and the best way to do that is to think of Christa Cairns not as your name but as you." Nikki felt a wave of relief so strong that she didn't understand it.

CHAPTER 56

Over most of the next fifteen weeks Nikki felt as if she were recuperating from one ten round boxing match after another. She was bruised and swollen and either in pain or sore. She endured rhinoplasty to shape and sharpen her nose, a butt lift that raised her buttocks and thinned her thighs, blepharoplasty that gave her eyes a more oval shape, and Botox injections that altered the look of her mouth and lips. Her cheeks were hollowed to accent the curve of her cheekbones. Her teeth were capped to enlarge them, producing a fuller smile. She had a series of injections stimulating melanogenisis, giving her complexion a darker hue. Through a combination of surgery and chemicals her fingerprints were altered. She dropped fifteen pounds and practiced lowering the pitch of her voice and more precisely articulating her speech. Contact lenses changed the color of her eyes to brown-green. Her hair grew out to shoulder-length and was styled differently and was now nearly black. Her eyebrows were darker and slightly thickened, and different make-up accented her more angular face and darker complexion. When the swelling and bruising and temporary scarring finally disappeared, she was a Latin beauty, Italian or Spanish and perhaps tinged two generations back with the color of a Moor.

The day before her scheduled departure her physician gave her a last, meticulous examination, and when he finished, he sat back and studied her for a long minute. Then he smiled and said, "Congratulations Christa, do you realize that you will be unrecognizable even to those who knew you well? They would have to look at you full face close up and," he emphasized, "be told who they were looking at. Then perhaps their minds might connect the dots. Short of that unlikely event, you are a different woman."

He meant of course that she looked like a different woman, and he had no idea that he had granted a more elemental permission. His words caused an intense emotion to well up and break over her like a wave, confirming the conviction that had gradually grown within her during long days in front of her mirror watching the transformation progress. *A different woman!*

As the wave receded, she felt its powerful undertow draw out and carry away from her deepest recesses layer after layer of tension accumulated over years of battling to keep her demons caged. Tired air rushed from her lungs until she had only enough breath for a single choking sob of gratitude for a relief she felt but did not understand. Then she drew a new, long breath that filled her lungs with the freshest air she could ever remember, and her heart pounded and her invigorated blood carried that freshness to every cell of her body. She felt lightened and unburdened and a smile formed on her mouth and danced in her eyes. Her clueless doctor basked in it and smiled back. "Why, you're welcome," he said.

That evening she sat on her small patio until well after sunset enjoying the sensation of being totally in the present.

Until darkness hid the shapes and colors of the gardens beyond her gate she marveled at their beauty and at the clarity of her vision. After dark the bird sounds and flower scents still rode to her on the back of the breeze.

When finally she dropped onto her bed, she fell into a deep sleep undisturbed until just before dawn when the dream came. She saw herself. She saw her stepfather extend his strong hand and grip her wrist and pull her to him. She watched herself. Separate, detached. She watched every horrible detail of those long-ago moments. She was a witness, not the victim. When she awoke, she remembered the dream and remembered that it was not just a dream, and she felt compassion and sympathy for Nikki. And she felt no shame.

Nor did she feel guilt about murdering four people. She was now an observer of those past events as well. They happened but they were disassociated from Christa's feelings and therefore not available for a moral audit. And as for revenge against Maria Isabella Loperena, she barely gave it a thought. *Revenge for what?* She asked herself. *Being the lover of a married man?*

She took a shower and then stood naked and dripping before the full-length mirror in the bathroom. She could not get over the beauty of the woman in the mirror. Not just the face, but the figure as well. That woman was strong and fresh and independent. *I don't need anyone,* she gleefully told herself. She thought of Virginia. *Particularly her!*

CHAPTER 57

There had been many long days when Nikki had been bandaged and uncomfortable and capable of nothing but sitting as quietly as she could. On those days television kept time from standing still. She initially thought she could get a clue as to her whereabouts by finding a local news station. "Havana Evening News," something like that. But the stations, all thirty-five of them, were American and included the major networks, cable news networks like CNN, Fox News, and MSNBC, some sports networks and movie channels.

She regularly watched the news, curious about what was being said about her and the effort to locate her. But what she saw and therefore what the world saw, was a Nikki shaped by Virginia's media campaign. Time and again, tall and sleek and imposing, Virginia looked out at Nikki from the TV screen and held forth about the "barbarous murders" and Nikki's "obvious madness." Nikki was "ill" and "dangerous" and "pathetic," a cruel and thankless creature who had betrayed the Congresswoman's trust and repaid her generous mentoring by robbing her of the husband she loved. Not to mention murdering three other people.

For the first eight weeks or so of her confinement, Nikki continued to be confused and hurt by this barrage, but it didn't turn her. She excused Virginia, telling herself that this was Virginia's way of diverting suspicion that she had colluded with Nikki. But as time passed and every glance in the mirror confirmed that she could actually become Christa, her intense devotion to Virginia bled out. The veil dropped, and she saw Virginia in a stark light. Virginia wasn't just diverting suspicion from herself. She was attacking Nikki to enhance her political career. *She doesn't care a fig for me,* Nikki realized. *I'm just another pawn on her chessboard!* By the time her doctor pronounced her "another woman," she was seeing Virginia's media performances through Christa's eyes, and Christa was offended and furious.

As she dried her lovely body on that last day at the hidden hospital she made up her mind. She looked in the mirror and said aloud, "So, Congresswoman Virginia Wetherill, do you enjoy telling the world who I am and what I did? Well get ready. Two can play that game. The difference is you can't hide."

CHAPTER 58

Owens knocked on the doorframe even though the door was open. He always did as a courtesy. Thad looked up, "Anything?" he asked.

"No," Owens said.

Thad shook his head in frustration, "Christ, it's been nearly four months! All we have is her car at O'Hare. As far as we know she hasn't tried to contact the Congresswoman again. She's just vanished. Not a whiff of a scent. She's making us look foolish, Owens. We've got money on the street. You'd think we'd get a snitch coming forward." He shut his eyes, took a breath and then looked again at his friend. "Well?"

The professor sat down and rubbed his cropped beard with the knuckles of his right hand. "Okay, maybe she killed herself when she learned she got fooled in Buenos Aires, but I don't think so. We'd have a body, and to me she's not suicide material. Thing is, we know she's got plenty of money so we can't count on a snitch with this one. She can hide herself and tweak her looks. Probably has a good new disguise and good new papers. She surfaces when she's ready, not before. Maybe she has already, and we just don't see her."

"Big help," Thad said glumly. "Enough to drive a drinking man to more drink."

They sat quiet for a minute. Owens then added, "Wetherill's been out there every other day talking to the press about how deranged Nikki must be to keep killing people, and how her own pleas for Nikki to turn herself in and get help aren't working and maybe putting her own life in danger. She's totally committed to the 'Nikki's-gone-nuts' theory. It's her ultimate defense if we get Nikki and Nikki sings."

"Well?" Thad repeated, "Is Nikki just going to fade into the sunset and live happily ever after?"

"Nope," Owens answered. "Nothing happy-ever-after about that one. She's driven, and we have to assume that Isabella is still in her cross hairs. It's a good thing you've been able to persuade her to stay put."

At this Thad shifted uncomfortably in his chair and slowly he said, "Ah, well, I'd say we have a problem there. She's coming to New York."

Owens' brow furrowed. "Oh boy," he said quietly. Thad knew that "Oh boy" meant Owens was really concerned. It was as close as he ever got to swearing.

"She feels she's postponed her fundraising trips as long as she can, and if she doesn't make an appearance soon and shake the trees, her contributors will find other causes. She feels the kids she's helping need her too much for her to 'cower in a corner forever,' as she put it. I think she feels guilty about the deaths and her atonement is to do everything she can for the kids even if that puts her at great risk." He paused, "Hell, maybe because it does."

"When is this visit?"

"When what?" Thad asked back, too deep into his concern to catch the words.

"When is she coming?"

"Week after next. Best I could do was extract a promise to keep as low a profile as possible and maybe Nikki won't know she's here. The sick irony is that Isabella walking the streets is the one thing that could draw Nikki out. It did once. Scares the hell out of me."

There was a silence. Then Thad shifted topics. "You think this time Moretti will honor the subpoena from Wetherill's subcommittee? Will he show next week?"

Owens answered, "So far his lawyers can't get this one quashed, so if he doesn't show, he's in contempt. He doesn't want to look like he has something to hide, so he'll show."

"Yeah, he'll show and make a statement about how he's being hounded and persecuted unjustly and that he personally would like to answer the questions and that his lawyers have advised him that he should take the fifth and that he reluctantly will follow their advice, etcetera, etcetera. He's smart and smooth. I'll bet he'll sway a few people his way." He paused for a moment, thinking. Owens kept his attentive silence.

Thad began again, "After all her hype about him, the Congresswoman won't get a thing. I can't figure what she thinks she'll gain. It'll take the wind right out of the sails of her investigation. Unless. . . Could she have something on him? Wouldn't we know?"

Owens shrugged, "Guess we won't have to wait long to find out. Should be quite a show." Again they were silent. Finally, for maybe the fifteenth time Thad asked the question that had bothered both of them for months.

"Owens, how the hell are we going to land the Congresswoman? Makes me sick to think she'll skate." Owens had nothing helpful to say, so, as usual, he said nothing.

CHAPTER 59

Thomas, one of Leonard Moretti's lieutenants, walked across the veranda of Moretti's home and approached his boss, who was speaking with three of the people whom Eleanor and he had invited for cocktails. It was a beautiful evening. The bright, sinking sun elongated shadows, and there was just a hint of a breeze.

"Excuse me, sir," Thomas said. "May I have a word?" Moretti had given standing instructions that when he and his wife were entertaining, he was not to be interrupted unless it was very important. He wanted their social guests to see them only as social creatures. He wanted everything observable about the Moretti's life to contradict the incessant rumors that he was a mob boss. *This better be worth the interruption,* he thought.

He excused himself with a gracious smile and an apology and walked to his study. Thomas followed and closed the door. Both men stood. Moretti looked squarely at Thomas and waited for him to begin. Thomas reached into the inside pocket of his suit coat and extracted an envelope. He did not immediately offer it to Moretti. Instead he said, "This was given to Clayton at the gate twenty minutes ago by a woman who described herself as a freelance reporter but declined to give her name. She asked that it be taken to you promptly 'because,' she said, 'it may bear on Mr. Moretti's appearance before the House subcommittee this coming week.' Those were her words according to Clayton. We have screened it for poison and explosives. It's clean. Clayton got the license plate of the yellow cab transporting her in case you wish to follow up."

Moretti said politely, "Use the letter opener on my desk." Thomas walked to the desk, picked up the letter opener, and slit open the top of the envelope. Then he handed it to Moretti, who took out the note it held, inspected the front and back, and silently read it.

Mr. Moretti, you do not know me. I know you are expected to testify before Congresswoman Wetherill's subcommittee in a few days. I have information I believe you will want to consider before you appear. I do not expect you to see me personally, but I will be at Tangerine at 232 Market Street in Philadelphia, tomorrow at 1:00 PM. I will be sitting alone, wearing a dark green suit, and I will have a white flower in my hair. Please send a trusted lieutenant. I will not object if he is wired; indeed, I hope he is, as I want no errors in his report of my message. I will not be wired, but you need not trust me on that. I will not ask your man to say a word, and I will not mention your name.

Moretti read the brief message twice. "Do we have her on camera?"

"Yes sir," Thomas replied. He walked to a computer screen on a table near one corner of the room "She arrived at 6:03," he said. He tapped keys for five seconds and stood back. Moretti watched a yellow cab approach the main gate. Clayton, the guard there, moved to the middle of the drive so the taxi stopped. Immediately a striking woman emerged from the back seat and walked up to Clayton and began speaking. *Has some Latin blood in her,* Moretti observed. He watched the woman hand Clayton the note. He could read her lips saying, "Thank you." She turned and got back in the cab. It backed up and drove off.

Moretti looked at the note again and for several seconds tried to get into the head of this woman based on the little he knew, her looks, the way she moved and carried herself, her choice of method to get a message to him, the way the message was written, and its subject matter. *This seemingly simple event was meticulously planned,* he concluded. *She thought about exactly what she wanted me to see and know. A trap?* He thought not, but would proceed as if it were. He had lots of practice at that. *Very well mystery woman,* he said to himself, *you gained your objective. You have piqued my curiosity.*

Finally, he looked from the note to Thomas and courteously said, "Thank you Thomas. You were right to interrupt me." That was a dismissal, and Thomas left. In the stillness of the library, Moretti decided how he would handle this curious matter. Then he fixed a smile on his face and returned to his guests.

CHAPTER 60

C hrista sat alone at a corner table. She touched the flower in her hair. She looked at her watch. Not quite 1:00.

To pass the time she reflected upon her experience since surfacing from her four-month ordeal. She recalled the unsettling moment she first walked on a street among a throng of people. *They're looking at me!* There was an instant of panic, but almost at once she realized that these were not looks of recognition of Veronica Patterson or of lust for Hot and Easy Mary Ellen. She had never drawn looks quite like these. They were in appreciation of her singular beauty and yet they were admiring and respectful. They made her feel good.

As long as Nikki could remember the stares of men, particularly, had only increased a sense of discomfort that she didn't understand. The few times she slept with a man she couldn't avoid feeling humiliated and found herself driven to exhaust him and send the message in no uncertain terms that he was disappointingly incapable of satisfying her sexual appetite, her feigned sexual appetite. She wanted to strip these men of power and pleasure and cast her humiliation upon them. But now she felt no disquiet. The looks she was receiving from both men and women made her proud and.... She struggled to identify the feeling. *How do I say it? Significant. That's it! Significant!*

She glanced at her watch again. Five minutes after one. No one had approached her. Several men had entered and met others and two sat at the bar, although not together. Each from time to time glanced at her, but she did not know how to read that.

Nothing happened for another five minutes. Then she sensed someone approaching from her right. Her flower was on that side of her head. She turned. It was a woman. *In her 50's probably, but well preserved,* Nikki thought. Well dressed and smiling, the woman held out her hand as she reached the table. "How nice to see you," she said pleasantly. "And so good of you to arrange this meeting." She sat down opposite Nikki and with hands in her lap leaned forward, "You know, my dear, this is such a noisy public place. Our friend would very much like to meet you himself, so I hope you have time now to come with me to his home. It is very lovely, and he is always such a gracious host."

Nikki thought, *it's not noisy here. Clever. If anyone had overheard or bugged this woman's words, they would have learned nothing.* But she was taken aback by the invitation. She was to meet the big bad wolf himself! She felt herself getting angry but wasn't sure why. She was also excited because she was sure that, face to face, he would understand that the information she would give him was real.

"Good," the woman said, without waiting for a response, and never offering her name. "My car is waiting, shall we go?" She rose and took Nikki's arm as if they were old friends. Half way to the door Nikki, curious, glanced behind her. Sure enough, the two men who had been sitting at the bar had also risen and were following them. She looked from them to the woman, whose expression was unreadable. Once outside, the woman led Christa to a waiting limousine. A man in a dark suit opened the back door for them, and both women got in. He then got in the passenger seat next to the driver.

As the car pulled from the curb, the lady said pleasantly, "It will take about half an hour to get there, so we have time to talk. What is your name?"

"Christa Cairns," Nikki answered, enjoying the thrill it gave her to say it.

"Tell me about yourself, Christa," the woman continued.

"I'm a freelance reporter. I happen to have information from Veronica Patterson that I believe no one else knows. That is all I would like to say right now." The woman looked at her closely, but continued to smile.

"When we arrive," she said, "you must undergo a search before you will be permitted to see Mr. Moretti. Are you carrying any weapons?"

"Certainly not," Nikki answered honestly.

Thirty-five minutes later Nikki was ushered in to as tasteful a drawing room as she could recall and she had seen many while working for Virginia. The two men who had been at the front door when she arrived looked and were dressed like middle management in a large company, not thugs. Nothing about this setting was consistent with her preconceived notion of Moretti and his environment. She had expected ostentation, not taste.

Moretti was standing as she entered. She could see in his face pleasure at looking at a beautiful woman. She could not get used to the fact that such a look no longer offended her, even from this very bad man. Moretti appeared to her younger than his age. She saw a slender, fit man with fine features, spoiled only by a slight sagging of his facial skin. His hair was gray-flecked, full and naturally curly. His smile revealed large, very white, almost but not quite, perfect teeth, so they looked natural. She thought of the beautiful new look of her own teeth. His tailored pinstripe suit looked more Wall Street than Italian fashion. He was neither fleeing from his Italian heritage nor shoving it into her face. He was simply urbane.

If he was consciously trying to construct an image, she could not tell it. What she saw seemed genuine, and that made his eyes even more formidable. In her life she had never seen eyes simultaneously so penetrating and impenetrable. The pupil color was something between brown and black. There was no way to gauge depth. The surface was infinitely deep, yet still surface, a visual contradiction. For an instant these eyes owned hers, a unilateral possession, as all possessions are. But it was only momentary. He in turn saw anger in her eyes and rejection of his attempted domination. Each sensed the other was formidable, but pleasantries were the rules of engagement.

Moretti extended his hand and said in a rich baritone voice, "I am told you are Christa Cairns. I do apologize Ms. Cairns. I have been admonished that when I see a beautiful woman, I tend to stare, and the eyes I was born with and with which I must live out my days fail to convey accurately the appreciation for beauty that I feel. That is a curse that has cost me many a conquest. At least that is my excuse for those many failures." When he stopped speaking, he smiled broadly.

Nikki was impressed by this layered speech, each thought building on the last and all calibrated not only to disarm, but to convey a warning: "I know myself better than you possibly could, so you will not take away from here any impression of what I say or do that I do not intend." *This is a formidable man,* Nikki thought. *And his network is efficient. I mentioned my name in the car and he greets me with it.* She had one other significant impression. *He's dangerous!* She thought of Virginia. *Good!*

She harnessed her anger and went about spinning her web without noticing that he too was spinning. She would discover that later. She took his offered hand, placed her other hand on her chest just below her neck, and tested his ability to discern when she lied. "You are an imposing man, and I must confess that your gaze is intimidating. I am a little nervous."

"Ms. Cairns," he replied, "For good or ill, God also endowed me with an acute ability to distinguish between candor and guile. You are not in the least nervous. So let us agree that the rest of our conversation will not be patronizing on the part of either of us." He extended his arm toward a sofa and said, "Please have a seat. Would you care for lemonade or water?"

"Neither, thank you," she said, sitting down and wondering if he would sit close beside her. He did not. Instead, he pulled up an elegant wooden-backed chair and squarely faced her. Close, but not intimately close.

Moretti began. "I understand you have something to tell me, a message from someone else."

"Yes," she said, looking straight into his eyes, challenging their power. "You obviously read my note. She called me. I have never seen her. She said she was using a phone card and would not tell me where she was, which hardly surprised me. I asked why she chose to call me. Her response was not flattering. 'Because you're a nobody,' she said, 'So your ego is less likely to be a problem.'"

Christa stopped to give Moretti a chance to comment, but he only smiled, giving nothing away, and said, "Please continue."

"Then she spoke like it was an order. 'Get your pen ready. I'm only going to say this once and no interruptions.' She identified herself as Veronica Patterson, Congresswoman Wetherill's Chief of Staff, who I'm sure you know is wanted for the murder of the Congresswoman's husband." She paused again. He said nothing again. "'Get this information to Mr. Moretti,' were her exact next words. 'He needs to know it before the hearing. I have no doubt he will know how to use it.'"

"Her next instruction to me was that I should not tell you how to contact me or locate me and to extract from you, Mr. Moretti, a promise not to follow me or try to find me. Patterson said it was because she may want to convey more information through me and can't risk doing so if you know my whereabouts.

"I was concerned that this might expose me to some criminal charge, so I consulted an attorney describing the problem hypothetically without real names. He assured me I would not be breaking the law since I have no idea where Patterson is or how to locate her. He told me to go to the police with what I do know as soon as you complete your testimony at the Committee hearings.

"I want to comply with Patterson's instructions so that I can remain in a position to get more information from her should she choose to use me. This is the biggest opportunity I've had as a reporter. I can sell the story when the time comes." She stopped and then added, "Will you give me that promise?"

Moretti nodded and said, "That all sounds very reasonable."

Christa added, "Ms. Patterson said you wouldn't keep it, but there's nothing I can do about that."

Then Christa gave Moretti damning information that only Nikki could know.

CHAPTER 61

The large room was nearly filled with spectators. Standing against the sidewall Thad and Owens watched and listened. The hearing opened with short speeches by several subcommittee members. Then Wetherill called Moretti to testify. He and Leonard Quill, his lawyer, took their seats before the microphones, and he was sworn in. He declined the invitation to make a statement before answering questions. There was complete but strained silence in the room. Congresswoman Wetherill opened aggressively. "Mr. Moretti, this subcommittee is happy that you are finally here. We note that you have waived your right to an opening statement, and we can only hope that further silence on your part will not be the watchword of the day. Let me, as Chair of this Committee, begin by asking you why you resisted so many subpoenas of this Committee? What are you hiding?"

If Moretti was going to invoke his 5th Amendment right to remain silent, it had to be now. He let silence speak for a long moment. He was acutely aware that all in the hearing room and all following the proceedings on radio, C-span, or the internet sensed how combative the Congresswoman was being right out of the box, so when he finally spoke, his voice was low and calm and his tone was measured and respectful, creating a contrast to the Congresswoman's delivery. But his words threw down the gauntlet and revealed secrets only the guilty would know.

"Madam Chairman, you asked your husband to turn on the overhead light in the car just before the shots that killed him were fired. I have a car with similar tinted windows. If the inside lights are on, someone outside can see the interior well enough to shoot the driver without shooting the passenger."

It took only a few seconds for those listening to grasp the significance of Moretti's words, and then involuntary utterances buzzed through the large room. Wetherill's eight subcommittee colleagues gaped. This was coming from left field! It had nothing to do with the question the Congresswoman had asked. But its specificity gave it force. Wetherill looked stunned. *What is this? How could he know about the light? Christ! Nikki's in bed with him!* She struggled for control, hoping her visible reaction would be interpreted only as innocent and understandable surprise.

Moretti continued smoothly, as if he were reading a recipe for cornbread. "Why, Madam Chairman, did you bother to turn the light off? Someone was shooting up the car. You were so desperate to get out that you threw yourself..." At this point, Wetherill regained her composure enough to pound her gavel and try to shut Moretti up. "Silence! Silence!" Unfazed, Moretti simply picked up in midsentence. "...into the back seat and then out the back door behind your dead husband." She pounded, nearly shouting now, "You are out of order, Mr. Moretti!" He kept speaking, "But you had the presence of mind to turn off the

light. Why, in that terrible moment? Why pause to turn off
the light? Why bother?"

For those watching and listening this was too good to be
true! Had it been a story no one would believe it! Wetherill
could hear the murmurs and feel the curiosity in the room,
and her instincts told her she needed to take back control fast
or God knows where this would lead.

She pointed the gavel at the witness. "Mr. Moretti, if
you think you can intimidate me or the other members of
this subcommittee with this sensationalism, you are sorely
mistaken. There is a question pending which you have
refused to answer. You are here to answer questions, not ask
them. I owe you no explanations, but it so happens I did not
touch any light switch. It was my husband's car, and I have
no idea how to work the lights. Now, that is going to be the
end of your little performance. This subcommittee will take
a ten-minute recess so your counsel can make you understand
how close you are to real trouble. When we return, I expect
to have answers from you, not questions. You will not enjoy
the consequences if this behavior continues."

She raised the gavel, but before she could bring it down,
Moretti began again in his quiet but strong voice, "Just
one more thing, Madam Chairman. If you did not turn the
overhead lights off, why is your fingerprint the freshest one
on the switch for those lights?"

The curiosity in the room was now palpable. There was
total silence, but many in the hearing room and watching
electronically fidgeted in their seats. The moment was too
pregnant with accusation for sitting still. Only Nikki, who
was watching on C-Span in the apartment in Embassy Circle
Guest House she had rented in the name of Patricia Miller,
had expected this surprising turn of events. But even she was
surprised by the detail of the fingerprint. She hadn't mentioned
it to Moretti because she never thought of it. He had simply

extrapolated from the facts she gave him. *But he has to be right,* she thought. *He's scary smart,* she warned herself.

Thad and Owens exchanged glances. Thad asked his partner, "We didn't dust the overhead switches, did we?" "We don't have prints from them, right?"

"Not that I know of. No need. Killer was never inside."

"Let's get it done," Thad said. Owens left the room and made a call.

The Congresswoman leaned forward over her reading glasses and followed her instinct to attack. Her green eyes and red mane were blazing. In a strong, confident voice she said, "Mr. Moretti, if you continue with this circus when we reconvene, if you say anything except in response to this Committee's questions, you will be held in contempt."

Moretti sat perfectly still, looking straight back and saying nothing. Two bull elephants had faced off in battle with neither giving ground. Two giant egos were trying to disembowel each other with rapier-edged civility. The Congresswoman banged the gavel, straightened, stood tall, and strode out with all the dignity she could muster. In her anger, she had looked hard into Moretti's eyes, intent on staring him down. But instead, those eyes had bored into hers until they reached the fear that hid deep beneath her talents.

As the Congresswoman strode out of the room, her staff members scuttling behind, Nikki replayed in her mind's eye every tiny movement of Virginia's face and body and every inflection of her voice. Only Nikki knew Virginia well enough to read her face, so only she had seen the deep fright in that supposedly indomitable woman. Moretti had reversed the roles of the two protagonists. He had become the cool inquisitor, Virginia the reluctant witness. Before the world, Virginia had just said she never touched the light switch. She had been caught on the record in what might soon be shown, if Moretti was right, to be a condemning lie.

When Owens returned, he said, "Our tech guys tell me there is every chance that a good print will still be identifiable after five months because the car's basically been sealed up as evidence."

"Good," Thad said, "Maybe we'll get a break." Then he stated the obvious, "Only one place Moretti could have gotten that information about the overhead light. It makes such sense!" Owens nodded, frowned, and once more demonstrated how cannily he could think a step ahead.

"Moretti knows he will have to tell us his source. He won't risk exposing himself to a charge of accessory after the fact or harboring a murderer. He'll have some story that will insulate him from knowledge of Nikki's whereabouts."

Thad added, almost in a whisper, "This guy has ice water in his veins. Can you imagine saying this stuff in public? He really wants to take the Congresswoman down."

"Chief, this is dramatic for sure, but I was convinced by the lengths he went to get Correa into Isabella's home. I'm sure he had her first secretary drowned. Nice guy."

Thad went in search of Leonard Quill to tell him not to let his client leave the building until they spoke about the source of Moretti's information. Quill said, "We expected your request. Mr. Moretti will be available when the Committee adjourns the hearings for the day. In the meantime I can assure you that Mr. Moretti tells me he has learned nothing that indicates Ms. Patterson's whereabouts. I would have contacted you immediately otherwise." Thad believed Quill. He did not believe Quill's client.

On the retreat to her office Wetherill displayed as much confidence and outrage as she could muster. She went immediately to her office bathroom and held a washcloth soaked in cold water to her face for a long time. Then, she looked into the mirror. She felt like stalked prey. *What the hell happened?* This was supposed to be her day, when she would either have Moretti make denial after denial under oath or take the fifth. Either way she figured he would look more like a thug and she more like she has information that he is a thug. Interest in her investigation would ramp up, and her fellow house members would be excoriated if they did not vote the funding to continue it.

Instead, Moretti became the examiner and had real information about the murder. *Christ, what the hell is that crazy Nikki doing?* All the way from the hearing room to her office, *idiot reporters*, as she secretly and contemptuously thought of them, hounded her with a stream of questions about Moretti's questions, not her investigation. She had created this public forum to take advantage of the public's love of scandal, knowing that the press and her constituents would believe she had more on Moretti than she really did. Now, *he* was using *her* to suggest that she was a murderer, *and*, she thought, *that's all the idiot press and public are going to think about!*

She looked in the mirror again and began to draw strength from her own reflection. After all, she was Virginia Wetherill. *No two-bit mobster is going to best me!* She took a deep breath and reminded herself that it was not Moretti's word against hers. Ultimately, it was her word against crazy Nikki the killer. *No way will John Q Public believe Nikki over me!* The greater worry was that Nikki was coming after her, indirectly and invisibly. That's what had rattled her and caused her to make that damn, stupid mistake about the light switch. For a third time she looked into the mirror, and she willed the concern in her face to turn into resolve. *Fight*, she said to herself. *Get out there and fix that fucking mistake! Get the goddam Genie back in the bottle!*

She used the toilet and washed. Composed, she walked confidently out to face the reporters she knew would be crowding the corridor just outside her office door. But as much as she coveted press attention normally, even she was surprised at the number of waiting reporters. The hallway was jammed. *Control this god damn scene,* she said to herself, as she smiled and held out her arms in an open and embracing gesture.

She pointed to an NBC reporter, whom she knew well. "You first, Jeanne." "Congresswoman, did you ask your husband to turn the overhead light on and then turn it off as Mr. Moretti claims?" She did not hesitate, "How I wish you all would not succumb to Mr. Moretti's ploy to divert these hearings. But okay Jeanne, the only light I remember on inside the car that night was the penlight I carry in my purse. As you have probably heard, I dropped a contact lens on the floor, and I thought that the point of light coming from the penlight would reflect off the contact lens better than the diffused light from the interior lights of the car.

My husband offered to turn the light on, that I remember. But I thought I'd find the lens faster without it. I was fishing for the lens when" – here she paused very briefly – "when the shots began." For the first time she sensed sympathy in the hall. *Go on,* she said to herself, *do it now.* "That car has a bewildering number of buttons, knobs and things on the dash and the ceiling and the console. I never drove it except occasionally at night, when my husband believed he had had too much to drink. We were very conscientious about that. On occasion I would start poking at things to try to get the inside light on, but," she smiled, "I'm challenged that way. Sometimes I hit the light button and other times I hit the wrong button, like opening the sun roof when it was raining." There was laughter. *They're buying it,* she thought. "And then Taylor would have to come to the rescue. So my guess is my fingerprints are probably on a bunch of the overhead controls, maybe even the overhead light. But I must tell you all, as I think about it I'm not sure what I did that night or what I asked Taylor. It is still a blur and I can't sort out the sequence of events very well. I do remember after the shooting I was petrified to be alone, I felt trapped. For all I know I could have groped for the light, turned it on, turned it off, who knows. I was looking for anything that would help me escape the terror I felt."

She blinked quickly three times, appearing to fight off tearing up, but she was telling herself, *Okay, now get on the offense, damn it.* She visibly took a breath and stood a little straighter. "But you know, Mr. Moretti's obvious attempt to distract you all suggests to me that he may be harboring a criminal. I'm concerned that Nikki Patterson may now be spiteful because I have publicly asked her to give herself up and get help. Moretti of course would do anything to disrupt this investigation. He may know where she is, or they may be acting together.

"I tell you, that bit about me getting out through the rear door? That's true, but I don't believe it ever came out, did it? I know I told Nikki. I wonder if she is feeding him a fairy tale that he wants to hear because it undercuts my investigation of him. I intend to confer with the FBI about this." That's where she wanted to leave it – she and the FBI working together, she on the side of justice. She looked at her watch. Then, with authority, she announced, "Now we must get back to these important hearings." As she strode toward the hearing room, she suppressed a grin. *So much for fingerprints!*

Word had gotten around that there were fireworks at the subcommittee hearings. When the Congresswoman and the other subcommittee members returned, the room was jammed to overflowing. Thad and Owens were again standing against the wall to the Congresswoman's left, where they could see many faces in profile rather than just a few full on. The Congresswoman pounded the gavel and asked for silence. Within fifteen seconds the room was quiet. She began, "This hearing is again in session. Mr. Moretti, are you ready to proceed?"

"I am," he said evenly.

She continued, "I still have the floor since my one question was never answered. However, I withdraw it for the time being because it appears from your unsolicited comments before the recess, Mr. Moretti, that there may be a more important line of inquiry. I remind you that you are still under oath. Do you know who Veronica Patterson is?"

A murmur rippled through the crowd like a small wave. Nikki leaned a little closer to her television screen.

"My understanding," he answered, "is that she is a person wanted for the murder of your husband and that she is...was your Chief of Staff."

"Do you know what she looks like?"

"I have seen pictures and video of her on the news."

"Have you seen her in person?"

"If I have, I am not aware of it."

"What does that mean Mr. Moretti?"

"Just that, Madam Chairman, I am not aware of ever being in her presence or laying eyes on her in person." At this, Nikki thought of Christa's looks, *her* looks, and her meeting with Moretti. She felt so safe.

"Would you recognize her voice?"

"I would not."

"Have you ever spoken by phone or through any other medium to anyone who claimed to be Veronica Patterson?"

"I have not, Madam Chairman."

"Have you ever spoken to anyone who claimed to have spoken to Ms. Patterson?"

"Other than yourself, Madam Chairman?" There was tension-easing twitter. The Congresswoman, feeling it was going better now, permitted herself a condescending smile.

"Yes, Mr. Moretti, other than me."

"I have." Murmurs were audible throughout the room, then eager silence again.

"Name the person, Mr. Moretti."

Nikki thought, *Christa Cairns is about to be introduced to the world! But the world won't find her until I am ready.*

Moretti demurred, "Madam Chairman, that is information I intend to give to the authorities when you permit me to leave here."

The Congresswoman pressed. "I instruct you to give this subcommittee the name of your source, Mr. Moretti." Moretti covered the microphone in front of him with his hand and leaned to confer with Quill. Then he straightened and addressed the subcommittee. "I am advised that this entire line of questioning is outside the scope of the subpoena to which I am subject; indeed, outside the scope of the charter of this subcommittee. So I respectfully decline your invitation to speak now and will give my information to the authorities."

The Congresswoman flashed an angry look at him. Then it was her turn to cover her microphone and confer with counsel to the subcommittee. There was a low hum in the room. In a moment, she turned back to Moretti and the overflow audience behind him. In a contemptuous tone of voice calculated to overcome the fact that she had just been told Moretti was right, she said, "Well, Mr. Moretti, your contention that you don't have to answer my questions didn't stop you before the recess from trying to question the Chair about matters you now assert are extraneous did it?"

"That is correct, Madam Chairman."

"So you raise the issue when it suits you, but refuse to discuss it when it does not, is that right?"

"Yes, Madam Chairman, that is correct. How could it be otherwise?"

A low twitter permeated the hearing room. Moretti's simple, straightforward and logical acknowledgement of the reality of the adversarial nature of the proceedings delivered calmly and seemingly respectfully washed out any implication of unfair play. The Congresswoman had just been out-maneuvered, so her next question, to which she had been building, had little sting. "And your purpose was to deflect attention from the vital business of this subcommittee, namely, your involvement in the drug underworld in our community, isn't that also correct, *sir*?" She made "sir" sound like a four letter word.

Again Moretti did not hesitate and calmly responded, "Madam Chairman, bringing me before this distinguished subcommittee does not further one iota the laudable objectives of this subcommittee's investigation. So, to answer your question, 'No.'"

"Really? Mr. Moretti," Wetherill asked exaggeratedly, "You just raised it for fun?"

"No, Madam Chairman, I confess I am not having much fun."

Frustrated by his coolness, Wetherill succumbed to the temptation to be argumentative. "Well then, Mr. Moretti," she said in her most sarcastic tone, "be so kind as to enlighten us. We are all on pins and needles. Why did you refuse to answer my question and try to obstruct this investigation by cheaply trading on my husband's death?"

Moretti was silent for a moment. The pause made the audience even more expectant. And it was during this pause that Wetherill realized she had made a devastating error. *Dumb open-ended question! But I'll look terrible if I withdraw it!* Then Moretti spoke, "Because Madam Chairman based upon information I have disclosed here, I believe that you are ..."

"Take care Mr. Moretti," the Congresswoman hissed, leaning forward, her red hair flaring, "take care what you say."

"...a murderer," he finished. "That you murdered your husband."

The room erupted, and the Congresswoman exploded from her seat. Pointing at Moretti with her gavel, she raged, "Disgraceful! You are in contempt! Every person in this room and watching across the country has now been witness to the depravity and rot that infests you underneath your expensive suit and affected manners. You are in contempt of this subcommittee, and you are contemptible, and you will pay dearly for this slander!" She started banging the gavel on the table before her. "This hearing is recessed until such time as this subcommittee determines the extent of the malfeasance this witness has just committed and the appropriate penalty." She pounded the gavel twice more and with long strides of long legs stormed out, her fiery red hair dancing. Some subcommittee members followed. Others hesitated as if not wanting to appear associated with Wetherill. Confusion reigned.

Thad and Owens headed towards Moretti and Quill, holding up their badges to persuade the pushers and shovers to make room for them. Thad reached Quill. He had to get close and raise his voice above the din of reporters swarming and thrusting microphones out and firing salvos of questions.

Watching this drama play out from the safe distance of a television set did not prevent Nikki's heart from pounding with excitement. *Beautiful!* She exulted. *Now you know what it's like to be called a murderer before all the world Virginia! Having fun? And I'm just getting started!* Before C-Span shut down its hearing room camera Nikki saw Thad approach Moretti and Quill. She smiled. *Moretti is about to tell Pennock about the small-time, "nobody" of a reporter Christa Cairns.*

Thad spoke over the noise of the crowding members of the press. "Desmond, we need to talk to your client immediately." Quill was prepared.

"Of course, Thad. May I suggest that you and Agent Owens join us in Mr. Moretti's limousine? It's handy, large enough, quiet, and private."

Thad's initial reaction was negative. *The FBI being seen getting into Moretti's limo? No way!* But it was immediately available and very private and he heard himself say, "We'll start there with the understanding that if I decide we should continue the questioning at headquarters, you will not object."

"Agreed," Quill said.

A moving gang of reporters surrounded Moretti, Quill, Thad, and Owens as they slowly made their way outside and down the steps of the Capitol to the waiting limousine. "No comment," was the only response they got to their many questions.

In the expansive back seat of the limousine, with the doors shut and the glass partition between front and back closed, it was quiet and private. Thad and Owens sat just behind the partition facing rearward while Moretti and Quill sat further back facing forward. "That was quite a performance, Mr. Moretti," Thad began. "Theater at its best. I suspect that went about as well as you could have hoped, but you needn't comment on that. We need to know every detail. Where did you get the information concerning the overhead light and the fingerprint?" He stopped and gestured for Moretti to begin.

For the next five minutes, Moretti, who had trained himself to have near perfect short-term recall, described his meeting and recited his conversation with Christa Cairns. Thad or Owens interrupted from time to time to ask a question or get a clarification.

When Moretti finished, Thad asked, "Did you get any contact information from Cairns?"

"She refused. She said that Patterson made it a condition of using her as a conduit that she, meaning Cairns, be hard to find until three days after my appearance before the subcommittee concluded in case Patterson wanted to use her again. She said after that time, she would go to the authorities or do whatever was appropriate. Cairns told me that since she had no idea where Nikki was, she really did not think she was withholding any material information by waiting that short period."

Thad frowned. "That may indicate nothing more than Nikki's cleverness and this Cairns woman's ambition to be part of a real story. But her elusiveness is, frankly, a little suspicious. We'd like to see the note Christa sent you. Cairns may simply be Nikki in disguise. She's damned good at that."

It was Moretti's turn to frown. "I regret to tell you that I threw it away. It gave no hint of what she would tell me, and I could not get very excited about it. I assumed her information would concern drug distribution since that is what the subcommittee hearings are about. It never occurred to me it would relate to Mr. Warner's murder."

"Are you telling us you don't know where Cairns is or have any way to contact her?" Thad asked.

"That is correct."

"That's disappointing. You strike me as a careful man who would hold on to such a note." Moretti did not respond. "You do like to throw things away, Mr. Moretti." Moretti didn't take the bait. He sat quiet and composed and looking at Thad. "All right," Thad said, "give us as detailed a description of this woman as you can, height, weight, features, color, voice, everything."

"I can if you wish." Moretti described Christa in as little detail as he thought was credible. It was much less than he held in his photographic memory. Owens and Thad listened carefully, trying to discover Nikki in the woman. They could not.

When he finished his description, Moretti added, "I might add that I have seen and heard Ms. Patterson on television newscasts several times, including her performance in the Congresswoman's garden when she essentially accused me of Mr. Warner's murder. Needless to say I carry with me a vivid image of her, and I would like to think I would recognize her notwithstanding the most sophisticated disguise. As for Ms. Cairns, I spent fifteen minutes conversing with her as close as I am to you now, Agent Pennock, and it never occurred to me that she might be Patterson."

Thad could think of nothing Moretti could gain from protecting Nikki. To the contrary, a captured Nikki might sing and bring down the Congresswoman. So from that moment Thad never questioned that Christa and Nikki were different women. He turned to Owens, "Anything else?"

Owens shook his head, "No."

"Desmond," Thad said, looking at Quill. "You know Mr. Moretti must give us a full statement about all this. Your choice; we can all go to our offices and get it done, or, since we've known each other a long time, I'll let you take Mr. Moretti's affidavit so long as we have it by 9:00 a.m. tomorrow, and," he raised a finger, "you must commit to me that if I think it doesn't fully cover everything we have discussed or if what it says suggests further lines of inquiry by us, you will produce Mr. Moretti promptly at my office so we can be satisfied we have everything."

Quill responded, "Agreed. Thank you for the courtesy, Thad. We'll get you the affidavit."

The limousine had been driven in a large circle during this interview so Thad and Owens were quickly returned to their parked FBI sedan.

The two lawmen were alone, Thad driving, when Owens' phone rang. He looked at the number and said to Thad, "Lab." He spoke with the caller about a minute, rang off, and looked at Thad. "There's a beautiful print taken from the control of the overhead light."

"Hers?" Thad asked.

"Yep."

Thad took it in. "So," he said, thinking out loud. "Nikki really called this Christa Cairns with real information, and the Congresswoman is guilty as hell." He paused and then shook his head. "How do we nail her, Owens?"

His partner replied, "If we're lucky, Nikki will keep feeding information to Moretti."

———

Moretti thought the interview had gone well. He was comfortable telling the FBI the exact truth about his meeting with Christa Cairns, and he was comfortable lying to them about everything else. *Of course I have the note and of course Cairns is Patterson,* he said to himself afterwards.

While Christa's story about a call from Nikki had been plausible, Moretti had been unwilling to accept "plausible" as fact. His success, to say nothing of his survival, was rooted in a profound pessimism and distrust of others. He rarely took action in reliance on the untested word of another. When Christa left his home after their meeting, he put a round-the-clock tail on her.

But most importantly for Christa's fate, she had been secretly photographed and filmed during her visit to Moretti's home. He had called in an expert who studied the images of Christa and compared them to pictures and film of Nikki collected from a variety of public sources. The expert selected images of both women that were then digitized so they could be manipulated.

It did not take the expert long to reach his conclusion. The key lay in spatial relationships of features. "Mr. Moretti," he concluded, "They are the same woman. I can describe to you the specific surgical techniques that, applied to Patterson, would result in Cairns' looks. It was well done. But what cannot be altered is size and shape of the cranium, distance between the bridge of the nose and each ear or specific points on the side of the cranium, and a half dozen other telling spatial relationships. There are enough identical measurements to create statistical certainty that we are looking at one woman."

So, within thirty hours of Christa's visit, Moretti knew she was Nikki, knew from the surveillance that Nikki had an apartment in the name of Patricia Miller, and knew where Nikki was every minute of the day. He had plans for the Congresswoman that importantly involved Nikki.

He wanted the Congresswoman disgraced before she got too close to evidence of his activities. He knew she had nothing solid yet. But Pennock's hypothetical question to him when they met at Moretti's home five months earlier had been on target. The Congresswoman was closer to hard evidence than she knew. As she suspected, Moretti was the "Don" of Philadelphia/Newark drug operations, including importing, cutting, distribution to the street, and money laundering. But what no one on the right side of the law, and few on the wrong side, knew was that he controlled the entry and initial distribution of hard drugs along the entire East coast from Miami to Maine, and he would dispose of as many people as necessary to protect that empire.

CHAPTER 62

When Thad got back to his office, his phone was ringing. "Agent Pennock," he said.

"This is Virginia Wetherill, Pennock. I saw you at the hearings today. What are you going to do about that outrageous slander and the accusations against me? And not just me personally, but the integrity of the office I hold. I want the FBI to make a statement that I am not a suspect, which surely must be the case."

Thad paused, he realized he should have expected this call, but he hadn't. "Congresswoman," he said, "That would be unusual. We make statements when we have something to say, not to referee fights between public figures. I need to think about this and talk to the Deputy Director."

Wetherill's temper was short. "Don't pussyfoot with me," she retorted in a raised voice. "I know the difference between a person of interest and a suspect. Unless you believe I am a suspect, you do a disservice to this country to let that underworld hack slander a member of Congress about something the FBI knows more about than anyone else. The press is having a field day with this, and if you won't get the job done, I'm going to the Director."

Thad's ire was up, and he wanted to slash back. He was tempted to tell her they had her fingerprint from the light switch on the overhead panel of the BMW and that she was a god damn liar and a murderer, but he resisted. Her request involved political considerations, not crime solving. It was not his call.

"Doesn't do any good to yell at me, Congresswoman. This is not my decision to make either way. One of us, me, Deputy Director Porter, or the Director will be back to you."

"For god's sake, Pennock, do the right thing for once," she said tersely and hung up.

His phone was not in its cradle more than two seconds before it rang again. He did not get the chance to say hello. "Jesus, Thaddeus," Lew Porter said, maneuvering his words around the ever-present cigar, "what's going on? You know I don't like surprises. The Director just shoved one so far up my ass I can read it! He's gotten calls from the office of the Majority Leader of the House and from the President's office, and they damn well didn't call to ask him to play strip poker. They want to know why this office says nada while a grease ball mobster slanders a certain red-haired – probably everywhere – duly-elected member of Congress with bullshit this office knows there's no proof of. Problem is we know it's not bullshit but can't prove it! What the hell have you gotten us into, man? Actually, I know too well the answer to that question. Just get us the hell out!"

Did he do that all in one breath? Thad wondered admiringly. The Congresswoman's heavy-handed methods irritated him, but the merits of the issue did not. "Lew, I just got off the phone with the Congresswoman myself. She demands that we whitewash her, but here's the thing. At that hearing, Moretti handed us a clue that we didn't have before. He got her to deny that the interior lights of the car were on at the time of the shooting. That's in black and white on the record. She denied having touched the light switch. But Moretti told her, and everyone listening, that her fingerprint is on the light switch. Then he went further and accused her of murdering her husband."

"I know all that," Porter interjected.

"Well then," Thad continued, "you know how that went down. It was some theater. But it turns out Moretti's information is accurate. The print's very clean and clear. She was to a certainty the last person to press that particular switch, and the light was off when the police reached the crime scene. That makes me even more certain that she was the mastermind. And, to me, the clincher is the source of the information. Nikki Patterson."

"Spell it out, man. I happen to be a genius, but even I can't get it if you leave out six steps of the analysis."

Thad continued, "Moretti told us he got the information about the light switch from a green reporter named Christa Cairns. Cairns told him that Nikki Patterson phoned her out of the blue and gave her the information to pass on to Moretti so he could use it at the hearing. So as far as we know the source is Patterson. But according to Wetherill's statement to us about what happened at the scene, the shooter was long gone while Wetherill was still on the floor of the car, which means the shooter, who we now know was Patterson, wouldn't have actually seen Wetherill switch the light off. She would only have known it happened if it had been part of a plan."

"Praise the Lord!" Porter said. "Yet another genius!"

Thad continued, so familiar with his boss's verbal outbursts that he didn't skip a beat. "Lew, I know that no jury is going to jump from that to finding her guilty of conspiring to kill her husband. But I don't think we've heard the last from Nikki Patterson. It's clear now that she wants Wetherill to go down, so I think we'll eventually look like fools if we go out there now in the Congresswoman's defense."

Porter barked back, "How the hell can we keep silent? Makes us look like we suspect the Congresswoman, and the Director's phone will never stop ringing. There won't be enough left of you and me to sprinkle on a pigmy's pussy! Let me think." There was silence for ten long seconds. Then Porter continued, "All right, if we don't have hard evidence that our Congresswoman was involved, we say something like, 'the prime suspect in this killing, Veronica Patterson, is still at large. The investigation and the search for her continue. At this point we do not have hard evidence that anyone else was involved, and anyone includes Congresswoman Wetherill.' What if we say that?" Thad actually thought it sounded pretty good, but before he could comment, Lew continued. "I think it's pretty good, so get it out right away. You do it."

"Yes sir," Thad answered.

"Wonderful!" Porter said sarcastically. "Tell me, what's considered a low blow when two lesbies fight? I can't imagine! Maybe when Patterson hears about your little press conference pulling the Congresswoman's ass off the griddle, she'll be so pissed she'll invite you to lunch and sell her beloved boss up the river."

———

And that is very close to what Nikki did. She had planned to call Thad anyway to open a direct link with him. That way she would take Christa out of the middle so no one would keep looking for her. But before she made the call she heard Thad's public statement that there was no evidence implicating Wetherill. She was hopping mad. *What the hell more do they need!*

Thad answered his cell phone and immediately recognized Nikki's voice. "Pennock, this is Nikki Patterson. I'm going to talk for forty seconds, then hang up."

"How do I know it's really you?"

"Thirty-five seconds. Want to waste more time? What the hell are you doing? You damn well know killing Taylor was Virginia's idea."

Thad quickly jumped in. "We got the fingerprint from the light switch, Nikki." He wanted to call her Nikki, be her buddy, her partner in proving the Congresswoman's guilt. He continued, "But it's not enough, Nikki, you have to give me something solid."

There was a slight pause, and then Nikki said, "From now on no middle man, no Moretti, no Cairns. I deal directly with you. I'm taking her down Pennock. Time's up. Don't bother tracing. The phone's a throwaway, and it's going into the garbage right now." She clicked off. She smiled Christa's lovely smile and congratulated herself.

Thad sat thinking for a minute. They'd heard nothing from Nikki for four months. Now she was back blazing away and seemingly bent on exposing Wetherill. He wasn't surprised. For four months, like everyone else who turned on a radio or television he had had to listen to Wetherill's media blitz against Nikki. He'd take his phone to the geeks and see if they could locate where Nikki made the call. At least then he'd know whether she was in DC, New York, or Oshkosh. His gut told him she was nearby. *Would she gun Wetherill down?* Maybe, but her actions so far suggested that she wanted to see Wetherill sweat for a while. And, he concluded, directing her fury at Wetherill had logic to it that stalking Isabella did not. He felt relief. It seemed much less likely that Isabella was still in danger.

Thad dialed in Owens. "Let's talk," he said when his partner answered. Owens knew this meant a strategy session in Thad's office.

"Be right there, Chief." The savvy veteran and his smart younger boss reviewed every aspect of the case looking for a new approach to the capture of Nikki. That remained the key now more than ever since Nikki seemed to be turning against Wetherill. Despite their efforts, they could think of nothing new and different. But they were about to get some help.

CHAPTER 63

The Congresswoman pounced on the FBI's public statement, which she of course touted as complete exoneration. She called her own press conference for one hour after Thad's statement. She had no idea what Nikki would do next to implicate her, but she saw the present moment as her best opportunity to shore up her defense and at the same time salvage her investigation of Moretti.

She rightly guessed that the press would be interested, but for greatest effect she wanted the venue to be a smaller, more intimate space where she could touch and be touched. She clearly had in mind the aloof image she had projected commanding the room as chair of the subcommittee hearings and berating Moretti. She wanted now to appear human, approachable, and open, once again the courageous fighter against crime, wounded by her husband's death but not beaten. She decided upon the corridor outside of her office on the Hill. The performance was classic Wetherill.

She began, "Hi everyone. I see lots of familiar faces. As you know, I believe Mr. Moretti is the leader of a powerful and deadly drug cartel. The people of Philadelphia and indeed the nation have now witnessed the extremes to which Mr. Moretti will go to obstruct and disrupt the subcommittee's investigation. His performance yesterday, and that's what it was, a performance, demonstrated that he has nothing but contempt for the system by which we in this country have developed a great nation. Instead of responding under oath to our questions probing his involvement in contemptible illegal activities, he accused me, without one shred of evidence, of complicity in the murder of my husband. Without one shred of evidence," she repeated.

"He also claimed to have been indirectly in contact with my former Chief of Staff, who as you all know became completely deranged and killed my husband and two lieutenants in the Argentinian National Police."

"When Mr. Moretti accused me of murdering my husband, I challenged him to come forth with any evidence. He refused and said he would give his proof to the authorities. Again, you all know this as fact. It is on the record. I'm told that immediately after I recessed the hearing, FBI agents Thaddeus Pennock and Robert Owens, who are in charge of the investigation into my husband's murder and who were present at the hearing, announced themselves to Mr. Moretti and his attorney and required immediate access to Mr. Moretti for questioning."

She paused here and visibly took a breath. The next sentences were delivered more slowly. She let her speech falter just a little, bravely struggling to keep from breaking down. She played her listeners like a piano. She loved it. "So, whatever Mr. Moretti had to say, the FBI learned right then and there." She had thought long and hard how she should pitch this speech, loud and angry, controlled "just-the-facts," or quiet, regal, vulnerable. She had practiced all three and liked the last approach best. The normally busy corridor was still, everyone awaiting her next words.

"According to the authorities, a person identifying herself as Veronica Patterson contacted a reporter and asked that reporter to give Mr. Moretti certain so-called information that the caller said only Veronica Patterson could know, namely, that just before the murder, I supposedly turned on the car light to give Patterson a clearer shot at my husband. You heard Mr. Moretti refer to that at the hearing."

Now her eyes flashed. "How absurd! The broken glass and bullets flew all around me. The glass cut into me. Is that not defense enough? But you in the media know so well how even the most outlandish, reckless, irresponsible falsehoods take on a life of their own. We have seen it happen time and again to public figures, and the cruel irony is that if the falsehood is sensational enough, it tends to stick regardless of how absurd it is, indeed, because it is absurd!"

Mini-lecture over, she returned to quiet, regal, and vulnerable. Looking up from her prepared statement, she continued in the righteous voice of the exonerated victim. "We all now know that Mr. Moretti had nothing and knew nothing when he accused me. An hour ago the FBI took the unusual step of making a public statement about who was *not* a suspect. I quote." She had it memorized, but looked down at her notes lending the statement more authority, and she spoke slowly and deliberately. "'We do not have hard evidence that anyone other than Ms. Patterson was involved in these murders, and anyone includes Congresswoman Wetherill.'" She looked up and took a moment to meet every pair of eyes she could while avoiding looking into any camera. *I've got them!* She told herself.

She looked down at her notes again. Like a composer writing "andante" or "allegro" indicating the tempo of her music, she had written in the margin of her speech such phrases as "with compassion." She had practiced "with compassion." Now, she began, "The tragic facts must be faced head on. So long as Veronica Patterson remains free, I cannot know what she might do next to try to frame me or even harm me, or, God forbid, kill someone else." She deliberately did not say, "Kill me." That would have been out of character for quiet, regal, and vulnerable. She continued, "We can only hope that she will be apprehended soon, and I plead with her once more, please, for your own sake Nikki, turn yourself in and get the help you so sorely need."

The next signal in her notes was, "with authority." She straightened herself, threw her shoulders back, and continued in a strong and confident voice, "As for Mr. Moretti, the subcommittee is seeking a court order holding him in contempt of its proceedings and requiring that when he is recalled to testify, and believe me he will be recalled, he not refer to matters relating to my husband's death on pain of prosecution. Mr. Moretti's performance yesterday proved one thing and one thing only. This subcommittee's investigation is getting close to exposing him, getting close to exposing the command and control apparatus distributing the illegal drugs that enslave our children and ruin their lives. I pledge to those children that the investigation will not be derailed. I will not waiver. Thank you. I'll be happy to take questions." Wetherill then parried questions for fifteen minutes. They couldn't touch her. She was riding high.

Moretti, watching the performance on television, was also pleased. Wetherill was linking the integrity of the subcommittee investigation to her own integrity, which, with the help of both Christa and Nikki, he was about to destroy.

CHAPTER 64

Nikki, comfortably hidden from the world in Patricia Miller's apartment, or so she thought, was in the middle of a workout routine when Christa's cell phone rang. She jumped. *Who knows my number?* She glanced at her watch, 7:45. "Christa Cairns," she answered, thrilling at the sound of her name.

"Why hello, Christa." The pleasant female voice was familiar, but she could not place it immediately. "I hope I haven't disturbed you." Then she remembered, the woman who met her in the restaurant and took her to Moretti's home.

"How did you get this number?" Christa asked guardedly. The woman responded evenly, "Oh that doesn't matter. I'm calling because Mr. Moretti would so much appreciate the chance to talk to you again briefly."

"I'm not in Philadelphia," Nikki said.

"Neither is Mr. Moretti. He's in Washington too." Nikki was startled. *What does she mean by 'too'?* "Well, I'm not in Washington," she lied.

There was a pause. Then the woman said, "Why of course you are Christa. You're in Patricia Miller's apartment. We'll pick you up at 9:00. That gives you an hour and a half to be ready." Nikki's jaw dropped. *How does she know? How could she know?* She felt panic start and transformed it into anger.

"That's not convenient. Have him call me. I can talk until about 8:45, and then I have another appointment."

"Oh dear," the woman said in a sympathetic tone, so different from the meaning of her words, "but that won't do. The car will be there at 9:00, and I am afraid that Mr. Moretti will insist upon it. He has traveled to Washington for just this purpose."

Nikki could feel the anger surge and did her best not to show it. "Mr. Moretti may be able to order you around, but not me. I'm sure we can agree on a mutually convenient time, but in any case I would first want to know what this is about. Understand, I am not going to see him at 9:00."

In soft, measured tones, the woman said, "The car will be there at 9:00, Christa, or should I address you by your real name, Nikki?"

Tiny starbursts of white light exploded in the sudden darkness behind Nikki's eyes, and she felt as if all of the blood pumping through her heart and lungs must suddenly be draining into her stomach. Her chest ached. She was dizzy. In an instant Christa had been reduced to nothing more than a sophisticated Halloween mask, and Nikki was Nikki again. A burden, lifted for too short a time, returned, and her shoulders sagged perceptively. The room seemed darker.

After a few seconds of silence the woman continued. "Now Nikki, it will do no good to try to leave. Men are watching just outside your little hotel – front and back. You may be comforted by the fact that only Mr. Moretti and a very few of his loyal employees, including me of course, know or even suspect that Christa and Nikki, and, oh yes, Patricia Miller, are one and the same. I'm sure you would prefer that others not learn of our little secret. Please be ready promptly at nine. Good bye."

The phone went silent. For half a minute Nikki was frozen in place. Gradually she got her mind working and assessed the damage. As she did so, she began to take heart. Moretti had somehow found her out, and it would have been so easy for him to tip off Pennock and have her arrested, counting on her to identify Virginia as the architect of Taylor's murder. But he didn't. That meant he wanted something, *something that included Christa!* That possibility held her together and breathed life back into Christa. It was what she wanted to believe, what her subconscious needed to believe. She filled the cracks in the dam with hope. *It's not over. I can still be Christa.*

She slowly went to the front door and opened it just enough to peer out. She saw two men in business suits by a car appearing to be engaged in conversation. They both turned to look at her. She shut the door. She showered, dressed, and waited for the car coming at 9:00.

———

She was taken to a suite at the Henley Park Hotel. Moretti greeted her politely as Christa, but she went straight to the point.

"How long have you known?" she asked angrily.

His eyes bore into hers, and his answer was equally direct. "Within a day of our first meeting."

"How obvious is it?" she asked.

"You must know very well that it is not at all obvious. It took precise measurements by a highly skilled technician working with pictures of Christa and Nikki and some very sophisticated software. The results are as conclusive as a fingerprint match, which," he glanced briefly at her fingers, "I expect you have made certain could not be made now. But if I can discover you, so can the FBI, a district attorney, or a prosecutor in a death penalty case. Actually," he continued, "I could simply send them what we have and save them the trouble."

"What do you want?" Nikki asked, trying to temper her anger. Moretti controlled his irritation at Nikki's apparent lack of fear, which he could not understand. Did she not appreciate the precarious position she was in?

He quietly said, "It is not 'what' I want, Christa, it is 'who.'" His reference to her as "Christa" gave her hope an agreement could be struck. He continued, "I believe we have a mutual objective. To this point, you have convinced yourself that you could bring the Congresswoman down somehow and still preserve your identity as Christa. That now depends. I owe you nothing, but as the saying goes, 'the enemy of my enemy is my friend.'" He put up his hand and shook his head sideways. "No, actually that maxim doesn't do you justice. You see, I rather admire you, your determination, and that is why I am going to give you your opportunity to eliminate – if that is not too strong a word – this irritant in our lives."

Nikki sensed it was smart to say nothing, but his words gave her hope that there was a way out. Moretti continued, "Your choices are now just two, and the only reason you have any choice at all is because of our mutual objective. The first choice is that I cause the analysis proving that Christa is Nikki to find its way to the FBI, while at the same time assuring that you do not escape before they apprehend you. But of course, that choice hardly benefits either of us since in a contest of credibility between you and the Congresswoman you would not win. Your other choice is to perform in a little play that you and I are going to write in which the Congresswoman will incriminate herself."

Nikki began to speak, but Moretti raised his hand. He would brook nothing from this arrogant woman. The fierceness of his gaze compelled her to be silent. He continued, "The benefits to you are twofold. First, you will have the revenge you so justly deserve, and a rather evil person will rot in prison. Second, I will keep your secret. In any case, Christa, there is nothing to negotiate. I made this trip to DC just for this meeting, and it has been a considerable inconvenience. Choose now. I have no patience for this. One or the other."

CHAPTER 65

Constitutional Gardens is a fifty-acre park bounded on the west by the Vietnam Veterans Memorial, on the east by 17th Street, on the north by Constitution Avenue, and on the south by a portion of the long and majestic reflecting pool that links the Lincoln and Washington memorials. Within the Gardens is a pond with a small tree-covered island reached by a simple, arching footbridge of wood. The island is rarely visited at night. Although a little light from Constitution Avenue penetrates, the trees on the berm beside the reflecting pool prevent light from the lampposts along the pool from reaching the island.

By 7:30 PM the sun had set and twilight had nearly faded into night. Congresswoman Wetherill quickly crossed the footbridge and approached Christa Cairns standing under the trees. Strollers on the walkways along the reflecting pool were on the other side of the berm and therefore out of sight and hearing. The few people standing or walking in the Gardens that Wetherill could make out in the disappearing light were also well out of earshot. As a practical matter, the two women were alone.

"Christa Cairns?" the Congresswoman inquired in a clipped, impatient voice. "Yes," Nikki answered. "You're the person Nikki Patterson contacted with so-called information that you gave to Moretti?" "Yes," Nikki repeated. "Well?" Wetherill asked, wanting to appear as impatient as she was, "Why insist on telling me first? Why aren't you reporting it to the FBI this very moment?"

These questions were for the benefit of any listening or recording device Christa Cairns might have hidden on her. Wetherill was taking no chances. She had seen little upside to agreeing to this blind meeting in the first place, but couldn't risk refusing it. The information Nikki had leaked to Moretti through Cairns had been dangerous stuff, and if there was more to come, she had to know what it was. She could always tell Pennock she thought she was helping to unearth evidence that would lead to Nikki's whereabouts. He could get as mad as hell, but what could he really do to her? *Nothing,* she had decided.

Answering Wetherill's question, Nikki said, "She would tell me nothing unless I did things her way. This is not my idea."

Wetherill had approached the island anticipating a meeting with someone other than Nikki. The woman she saw in the dim light did not remind her of Nikki. Therefore, it did not occur to Wetherill to look for Nikki in her. She believed she was dealing with some lightweight reporter with an agenda.

"Well Christa Cairns, why do you feel you must keep a promise to a murderer? I suggest you take this so-called evidence right to the FBI where it belongs. I have no interest in trumped up facts and lies." Wetherill was still playing to a hidden recording device.

"I may well end up there. She said she wanted you to suffer." Wetherill felt a stab of fear, but she recovered quickly. "All right, if I can't persuade you to do the right thing, go ahead. I'm all ears. I eagerly await proof that I did something I didn't do. Just what did this crazy woman have to say?" *Crazy am I!* She shouted silently. *Oh, you are going to pay!* She paused to control her anger and then said in a measured tone, "I'm to begin by asking you a question." "Well?" the Congresswoman demanded, consciously putting her right hand on her hip and tapping her left foot. Nikki asked matter-of-factly, "Have you had anyone on the couch in the library since Nikki left? Did you do that special thing you do with your middle finger?" The questions arced between the two women like a strong electric current and consumed the oxygen in the air that Wetherill was trying to breathe.

Those searing questions were not in Moretti's script because Nikki didn't mention to him her affair with Virginia. But Nikki rather liked improvising. The Congresswoman stared at Christa with the dazed look of a prizefighter struck by an unseen roundhouse. She suddenly felt exposed, as if all her clothes had been stripped from her. *Those intimate things,* she thought. *God, Nikki must hate me intensely. She's totally out of her mind!* But her combativeness and survival instincts kicked in. *Bluff,* she demanded of herself. She mustered a bold voice. "Is that little piece of smut why you brought me all the way out here? That's disgusting. I have no idea what you're talking about."

Then in her own voice, one that Wetherill knew so well, Nikki said, "Oh, but you do Virginia."

Startled and confused, Wetherill reflexively said, "What? Say that again." Nikki repeated her words exactly, but in Christa's voice, toying with Wetherill. Although suspicious by nature, at that moment Wetherill needed stability and safety. Besides, there was no logical explanation for what she first heard. So she attributed it to her imagination and dismissed it. She regrouped.

"Look Cairns," she said, "you asked to meet me. Tell me what you know or want. Is it money? Your problem is you don't have anything to bribe me with, and I wouldn't pay a bribe anyhow."

In Christa's voice, Nikki continued, "Did you know the police found your very fresh and clear fingerprint on the interior light switch of your husband's BMW?"

Wetherill scoffed. "If they did, I covered that with the press. That's going nowhere. Whatever you think you know is going to have to be a lot better than that."

"It is," Nikki said. Then, she raised her left arm. In her hand was a small envelope. Wetherill looked at it, then looked at Nikki and waited. She refused to appear curious. Finally Nikki said, "Nikki gave me this. A small tape from a miniature tape recorder?"

"I can see what it is. Low tech stuff for this day and age."

"Nikki said it's a tape from the recorder she used to dictate letters and notes. The one you gave her. She said the recorder can pick up someone speaking thirty feet away.

Wetherill looked at the envelope again. Her eyes narrowed. She thought of her many private conversations with Nikki.

"So this is some shoddy attempt at blackmail after all?"

"No, just proof."

"Ah, proof is it?" Wetherill asked sarcastically, "Of what?"

"That you murdered your husband."

"Ha! There's no such thing."

"Well, Nikki told me that this is a recording of your intimate time with her in your library after the press conference at which you had Nikki tell her story. I listened to it. Your voice is unmistakable. You talked about the murder. Nikki said she would do anything for you, and you replied that by killing Taylor she had already done all you would ever ask of her. It's right here." She held the envelope between her thumb and index finger so more of it was visible.

The recording had been Moretti's idea. He knew Nikki and the Congresswoman had to have planned the murder together. He told Nikki to select one of the conversations in which they spoke of the murder. Christa Cairns would then identify that conversation to Wetherill as the one Nikki recorded.

Now Wetherill could not take her eyes from the envelope. Her mind was racing. *Christ! She recited exactly what happened!* The instinct for self-preservation now dictated her conduct, overriding her usual cleverness and guile. "Let me see that!" she commanded, grabbing at the envelope. Nikki pulled it back but then held it out again. Wetherill snatched it a little too quickly.

"Sure, go ahead. Take it. I know you'll want to hear it for yourself, hear your voice." Then Nikki put her hand in her pocket and pulled out another envelope. "But you can't have this copy or the other ones I have."

To Wetherill this whole scene was beginning to resemble a bad novel. Her legal training kicked in, and she thought hard to get the analysis right. *Recordings can be faked. Cairns hadn't been in the library. She can't authenticate the recording. Only Nikki can do that. I just deny it all and say it's a fake. That's got to be right.* She felt better. *This lightweight isn't going to screw me over!*

Nikki, slightly adjusting the heavy-framed glasses on her nose, continued. "So now you know why I contacted you. What is it worth to you to have the original and all the copies?"

Wetherill was now smirking. "So, it's money after all. You're nothing but a petty thief and a bad one at that! Those tapes are worthless. If you had a thousand of them, they would still be worthless. Voices can be faked. No court would admit them into evidence. Even if they weren't faked, the only person who could authenticate them is Nikki and that would require her to turn herself in. I won't pay a dime for them, so you can jump off a bridge."

Nikki was getting hot now. "What makes you so sure Nikki wouldn't give herself up to see you rot in jail?"

"No one is that crazy, even crazy Nikki!"

At this, Nikki's rising anger exploded and something snapped. She suddenly felt imprisoned within Christa Cairns. She was being crushed. She was not Christa and never really had been. Christa had been flight, and furious Nikki no longer wanted to flee. She was Nikki! If she were immolated in the flames of anger and shame that raged within her, so be it. *But, by God, I will have my revenge!* She was about to go way off script, but she didn't care. In the voice so familiar to Wetherill she slipped the stiletto in, "Oh, I think you are sadly mistaken, Virginia."

Wetherill flinched, muscles contracting involuntarily. That voice was undeniable. She was struck dumb. *What is this?* With dread, she inched closer to see Christa clearly, the chill returning to her chest. Nikki also leaned forward so their faces were very close and finally said aloud what she had so long struggled to deny. "You never loved Taylor, and you never loved me." That simple, condemning utterance could emanate from only one source. Wetherill stared hard at the face.

"Nikki?" she asked, incredulous. Then her mind connected the features that plastic surgery had not altered and an involuntary cry escaped from her throat. In a half-whisper she uttered, "My God, it's you."

Nikki felt a surge of satisfaction. "Yes, I am me!" she exclaimed. "You asked me to kill Taylor! I did what you wanted done. And now you tell the world that I'm crazy?"

In the shock of the moment, Wetherill, always so careful, made her fatal mistake. "I didn't make you do it. I just asked. We agreed it was the best way to deal with the photographs, but you wanted to do it. I didn't make you."

"Hah!" Nikki exclaimed. "You knew I loved you and would do anything for you. Of course you made me do it!" Then her tone abruptly changed. She said matter-of-factly, as if she were ordering paint colors, "You said it yourself. I can authenticate the recording. It will be admissible in court. But you and I both know all I need to do is make it public, and your political enemies will do the rest. You're going to be ruined." Nikki thought back at how Moretti enjoyed writing that part.

Wetherill, the ultimate political animal, knew that Nikki was right. She thought of the small revolver she carried in her purse for protection, but rejected the idea. She asked bitterly, "What do you want for all the tapes and your silence?" With that question, she gave Nikki and Moretti everything. Nikki would have preferred to walk off right there. She didn't like this part because it was all about blackmail, but she knew Moretti would find out she hadn't finished so she continued with his script.

"Well now," she said, "you almost took too long. I was completely out of patience and still am." She wasn't really, but it was in the script. "Two hundred fifty thousand cash," she said.

"What!" Wetherill exclaimed.

"Wrong answer," Nikki said, ad-libbing again. "It's now three hundred thousand, and that's a bargain for getting rid of Taylor. Do you want to keep negotiating?"

Wetherill bit her lip to keep from saying something that might raise the price again. "Okay," she finally said, "I'll pay you two hundred fifty."

Nikki rejoined, "I'll treat that as a slip of the tongue. You meant to say three hundred, right?"

Wetherill paused, trying to control her frustration. Then said simply, "Yes."

"Good. You don't happen to have the money with you?" That was an ad-lib. Nikki was enjoying this again.

"Of course not!" Wetherill snapped.

"Then you have twenty-four hours to..."

"I need forty-eight." Nikki thought for a moment. It really didn't matter because Virginia was likely to be in jail in forty-eight hours, and Nikki would never see the money anyhow.

"Forty-eight," Nikki said. "All in hundred dollar bills in a nice suitcase, and no sequential serial numbers please. I'll contact you about where and when to leave it. Oh, and you won't get the tapes."

"What!" Wetherill exclaimed for the second time, but Nikki just continued ordering paint colors.

"I'll destroy all but one. That one I'll keep just in case I hear that the FBI thinks that Christa is Nikki. That's our little secret."

"That's not the deal!" Wetherill shot back.

"Listen," Nikki ordered, "If I told you I'd handed all the tapes over to you, you would never know if I kept one out. What you're buying is my silence, and what I'm getting is the money and your silence. That's why the deal works. Take it or leave it." She extended her hand for the envelope.

Glaring, Wetherill said, "Calling you crazy was to help you! If you're captured, you can plead temporary insanity." Nikki glared at her and then slowly, bitterly, gave the only response there was.

"Help me, Virginia? Help me? When did you ever do anything to help anyone but yourself?" In the silence that followed she again motioned for the envelope with her hand. Wetherill slowly raised her arm and extended her long fingers. The envelope seemed suspended between the two women for an instant, and then Nikki's fingers closed on it.

Slipping it into her pocket, Nikki gestured back toward the footbridge and said, "You go first. I'll wait here a few minutes."

Wetherill looked at her in the dim light, "I could kill you right now, claim self-defense, and no jury would convict me."

"Sure," Nikki responded. "But would you win the next election?" The question hung in the air between them, as the envelope had a moment earlier.

"Bitch!" Wetherill spit out. Then she turned on her heels and moved quickly to the footbridge, crossed it, and hurried off into the night, knowing that for the first time her political future was no longer in her hands alone. She had no idea how right she was.

Nikki waited. Nothing moved for three minutes after Wetherill disappeared into the darkness. Then two men who had been well concealed crossed the bridge onto the island. Each carried a duffle bag. When they reached Nikki, one of them said, "Coast is clear." Nikki removed her glasses. As the stems came into view from under her hair, their unusual thickness was noticeable. She handed the glasses to one of the men, who carefully put them in a pocket of his jacket.

The other man handed Nikki the bag he carried. "One hundred thousand in hundreds," he said. "You've never seen us, and we've never seen you."

The man still holding a duffle said, "By the way," he tapped the duffle, "this night vision telescopic camera caught the whole thing. Even better than those glasses you wore. Got both of you."

"Yeah, thanks for including me," Nikki said absentmindedly. Something happening within her had her attention. The same man said, "You went off script, but it really blew her mind. Better than we ever expected. He'll be pleased." Nikki mustered a shrug. Moretti's men said nothing more and left.

The plan was for her to wait three minutes before leaving to insure that no one would see them with her. But she wasn't counting. She was bone weary, and she felt the isolation of the dark little island. She was a dark little island. She had just sacrificed Christa to dispatch Virginia, and with both gone she was utterly alone in the world, connected to no one by love or hate. Without Christa to protect her, the awful shame, always ready, began to pull her down. Always she had fought against it, but this time had been different. She had made a deal with Moretti that let her keep Christa's true identity safe. Yet she had just given that identity away. *Myself! And On tape!* And now she was only Nikki. Bare and unprotected. *Why didn't I fight?* She asked herself. *What have I done?*

She was sinking and didn't resist. All the strain and tension that had characterized her life before Christa bore down on her again. She felt weary to the bone. *You're too tired,* she told herself. *Let it go. Give it up.* She thought of death and welcomed it. Her only way out.

But just as a darkening sky suddenly makes previously undetectable heat lightning faintly visible in a cloud, her blackening mood made her aware of a faint burst of energy she would not otherwise have detected. *What?* She asked herself. She could feel it. Some little thing nagged. *Forget it. Let it go,* she told herself again. But it wouldn't go. She concentrated on sinking, but that was not how sinking worked. It decided.

A thought fragment came to her from nowhere. *Unfinished business.* She was curious. *What does it mean?* Curiosity meant she was fighting again. She focused on it. *Is it Moretti?* Her concept of justice ranked Moretti high among cruel and despicable bastards, but his disruption of her life had been reactive. Virginia went after him, so he retaliated with the photographs. She, Nikki, tried to use him to bring Virginia down, and he outsmarted her. *No, not Moretti,* she told herself.

Now she was thinking only as Nikki thought, all traces of Christa except the mask now gone. Then it came to her. She knew her unfinished business. Her stepfather, who despoiled her just to assuage his sexual appetite, had escaped her revenge because she had dallied. But he had not been the only one to wreck Nikki's life in selfish pursuit of sexual pleasure. And that person was still out there. She had escaped once. "The Whore won't escape me again," Nikki vowed to the night.

She strode from the darkness of the island to the lighted city streets and hailed a cab. She needed to plan to do what was necessary. *After necessary,* she told herself, *everyone and everything could go to hell.*

CHAPTER 66

T had was deep in a beautiful dream. Isabella and he were in the first flight of foxhunters galloping across a rolling pasture with eighteen couples of foxhounds in full cry two hundred yards ahead pursuing a large and healthy red fox. The disciplined hounds were following by scent, not sight, yet they were together in a tight pack. The riders could hear the huntsman blowing "gone away" on his horn as he galloped hard to stay with his hounds. The sound of the horn gradually became central to Thad's dream as it turned more and more into a ring. Then it was only a ring, and it pulled Thad to the surface. He mechanically reached for his bedside phone and sleepily said, "Pennock."

"Fifteen seconds, so just listen," Nikki began.

Moretti had ordered Nikki to alert Thad to the recordings, take credit for setting up the trap for the Congresswoman, and keep him out of it. That was fine with Nikki. It gave her an opportunity to convince Thad that she was no longer hunting Isabella.

"You're going to get a video delivered to your office early this morning that will blow your mind," she continued. "Virginia admits she planned Taylor's murder. She has no idea I was taping her. She's done it to herself. What a fraud she is. Wish I could be there to see her face. So long Pennock. Have a nice life. I plan to." The phone went dead.

Thad slowly lowered the receiver, repeating in his gauzy mind Nikki's message until he had it clear. What he didn't have clear was why her voice sounded so.... devoid of emotion. He looked at his watch, picked up the phone, called Owens, and, sure enough, after only two rings Owens answered. He told Owens about Nikki's call and then said, "Let's be at the office by seven-thirty."

CHAPTER 67

A t 8:00 the next morning, one of Moretti's men stopped
a teenager on the sidewalk two blocks from the FBI
building and offered him $50 to take a small suitcase there,
warning him that he would be watched. The young man
jumped at it. Taped to the suitcase was a letter to Special
Agent Thaddeus Pennock, Chief of the Washington, DC
office, and marked "CONFIDENTIAL." It contained a
DVD of the clandestine meeting, the sophisticated night
vision cameras and microphones that had recorded it, and
the original memory cards containing the original digital
record.

Owens and Thad watched the DVD straight through with
no stops or comments. The images from the camera glasses
Nikki wore showed Wetherill's face and upper body clearly and
recorded the words of both women. Unknowingly, Wetherill
had been looking right into the lens of that camera. The
quality of the images and sound from the remote camera and
mike was more than adequate to identify the Congresswoman,
particularly because her voice was so distinctive.

The close up camera content was burned onto the DVD first. When the off-camera voice changed from Christa's voice to Nikki's, Thad and Owens shared in the amazement that they saw written on the Congresswoman's face. They watched, fascinated, as this seemingly invincible woman recognized Nikki and, thrown off balance, spoke of her central role in her husband's murder. Then the entire scene was repeated as recorded by the remote camera, and the two men saw both women. They were astonished at the transformation of Nikki's appearance. They would never have suspected that the person they saw was Nikki.

They were equally impressed with Nikki's performance. She had played to Wetherill's weakness – her need to win not just every war, but every battle in every war. *Probably the only way she could ever be caught,* Thad told himself.

When the disc ended, Owens hit the stop button, and Thad said, "Lew needs to know ASAP so he can report to the Director and be planning for the political side of this while we figure out how we want to get the cuffs on her."

As they walked the halls to the Deputy Director's office, Owens said, "He'll want to know where the tapes and this equipment really came from." Thad knew what he meant.

"We tell him what Nikki told me when she called me." He chuckled and added, "Jesus, I assume it was Nikki. Who knows who's real in this case? Then we tell him what we think."

Owens picked up the theme. "Moretti uses Nikki to take down the Congresswoman. Either she disclosed to him that Christa was Nikki or he figured it out and used it as leverage to persuade her to trap Wetherill." Thad nodded in agreement.

"Moretti lied to us. If we can take Nikki alive, maybe she'll rat on him. Then at least we'll have him on harboring a murderer and aiding and abetting a murderer after the fact."

They were approaching Porter's office. Thad said, "Odds are there's nothing on that video equipment we can trace back to Moretti."

"Probably right," Owens said, "but you never know. Yesterday I thought we'd capture Nikki because she needed to stay above ground to get back at Wetherill, but I figured we'd never get Wetherill. Today, well, we have Wetherill cold, but may never get Nikki." He paused and then imparted some Owens' wisdom. "We're always assessing our chances based on what we can do with the information we have. But then out of the blue, no thanks to our efforts, the criminal or his world just hands us the key to the kingdom."

"Well, it's a good thing this particular key fits this particular lock perfectly because our red-headed, green-eyed dragon will probably make a ruckus they'll hear in Tasmania."

It took Lew Porter about a minute after seeing the video and only one "son-of-a-bitch!" to direct Thad to "take it to Jake."

The District Attorney for the District of Columbia was skeptical at first. The electronic evidence had not come with any chain of custody or with a live body to testify about who took the videos. But after studying the tapes, he was convinced. The lady was the Congresswoman beyond any reasonable doubt. She could yell, "fake" from the dome of the capital, but since the two videos recorded the same event, each authenticated the other. They would get into evidence regardless of her lawyers' efforts to keep them from the jury. Jake was on board with first-degree murder.

Later that morning Thad and Owens had a final "go ahead" meeting with Lew Porter and Jake in Porter's office. "Unless those videos turn into pumpkins at midnight," Porter said, "one distinguished Congresswoman is going to jail for a long time." They discussed details of needed steps prior to the arrest, and then Thad spoke.

"If we're through cocking the hammer, I want you to hear an idea I tried out on Owens. He thought it was worth considering."

Porter looked at Owens. "Hell," he said, "I like it already!" He liked it even more after Thad spun it out.

CHAPTER 68

Congresswoman Wetherill paced her office on the Hill. Her thoughts bounced back and forth between what she should have done, *shoot the bitch,* the Beretta in her purse flashing through her mind, and what she should do next. *What's the worst case?* She asked herself. She finally decided the worst was Nikki leaking more information to the police, maybe even the tape, *if it's real. If only I knew for sure it wasn't, I could call Pennock and tell him everything about last night...almost everything. I'd be the one to expose Christa Cairns as Nikki.* But she didn't know for sure, and she would be risking her political career. That was the clincher. She stopped and took a deep breath. Her bet was on Nikki never getting caught. *Out of my hands,* she realized. *Get on with it.* She stopped pacing, leaned one hand on her desk next to the telephone, and, looking at nothing in particular, returned to thoughts about what to liquidate to raise $300,000.

She jumped when the phone rang, and she took a few more rings to gather herself before answering. Thad, waiting on the other end, thought back to Jake's reaction to his idea. "You really think she'll buy that crap?"

Thad had replied, "She has no option. She knows that if we have Nikki, Nikki will try to nail her. She wants it all to go down with her spin on it – 'deranged, crazy Nikki trying to destroy me out of spite because she thinks I abandoned her.' No. The Congresswoman has to come, and once we get her here, the key will be to get her to consent to the session being recorded."

Porter had interjected, "What if we don't get what we want?" Thad answered with a question, "Is there a downside? I don't see it."

"Who's in the room?"

"Owens and I. We don't want her distracted by having to psych out someone new. The rest of you and the two formal witnesses would be behind the glass. Come on Lew, nothing to lose. Take the shot." Porter shifted his perpetual cigar and said to no one in particular, but clearly meant for everyone, "Could turn into a circus, a one-pretty-pissed-off-Congresswoman circus." Thad knew that meant, "let's go."

After four rings, the Congresswoman picked up. "Yes?" she said, sounding more irritated than she wanted to. *Get it together Wetherill,* she told herself. Thad was surprised the call had not been filtered through her staff.

"Congresswoman Wetherill, this is Agent Pennock." He did not stop. "I hope you are available because we've had a significant development." *A trap?* she thought.

But she said, "I will make time, Agent Pennock," satisfied now with the even tone of her voice.

"We have Nikki." He stopped. The Congresswoman waited a moment to make sure she was totally into her role. She couldn't give any hint that Nikki's capture was a danger to her.

"Oh thank goodness," she sighed. "Now maybe this whole nightmare will end."

Thad picked up the theme. "Yes, you can't imagine the heat I've taken as this has dragged on. She's been so clever, so slippery, but I guess confidence in her change of identity into Christa Cairns made her a little careless." Silence again for a moment.

"Her what? Change into whom? I'm not following you." Completely in her role, Wetherill had not been tripped up. If she had not asked those questions, the omission would have given her away. Thad begrudgingly gave her credit for that.

"Yes," he said, "She had plastic surgery, lost weight, and did some other things. She really looks different."

"How did you find out?"

"Actually, I can't tell you that, not now anyway. But we really need your help."

"My help?" she asked warily.

Here goes the bullshit, he thought. "Yes, your help. She's not admitting to being Nikki. Her fingerprints have been altered. We can't get a match, and we can't get an order to do the physical testing to prove she is Nikki without a sworn statement by someone who knows Nikki well. Sounds crazy I'm sure, but we'll have to let her go unless we have probable cause for such an order. They aren't issued lightly because the tests involve touching her body, getting DNA samples, strapping her down if she resists, that sort of thing. My saying she is really Nikki, or some other officer of the law saying it, won't cut it. But you know her better than anyone, and if you can say it, I think we'll get the order. So I need you here to look at her in front of witnesses and see if you can honestly say Cairns is Nikki. Then we can arrest her as Nikki and have the time to have the experts confirm it."

He had spoken quickly with as much authority in his voice as he could muster. He did not give her time to question or comment. He kept on. "How soon can you be here? This is important. Fifteen minutes?" She didn't bite yet.

"I really don't understand. Has she admitted to being Nikki?"

He was getting worried. "Oh no. That's why we need the order."

"But if she doesn't look enough like Nikki to get an order and you can't get prints, why do you think it's Nikki?"

He could only stone wall. "I wish I could tell you now, but I can't. We need you."

There was silence for long seconds. Thad was tempted to fill them. Silence wasn't good. But he could only repeat his thin story and that was worse. He shut his eyes tight and waited. Finally she said, "You know I can't get there that quickly. Maybe half an hour or a little sooner." Thad exhaled. He hadn't realized he'd been holding his breath. *The hook set,* he thought.

"As soon as you can. I'll have an agent waiting for you at the main entrance. Thank you, Congresswoman. You're right. Maybe this will end it all."

Before he could ring off, she asked, "What if I can't tell? Can't recognize her?"

"Nothing lost. Please be here as soon as you can, and thank you." He rang off, not wanting her to have time for second thoughts or probing questions. He turned to Owens, "She took it, but just in case, radio the tails. If she goes anywhere but here, have them arrest her." *We screwed up bringing Nikki in. Not this time!* He kept this thought to himself.

Thirty minutes later, Owens and Thad sat in silence at the main table in interrogation room 2. On a stand against one wall was a forty-eight inch flat screen television and DVD player containing a disc that FBI techies had burned using the data on the DVD delivered to Thad. The original had the entire meeting recorded by Nikki's eyeglasses camera first followed by the meeting as recorded by the remote camera. The techies' disc jumped back and forth between cameras, showing fifteen seconds of action recorded by one camera followed by the same fifteen seconds recorded by the other. The remote control lay on the table close to Owens' right hand.

The interrogation room was designed so that everything that occurred could be taped and observed. Four cameras looked down from the ceiling where it abutted the midpoint of each of the four walls. About two-thirds of the wall directly behind the television was a one-way window fronting an observation room. Five people waited there for Wetherill to arrive – Lew Porter and two FBI agents, and the Majority and Minority leaders of the House of Representatives.

Porter had called the two House leaders and told them that there was a matter of urgency involving the conduct of a prominent House member, that time was of the essence, that it was to be totally confidential, and that only certain FBI officials on a need to know basis and the District Attorney's Office were aware of the matter. They were told that they would witness an event about which they would later be asked to testify. So as not to taint their testimony they could be told nothing further now.

He asked if they would make themselves available as soon as possible. His ace was telling each of them he was calling the other. Both readily agreed. After all, they were politicians. Each figured that at some point in the future, when it could be made public, whatever "it" was, there would be political hay to harvest. Besides, neither could afford turning down the request knowing the other might accept. Thad's call to Congresswoman Wetherill was keyed off of their arrival at FBI headquarters.

When the cars tailing the Congresswoman reported that she was about to enter the parking garage of the FBI building, the witnesses took their places. They received another alert one minute before she was expected to be at the door of the interrogation room. Fifty seconds later there was a knock, and the agent escorting the Congresswoman opened the door and motioned her in, then shut the door after her. Wetherill, in a tailored, green tweed suit the color of her eyes and a white blouse and green and yellow silk scarf quickly surveyed the room. She had had enough time to think through her situation. She had only one way to play it. She would tell Pennock that she couldn't recognize Nikki. She told herself, *maybe then she'll return the favor and not sell me out.* She wasn't worried about going to jail even if Nikki ratted on her because it would still be her word against crazy Nikki's, but she wanted to preserve her political career if possible.

She walked in confidently and held out her hand. Cordially, but all business, Thad said, "Thank you for coming on such short notice." The Congresswoman was all business too.

She shook hands saying simply, "Gentlemen." With no pause, she looked at Thad and asked, "Where is she?"

Thad wanted her busy with no time to rethink whether she should cooperate. Moving more quickly than normal to convey the impression that Nikki would appear soon, Thad directed her to the table and to the chair facing the TV and the one-way mirror behind it. He sat to her right facing Owens, who sat to her left, both men about four feet from her. "They are bringing Nikki in now, Congresswoman," Thad answered. "But for this to go right and give us a clean arrest, do you see these four cameras and this large mirror?" He pointed at them as he spoke. "We need to have what happens observed and taped. Okay with you?"

This was the critical moment. If she were thinking like a lawyer, it would occur to her that her permission was not important unless they expected something to occur that would incriminate *her*, not Nikki. But she had already decided her best bet was to appear cooperative, so she was focusing on that and missed the significance of the question. Inside she answered, *none of this is okay with me, asshole!* Aloud she asked, "People are behind the mirror?" He could handle this question, but not the logical next one. He couldn't let her have time to ask *who?* If he lied about who was there, it would taint the whole necessary consent. If he told the truth, she'd know she was the target.

"Of course," Thad answered. "Best to have witnesses. It's routine procedure. Are you ready?"

She looked at the mirror quizzically then caught herself. *Don't look concerned about that for Christ sake!* She turned to look at Thad, "Let's get on with it." On the other side of the mirror Porter, who had forsaken his cigar in the small room, blew out his lungs through puffed cheeks.

Gesturing toward the television screen, Thad said, "You need to see something first." Before she could ask, "Why?" he nodded to Owens, who immediately hit the "play" button twice, and the dark screen came alive. Ten minutes earlier, Owens had paused the disc at just the point where Wetherill spoke of her role in her husband's murder.

In the first few seconds, the witnesses behind the mirror watched Wetherill orient herself. Her brow furrowed as she recognized her face. Surprise registered when she heard the fateful words she had foolishly let slip, and it dawned upon her that Nikki had recorded their meeting. A look of shock swiftly followed as the significance of the existence of the tape hit home. Finally, they saw her face distort with rage. "God damn!" she roared as she pushed away from the table with both hands and shot to her feet. Her body was rigid. Her fingers were balled into fists, but she could not take her eyes from the screen. "Pennock!" she yelled, fixated on the screen. "What is this? What the hell are you doing?"

Then the video shifted to the same scene captured by the remote camera. The Congresswoman, confused but mesmerized, leaned towards the screen and therefore towards the observers behind the mirror. Her jaw dropped as she clearly saw and heard both Nikki and herself. *Somebody else was watching us? Taping us?* Then she tore her icy eyes from the screen and cold-burned them into Thad, who sat looking up at her, motionless and infuriatingly calm. "That's entrapment, you bastard! I'm having your ass and your badge for this!" Thad sat quiet and unmoved. He knew it was not entrapment. The police had not been involved. He also knew that with every word and gesture she was confirming her guilt, and it was all being recorded and witnessed.

Wetherill wanted no part of these sounds and sights that were condemning her. She turned her blazing eyes to Owens and pointed to the remote control in his hand. "Shut that off!" He did not move or speak. She lunged down the table and grabbed at the control, yelling, "Turn it off! Turn it off!" Owens easily wrenched the control away from her, but in the process one of them hit the pause button, freezing on the screen the exact instant Virginia handed the envelope back to Nikki.

When the Moretti lieutenant operating the remote camera had seen Nikki put her hand out, he had zoomed in to insure that the item exchanged could be recognized. So the still picture was a close-up.

It shocked Wetherill. She stared at it, stock-still and speechless. The swift transition within the room from motion to stillness mimicked the screen. Both were now in freeze frame. In another context the picture on the screen could have been photographic art, a slightly gauzy black and white photograph, tinged green by the night vision optics, of Wetherill's magnificent long fingers extended toward Nikki's with the wispy envelope almost suspended in the air between them.

But this was ugly life, not art. The clandestine exchange, secretly captured for the entire world to see, symbolized like nothing else could the original devil's bargain Wetherill made with Nikki to murder Taylor Warner. The observers behind the mirror were looking directly into Wetherill's face, and each saw there not fear or anger but sheer desperation as Wetherill was compelled to look upon a profound truth she needed to evade but could not.

Five silent seconds stretched to ten. Then the stiffness left Wetherill's posture. Her back rounded, and her shoulders slumped. Slowly, without speaking or taking her eyes from the screen, she sank into her chair. The onlookers watched fixated as her head fell back over the chair back as far as her neck would permit. Her blazing red hair fell toward the floor, strong scarlet curls bouncing until they reached an accommodation with gravity, and then they hung still. Her widening eyes stared upward. Then she slowly raised both arms straight up until her elbows locked in the air. Her hands opened and she reached in vain for what even those long, magnificent fingers could no longer touch, let alone possess. From deep within her breast an eerie sound started quietly and grew to a chilling wail made all the more unearthly by her stretched neck's constriction of her throat.

The wail seemed unending. Finally her lungs emptied, and the sound faded, leaving an unsettling silent echo rather than simple silence. Slowly, very slowly, her arms fell until they hung limply, her fingers slightly curled and still just above the floor. At the same time her head drew up and then fell forward, again as far as her neck would permit. Her hair followed, covering her face like a red curtain descending at the end of a play. Then she was perfectly still.

No one moved for almost ten seconds – a very long time in that charged atmosphere. To those watching it was frightening. Each observer felt that at some level the form slumped motionless in the chair was deserving of compassion.

Who Congresswoman Wetherill really was and who her unquenchable ambition drove her to be had long since become indistinguishable. If the video had not accidently paused but instead had continued playing, she might have continued raging at Thad and Owens and fighting and denying the undeniable evidence of her guilt playing out before her in the belief that she ultimately would overwhelm her predicament by sheer will. But it did pause, and the image frozen on the screen gripped her and forced her to see a truth she could not explain away or blow past. She was a fake, an expectant flower that proceeded directly from bud to rot, devouring itself without ever opening to the world. And the world was going to know. Lacking any clever defense or explanation with which to mesmerize her public, she simply walked off the stage.

Thad was shaken, but he was the first to move. He dropped his gaze, slowly rose, and touched the Congresswoman's shoulder and, bending down, looked into her face. Her eyes were open but blank. She was breathing regularly but was so still that Thad thought she might be in a clinical stupor. Owens' fingers moved, and the television screen went dark. Then he quietly stood, also focusing on the still figure drooped in the chair beside him. The movements of the two agents had no effect on Wetherill. Thad quietly went to the door where a female sergeant waited. "I didn't think to have a doctor handy," he said.

"We did," she answered. "We thought she might need a sedative. Lord knows what she needs now. The doc should be along any minute."

"Stay with her," Thad said. He looked over his shoulder at Owens. "Better if you stay too until we know what her condition is." The sergeant moved into the room. Thad looked once more at the still figure. The blaze seemed to have leached out of her great mane of hair.

Thad approached the observation room door as it opened, and those in it somberly began to emerge. Thad held up a hand. "If you don't mind, let's go back in for just a moment. It's as private as any room we have." No one protested. When all were inside and the door shut, Thad looked at each burdened face and noted how ashen the two politicians were. Indeed, he was concerned that the minority leader might be ready to pass out. She had beads of sweat on her upper lip and forehead. He said to all of them, meaning it really for her, "You may wish to sit for just a moment." She did, after turning her chair away from the window.

Porter was the first to speak, "Christ!" Then he looked at one of the other agents, who was a legal expert on rules of evidence. "Tom, you saw we got her consent? She had no idea what she was going to see. Are we okay?"

Not hesitating, Tom answered, "With the live witnesses here, it may not even matter, but it was by the book. The tapes of this..." He paused and searched for the right word to describe what he had witnessed, but it did not come, so he simply gestured towards the room ".... are admissible." He continued, "As to the tape playing on the TV, the audio was loud enough so the video can be identified by the sound, even if the camera behind her couldn't pick up what was on the TV screen."

"We tested that. The camera picks it up," Thad said.

"Well, we can't ask for more than that."

Porter spoke again. "Before we go on..." He paused and began again. "I've been in this business for some time and I've seen a lot. The Congresswoman is a cunning, ruthless murderer. I've watched her type executed and felt no remorse." He took a breath. "But I have never seen a self-execution like we just witnessed. I'm trying my best not to, but I find myself pitying this woman, and I don't find that a contradiction." He shook his head as if to clear it. Thad couldn't remember his boss stringing together that many sentences with that many words without at least one being off color. Then Porter said, "All right, Tom, let's wrap this up in a nice pink bow."

The agent addressed the two politicians. "We will need you to go into separate rooms with a witness we'll provide so you can dictate to a stenographer every detail of what you saw and heard from the minute the Congresswoman entered the room to the time Agent Owens turned off the TV monitor. You will then be asked to read it, make any corrections, and sign it. That may seem like a formality now, but remember who Congresswoman Wetherill is. By the time she is arraigned, she most likely will have recovered and be hell bent to fight. You know as well as anyone how formidable she can be. She's trumped up a lot of sympathy out there. Also, please say nothing about this to anyone and walk away from anyone who wants to discuss it with you until you have testified. Any questions?" There were nods of agreement. The typically gregarious politicians were quiet as they walked from the room, shocked by the impact of the drama and by the fall of their high-flying colleague in the House.

Thad and Porter returned to the interrogation room. The doctor had arrived and was examining Wetherill. She had not moved. They stood near the door and motioned Owens to join them. Thad asked, "Is she awake and talking?"

Owens answered, "She's answering the doctor's questions when he presses her."

"Her answers make sense?"

"Yes," Owens said.

"Ask the doctor if she would comprehend them if you read her her rights. If he says 'yes', go ahead. If not, make sure the doctors and others with her know that as soon as she can understand it, it gets done. I don't want her blurting out something useful to us that we can't use."

"Understood."

Porter added, "The next step is up to the docs. If she's sent to the hospital, full security detail. If no hospital, she gets her own cell with suicide watch. Either place, no access except the doctors and her lawyer unless Thad or I or Jake says otherwise." Owens nodded his head in agreement. "Shit," Porter said, "Her lawyer's gonna earn every damn penny of his fee. She'll pull herself together and be ready to fight like hell. He'll have to convince her to plead to second-degree murder, if the DA gives her that option. Can you see her agreeing to that?" He answered his own question. "Hell no! Combat pay, that's what that poor guy will deserve. God damn combat pay!"

Thad and Porter walked together to Porter's office. Thad's adrenalin was leaking away, and he was tired. He said, "Lew, give me a minute?" They both sat down, and Thad exhaled heavily.

"Well?" Porter asked, taking a fresh cigar from the humidor on his desk and slipping it between his teeth.

"Given that this worked out pretty well, I'd like to take the weekend off. Isabella's flying from Buenos Aires to New York tonight. She has a fundraiser there tomorrow, but she's planning to make the eight pm train to Philly tomorrow night. I'll pick her up, and we're spending the weekend at the farm. Anything I really need to do, including the paper work, I can finish up tomorrow."

Porter looked at him, moving the cigar from one side of his mouth to the other and back in one continuous motion. Hearing no response Thad continued, "Lew, you don't need me here. The press will go nuts when this story breaks, but, hell, you were right there. Besides, you love that stuff, at least when we look good! You can get along without me."

Porter silently continued to look at Thad and then blinked twice and frowned. Solemnly he said, "Jesus, Thad. I don't know. Get along without you for two whole days? This fucking place just might fall apart without your invaluable presence. Not sure I can risk leaving the nation's ass exposed for that long."

Thad grimaced. "Christ, I did sound all important, didn't I?" Porter grinned through his cigar and turned his palms up as if to say, "Well?"

What he did say was, "I seem to recall that Superman took occasional weekends. Don't worry. When the Director asks me where you are – I'm sure he'll notice the gaping hole in our security net – I'll tell him you are on special assignment enforcing the Monroe Doctrine and cementing relations between Argentina and the good old U.S. of A."

CHAPTER 69

It was after 10:30 the following night when Thad turned his car into his driveway. Isabella was in a deep sleep in the seat next to him and had been asleep for twenty minutes. The headlights threw out just enough light to the side to illuminate a portion of the fence bordering a horse paddock on the right and a portion of the grove of bushes and trees on the left that eventually gave way to lawn. Soon the high beams played on the 1811 brick Georgian farmhouse that was the only real home Thad had ever known. Invisible in the dark behind and to the left of the house by 150 yards was the 1810 fieldstone bank barn that now housed only Thad's four horses and Oscar and Oreo, playful cats that kept the barn free of rats and mice. Just beyond the barn to the west were three small horse paddocks and south of the barn was a ten-acre, fenced pasture with a two-acre pond. Beyond these enclosures to the south and west were crop fields that ended at the edge of woods that began about 500 yards south and west of the barn. An extension of the upper level of the barn served as a garage.

Although Thad was tired, it was a good tired. The extraordinary woman he found himself in love with was next to him, and he experienced the serenity he always felt returning to his home. The farm and surrounding country had not much changed in his life time and represented for him a continuity that gave meaning to individual lives and sustained his conviction that despite the moral corruption he fought every day, there was more good than evil in the world.

Approaching the house, Thad decided to stop in the circle in front rather than put the car in the garage. He endured with a smile the familiar pang of guilt he felt every time he postponed or pulled up just short of completing a task, however insignificant. *Damn Quakers,* he said to himself. Isabella woke when he stopped the car and turned off the ignition. She raised a sleepy face to his and kissed his cheek. "Here we are," he said. "You finally get to experience for yourself my little corner of the world."

"Tomorrow," she replied with a smile. "Tonight I just want to experience you." She kissed him again. He got out intending to round the car and open her door, but she didn't wait. She had dressed comfortably in slacks and walking shoes for the train ride and bounced out and met Thad at the trunk. He lifted out their luggage and his shoulder holster, which he had taken off when they started their journey. He didn't disturb the rifle lying in the back of the trunk. It traveled with him.

There were no stars visible, no lights on in the house, and the houses of the nearest neighbors were a quarter of a mile or more away and masked by trees in full leaf. The only light came from the courtesy light in his car, which shut off seconds after he shut the trunk. In the darkness, he took Isabella's arm, drew a deep and exhilarating breath of the country air and looked up at the deep black of the night sky. "No neon lights out here," he said to her.

"Then I'm lost without you," she said playfully, snuggling closer. He did not need light. He guided her the ten yards to the four wide stone steps leading up to the brick terrace that ran the length of the front of the house and extended around to the south side where it expanded into a large oval that overlooked the south lawn and the Ha-Ha wall and pasture beyond. He loved the old brick of the house and marveled at the fact that it had changed little since laid here more than two hundred years before.

They reached the tall front doors. The outer one was a single pane of glass, framed by wood painted a deep ivory. Behind it was the main door of stained white oak almost as old as the house. Thad set down his bag, notched his shoulder holster under his left arm, and reached for the brass knob of the unlocked glass door. The tiny, dancing dot of bright red light he caught in his peripheral vision was on the brick to his left only an instant before darting right and disappearing because Isabella's body blocked it.

He reacted instinctively. He wrenched Isabella to him the instant before the glass door noisily shattered, nearly drowning out the report from the rifle. "Thad!" Isabella yelled. "Down and run!" he shouted back, crouching and running while pulling her between him and the house so any bullet that found her would have to find him first. *Nikki!* He told himself. *Right-handed!* He was already thinking tactically. He knew it was marginally harder for a right-hander to rotate a rifle to the right than to the left and still aim accurately at a moving target. He heard the second round an instant after it smashed into the brick just behind his head, and he felt the sting of displaced brick dust as it flew into the left side of his face. "Ouch!" He heard Isabella say at the same time, her voice now more mad than fearful. She raised her left hand to her face reflexively in response to the pain from the brick dust.

They had nearly reached the corner of the house when Thad felt a third round rip his jacket a fraction of an inch above his hunched shoulders and slam into the brick, exploding more stinging dust into both of them. *High caliber, semi-automatic,* ran through Thad's head. Then they were around the corner and heading for the back to get the house between them and the shooter as fast as possible. Thad prayed Nikki was alone and that he wasn't running Isabella straight into an oncoming bullet. When they reached the back of the house, Thad shouted a whisper, "Come on, to the side of the barn!" And he ran as fast as she could. *She'll be faster if I let go of her arm,* he thought. But he could not, however rational it would have been. She was his to protect. *No shots,* he thought thankfully.

He hoped to hear tires screeching and a car speed away. But the only sounds were running sounds and Isabella's breathing. He thought about Nikki's military training and marksmanship awards. *Damn, this is trouble!* He told himself. His mind raced. *Which way is she coming?* They were almost to the corner of the barn. He stole a glance at Isabella and could make out the determined look on her face. *Some tough lady,* he thought admiringly. But he quickly focused back on their predicament. *She is surely dressed for night-stalking, maybe even night vision goggles. Has that damn laser scope.*

They reached the edge of the barn. "You okay?" he asked.

"Yes," she replied. She was in control and not breathing hard. She kept herself in shape. "Let me run by myself, I can be faster."

"All right, but stay right behind me. In this dark you could run into something, besides we don't want to provide any wider a target than we have to. We're heading for the woods. I know them, she doesn't."

"It is Nikki, isn't it?" She spoke it as a question, but needed no answer.

"Climb here," he said, "and there will be another three-rail fence in about fifty yards." Isabella agilely vaulted the fence.

She had never before heard the whine of a bullet passing close by, but as she landed on the far side she knew that was the sound she had just heard, and she sensed that the round barely missed her ear. "Christ!" Thad whispered. "Run and weave!" In no time they covered the fifty yards. "Fence coming up," he said over his shoulder. Isabella was right on his heels. *In a foot race she'd clean my clock,* he thought as they quickly got over. "Now it's a fair distance to the woods. You okay?"

"I'm just glad you brought your gun." Isabella replied. Thad looked with surprise at the shoulder holster in his hand. He had been so intent upon Isabella's safety that he forgot he was holding it. He ripped the Glock 22 from its holster, threw the holster down, and took off, no longer worried whether Isabella could keep up.

In the soybean field they were totally in the open. He tried to zigzag. She followed. He could feel wetness thicker than sweat dripping from his left temple, and the pain from the brick-dust burns on his neck surprised him. Not slowing, he drew his left hand over his neck and left ear to check if he'd actually been hit. He moved his hand to his forehead and felt a stab of pain as he inadvertently pushed on a shard of glass embedded there. His fingers plucked it out, and he could feel the bleeding increase slightly.

They were gaining on the woods. Another two hundred yards and they would be there. Looming as a darker black than the night, the woods looked impenetrable. But he knew them, and that knowledge was their only advantage, however small. He heard another shot, and because he heard it he knew it missed him. *She can see us!* He also knew it missed Isabella right behind him because if it hadn't, he would have heard the sickening sound of the slug plowing into her body. Then, they reached the woods and plunged into the darker darkness there and on to a narrow horse trail. "Be right behind me," he ordered, "arm up to your face!" He had to slow down to a careful trot. He moved with his left arm up protecting his eyes from branches. When he calculated he was about forty yards or so deep, he slowed to a walk. He spoke to her without stopping. "We have to walk to move as noiselessly as possible. Try not to snap any twigs. The sound really carries."

If Nikki has night vision, she can move faster and quieter in the woods. No way to know, he thought. He hoped she hadn't heard the little noise they had made so far.

Moving silently demanded nearly all of their attention, but Thad was visualizing the familiar terrain. He was thinking of a hiding place or an escape route. He knew, if Isabella did not, that his Glock was little comfort. *If she's close enough for me to use it, Isabella is already dead.* His breathing seemed loud to him. Isabella was soundless. *She's showing me up at my game!* A hint of annoyance at that flashed across his competitive mind and disappeared. In another one hundred yards he knew he would come to the creek. The water varied in depth from six inches to two feet. The creek banks were twelve to fifteen feet wide at the top, but the creek bed lay three to four feet below the floor of the woods, sometimes even lower, and that could afford some protection.

Although it meandered, the creek ran generally perpendicular to the direction they were moving. So Thad had to decide whether to turn left or right or cross it or move in it. Without thinking of it as a formed plan, he reached the creek and quickly lowered himself down the muddy bank as silently as he could. Isabella followed. He crossed and scrambled up the other side, ran eight or ten feet and stopped. She was right behind. He turned, "Backtrack down the bank and into the creek again." She understood and without pause did so. It struck Thad that they were mimicking a ploy foxes used to hide their scent and confound pursuing hounds.

Once back in the creek, they crouched below the top of the bank and shuffled crab-like as noiselessly as they could downstream to the right. They continued this way for about one hundred fifty yards. Thad could not believe how exhausting it was! He couldn't control his labored breathing and silence it. *Can Nikki hear it!* Isabella looked unfazed by the effort and not winded. *How does she do it?* He asked himself. They soon came to a point where the creek bed sharply turned almost ninety degrees to the right for about forty feet and then cut back to the left almost ninety degrees, forming a lazy "S" for those thirteen yards. He didn't know what phenomenon caused such a double bend, but he was glad of it.

As good a place as any, he thought. They rounded the turn to the right and just where the streambed turned back to the left, he stopped. Controlling his heavy breathing as best he could, he looked at Isabella and put a finger to his lips, then pointed with two fingers to his eyes and then to the creek bank. He raised himself just enough to peer over the edge of the bank in the direction they had come. He was looking through stringy grass about eight inches high fighting to survive next to the creek in the shade of the woods. He could see better through this close screen than he could be seen, but the darkness robbed him of this advantage. He could see nothing in the darkness beyond about forty feet. Ultimately they must rely on their hearing.

He was torn. A part of him wanted to tell Isabella to continue downstream then cut back through the woods to the house. But he didn't know where Nikki was, and if separating himself from Isabella got her killed, he could never forgive himself. He dismissed the idea.

At least this spot brings the Glock into play. If Nikki was following them down the stream bed, she would not see him until she rounded that first bend, and he would then be close enough to her that maybe, just maybe, his puny little weapon could do some damage. But if she was coming up the stream the other way, well, the best they could do would be to move fast back the way they came, get around the first bend and wait for her there. Problem was, if they heard her coming that way, she probably would hear them retreating, and they would lose the element of surprise.

He bent to Isabella's ear. "I'm going to stay right here against this bank. If she comes down the stream after us, she has to round that bend, and I'll have a chance with this," holding up the Glock. "You crouch over there. He gestured towards the opposite bank downstream of them just around the second bend. She can't see you there unless she gets by me or she comes the other way in the stream, which is unlikely. You'll hear her if she does. If you see me go down, run for it. You're fast and will have a good chance." Isabella said nothing. Her hand found Thad's cheek touching the blood there. She moved her face to his so their eyes were nearly touching. She wanted to see his eyes as clearly as she could in the darkness so hers could tell him the feelings that were in her heart.

She softly kissed his lips, turned, and silently moved downstream to the far bank just beyond the second turn. There she crouched, looking back toward him. They were no more than eight yards apart and in plain sight of each other but for the darkness. As it was, each saw only the shadowy silhouette of the other, and the danger approaching was so dire that neither could help the other. They might as well have been a hundred miles apart.

They waited – fifteen seconds, thirty seconds, forty-five seconds, "Crack," the unmistakable sound of a twig snapping under foot upstream, maybe fifty yards, and then a muffled splash. *She's entered the stream!* Thad shot a glance towards

Isabella, but could only see shadows. *She must have heard it!* Then to his dismay he saw that Isabella had left her protected spot and was moving toward him. He glanced quickly up over the bank in the direction of the snapped twig then back to Isabella as she reached him. "What are you doing?" He scolded in a harsh whisper.

She touched his face again and whispered back, "We know where she is now, and I am not leaving you." His response was tinged with frustration.

"There is nothing you can do here but die for nothing! Get back there! In fact, get out of here. Keep going down the middle of the stream. This is the perfect chance for you to get away."

When she answered, her voice was calm, "I decide if it is for nothing Thaddeus. Besides, your plan is a good one, and we are going through this together and walking out together. Now get the job done, my hero!"

He marveled! She was so different than any woman he had ever known, so courageous that she could inject levity into their plight and calm him and shore up his own courage. He felt a surge of love, and he was totally ready to fight. He motioned her to get behind him flat against the bank so he would be between Nikki and her when Nikki rounded the corner.

They remained motionless in the shallow water, knees bent, so their heads were below the top of the dark creek bank. Thad had his Glock in his right hand pointed upward. Lowering it to shoot was quicker and more accurate than raising it. Thad was cold, and his bent legs were rapidly tiring. He would have to straighten them soon. He estimated that at least two minutes had passed since they had heard the twig snap. The only sound was the gentle gurgling of the slow moving water over small rocks. That sound had always been peaceful and welcoming to him. He wondered if it ever would be again. Now it was Nikki's ally, masking the sound of her approach.

A minute more passed. Isabella was absolutely still. Thad's brain registered wet and chilled feet. His bent knees complained louder and began to shake. *Maybe she's gone,* he thought or, rather, hoped. Then he heard it, a different water sound. He glanced back at Isabella. She had heard it – a quiet "swish." He pictured Nikki's foot and ankle pushing water aside as she slowly moved toward them in the creek without lifting her legs. The sound again. So quiet. Almost not there. Almost.

Now that it was about to happen, he felt behind him to touch Isabella without moving his eyes from the direction of the sound. He wanted her close. He pressed his left shoulder against the creek bank to give himself the steadiest aim. It was moist and slippery. His bent knees were burning and shaking from the strain, but his upper body was still. He worried that the distance was too great for him to take Nikki out with the Glock before she got shots off with the cannon she was carrying. He thought of Isabella taking a round. *Not going to let that happen!* He knew Nikki's training, so he knew how she would round the corner. He visualized her movements. Her rifle would be up. Again he was thankful she was right handed. *She will have to get her body all the way around the turn to get a straight shot at me!*

She was moving closer, approaching the bend. *Here we go,* he thought. He brought the Glock down slowly. He fully extended his right arm and grabbed his right wrist with his left hand. He aimed at the bend. The Glock felt like a toy. *She has to be just around the corner. Why is she so damn slow!* Then the soft swoosh sound began again. Straining to see, Thad could just make out a change in the shade of darkness at the bend in the creek bank, just a sliver of blacker black as Nikki inched the rifle barrel beyond the corner. The blackness Thad saw began to rotate slowly toward him. His mind's eye raced forward envisioning Nikki's left shoulder, then her upper body and her head. *Will she turn quickly or continue moving slowly?* He took a breath and slowly exhaled. He looked straight down his extended right arm and over the barrel of the Glock to the growing shape at the bend in the creek, with the dark mass of brush and trees beyond it. *Be enough weapon,* he prayed.

He slipped the safety. Suddenly, the brush and trees on the bank behind the barrel of Nikki's rifle came noisily alive! Branches crackled, bushes and larger limbs swooshed, and hoofs pounded on the moist ground.

Immediately the rifle barrel disappeared back around the corner and two then three flashes of light appeared followed by the noise and concussion of the shots. Then Thad and Isabella could hear Nikki running, splashing back up the creek the way she had come, no longer concerned about giving her location away.

Thad knew instantly what had happened. Deer had come cautiously down to the water's edge in the cover of night to drink. Because Nikki had been moving stealthily, they had not sensed her presence until they were so close that they were startled into a panic. The commotion continued, but with ever decreasing intensity, and then it finally stopped. Without having to look, Thad knew that one or more deer had been hit and had taken time to die. The lucky deer were well away, and the unlucky one or two were now even further away.

Nikki was furious. She ran splashing up the center of the shallow creek until she reached the spot where she had entered it. There she climbed the bank and headed back through the woods toward the pasture. She had to assume Thad had a phone, and he would now have a moment to call for help without giving his position away. She relished going one on one with him if she only knew where he was, but did not want to fight the entire Pennsylvania state police force to get another shot at the Whore. *Get to the car,* she decided, *and make a plan.*

She did not have night vision glasses. She moved as fast as the dark night would permit, quite sure that she was accurately retracing her steps. She moved with the rifle slung in her left arm and her right arm up to cover her face as she swept through the unseen branches. Sensing she was getting close to the edge of the woods, she quickly moved ninety degrees to her right for about twenty yards. She could half see, half sense the mass of a large tree just off to her right, and she flattened her back against the trunk, her body facing the pasture. She took a deep breath, held it, and listened as intently as she could. Innocent night sounds reached her ears, the light wind stirring and a bird calling, but nothing she could associate with moving humans. *Where the hell were they?* She knew Thad had at most only a handgun, so she was not worried about getting shot while she was retreating. She crouched, and with the rifle held in front of her, moved to the edge of the woods and struck out to the right at a run.

As soon as Thad heard Nikki splashing away from them, he reached out for Isabella's arm and said, "We're getting out of here. Follow me." They hoisted themselves up the bank and struck off as quickly as they could through the woods in a straight line back to the pasture. *Nikki will be well to our right,* he thought. They moved without much regard for noise so long as they could hear Nikki making noise. When that stopped, they stood still for a brief moment, listening. All was quiet again, so they too slowed and moved silently. Thad's senses were on high alert. He now felt that the Glock afforded real protection and attributed that to no longer being hunted.

He did not know whether Nikki was going to retrace her steps by crossing the pasture to the barn, then go around the right side of the house, and then to wherever she had hidden her car, or move further to the right, staying in the woods, eventually bending to the left all the way to the road. He thought those were her only real options. He did not think she would come in their direction and pass left of the barn and house because on that side there was little else but open country and no good place to conceal a car. When they reached the woods' edge, Thad said, "Look to the right in the pasture and along the woods line. See anything moving?" They peered into the darkness, trying to adjust their eyes. Then he made out the moving black shape, maybe two hundred fifty yards to his right and a hundred yards into the field of young corn. She was running. "See her?" he asked Isabella as he pointed.

"Yes, I think I do. She's running."

That changed the calculus for Thad. In the open field and running away, Nikki would rightly believe danger could only come from behind. So, if he followed her, he would again be in the danger zone where her rifle would be deadly, his Glock useless, and he could not maneuver to take that advantage away.

"Follow me." He jogged to his left along the woods line for another fifty yards then broke across the wide soybean field in a run to the paddock fence to the left of the barn. Isabella was right alongside. With no gun to their back they breathed easier, and it did not seem to take as long as their flight to the woods. Then they were quickly over the first fence, across the paddock, and over the second fence to the back lawn about eighty yards from the main back door of the house. But that door was exposed to the south and the field they had seen Nikki in. Thad thought, *we'd be stationary targets for the seconds it would take me to unlock the door.* Instead, he sprinted more to the left and onto the little porch outside the mudroom. Thad unlocked the door, and they quickly entered the comforting space.

They threw their arms around each other, relishing the feeling of deliverance that washed over them. Had they the ability to read each other's thoughts, they would discover that each was thanking God for protecting the other. They kissed with a fervor fed by the welcome release of tension. Then Isabella put her lips to his ear. "Do your future girlfriends a favor, Thad. Wait till morning to tour the property."

Squeezing her tight he said, "She fooled me. I thought she was no longer after you. I damn near got you killed."

"Why?

"It makes no sense," he answered. "I have no explanation."

This interlude lasted no more than thirty seconds, but it had been necessary. Now, however, was decision time for Thad, stay with Isabella or go after Nikki. It was not even close.

"Better leave all lights off," he said. He opened a cabinet and took a flashlight from the shelf. He played it on the tile floor. "Follow me." He led her into and through the kitchen and paneled pantry that opened to the dining room on the left and to an anteroom straight ahead. They went straight into the front hall and through a door under the stairway into the library. To the left of the large fireplace was a paneled gun case. He opened it and shone the light on the racked rifles and shotguns. "Which of these are you most comfortable with?" he asked. Without hesitating she replied, "The over and under 20 gauge." He took it from the rack and handed it to her. She immediately opened the breach and waited. From a large drawer beneath the rack Thad took a box of 20 gauge shells, opened it, and handed her two. She quickly loaded, put the gun to her shoulder for a moment, and brought it down. "Feels fine," she said.

Thad continued, "The rifle I want is in the trunk of the car." "Have your cell phone?" he asked.

"Yes, who do I call?"

"Do you still have Owens' number?"

"Yes."

"Call him, tell him what's happened. Ask him to get help out here. The state police barracks in Avondale is only about four miles from here. Tell him I'm going after Nikki. She will reach her car in a couple of minutes. No idea which direction she'll go. He paused. She knew what was coming. "I've got to do this," he said to her.

In the creek with death bearing down on them, she had refused to obey him and insisted on being at his side. But she knew this was different. This is what he did. It was not just his job but also his life, and she would be in the way. "Come back to me," she said.

"Here's the flashlight. Keep it aimed down, go anywhere you're most comfortable in the house, get a drink of water, keep the box of shells with you." He paused, looking at her in the soft light. "I will be back. Count on it."

"Don't worry about me," she said. She kissed him again briefly and intensely.

"I've never known anyone like you," he said softly. Then he was gone into the night to hunt.

CHAPTER 70

He coupled his seat belt behind him. He wanted freedom to move, aim, shoot, and drive without the annoying, repetitive "ding" ordering him to buckle it. He lowered all four windows. *Don't need glass flying around.* The Colt AR-15, 5.56 mm rifle he retrieved from the trunk sat across his upper body, the butt resting on the inside of his right thigh, the stock cradled in the crook of his left arm, and the barrel jutting out the window. *Like Nikki stalking Warner,* he thought. He started the engine and, driving with his right hand, rounded the circle and headed out the driveway toward Townsend's Bridge Road. Once again he had the advantage of familiarity with his surroundings. He did not need lights to move at a decent speed.

The driveway had several gentle bends in it, but generally headed a little left, further away from the place Nikki likely hid her car. *Probably can't hear my engine,* he thought. In just under a quarter of a mile, he reached the road and switched on his lights before turning right onto it. He calculated it had been about four minutes since Isabella and he had entered the mudroom. If she had been jogging fast, Nikki would have already reached her car and was on the road. He decided he needed to know if she was ahead of him. He pressed the accelerator and was soon going 55, on the brink of reckless for this winding gravel road. He sped past the area where he thought her car should be if it was still there. He saw nothing in his headlights. He kept moving, pushing a little faster.

He came over a slight rise to a long straight stretch, after which the road curved to the right and ended at Pennsylvania Route 82, where there would likely be more traffic and Nikki could slip away. Ahead he saw taillights for two seconds before they disappeared around the curve. *If she's looking in her mirror, she'll have seen my lights,* he thought. His intuition told him she knew he was coming. He floored it, and the speedometer reached 80. Ten seconds later when he slowed enough to round the curve, his lights illuminated the stop sign ahead at the junction with Rt. 82. No car in sight. He looked left and right as he closed the distance to the stop. An 18-wheeler with a car behind it was moving away to his left. *That could be hers,* he thought. *The distance from me is about right.* Then he looked to his right. There was a car there too, also moving away. *Could be her,* he thought. *Which way?* Then he got it. *Why would she pull out behind a big truck and still be there?* He knew she wouldn't. She would have passed it, and let the truck screen her. He turned right, peddle to the floor and tires screaming.

Five seconds later he was surprised to see red brake lights shine on the car ahead and then see all red lights disappear and yellow-white headlights rotating to the left until they were facing him. The car had done a quick U-turn and was now coming toward him. His intuition shouted, *She's coming for you Pennock!* The two cars were closing fast. He knew that stopping would give her a real target. Speed was his friend.

He grabbed the steering wheel in his left hand, and with his right arm, worked the rifle butt up to his right shoulder. The stock still rested on his left arm. His eyes never left the lights of the car racing toward him. He clicked off the safety and got his index finger onto the trigger. *Knights jousting in a medieval tournament* flashed through his mind.

He moved his body against the car door and his right shoulder as far back as he could. He wanted to aim as far forward of his car as possible to cut down the lateral correction needed to hit someone speeding past at maybe 140 combined miles per hour. Both had their high beams on, and in the blinding light and with the speed and the awkward firing angle, aiming and timing were largely guesswork. They took their shots within a fraction of a second of each other. In the next instant Thad felt a slug slam into the support beam between the front and back seats on the driver's side, and then came the report of her rifle. He had no idea what, if anything, his shot hit. As the cars sped first toward each other and then away, the Doppler effect made the roar of the cars and the sound of the rifle shots surreal.

This is nuts, he thought. But he grabbed the wheel with both hands, letting the rifle bounce in his lap and on his left arm. He braked hard until slowed to about 10 miles an hour. Any faster and his next maneuver could flip the car. He swerved to the right shoulder and forced the wheel into a hard left. The car spun around facing the other direction. *Thank goodness no other cars in sight now,* he thought. He floored it. She had been a second faster and was already bearing down on him. About one hundred fifty yards out, a hole burst in his windshield just to the right of his right ear, and behind him his rear window blew out with a shattering sound. He felt tiny glass fragments hit his right ear. He instinctively shut his eyes as a protective reaction to flying glass, but he knew it had been too late to do any good. He had just been damn lucky.

He had only an instant to marvel at how she could get off so forward a shot. *Did she blow out her front windshield? Did my shot do it?* She was no more than twenty-five yards in front of him when the angle permitted him to take his shot. Again, he heard and saw nothing other than the report of his rifle. "Damn!" He muttered under his breath, thinking, *I'd do better with the little over-and-under Isabella has!* Through his rearview mirror, he could see that she was already preparing to turn again and so did he. When he was around and trying to pick up speed, he sensed something was different. His intuition screamed at him. *She's in your lane, Pennock! She's not going to pull out!* He had two seconds to decide. He gripped the wheel with both hands, letting the rifle bounce across his body again. He swerved right to the shoulder and immediately back to the left, just as she was reacting to his move to the shoulder. It was a football running back juke. They passed so close that her car grazed the back fender of his. Any greater impact and the stability of his car's rear end would have been lost. They sped away from each other until they could once again harness the speed and turn around.

Thad was now in a fury. "Enough!" he shouted into the night. Instead of reversing direction for yet another charge, he brought his car to a squealing halt across the road. Four hundred yards away, she had turned her car and was now roaring toward him again. He jumped out, ran around what was now his barricade, leveled the rifle on the car's hot hood, and aimed. He figured he could get off two maybe three good shots. He looked through the night scope, which was now a handicap. The bright light from her high beams was diffused over the whole lens. With her headlights as his marker, he fired where he thought the steering wheel and thus her body should be. But there was no sign of a hit, and the car kept coming. He fired twice more as the car bore down. Now, even if he killed her, the car would keep coming. It was at high speed and no more than eighty yards away. He dropped the rifle and then leapt away towards the ditch to his right. He did so without taking his eyes from Nikki's car.

To his amazement, he saw that she had anticipated this. She was not going to crash into his car. She was going to run him down! He dove for the ditch. He could hear himself yelling, as if that effort would propel him farther and faster.

"Ditch" was a grand word for the depression in which he landed. It was no more than two feet deep and ten feet wide. Somehow he knew enough to drop parallel to the road and close to the roadside wall of the ditch. He hit the ground as the front fender of Nikki's SUV broke the plane of the ditch. He felt the heat and vibrations of the undercarriage passing an inch or two above his head and his ears filled with the roar of the motor and drive train as they screamed past. As fast as the SUV was moving across the earth, gravity had the final say. In the next instant, he could feel through the ground beneath him the impact as the front wheels slammed into the top nine inches of the opposite side of the ditch. That's all it took to trip the SUV.

The impact transferred forward forces to the slightly higher back end. The rear rose into the air, and the car began a somersault. When the back end crossed the vertical line and kept moving, the front end lifted into the air, and the car was airborne upside down. The back end hit the ground first, and the car twisted and viciously rolled four times, spewing metal and glass before finally coming to rest on its bent and shattered right side. Steam hissed and what was left of the engine crackled, but there was no fire. There should have been, but there was not. Thad was on his hands and knees in the ditch staring at the awful sight. He did not remember raising himself to that position, but there he was.

He heard the screech of brakes as an 18-wheeler strained to stop. The driver leapt from his cab with a fire extinguisher in his hand and started running toward the car. Behind him a pickup turned off the road and drove through the ditch and up to what was left of the SUV, playing its head lights on it. The driver jumped out with a flashlight. By now Thad was up and running to the car. He got there just as the man in the pickup did and just before the long hauler. The front windshield was gone. The man played his flashlight into the front seat and froze it on a mutilated body. "Sweet Jesus," he murmured.

"I'm FBI," Thad said. "Get close and keep the light on her. Can you do that?" The man swallowed and managed an "okay." Thad got on his knees on the ground just where the glassless windshield, now pointing straight up, met the SUV's hood. He put both hands on the edge of the windshield frame to brace his body and leaned in. The man stood above him, shining the light down. Nikki was face up. Her head and shoulders lay against the passenger side door flat on the ground. Her face looked skyward out the driver side window. The rest of her body was above her head but compressed and crumpled unnaturally to her right off the seat in the space between the seat and the dashboard. Thad backed out enough to reach up a hand and say, "Give me the light." The man did.

Thad leaned forward again, this time with head and shoulders through the windshield cavity. At the same time he could hear the pressure releasing from the fire extinguisher as the long hauler hosed down the engine to prevent a fire. Thad played the light onto Nikki's face. He had a double shock. The face was a bloody mess, and it was not Nikki's. He realized that since the first shot at Isabella, a seeming century ago, he had known their stalker was Nikki, and the danger she represented caused his mind's eye all that time to see her face. He was not prepared for the shattered face of Christa, now marred by swelling and a huge and bleeding gash running across her entire forehead and down her left cheek nearly to her throat. It dwarfed her many other cuts and contusions.

Without the restraint of a seat belt, the deployed airbag could not keep Nikki's body pinned as the car somersaulted and rolled. She had been slammed against one part of the breaking up interior and then another and was sliced up by her rifle turned errant missile inside the tumbling cab. From the position of her twisted body, Thad was certain she had broken her lower spine. Her left leg was clearly broken. Blood trickled from her mouth and left ear, signaling head injuries. But her eyes were unscathed. They were open and reacting to the yellow light.

Thad turned the light beam to his own face. "Nikki," he said firmly. "Nikki, can you see me? It's Agent Pennock. Can you hear me? It's Agent Pennock." Then he turned the light back to Nikki's face, keeping it out of her eyes. Her eyelids flickered, reacting to the light, and she mouthed a word he could not hear. He leaned in further until his ear was close to her mouth. Blood covered most of her teeth. "Can you talk to me Nikki?" This time with his ear close he heard a faint "Yes." He turned his head to look at her and could see her painful struggle for even a little breath.

He knew she was dying, but despite this, or perhaps because of it, he needed to know. "Why kill Isabella, Nikki? Why her? Why didn't you escape? You're good at it." As he was saying this, he was searching her eyes for the answer, and he noticed them begin to lose focus. She was slipping away, but he still could not suppress his anger and he wanted the answer. His voice was quiet but it came out a command, not a plea. "Tell me! Why kill Isabella?" In his eagerness, he bent even closer, so his ear actually touched her lips. Her next words were not spoken but breathed, a simple question in answer to his.

"Escape where?" That was all, except for her fight for a breath. Thad didn't move, hoping for more. He sensed she was not finished. But a gurgle in her throat caused him to turn and look at her face.

He was astonished! It was completely transformed! Her eyes were clear and shining, fixed upon something that only she could see in the night sky visible through the open window above her head. Through the gashes and blood she was smiling and her expression was rapturous, as if she were not just seeing but also comprehending a wonder.

He felt her left arm move, and then he felt her fingers in his hair. She used them rather than her battered arm to crab her hand up the side of his head and then behind it. Her fingers closed with strength he could not believe possible from her broken, dying body. Her fingernails dug in as her grip tightened and then tightened more. Her eyes seemed to widen even further. Her hand in place, she pulled his head toward her. He resisted at first, but something told him to let this happen. He relaxed, and she drew his head down past her face to her shoulder, cradling it there as she would a baby's. He could not see her face now, but through her embrace he could feel tremors riffling through her body. With great effort, she expended her breath on a blood-choked but joyful proclamation to the world she was leaving. "I know... Now I know... I didn't ask... I didn't!"

Then he felt her grip relax and her life depart. Nikki's words made no sense to him, but he had no doubt she had experienced some ecstasy for the fleeting seconds before she died. He pulled back to look at her, and her clutching arm fell away. He played the light on her face a last time. Although bloody, swollen, and broken, it still shone. *Peaceful*, he thought. He reached forward and closed her eyes.

He looked hard, hoping to see something that would explain her. He recalled Owens' question to him on the train many months before after their meeting with Moretti. "What do we really know about Nikki Patterson?" Since then they had learned many facts, but they didn't explain her. He heard himself asking aloud, "Who were you?" He listened to her silence for a moment, frustrated by the mystery but no longer angry.

He became aware of wailing sirens drawing closer. Colors from the rotating roof lights on the approaching police cars danced on the twisted metal of what had been the SUV. He thought of Isabella, now truly safe. Then he rose and clicked off the flashlight, relegating to the dark night Nikki's body and Christa's face.

He handed the flashlight to the man. "You know her?" he asked.

Thad shook his head, "She's a mystery." He turned and slowly walked toward the whirling lights.

EPILOGUE

I sabella and Thad, dressed in riding boots, britches and hunting coats, left Thad's house and walked arm-in-arm to the barn in contented silence. Each was privately savoring the previous night. They had reached the age where lovemaking was its richest. They were still young enough that fire burned in their bellies yet mature and experienced enough to delight in unselfconscious experimenting and the pleasures derived from simple touches, gentleness, and patience.

They had no idea where their relationship was going. The chemistry between them was greater than either had experienced before, so they appreciated it as something valuable to be nurtured. But their independent lives were also full and rich and separated them for weeks at a time. Neither knew whether this arrangement could survive long term, but their time together yielded ever deeper and richer feelings and so long as that continued, the inconveniences seemed slight.

They were not halfway to the barn, however, when their hearts and minds were highjacked by the beauty of the day in horse country. The sky was that deep blue possible only when the barometric pressure is high and there are no clouds at any height. The air was thus perfectly clear, causing pastures, fence lines, trees, pond, and grazing horses to stand out in greater relief, contours to be sharper, and colors to be more vivid. In the fields, the last of the corn had been harvested, winter wheat was sprouting green shoots, and the browning of the soybean plants signaled it was nearly time for them to yield their beans. The very center of the pond was painted the sky's blue but near the edges the surface reflected the greens, browns, reds, and yellows of late-October's changing leaves. Those leaves rustled in a gentle breeze, providing accompaniment to the mingling, varied songs of birds busy in the trees.

Three couples of fat geese pecked in the pasture, never far from the safety of the pond. A single blue heron stood stock still on one stick leg in six inches of water near the pond's edge, waiting stoically for an unsuspecting fish swimming down its own meal of plankton or tiny skating bugs.

In the barn Fidel, Thad's long-time, loyal friend and employee, was tacking up the two hunters that Thad and Isabella would depend upon to meet all the challenges of the day's foxhunt and see them safely to its end. Thad's other horses were grazing, and Thad looked upon them for the ten thousandth time as if for the first. These special creatures were in his blood, a condition impossible for someone not so infected to comprehend.

The beauty of the day and the countryside and the lovers' anticipation of a view of a magnificent red fox speeding to safety, the sight of the hounds chasing in full cry, and the feel of their powerful galloping mounts beneath their gripping legs – all these blessings of life were in their own way every bit as rare and worthy of worship as were their feelings for each other. And, as it turned out, the day did not disappoint.

That evening Thad sat on the brick terrace looking out over the fieldstone Ha-Ha wall seventy yards away and into the green pasture beyond where his horses, as always, grazed near the pond. Isabella had departed to continue her scheduled fundraising, but she would return to him before flying back to Buenos Aires. The stately, old sycamore trees that towered over the house threw long shadows onto the lawn, announcing the sun's imminent departure behind the woods to the west. It was a tranquil time. The physical exertion and mental excitement of the chase earlier in the day left Thad completely relaxed, and he closed his eyes.

As often happened, he thought of that wild night four months earlier when Nikki came so close to killing Isabella and him. Her last words, "I didn't ask...I didn't..." *What did she mean?* His intuition, which had an opinion about almost everything, told him only, *you'll never know, Pennock. Put it to bed.* So, he did. At least until the next time.

He thought of Isabella and of how fortunate he was in all things – love, health, home, occupation, and friends. It was quite a list. He gave silent thanks to his particular God, who over the years had gradually taken form as a moral imperative demanding that he cede the center of the universe and strive to be grateful and humble in all things. At this he knew he was still an aspirant.

In this mood he had the romantic notion that all was right with his world and so he raised his glass to it. But then he lowered the glass without drinking and softly said aloud, "Not quite, Pennock." His thoughts went to Congresswoman Wetherill, whose crime had earned her a plea-bargained thirty years in prison, but who surely had gotten one thing right. Moretti, a clever and ruthless bad guy who was the mastermind of a thriving trade in illegal drugs, was still out there. And catching bad guys made Thaddeus Ignatius Pennock glad to get up in the morning.

Acknowledgements

I
f you enjoyed this book, it is due in large part to the
contributions of many wonderful people, including my
insightful editor Virginia Beards, a published poet, who was
irreplaceable; authors Anne Hambleton, Andrew Jefferson,
and Peter Ernster, who gave me invaluable advice about the
publishing process; the erudite ladies in the You-Don't-Have-
To-Read-The-Book Book Club, who mercilessly critiqued
it and then gave a thumbs up; my long-time assistant and
friend Gloria Connell, who cheerily put up with change
after change; Elizabeth Clark, whose perspective influenced
the tone of the story; David Stewart Brown, a brilliant
young artist who designed the book's cover; Nita Greer, my
irrepressible marketing and design consultant; my brother
David, who corrected my many grammatical and punctuation
mistakes (If you discovered any, I get to blame him); my son
Michael, who is an expert on firearms; my brother Fred, also
a published poet; and all my children for their suggestions
and unwavering support. I am also indebted to Ernest
Hemingway. His genius is far beyond my poor talents, but the
clarity, power, and simplicity of his best writing are inspiring.

Please visit my website -- www.clipperlamotte.com -- and tell me what you think of *Necessary Vengeance*. I'll pass your comments on to Thad. And if you enjoyed it, please tell your friends.

90625127R00234

Made in the USA
Middletown, DE
25 September 2018